MERGEWORLD

BOOK TWO

Titles by Mason Elliott

The Spacer Clans Adventures, Cycle One:

NAERO'S RUN
NAERO'S GAMBIT
NAERO'S FURY

The Spacer Clans Adventures, Cycle Two:

NAERO'S MASTERY*

The Citation Series, Cycle One:

Naero's War, Book One: THE ANNEXATION WAR
Naero's War, Book Two: THE HIGH CRUSADE
Naero's War, Book Three: NAERO'S TRIAL

The Citation Series, Cycle Two:

Naero's War, Book Four: THE GAMMA QUADRANT*

Short Fiction in Ebook Format

THE PERMIT

Fantasy with Author Garan R. R. Faraday
MERGEWORLD, BOOK 1
MERGEWORLD, BOOK 2
MERGEWORLD, BOOK 3*

(*Forthcoming)

MERGEWORLD

BOOK TWO

Mason Elliott
&
Garan R. R. Faraday

High Mark Publishing

High Mark Publishing
www.highmarkpublishing.com

Seattle & Portland,   Chicago,   London

Mergeworld

Book Two

by
Mason Elliott & Garan R. R. Faraday

Trade Paperback Edition
© 2014 by Mason Elliott & Garan R. R. Faraday. All rights reserved.
Published by High Mark Publishing
ISBN 978-1-930451-11-7
Watch for other titles by these authors in the future.

Cover Art by
Mike Leonard
madmanmike.deviantart.com

Edition Notes
If you do not see this edition note here in this spot on the copyright page and
on the very last page of your ebook or print version of this title, then you are
not getting the final, polished version of this novel that the publisher, editors,
and author intended for you to receive. Please contact either the publisher or
the author via their emails or websites if you do not see the following update
code:

High Mark Publishing Update Code K2428E

1

The sun was shining high the next day in a bright blue sky. But it might as well have been a big black rock hoisted in the air on ropes, as far as Mason Tyler was concerned.

He had flipped around in his comfortable bed like an oiled jackknife. A real bed, too: box spring, mattress, pillows, soft blankets, and all.

With the woman he loved dead and buried in some nameless grave, there was no comfort for him to find—any place—anywhere.

The defenders of Michiana had won the initial war after the dimensional cataclysm that had messed up both worlds—as well as technology and magic. What people called the Merge.

Yet that victory remained hollow, for all the good that it did Mason. So many other people had died, but with his beloved Tori gone, Mason felt as if someone had gutted him like a trout. Just taken a jagged knife and carved out his insides, snapping his ribs, to allow the cold wind to twist and whistle right through his empty core as it would.

He didn't want to get up or go out that next day, so he didn't.

Why? What good would it do to get up out of that rotten bed and do anything at all?

At last he did get up briefly to use the toilet attached to the room; there was no sink, for some weird reason. He still cared just enough not to want to wallow in his own filth, but that was about the extent of his concern. He figured he had a couple of water bottles and the stale water in his belt canteens tide him over.

He could hold out in his room for a spell.

He could hole up there and shun the world for at least a while.

Mason kept his door good and locked, and then shoved a dresser in front of it, for good measure.

Friends and other people pounded on the door and tried to talk to him.

He didn't listen, ignored them, or told them to go away and stay the hell away from him.

Tori was dead.

They yelled at him.

He stopped listening.

Tori...

He mourned for his beloved and recalled every sweet memory, everything he knew about her. Her hair. Her smile. God almighty...her sweet smile. The way she looked at him and the way he felt when she looked at him like that. As if he were the king of the universe with her beside him.

He didn't need anything else, had never wanted anything or anyone else. Not money. Nothing. Not a goddam thing.

Together, they'd had no need for anything or anyone else but each other.

He thought of the way her pretty brown eyes would open up in the morning after he had been patiently watching her just breathe beside him, for a long, long time.

How lucky had he been? It was like watching an angel breathe and sleep.

He thought of the light that came into Tori's eyes when she looked up at him and she smiled that smile of hers.

Mason couldn't take it. He broke down alone and sobbed for all he was worth, which, at the moment, wasn't all that much.

When a person was alone with himself, he could do and be whatever he damn well wanted. He could let his emotions gush out of him like blood from a gaping wound, until he was completely spent and drained.

Time passed. It got dark again.

More pounding on the door.

He drank water.

He hit the pot.

Four days like that passed. Then, even after careful rationing—he was out of water, and wasn't about to play dog and drink from the toilet.

Damn it.

2

He jumped when Thulkara broke the wooden door down with ease and shattered that dresser–as if she were bulldozing through dry crackers. The Thul warrior goddess simply passed through the flimsy obstacles as if they were nothing, and shook off the pieces and splinters.

Blondie and Major Avery came in right behind her, their faces set.

"You can't stay in here forever, Mace." Blondie told him.

He stood up from his bed calmly. "I know that. I just needed some time, so I took it. I was about to come out, before Thulkara got the idea to remodel the entire place."

A person couldn't mourn forever, either.

Tori had loved him, and he her. She wouldn't want him to stay miserable and depressed about her for the rest of his days.

Actually, at that moment, he was pretty darn sick of being in that damn room.

He reeked. And the room reeked right along with him, after four days.

"Whew!" Thulkara said. "By the Powers! Open the windows and air this skunk hole out. And the skunk had better take a bath, too. Before we give him one. We knew you weren't dead, Mace, because the guards could hear you moving around still and you flushed your toilet."

"I do need a bath," Mason said flatly in agreement.

"Granted." Major Bill Avery was actually the one who went to the two windows, pulled back the curtains, lifted the blinds, and opened the sashes to let in fresh air. "I imagine you'll be a little hungry, Mace."

"I think I will be, after I bathe and get dressed. Thanks, Bill."

"I'll have your regular gear washed and dried, and fresh clothes sent to the bath house nearby. I think it will do you good to make a fresh start. Then you and your friends can grab some chow. When you're ready, afterwards, we can talk."

Thulkara placed both of her hands on his shoulders and held his eye for a moment. "Mason Tyler, you know we're all very sorry about the loss of your woman. You know that, right? We're your friends, your family, and we're here for you, my brother."

Mason sighed and rested his hands on hers. "I know every bit of that. Thank you all. But this is still pretty rugged for me, and I just have to work through most of it on my own. When I need you guys, I'll let you know."

"We can also let you know that," Blondie said.

Major Avery nodded and left the three of them alone.

The silence became uncomfortable very quickly.

"So…" Mason said, not really knowing what else to say. "How are you guys doing?"

"Fine," Thulkara said.

"Pretty good, I guess," Blondie added.

3

Lots of help there from those two.

Thulkara shook her finger. "The signs have been troubling me, of late," she noted.

Blondie groaned and rolled his eyes. "He we go, with the daily superstition report. A grasshopper farts...and spells doom for all."

The warrior goddess shrugged. "Ignore the signs and suffer the consequences. How can you deny them? Birds flying in the wrong direction for this time of year. Snakes fleeing north in large numbers. Groundhogs, raccoons, fox, and deer–even wolves, hillcats, and bears, passing on from one area and into others, avoiding the south, north, and west–always pushing east."

Blondie sighed and crossed his arms. "And I say they're simply adjusting to the Merge. There are many dangers in the wilds, especially now for the beasts of the forests, who will only be seen as food."

"Any good news?" Mason asked.

Thulkara's face brightened suddenly. She whipped a battered sketch pad out of her shoulder bag, anxiously shoving it into Mason's hands. "Now that I have more time, I've been taking drawing lessons to go with my painting classes. I'm getting pretty good. Look, look!"

The Amazon was clearly proud of her artistic skills. Mason flipped through several very fine pencil sketches–all of them quite good, in fact. Blondie looked over his other shoulder.

The subject matter was slightly disconcerting.

"A Thul splitting a gozog's skull in half like a melon..." Mason noted.

"Yeah, look at the brains!" Thulkara added, eagerly.

He flipped to the next. "A Thul splitting a mor-kahl down the middle, from head to groin."

"Note the bursting entrails and exploding groin." She said proudly.

He could have nightmares about it when he slept next. "Can't...miss 'em. Hmmm...and next we have–a Thul cutting down several torgs and ka-torgs with one stroke. Impressive. Look at their hideous faces, twisted in agony and death."

"I'm starting to detect a certain theme at work here," Blondie noted.

Thulkara raised and shook both hands. "Now mind you, these are just pencil sketches. Wait until I get my studio set up and I paint them all, in vibrant color!"

"Ooh..." Blondie said, "look at the one with you ramming that spear up through the necromancer's nether regions and out his shrieking mouth. I want that one on my wall. Be sure to use lots of scarlet."

"Yeah, I think I'll have to," Thulkara said.

"What about some landscapes?" Mason suggested. "Maybe something peaceful and serene? Still-lifes of fruit baskets? Baby birds in a nest–bunnies?"

"I like these," Thulkara flatly said. "I'll have you know that I find art extremely relaxing."

Mason's eyes popped at the hyper-violent sketches.

Relaxing?

"What about those voice lessons we tried to arrange for you?" Blondie asked.

"Yeah," Mason said. "What happened to those? You like to sing...so much."

"Voice lessons?" She laughed "Yeah, you guys are so funny. I knew you were just kidding. My voice is great. But I still need to become a better artist."

Behind Thulkara, Blondie shook his head and mouthed the words, "Not kidding!"

Mason handed the sketch pad back to her. "Cool stuff, Thulkara."

"Thanks." She beamed with pride and put the pad back in her bag.

Blondie scratched his head. "You know, Mace, I could use a bath, myself. How about I go with you and we can talk?"

"Blondie, I might not have much to say yet."

"Good, then I won't have to work too hard at listening."

"I don't mind joining you guys," Thulkara said.

Mason and Blondie both looked at each other and paled.

"Uh, maybe not this time," Mason noted.

Thulkara emitted a booming laugh and smacked them both on the back, nearly driving them off their feet. "You little boys don't have to worry about me. I have no fear of being naked like your peoples do. How silly. Why with Thulls, we hardly wear clothes at all until we're ten or eleven. And even as adults, the men and women take turns bathing in public for each other. It is considered great sport! Every week in the summer, and every month or two in the winter!" She roared with laughter once more.

Mason felt sorry for the Urth human populations around Detroit/Tornhold–on bath days. Thousands of buff Thulls taking turns basking and strutting around like seals on the beach? All jeering and poking fun at one another. That certainly would be a sight.

He still was at a loss of what to tell Thulkara to put her off.

Blondie came to his rescue.

"Now, Thulkara, Mace just found out his beloved is gone. His people aren't like yours. It would be cruel to get him all...excited, while he is still in his time of mourning."

Thulkara thought about that for a moment, and her face went blank. Then she burst out laughing even harder and had to leave the room before she couldn't stand up any longer.

The hot, soapy water out in the bathhouse did feel very good when Mason lowered himself slowly into it. He only slightly winced and hissed.

Blondie was already relaxing in his steaming tub and saying nothing but "Mmm…"

A long while passed.

Mason liked that about his friend. Blondie could be stoic and silent a good deal of the time. A good trait to have in a companion.

In the end, it was Mason himself who finally said something to break the silence. "Well…what else have I missed?"

Blondie sighed. "Not that much. People are scurrying about, after the war. Everyone's trying to get settled and find a place for themselves. People searching for family and friends, again. Like you, everyone's mourning their losses."

"What about you, Blondie?"

"I don't remember everything that I've lost, so I can't mourn much of anything, yet."

More time passed.

"How's Jen?"

Blondie smiled and started washing his shining, golden hair. "As bitchy as ever, demanding, and giving everyone fits—but she's the craziest lover in the sack I have ever known. She makes me crazy about her. I think I might just keep her around for a long while."

"Anything else going on in that golden head of yours?"

Both of them looked at each other and laughed.

It seemed as if it were the first time Mason had laughed in years. Although he knew that wasn't true. It had been less than two weeks since the war ended.

Blondie went under for a rinse and came up spluttering. "My sorcerous powers are rapidly returning, Mace."

He lifted both hands and they glowed slightly. He transformed the steam into dozens of floating, glowing globules of water. "I'm recalling what it is to be a mage, and I'm even more formidable than I had originally thought."

Instantly, the globules snapped into the shape of icy daggers and sped toward the far wall.

Blondie clenched both fists crossed in front of him, and then violently thrust his open hands before him.

The glittering energy knives burst into dozens of shining explosions, then winked out as he dispersed their enormous power as quickly as he had summoned it.

Blondie was in complete control of his abilities. It was a terrifying demonstration of raw skill and power to behold.

As a sorcerer himself, Mason knew very well that if his friend had unleashed those powers, full force, he might have taken out the entire building. Or a large unit of troops.

"Damn, Blondie. That's amazing!"

His friend grinned. "And that's not all, Mace. Some of my telepathic mage powers are returning, stronger than ever. And yet I can still mask my own mind completely from others. I've been spending some of my free time snooping in on that batch of mages we've captured. They still won't talk to anyone, but from what I can tell, they sure want to escape something fierce. They are bored to the point of weeping."

"I would be, too, if I were them—locked up, tied up, and gagged all the time." Mason finished scrubbing himself and rinsed.

Blondie waited for him to stop spluttering and cocked one eyebrow. "That's another thing, Mace. The enemy isn't done with us, or with Michiana for that matter. This war isn't over, not by a long shot."

Mason sighed heavily. "No, I guess it wouldn't be."

"Mark my words. When their friends get around to hitting us again, it's going to be much worse than before. They won't underestimate us this next time around."

"Do any more of them recognize you, Blondie? If you were one of them before, why won't any of them talk to you? Can you find a way to trick them into doing so?"

"I've tried a couple of times, even using different angles, but until that necromancer named Gultor gives the word to the others, none of them are going to risk it. The others are afraid of him."

"What if we remove the necromancer from among the others?"

"Mace, you could kill Gultor now and it still wouldn't make a difference. He's given an order, and the others must obey. But I have something in mind. Something drastic."

Mason raised one eyebrow. "Oh? I hope you've kept Bill in the loop on your plans."

Blondie shrugged. "He knows enough, for now. I wanted to go over some of it with you to work out a few things before I took my plan to Major Bill."

"We have thirteen enemy mages prisoner now, Blondie. That's a lot. If any of them ever do break free, they could cause a lot of damage before we put them down. We can't underestimate them. They are not dumb."

"No, they are most definitely not. They know they're being watched and listened to, very closely. Second, they can already talk to each other all they want. They're not going to get lonely. And third…"

His friend hesitated. Mason stared at him.

Blondie seemed deep in thought. "And third, they can't reach me with telepathy, and so they think my powers are still down from my head injury. But they've all seen me working with the enemy, so they just naturally assume that I am now a traitor. They don't care about anything I say. I have fought against them directly, and even wounded and killed many of their number. They despise me much more than all of you. To them, I am more than an enemy. I am a traitor."

"I suppose that would be the case, Blondie."

"When, not if, they do bust loose–even more than escaping–their primary plan is to kill you, Thulkara, and especially me. That is their goal. Then they will attempt to get away after they have made sure that all of us are dead, and anyone else who gets in their way."

Mason laughed.

"What's so funny, Mace? These people are damn serious, and right dangerous. They want our asses dead almost as bad as they wanna get away. They mean business."

"Well, they might take you and me down…but just how in the hell are they going to take down Thulkara?"

Both of them had a good laugh at that.

"Mace, like I said, I do have a plan to perhaps open them up and get them to talk. I wanna run it by you first, and then Bill. It's going to be risky in a lot of ways. But we can't wait for their comrades to hit us again. And we can't let them bust out on their own. Eventually, believe me, they will devise a way. We need to know at least some of what they know, and why they are doing what they they do."

Mason looked at his friend curiously. "What do you have in mind?"

"Well, what if I was to offer them what they may want even more?"

"More than our heads in a sack and a ticket home?"

"That, too. No, what if we inform them all that since they are pretty much useless to us, they are going to be executed? To them, that would seem logical on our part. Under the threat of death, we might be able to get a few of them to crack."

Mason considered such a ploy. It could work, in part. Even if a few of them turned, it could be a major coup.

"I'm still not convinced, Blondie. What if they call our bluff and Bill doesn't go for it? Where are we then?"

"No worse off than we were before. But we have to try something. Even letting them go and sending them back to the enemy would be better than just keeping them locked up, until they find a way to bust out and kill a bunch of our people. A breakout is going to happen, trust me. This many enemy mages together is dangerous."

Blondie got out of the tub and started drying off behind them.

Mason was still enjoying the soothing properties of the hot water. "All right. Let's say I agree with you. How do we make your plan work?"

"We have to sell it, Mace. Tell me true–do you think Bill would actually let us execute one of them? I was thinking maybe the necromancer."

"Hmmm…I don't know, Blondie. Bill would definitely hang or shoot them before just cutting them loose. He knows how many of our people those enemy mages killed during the war. He would never return powers like that into the enemy's hands—even if he was ordered to do so. But I still don't think he'd just take a prisoner out and kill him for no reason."

Blondie started to put his clothing on. "It would be for a very good reason, Mace. To trick and deceive the other twelve."

Mason rose, stepped out his tub, and reached for a towel. "I think you're starting to scare me a little, Blondie."

"What? It's just a necromancer? We'll never turn a dangerous cultist like that one. Most nations kill them on sight, once they are exposed. Wait until you have more dealings with them. Then you won't be so squeamish. That necromancer will not hesitate to kill anyone. They like killing."

"And that means that we should just waste him?"

Blondie nodded. "Sure. Let me explain it this way, Mace. Necromancers take a very dark path to become who and what they are and gain their abilities. They are fanatics, devoted and obedient only to the Dark Powers. They are not like normal people. Necromancers delight in torment and death. They routinely perform human sacrifices to their Dark Ghods. They drink the blood of the innocent. They relish the taste of human flesh. And they are masters of deceptions and lies. That is how they flourish. They pose as regular people."

Mason had his boxers on and pulled into a clean T-shirt. "Then my people would try them for their crimes and execute them."

"Necromancers are a walking atrocity. Mace, do you know what the Dark Khabal would have done once they defeated South Bend—or all of Michiana, for that matter, as they intended?" Blondie pulled his left boot on.

Mason sighed and got his pants on. "I have a feeling you're going to tell me."

"The necromancers would have held what is known as a Great Dark Ritual to celebrate their victory. On a high hill, they would prepare the site and encircle it for all of their hosts to watch. Then they would all get naked and cover themselves with dark symbols, sigils, and spells from their secret language, taught only among their kind. Then they would take up their sacrificial knives and kill six hundred and sixty-six carefully selected prisoners from among the captives of the people they had vanquished. All ages, from babes to the oldest.

"Half of the sacrifices would be male, and half female, performed as the victims are still alive and screaming. The necromancers would cut out the beating hearts and bite into them. Then they would mutilate the bodies and cast the pieces into the burning rings of darkfire set up all around the hill at six levels. The hill would turn red with the spilled blood that flowed off of the dark altars. They would make a great burnt offering of the prisoners and their souls to the Dark Ones—the Fallen. And once the fires and the reek of the smoke died down, they would all feast on the defiled, roasted flesh until they were bloated or even puked out their guts. Them, and all of their servants—including the darkspawn, the monsters. That is how the Dark Khabal marks and celebrates its major victories."

Mason shook his head, buttoning his shirt. "That all sounds pretty horrible. I can see why your people in the Old World killed necromancers on sight."

"Indeed. In the ancient days, the Dark Khabal had cults in each of the six nations, and were the cause of many wars. Until finally, the leaders of all the lands banded together and led a great crusade to sweep over the world and wipe them out. But always the dark cults manage to survive somehow, hiding among the people, growing to become a threat once more. And now it has come to pass among the colonists of the Sylurrians."

"Blondie, do you think the Sylurrians in the Old World even know what is really going on here, in the New World?" Mason slipped his second boot on and stood up in it to adjust his foot.

"Perhaps not. Those who do are most likely part of the cult, and most of them came across the sea, I imagine, to support the cult's efforts in the colonies. My guess is that those here who did not wish to join the cult—like my parents—were all systematically eliminated. That is why the Dark Khabal acts so openly now. And now, with the Merge, it could be years before the Sylurrians in the Old World really find out what has happened here. And by then, it will be too late. All many reasons why the life of one necromancer does not mean so much to me, Mace. Our life—all life means nothing to them. If they could, they would sacrifice all of us to the Dark Ghods."

"Then that is why we must never let them win," Mason said. He strapped on his Spiller & Burrs in their custom holster rigs, and tied them down on his legs.

Blondie frowned, and nodded sadly. "Yet they have grown and continue to grow in great strength, my friend. It is highly possible that we will not be able to prevail against them. That is what our captive mages all believe."

Mason tried to laugh. "And look where they are."

"For now," Blondie warned.

Several blasts rocked the militia camp at that exact moment, from the direction where the enemy mages were being held. Horn calls blared and voices shouted the alarm. A battle had already erupted.

Mason and Blondie grabbed their hats and ran out.

2

Back on the militia practice fields, some flashy popinjay from one of the other battalions was putting his brag on in front of the troops. The guy apparently thought he was Zorro or something. He kept boasting about his skills with a blade.

David studied the guy's garb. Classic.

Polished, thigh-high boots, black tights, white fencing shirt, poufy sleeves, leather fencing vambraces, supple leather fencing gauntlets tucked into the red silk sash around his narrow waist. Elaborate, metal-studded rapier belt, Italian rapier, main gauche, several throwing knives tucked in here and there. A fancy, embroidered baldric. He even had a black half-cape, lined in black velvet. The entire outfit topped by a cocked cavalier hat, complete with ornate hat band and bright feathers.

Real, flourishing feathers.

On top of that, the popinjay did look to be in top physical condition. And he had a pencil-thin mustache to boot.

Could David really slam this guy? He himself went around dressed in armor.

The popinjay bowed with a flourish and a sweep of his hat to the assembly of sweaty, dirty militia troops on the practice field, who mostly blinked and looked stunned and bewildered by the guy's mere presence.

"I have come from Elkhart to instruct you all, you lucky, lucky persons, in the art of the sword. Of course. I, am Alejandro Maximillian Aguilar: the Eagle of the Southwest. Three-time Champion Swordsman of the Combat Sport Fencing Association, a fencing instructor, and sparring master for what would have been the next Olympic Team.

"I personally led the charge that cut down the gozog and mor-kahl shock force and shattered the enemy retreat to the south." He raised his hands as if in response to applause. There wasn't any, of course, but that didn't stop this guy.

"Thank you. Thank you. You are, too kind. It was the least that I and my flashing blades could do for the sake of humanity, not to mention the vigorous and everlasting love of beautiful, señoritas everywhere."

David felt his own mouth drop open. He walked over to where Jason Inada stood with a knot of guys wielding bokken and practicing Japanese style swordsmanship.

"Jason? Is this guy for real?"

Jason rolled his eyes. "I'm afraid so, Dave. I don't know what's bigger: his head, his mouth, his opinion of himself…or that rolled-up sock he keeps in his tights,"

They all chuckled.

It did in fact, *look* like a sock.

"But his militia commander from Elkhart swears that he's a genuine death dealer with a blade."

David smiled. "Sounds great. Then why don't we give this guy a little workout? You know, to see what he's made of. If he checks out, maybe we can recruit him for the Blackhawks."

Jason nodded. "I'm game. We can put him through his paces. But they say he's pretty tough."

David picked up a wooden practice sword. "We'll know how tough he is in a couple of hours."

By dusk a few dozen of them remained on the practice field, rolling around, laughing, bruised, bleeding and battered in the dirt. Broken practice swords and weapons littered the area.

Alejandro Maximillian Aguilar sported a black eye, bloody nose, split lip, and countless bruises. He looked coated in dirt, his poufy shirt and his tights were ripped, and all of his feathers had broken off his crumpled cavalier hat.

David and Jason laughed along with them all, more or less in the same condition. By then they were all so sore and exhausted they didn't want to move. For warriors, it was a good feeling.

The Eagle of the Southwest tilted his head back and laughed even more.

"Ah, my friends, my friends. *That* was indeed a practice session. A truly inspired sparring match…after match…after match. Gracias. Gracias, amigos."

David winced. "Al, my troops and I would be happy to go into battle with you anytime, anywhere. We all learned a lot today. You have moves and techniques that I've never even seen before. And I've seen a lot."

"I agree, in every way," Jason added.

"My friends, you are too kind. I could say the same for all of you, but I'm afraid…that you will have to carry me somewhere. For I believe that I am somewhat creepled."

They spluttered and burst out roaring with laughter. Tears shot out of their eyes like water from drinking fountains.

"Seriously, my friends. I am quite creepled; I do not think that I can walk."

David finally regained the ability to speak.

"Then, Al, I hope it doesn't get too cold tonight, because I can't get up, either. We're SOL, so why don't we just camp out here?"

"If we're lucky," Jason said, "maybe someone will throw some blankets over us."

"To hell with that," one of the troops said. "I'm gettin' home if I have to crawl there."

Finally Jerriel walked up, staring down at them all with a very confused expression on her face.

"Daeved? Are you and these oothers hurt?"

"Only my pride, Jerriel. Only my pride. Please. We're all beat up and exhausted. Can you get some of our people to help us get home?"

"Verry well. You and your friends are verry strange, Daeved."

"I know. I admit it. We sure as hell are. Hey, meet our new friend, Al. Say hello to Jerriel, Al."

Alejandro struggled to get to his feet. He could barely do that much. "My beautiful lady, forgive me for being seen in this wretched state. Could I stand without holding onto something, I would gladly kiss your lovely hand and praise you with poetry and song. But alas, these filthy bastards have creepled me!"

"Creepled?" Jerriel said.

They all burst out laughing again, until they could hardly breathe.

Mason finally recovered. "Al, you gotta stop with the 'creepled' stuff. You're a mad man with a sword, but you're killing us with that word."

"Why? What did I say? Creepled?"

It was several minutes before they were all taken home. They carried Al away on a stretcher, but like the rest of them, he'd be fine after a good night's rest.

"I'm going to be sore as hell tomorrow," David warned Jerriel. "But it was a fantastic practice. You don't often get to work out with people of that caliber. So, how did your magic class go today?"

"S'okay. And here I was worried that I ran late. And yet I had to come looking for you."

"Yeah, I guess we both got carried away."

"I'll clean you up with magic when we get home, Daeved. You stink."

"Yep. I sure do."

At home, David moaned on the couch after dinner, trying not to move.

Jerriel spent time trying to decipher and unlock more of her father's magical journal. She also turned her mother's soulstone over and over in her hands. Occasionally it would flash with some kind of magic force.

"Any luck with your father's notes?"

"Somewhat," Jerriel said. "He talks about his growing fears that the Dark Khabal had infiltrated the colonial forces. Of course, now we know that they have. But back then, our people were so busy defending the colony of Vaejan against the monster hordes. The city was nearly overrun on several occasions. My father was one of the champions who helped beat them back. He sent my mother to the Old World to address their mutual fears. Then, when my mother's ship sank, and she was lost, my father both grieved and became increasingly paranoid."

"Sounds like he had good reason," David said.

"Yes. He took a chance on sharing his fears with High Magus Gorrial Lankorro. The Magus tried to reassure my father that his concerns were still minor compared to the constant threats they faced. Once Vaejan was secure, they could then root out the Khabal. The monster hordes launched the most massive assault on the city state we had ever seen in an attempt to wipe us out."

She paused and lowered her eyes, and took in a few sharp breaths.

"Jerriel?" David asked her.

"You have to understand, I was already mourning the loss of my mother. My father had to leave for the front lines of the battle to help defend us. He gave me his journal and some of the keys to decoding it. He told me to protect his writings, and my mother's soulstone, which she had given to me before she left. My father said that if anything happened to him, I was not to trust anyone. Not even my own brother, who was apprenticed to the High Magus. He warned me to leave Vaejan, and steal away. I swore to him that I would use my powers to travel unseen, just as he had taught me, and reach my mother's kin in Kellendra. He told me that everything would be explained in his writings, and that if something ever happened to him, it would prove that his worst fears were all true."

"And have you deciphered enough to know what all of that is?" David asked.

Jerriel shook her head. "I'm still sifting through it. My father was a mage genius, so even with the magical keys he gave me, translating his magical codes is a tedious and difficult task at best. My older brother was so much better at this sort of thing than I ever was. But I have done my best, and the glimpses I have had are terrifying."

"How so?" David said.

"My father feared that...that the Dark Ghods were conspiring to cripple or destroy Tharanor somehow. It all had something to do with the Six High Mages, other dimensions, transport magic of every variety, the Spectral Keys, and their Spectral Guardians. Much of that knowledge was thought to be lost during the eons of the Ancients."

David sighed. "Jerriel, none of that means very much to me."

"They speak of things from the depths of Time, when the universe itself and all the worlds were created. Only the High Mages of Tharanor would know even a part of such secrets, and would guard them all with their very lives. In the wrong hands, such ancient and powerful knowledge could be devastating."

"But you say this Gorrial—this High Magus character—was one of the Six High Mages, and he's now leading the Dark Khabal?"

"Yes, that would indeed explain much. But I only know the legends of all of these matters. My parents studied the Ancient Mysteries all their lives. I think my father and mother learned all that they could about them, and the facts are contained deeper within his writings. I must continue to study and learn from his vast store of knowledge and wisdom. He told me that I must get his journal, or a translated copy of it, to the Sylurrian and Marrandorian royals back in the Old World. The other five High Mages needed to be warned, unless they proved unfaithful as well."

"We can't even get ten miles outside of Michiana," David said. "How are we going to do all of that?" Reaching the Old World sounded impossible. Like trying to go to the moon.

"First I must unlock and decode all of the journal," Jerriel said. "Nothing can be done until then, in any case. But, perhaps we can find some way to send word to Kellendra and Tornhold. They would help us, and relay word to the continent, if they could, and if they knew we were here."

"What about your older brother, Jerriel? You said that he was working for the enemy now. You were fleeing from him and the Khabal when the Merge struck, isn't that right?"

She nodded. "Yes. My brother had been gone for almost three years or more. I hardly saw him. He was supposedly working very closely with the High Magus. Then, when our father was killed at the front lines, he came to me and demanded that I help him find father's journal and mother's soulstone. He told me that the High Magus had need of them. I put him off, saying that in my grief, I did not know or care where such unimportant things were. And that he was free to seek them out on his own. My brother chided me for being naught but a silly, weepy girl. We parted in anger, and I fled that very night. As I did so, I thought several times that I was being pursued, and that the pursuer might be my brother, or the Khabal, or both. I did not take any chances."

Jerriel chuckled slightly.

"What's so funny?" David asked her.

"Hiding, eluding, and passing unseen was one of the only things that I was ever better at in magic than my prodigy older brother. He was always stronger, smarter, and learned things faster than myself. I was just thinking about when we were children. Even back then, I could use magic to confound and escape from my older brother. He could never find or catch me. It used to drive him crazy."

David smiled. "I'm just glad you got away this time," he told her. "Keep working on your father's writings. We need to know what he was trying to reveal."

"I agree," Jerriel said. "My parents gave their lives to get me safely away with these two artifacts. They must be of vital importance. I must learn how to use them both to help us now, and defeat our enemies, whoever they turn out to be."

3

"Several of the enemy mage prisoners have escaped," a runner came to warn them. The young trooper looked terrified.

Mason drew his Spillers. They would have to be enough. After the bath, he didn't have all of his other guns. And there wasn't time to go after them.

It also worried him that he still felt—off his game, somehow. Something was still very wrong with him, but he couldn't figure out what. Perhaps that was merely what sorrow and depression felt like.

Blondie shook the terrified runner. "Calm down. Tell me what you know. Which prisoners? How many of them?"

"S-six, six, I think. They tried to free the rest, but the guards on the scene shot two down. Then the enemy mages fled this way, and started killing everyone they could find with magic."

Troops screamed, and close by to the west, magic blasts went off, and the sounds of battle and further bursts of magical rapidly sped their way.

The runner continued to stammer, "The tall n-n-necromancer is leading them. Five others. I don't know their names. As soon as they broke out, the duty officer sent me after you two and the Thul woman."

Blondie let the runner go. "Try to find the Thul. Go. Keep spreading the alarm."

"Yes, s-sir!" The young runner looked only too happy to keep running.

"They're coming for us, aren't they, Blondie?" Mason asked, hefting his Spillers.

Blondie clenched both fists, and violet magefire flared up to his elbows. "Yep. Just like I said they would. How do you want to do this, Mace?"

"Hmmm…too many to hit them head on. Let's go at them from the flanks. I'll hit them on the left."

His blond friend nodded. "Then I'll take them on the right. The necromancer's going to be the toughest of the lot. Let's peel off the other five, if we can, and then take him on together."

"Sounds good, Blondie. Let's ride."

They skirted around to either side, trying to stick to cover and stay out of sight. Mason quickly lost sight of his friend.

It did briefly occur to him that this would be an excellent time for Blondie to turn on them all, and help the mages make good their escape. But at this point, Mason had no choice but to keep trusting his good friend.

Blondie said that his abilities were returning.

He could tell them anything he wanted. How would they know if it was the truth or not?

From the sounds of things, the militia troops were putting up a pretty good fight and delaying the enemy at least somewhat. Each precious second they could hold them back, more troops would pour in.

Yet even as Mason got into position to attack, the enemy mages continued to push through, causing death and destruction all around them, and leaving many casualties in their wake.

Startled troops could slow the enemy down, but they would be hard pressed to stop six enemy mages bent on a rampage of devastation.

They were lucky that it wasn't all thirteen of the mage captives on the loose.

At Blondie's urging, Major Bill had spread several of the captive mages out to other nearby, secret locations—beyond the limited range of their prisoners' telepathy.

Mason spotted the enemy. The necromancer strode out in front with another sorcerer. A pair of enemy wizards marched slightly behind them on either side, guarding their flanks and watching the rear.

Blondie stepped up and raked the enemy left and the middle with violet lightning that knocked four of the six off their feet, and stunned the two flankers.

The first flanker on the other side turned to attack Blondie. The second one raised his hands and his eyes got big when he saw the Pistolero step out and aim both of his pistols.

Click! Click!

Nothing. Mason's guns wouldn't fire. He cocked and pulled the triggers again.

Nothing.

By then the one mage was charging Blondie, exploding anything that was made of wood around him. He sent the shards and splinters and whirling debris at Blondie, while the necromancer and the other sorcerer still looked dazed and tried to regain their feet. And the mage facing Mason shot greenish-yellow flames out of his hands at all before him.

Mason dove out of the way, tucked and rolled out of sight, and then crouched and ran. The enemy wizard would be on him in seconds.

Finally he came to a building and ducked inside. He scrambled out of sight into an adjoining back storage room and ducked down. He tried his guns again. Still nothing. Why was this happening,? Now of all times?

Blondie needed him out there.

Maybe if he reloaded. Yeah, that would do it.

Slowing his breathing, doing his best to stay calm, he broke out his spare cylinders for his guns and swapped them out. He was fast at it, but every second counted.

He went back out into the fight. As he expected, the fighting quickly turned Blondie's way, and blasts of magic nearby showed where the foes were pursuing Blondie hard and blasting everything around him. Blondie fought back as best he could, but from what Mason could tell, his friend was outnumbered four to one.

He raced that way, not even trying to stay under cover this time. He had to catch up quickly, and take them from behind, if possible.

Mason sped around a building and almost slammed into the same enemy mage as before. This one seemed to be holding back and protecting the rear of the other three while they stalked Blondie.

Mason had intended to shoot them on sight, but he clobbered the mage from behind now that he was right on top of him. The mage grunted and dropped, unconscious.

Pistol-whipping worked better in this instance. Mason dragged the mage back out of sight and quickly gagged him, and bound his hands and ankles behind him.

At this distance, Mason would not have any trouble taking out the other three with one or two shots, once he spotted them again. And their spells gave them away when they fired. Hopefully, Blondie was staying ahead of them.

Mason rushed forward once more, spotted several troops closing in with bows and crossbows, and motioned for them to go around and close in from one side or the other.

Finally he spotted the necromancer and the one wizard, crouched down and making plans of some kind.

Mason took aim at them with both barrels.

Click. Click.

Crap, not again. What the hell was going on?

Even worse, the necromancer turned and locked eyes with him.

"There's the other one. Let's get him!" All of their hands glowed with magefire.

Mason turned and ran for it. Dark lightning and exploding ice covered the area he had just been in.

His foes were right after him. Archers tried to fire upon the mages, but they swept the troops away from their positions with blasts of power.

A stone or outcropping of brick caught the toe of Mason's boot. He hurtled down upon his face, and tried to roll back up to his feet.

The third enemy mage stepped out right in front of Mason.

Now, the three of them had him fairly trapped.

"Kill him!" the necromancer roared.

The wizard still hesitated an instant. Then he prepared a spell, his hands beginning to glow brighter and brighter.

They were only a dozen or so feet away. Mason hurled his useless pistols at the wizard.

One missed as the fellow dodged to one side.

The other smacked him squarely in the face and dazed and bloodied him.

Mason expected to be cut down from behind by the other two enemies any second.

He glanced back just as the two stood ready to unleash their spells.

A net of lightning fell over both mages. Blondie rushed in, directing it right over them.

The mages tried to shield themselves.

Then the eleven o'clock express named Thulkara charged in and smashed into both mages. One she swatted away like an insect with the back of her gauntlet. The wizard flew through the air, slammed into the wall of a building, grunted, and dropped into a heap on the ground.

The necromancer she rammed into the earth with her shield.

He did not get back up. There wasn't much that could from such a blow.

Blondie came running up to Mason, a worried look on his face.

"What happened, Mace? For a moment, I was worried they got you. Then I saw you having trouble with your guns. Why aren't they working?"

Mason sighed heavily and shook his head. "I wish to hell I knew. I dunno, Blondie. They just don't seem to work anymore."

"What's this?" Thulkara said. "Mace's magic isn't working?"

Troops rushed in to collect and secure the prisoners.

All of the escaped mages were recaptured and accounted for. Two were killed during the breakout, shot repeatedly with arrows and crossbow bolts. Of the other five, four of them were in pretty bad shape. The six who never made it out of their cells were spread out even more, and kept under heavy guard.

Thus began a very heated discussion with Major Avery. It was obvious that the necromancer was the ringleader.

Nine militia troops had been killed outright. Thirty-one more troops had been wounded to various degrees.

At first, they spoke about what to do with the mages. Blondie told Major Avery his plans, and they discussed the matter extensively.

During all that time, neither Blondie nor Thulkara said anything about Mason and his problem with his Wild Magic.

They were waiting for him to broach the subject with the militia.

When they reached a lull, and some food and drink was being brought in to the meeting, Mason just blurted it out.

"Bill. There is something else very important that you need to know."

"What is that, Mace?"

"My guns don't work anymore. My powers have stopped working. I have no idea why."

Major Bill Avery's mouth hung open.

"Damn it all. This is pretty serious, Mace. Are you sure?"

"Pretty damn sure."

They stopped what they were doing, went out with the reloading team on duty, and tested all of Mason's guns that had worked before.

Nothing. Not even a spark.

"How can this be?" Major Avery said. "Blondie, does any of this make any sense?"

"Bill, nothing about Wild Magic makes any sense. It might work for a thousand years. It could shift and go away in a second, for no reason at all."

"We could wait for the next thunderstorm at that lake," Mason said. "I could take a swim in that water again with my gear if the lake starts glowing again with Wild Magic."

Bill looked very discouraged. "It's worth a shot. I'm willing to try anything at this point.

"It could be emotional," Blondie said. "Mason's still in shock and depression from Tori's death. His mental state could affect his abilities."

Major Avery glanced between them. "Do you think that's the problem?"

21

Blondie threw up his hands. "I don't know. I'm grasping for reeds like the rest of you. But when I was fifteen, my dog died and I was sad for a few weeks. During that entire time, my powers failed me, and would not work. Other sorcerers have suffered such lapses at times. It is not unheard of. Unlike wizards and other mages, our powers are greatly affected by our moods and emotions. Our abilities are part of us, tied directly to us and all that we are and experience."

"Then we'll send Mace to a shrink. We'll try to cheer him up."

"To hell with all of that. That's the last thing I need. No, wait a minute," Mason insisted. "This is me and my life we're talking about. The problem is, we don't have any idea what's going on with me. For all we know, my powers could return ten minutes from now. Or else they've simply dried up like one those magic pools; here today, gone tomorrow. They might not ever come back."

"Well, let's just wait and see, then," Bill said.

The next morning, Mason tried one of his Spillers.

Nothing.

And nothing for the next two days after that. Each morning, he tried one of his guns.

Nothing worked.

At first, Mason felt even stranger, strapping on his armor and guns each day, living a lie, keeping up appearances for the sake of the military. His gear never felt so heavy to him before, but now, for some reason, it all did.

His steps felt like lead, even though he was in perfect physical health. His feet seemed to drag when he walked.

The ground held his interest, and he stared at it. His head felt heavy, too—like a bowling ball stuck on his neck. He felt no need to look up at the sky. The sun was still bright. The sky was still blue. What of it?

It had to be connected to Tori's death. He still felt depressed about it all, and there was no remedy that he knew of.

Major Bill said that Mason and Thulkara could stay on with the guards, protecting Blondie's efforts to locate and train more mages throughout Michiana. Now they were in the business of making and protecting mages.

Mason took to just wearing his Spillers for show, and added a short sword and a hunting knife to his belt. Now he guarded Blondie's back, and Blondie took center stage as Michiana's primary mage.

It was all something to do to keep busy, other than sit in a room somewhere and be depressed. To hell with that.

22

4

Another few days passed rapidly for David and Jerriel. The last part of spring grew slightly warmer but also very wet at certain times. There was always more to do, and not enough time to do it in.

Language sessions, training sessions, and meetings abounded. Then there was militia duty with the troops at guard posts and patrolling the borders. They helped negotiate trade deals with the other enclaves, and even pursued and captured criminals.

Jerriel did take time, with help from Robert Billings, to enchant the rest of David's weapons, a few for General Dirk Blackwood and some of David's friends—even a set of daisho for Steven Hayward on his fifteenth birthday, the young warrior who had save both David and Jerriel, on several occasions.

Steven looked extremely happy with that gift, which came with another hug and a kiss from Jerriel. That always made everything better.

Jerriel and her mage screeners discovered more mages and even a few more fledgling enchanters for her training group. They took to assisting her and Robert Billings in their daunting task of enchanting basic magical weapons for the Blackhawks. In time, they would all become capable of enchanting weapons and artifacts on their own.

Dirk wanted the Blackhawks to be the first elite militia unit that could wield enchanted weapons.

Working together, the Urth humans of South Bend started to get a handle on their internal and border security. A few of their long-range scouting patrols even managed to return—or, at least, what was left of them. They warned of multiple, lethal dangers awaiting travelers in the wilds.

Many other exploration patrols, unfortunately, were never heard from again. Michiana remained cut off from its neighbors, and the greater outside world.

Dirk Blackwood and the town council held regular briefing sessions for the militia commanders, their various think tanks, and the council advisors.

"First of all," Dirk told them, "not a single scouting unit that we've sent toward what used to be the Chicago area has made it back. We haven't had contact with anyone west of what used to be New Carlisle, or east of Goshen. And we've stopped sending anyone out those ways to avoid further losses. Anything beyond fifteen to twenty-five miles out is dark to us—a dead zone. We have no knowledge of what's going on out beyond there, and that is not good."

He pointed at a regional map of Illinois, Indiana, Michigan, and Ohio.

"Outside of our town defenses, roving bands of monsters still raid and cause chaos at will, for days into the wilderness in every direction. We're contemplating sending out larger, better armed units of long-range troops to confront and take out any such threats wherever they can find them. Such dangers could pose great harm to future crops before they can be harvested. And they will keep other stranded groups of humans from reaching us. We cannot risk any of that.

"Meanwhile, we can only guess that tens of thousands of humans still might survive in pockets, huddled together for protection in places further out such as Benton Harbor, Kalamazoo, and Walkerton. We cannot leave them to fend for themselves.

"Some scouts have even made contact with other survivors, who report that there are other surviving, isolated enclaves around Battle Creek, Grand Rapids, and Lansing.

"We still haven't heard anything directly from Detroit or Toledo, where it is rumored that both humans and colonial Tharanorians are probably also still holding out. They could be in a situation much like our own, isolated and under siege. But again, the time window since the Merge still hasn't been very long. Such alliances could prove useful, but only after actual contact has been made. Yet we are guessing that even the Tharanorians, who are used to magic, have probably suffered ill effects and confusion from the Merge and its disruption of magic."

Someone called out from the council. "General Blackwood. What has the militia done to ensure and protect our food production? Food rationing within the city has already begun, and it is extremely unpopular among the general public."

"Security in the region continues to be a major concern. You can talk to the agricultural people and the Food Supply Department, but we believe that we already have enough basic supplies to get us through the year and all the way into next spring, if we are forced to. But it will still be pretty grim. We're talking about emergency rations of beans, rice, oil, flour, cheese, corn, and soy beans. Survival rations, barely enough to keep people from starving. But at least we could stretch it that far and still make it.

"But the militia and the council fear another darkspawn attack before we can raise and harvest fresh crops. Our enemies might burn or destroy our crops in the field before we can gather them. Another horde could trample our crops at night and cripple us without ever attacking our troops directly. That's why we need alliances with other groups to help patrol and protect more of our area. We don't have the forces to patrol every sector at once, and still protect the town and maintain internal security."

"So what do you propose?" an advisor asked.

Dirk pointed to Elkhart. "In the short term, we're in the process of negotiating treaties with Elkhart. They are the next closest, largest population of humanity. But they're currently a mess. We'll try do the same with any other enclave willing to cooperate with us and respect the rule of law. That won't be easy. This Dragon Cult in Elkhart is dangerous and spreading rapidly, from what we hear. Too much so.

"We might be forced to fight a war against them in the very near future, and the Elkhart street gangs are on the fence, too. They're quickly becoming mercenaries. They sell their muscle to anyone who will pay and supply them with food, weapons, liquor, drugs, and women."

Dirk sighed and shook his head.

"The Dragon Cult is descending into mass human sacrifice and murder—even children are not spared, it is said. We can't allow such atrocities to continue. Once our alliances are in place, it may become necessary to send a large army to Elkhart in order to do away with the source of this vile cult, a rather large and nasty red dragon that has mated with a blue dragon. We cannot have our skies filled with these monsters and the spread of this cult. They cannot be allowed to breed and produce more of their ilk. We have seen enough dragons and weird

25

monsters in the area as it is. Jerriel, can you advise us any further? We don't have much experience in dealing with dragons."

Jerriel stood up. "Commander Blackwood. I'm afraid I'm not very well versed in all the many nuances of dragonlore, but I would advise that you move quickly. A true dragon has four legs, wings, and vast intelligence–especially involving magic. There can be various drakes, serpents, and wyrms–some even with dangerous breath weapons, but they do not have wings. There are smaller dragonets and winged serpents, much like dragons, but tiny in comparison. They range in size from that of a songbird to that of a falcon. Many dragonets eat fruit, plants, or fish. They can use magic, but they usually have no more intellect than an average, clever person.

"I have heard that true dragons breed slowly and they are extremely proud and independent. Once hatched, it takes almost a century for them to reach their full size and strength–where they are the most dangerous. But in one year's time, a dragon hatchling is larger than a man and can fly. In ten years' time, a dragon leaves the nest of its parents. It is much larger by then, learns to use its breath weapons, and can travel interdimensionally–in some cases, even through Time–in order to escape danger, usually from other dragons. Dragons even see other dragons as potential food.

"Immature dragons will instinctively find a place where they can mature in peace, and may return briefly to where they were hatched, once they are fully developed. Young dragons are often nomadic, hunter-explorers. They are extremely intelligent and perceive magic intuitively, yet most of them become amoral and opportunistic. Some dragons can be reasoned with, if properly approached. They can intimidate the weak-minded and use many magicks and enchantments at will. Some few of them do enjoy being worshipped as gods by other, lesser creatures–but this is generally frowned upon by dragonkind. Others despise contact with most other sentients–even other dragons. There's a lot of room for variation in between.

"The vast majority of dragonkind will eat any kind of meat if they are hungry, and a hungry dragon is well known to be both ruthless and voracious. They see themselves as the undisputed, top of the food chain. When attacked or roused to anger, dragons can be both very destructive and extremely difficult to kill, as you might expect."

David stood up to speak. "Some of you might recall that I had a brief meeting with a green dragon, or forest dragon: Shavalkathar. He offered to speak with Jerriel if we traveled to his lair, a week to ten days west of here. We've talked about it ever since then, and we think that it's time to make that journey and have that meeting. This dragon wasn't openly hostile to us and, in fact, seemed rather amused and interested in our situation. Jerriel thinks that he could be a good source of much-needed information and, possibly, with limitations, a potential ally."

26

Someone in the crowd stood up and protested. "Why should we ally ourselves with one of these monsters? A dragon? They sound just as evil as the demon."

Jerriel shook her head. "You cannot think of dragons that way. They are very different from demons. They are unlike any other creature you shall ever deal with. And if you think that they answer to you and your laws, you will be gravely mistaken and sure to run afoul of them. They are dragons. By themselves they are neither good nor evil; nor do they see themselves or their actions bound by anyone's petty limitations. They are forces of nature in their own right, free agents who act as they will. If treated properly, and with respect, they have been known even to be friendly and helpful to humans at times, especially if that is in their best interests as well."

"It still sounds like a devil's bargain to me," another advisor said.

David raised his hands. "Look around us at what we face. We don't have a lot of choice, and most of all, we need information. We can't expect that all of these beings and creatures are going to do what we want them to just for our sake. This dragon we have mentioned has done us no harm. He hunts over hundreds, perhaps thousands of miles, and has seen much that we need to know about the region, the changes after the Merge, our foes, and any survivors still out there. It might even know of ways to cross over to the other side of the Merge. We cannot pass up such opportunities. We must make contact with him and, even if we cannot make him our friend and ally, we should keep him from becoming yet another enemy. We have far too many of those as it is."

"What do you propose, Captain Pritchard?" one of the council members asked.

David looked a bit confused. Dirk had told him the trip was already approved. "That Jerriel and I, and one or two hand-picked companies from the Blackhawks, will set out tomorrow. We hope to return within approximately two or three weeks to make a full report on our findings to the town council. By that time, we should know much more about what is happening outside of our town and across the region."

Voices rose up both in support and against such a mission.

"Jerriel is our only high-level wizard," some complained. "The only Tharanorian we have contact with."

"We cannot risk her getting captured or killed. You said that the demon and other enemy wizards were after her. We still don't know why."

"The council has spoken already on this matter," Dirk reminded the dissenters. "The time for debate is over. The vote has been made and approved by the militia. This mission will proceed in secret and must be kept secret. Preparations have already begun."

David and Jerriel spent most of the rest of that day checking over equipment and supplies for their journey.

Dirk interrupted them four hours later. He brought a thirtyish couple around to them, Kyle and Melanie Emerson.

"I thought Jerriel would like to meet the Emersons," Dirk informed them. "They keep pigeons as a hobby—messenger pigeons, in fact."

Jerriel gave David her confused look. "Pigeons?" she asked.

"Birds used to send messages back and forth between cities—like doves, but larger."

Jerriel's eyes brightened. "Yes, yes. The peoples of Tharanor train various hawks, falcons, owls, and ravens to carry messages in the Old World. Where are these birds trained to go?"

Kyle Emerson smiled. "I have a sister named Laura who lives in Toledo, Ohio, with her husband and family," he said. "Or at least they did, before the Merge. We used to send birds back and forth every week, just for fun and practice. But no birds have reached us since then, and we only have one left that could make the trip. And what if our people are on the other side?"

Kyle's wife Melanie joined in. "It's about a hundred and forty miles, as the pigeon flies. Depending on the bird and the weather, we could send or receive a message in one to three days, if a hawk or something else didn't get them along the way. We didn't want to risk it, until we learned in the paper that the authorities were looking for ways to contact the other cities. We decided we had to help."

"Wonderful!" Jerriel said. "I will immediately prepare a message for Kellendra, to be taken to my mother's people there. They must be made aware of our situation here and also be warned about the Dark Khabal in Vaejan. Thank you, good people."

Jerriel shook both of their hands and raced off to pen her message. David and Dirk spoke with the Emersons about the possibilities of setting up messenger pigeon service within Michiana and beyond. It all sounded feasible.

Dirk, David, and the recorders present all took notes. In the future, such communications could be vital.

They were still discussing such matters when Jerriel returned almost an hour later, with her carefully prepared message, penned on both sides of a small scroll of paper.

Kyle Emerson hefted the scroll in his hands. "Do you have a postage scale or something the measures ounces?" he asked Dirk.

Dirk actually produced one. Kyle zeroed the scale and weighed the scroll. "Good. A little over two ounces. That should be fine."

"The birds can carry up to two and a half ounces without much trouble," Melanie added. "We'll send our bird out to Toledo today. It should reach it within one to three days. Hopefully, there will be someone there to receive it."

"We hope so, too," Jerriel told them. "Again, thank you, good people. This could be very important."

They said their farewells. Dirk led the Emersons out to do their duty, talking all the while with them about the new messenger bird service he wanted to establish.

"What did you say in the letter?" David asked Jerriel.

Jerriel smiled. "Everything that we needed to tell them and warn them about. I asked them to send word to the Old World, and to send help our way, if they could. And to contact the other colonial city states. With the Khabal here, this could very well mean a much larger war between the new colonies. All of the six nations will respond, once they know."

David shook his head. "There's a lot riding on that little bird getting through," he said. "I hope it makes it."

"Me too," Jerriel noted. "Come, Daeved. Our path takes us to the dragon, and the wilds hold many dangers."

5

Mason tried everything he could think of to revive his powers.

He spent hours with four different counselors, sorting through his feelings and his depression. He tried a couple of antidepressant drugs, but they made him sick, loopy, or actually want to kill himself—in creative ways.

Next, Blondie performed a bunch of magical tests on him, now that the Sylurrian's own magical knowledge had returned.

The militia actually gave Blondie an entire old warehouse to use for his new magical laboratory. Blondie filled it with stuff within that first week.

After two days of tests, his sorcerous friend had no answers for Mason. "I still think the problem is in your mind, Mace," Blondie told him. "But I can't be sure. Even my people don't know that much about Wild Magic or all of its effects. Yet for whatever reason, your powers are gone. I have no idea if they will ever come back."

It was a beautiful spring day with a nice breeze somewhere between cool and warm.

Mason looked out at the white clouds in the blue sky.

Life after the Merge was going to go on with or without Tori Nelson, without Mason Tyler–and with or without the Pistolero. In fact, it was already clipping along without a whole lot of folks.

It was his choice what he chose to do next.

He let out a breath. "I wanna join the militia."

Blondie looked at him, at a loss, as if he didn't understand what Mason was saying. "What? Mace, we've both been a part of things all–"

"No, we weren't, Blondie. We never signed up. We never took the oath. We never joined anything. I rode and fought alongside the militia, but I was never officially part of them. Now I wanna join up. I wanna be a trooper, just like anyone else."

Blondie sighed. "All right, easy enough. I don't see why you need to make a big deal out of this. Bill offered us commissions several times. You'll become an officer and–"

"Nope. No easy commission just handed to me. I don't want to be an officer. Just a regular recruit, and then a trooper, like anyone else."

"Mace, whatever else happens to you, I have a very strong feeling that you are never going to be just like everyone else. Why do you feel like you have to do this this way?"

"I can go to Bill on my own, if you don't want to be involved."

"I didn't say that, Mace. I hate it when you act all stubborn and bull-headed like this. You wanna play soldier? Then go right ahead, if that fills out your time. But there are too many people out there–including our enemies–who would like nothing better than to get a hold of you somewhere by yourself, and take you apart like a puzzle–piece-by-piece. Is this your way of ending it? Giving others the chance to kill you?"

Mason grabbed Blondie by the front of his duster. "What the hell do you care, Blondie?"

His friend actually looked hurt and wounded for a passing instant, and Mason felt sorry for that. "Because you are my brother, Mace. And just as you have done, countless times, I would step up, stand in your place, and face down Death itself for you. Go ahead. Join the militia. Do all that you think you need to do. But I will demand that Bill attaches you to my private guard, along with Thulkara. None of us are going to stand by and do nothing, and watch you go off on your own, where too many others can get at you!"

"I never said I wanted to die, or let anyone kill me, Blondie. That's not what I'm after. Trust me."

"Then what are you after, Mace?"

He let Blondie go. Mason paused, and thought some more.

It seemed as if everything that had meant anything to him had been taken–stripped away from him.

"Blondie, I might not even know just yet what the hell I'm trying to do or find. But whatever it turns out to be, let me do it on my own, in my own way. How's that?"

Blondie nodded. "That's fine. As long as it doesn't get your dumb ass killed. Now, will you suck it up and go along with me to throw a scare into these other enemy mages?"

"Sure. What the hell do you want me to do?'

"Nothing much. Just stand around and look pissed off and ready to kill everyone around you."

"That's easy enough. Why the hell are we still yelling?"

"Because you were yelling at me, you dumb bastard!"

"Oh…" Mason said. "Sorry."

Several minutes later, Blondie put on a show for the six remaining enemy mages, five of whom never made it out of their cells. The other five were still laid up with their various, critical injuries.

The militia still didn't know if the necromancer was going to make it. He could go either way.

All of the captives were male. The Dark Khabal only recruited men as battle mages. The females mages who joined them were recruited differently and used in various ways by the cult to advance their power.

Blondie said that female necromancers were a rare and extremely vicious breed. When they swore their Dark Oaths to the Fallen, they did so over the sacrificed corpses and souls of men or even lovers and husbands whom they had loved—or worse still, their own children. They hardly ever exposed themselves, and that was often how the cult itself managed to survive—passed on by its women.

Major Bill helped them put on their little drama. Blondie would do most of the talking, after Bill said his piece.

They held it within one of the newly appointed outposts in town. This one was still under construction. Each such outpost would garrison a handful of rotating companies along key defensive lines. They were technically forts, constructed from brick, stone, debris, or fresh concrete as needed. Two such forts would anchor the ends of one of the old defensive lines.

Eventually, the plan was to build more such forts along those same lines, and defensive walls between each of the forts, or gatehouses, as needed.

This one was going to be the first, running just west of Bendix Road, and south of Ireland Road, along the old third defensive lines out those ways, and curving together where they joined up.

The partially constructed main keep of the first fortress formed a perfect arena to stage their little drama within. Several hundred militia were gathered together there, silent, grim, and bristling with weapons.

"Bring out the prisoners for sentencing under summary military justice," Major Bill announced, for all to hear.

Blondie had explained to them that only under the threat of death would any of the enemy mages possibly break down and try to save their own necks. And it might only work on the younger battlemages, who hadn't taken the Dark Oath or sought to become necromancers yet.

No one from any world wanted to die uselessly, for no reason. That much was human nature.

The six enemy mages were paraded out, shackled heavily, with gags over their mouths and black hoods over their heads.

The hoods were yanked off, and so were the gags. The six young men blinked at the sun and sky—at the gallows of six nooses waiting for them on the raised platform in front of them.

Around them, all they could see were the grim faces of hundreds of enemies staring back at them. Faces of troops whose friends and family they had helped kill and maim.

Major Bill spoke once more. "Under the Code of Summary Military Justice, established by the Militias of Michiana, these six enemy mages have lived out any value or usefulness as prisoners of war, and shall be executed as dangerous enemies of the state upon this day."

They were led up onto the platform and stood before the gallows. Executioners placed the nooses around their necks and prepared them to be hanged.

All six of the mages showed some sign of fear. Four of them shook visibly. Three of them openly wept. Only one of them seemed to go into one of their trances, and kept his eyes closed tight the entire time.

Mason swallowed hard and resisted his own very strong urge to rub the scar on his own neck from his near-hanging at the hands of vigilantes.

"These enemy prisoners did conspire to lead and execute a breakout and escape from their captivity," Bill noted. "This resulted in the loss of further militia lives, and many wounded. For these and their many crimes, let them be hanged by the neck until dead, and their bodies burned and disposed of in an unmarked mass grave. As soon as their five comrades are fit enough for execution, they shall be hanged and join them as well. May God have mercy upon them and their souls."

The wind whipped up suddenly and rippled through the captives' clothing. The six mages stood there, fully expecting to die.

A long, grim, terrible moment lingered.

"Enemy mages, our prisoners, you who have never spoken to us before," the major told them "This is you last chance. Do you have any final words that you wish to speak? Anything that you would like to say, before your sentences are carried out, and you meet Death?"

Two of them sighed and whimpered.

"Speak now, or be forever silenced!"

Blondie rushed out and lifted a hand to Major Bill. "Major, these men are our foes, that much is clear. But they were also my brothers, once, from my own nation. I alone understand them and their ways. Please, I beg of you, dread commander. Do not do this thing. It is the right and duty of every prisoner of war to seek to escape and return to his own forces. What they have done, they did so in the line of duty to their superiors. I still ask for mercy for these prisoners of war."

"Stand aside, or share their fate!" Major Avery snarled. Several dozen militia archers and crossbows suddenly pointed at Blondie, who remained defiant. "The sentence shall be carried out. These wretches have been given their final say."

"No!" Blondie yelled. "Allow me but to speak with each of them before they die. At least let someone from their world share words with them before their lives are ripped from their bodies. They may have a final request, or a message that they wish to have sent back to someone."

The major hesitated. "Very well, be quick about it then."

Blondie went up onto the gallows toward the condemned.

Mason followed his friend up, keeping both of his now useless pistols trained on his friend's back.

But the enemy mages didn't know that those pistols weren't working anymore.

Blondie went to Gellonar first. The wizard who had shown reluctance all along, but had been part of the escape attempt. "Gellonar, they are going to kill each and everyone of you. I tried to negotiate some other punishment, but the escape attempt royally pissed off all of these Urthers. They want all of you dead."

Gellonar nodded, and hung his head, resigned to his death.

"But listen, there still may be a way out."

The man stared back up at him and his mouth hung open. Finally he spoke. "What must I do?"

"Renounce your leaders. Offer to help them. They are desperate for information on us!"

"But…they are the enemy."

Blondie glanced back at Mason, and then leaned in to whisper at the condemned man so that only they could hear. "What does all of that matter, once you are dead? Lie to them. Make up something to appease them. Tell them anything they want to know. Offer to help them, and make some show of it in the days to come. Once they begin to trust you, just like myself, you can bide your time, and choose the right moment for your escape, when they least suspect it. I will help you. But nothing will work if you simply let them kill you. What higher purpose will that serve?"

Gellonar hesitated.

"What say you, Gellonar? Speak or die."

"What must I do?"

"I will ask for you all to be given a chance to cooperate with the Urthers. You must agree to do so and then follow through. That will at least keep you alive for a while. Let me speak with the others. Stand ready."

"Very well."

Blondie went to each of the condemned mages and spoke to them, telling them something similar. Mason followed along in the same fashion.

Five of the six seemed receptive to his plan. Only Zanjan ignored Blondie and his words, keeping his eyes closed and staying in his deep trance, awaiting death.

Blondie left them and went to speak with Major Avery.

Very quickly, the captives were all gagged and hooded once more, and shuffled off to separate holding areas where they could not contact each other.

After the militia separately questioned the five prisoners thereafter, four of them agreed to cooperate, promising no further attempts at escape, upon pain of death. Major Avery explained to them that once the militia had learned all that it could find out from them, as prisoners of war, they would then be released to go wherever they wished. Or they could remain in Michiana itself.

Blondie had done it, that snake. He had tricked four enemy mages into cooperating and spilling their guts.

Now the real interrogations could actually begin.

Mason spoke his recruiting oath later that evening after dinner, and was given his orders to report for ongoing basic training the following day.

That was it. He was now officially in the militia.

Blondie laughed and said that Mason could join them for some of the initial interrogation sessions later that same day, in the afternoon.

Thulkara rubbed her hands together eagerly, and said that she would be certain to come train with Mason's unit at some point.

Mason promptly began to wonder if he had made a grave mistake in signing up.

6

David and Jerriel's exploration company left the outskirts of South Bend very early the next day while it was still dark, far to the northwest. They skirted the north side of what was left of the east-west toll way. Few houses remained out that way. Most of the dwellings there had been burned out or abandoned during the monster attacks.

David, Jerriel, Jason Inada, Alejandro the Eagle, and two full companies—two hundred Blackhawks—went into the wilds. They wore new uniforms, armor, weapons, and gear. They carried enough supplies for three weeks.

David liked the new, militia field plate armor. The various pieces were made either of metal or high strength plastic to reduce weight. The final version proved to be a light, serviceable design, patterned after his own original armor, and not without some flair. It provided the wearer with good movement, protection, and flexibility. The weight distribution ratio was almost perfect.

There was a good range of vision in the helmets, and comfortable foam rubber padding in all the right places. The helms could be removed easily enough, but not knocked off by a blow during combat.

Their new armor had added bonuses such as dexterous gauntlets, and good armor for the legs, and especially the feet, that went over boots. Overall, the new suits offered very decent protection from head to foot. They had also been well-designed for use with military-style packs, for carrying and securing lots of gear and weapons in a variety of load bearing configurations.

David and the troops had tested several versions around town while on patrol. Nothing was left shiny. Every suit was primed, painted in a broken camouflage pattern, and sealed with a flat, non-reflective polymer to inhibit rust and corrosion.

Each trooper could fine tune his or her own suit of armor and load bearing gear to their own personal liking. Everyone but Jerriel marched out carrying about eighty to ninety pounds, but as they used up their supplies, that weight would decrease.

For weapons, each Blackhawk trooper had a six-and-a-half-foot spear, with a pointed butt cap. Next came a sword, usually a longsword or katana-style weapon of high carbon steel, a short sword or long fighting knife as backups, assorted hunting knives and hatchets, or tomahawks such as David's.

Many troops also carried a new, light plastic shield some genius had devised that could fold up to one quarter of its size for easy packing and carrying. In combat, it could be used half-size, or folded out and locked into place to form an effective shield wall. The plastic was more flexible than metal, and stood up well to blows and arrows. It had a small, round, hard plastic shield boss to help deflect weapons, and hard metal stripping around the edges to protect it from splintering.

A full third of the company were also archers, and carried strong short bows, composite wheel bows, or light crossbows—and four dozen war arrows or bolts. David had his light crossbow, and many of the other troops also elected to carry some kind of missile weapons. A few carried those modern crossbow pistols. This would give them additional firepower in a pinch if they needed it.

From all reports, the wilds were incredibly dangerous, and the company went into it heavily armed and armored. Alejandro wore a morion-style helmet, breastplate, and arm and leg armor that looked very flexible. He looked a lot like a Spanish Conquistador.

Since her head injury during the one battle, even Jerriel had the armorers fashion a light, padded metal arming cap for her to wear on her head for protection, with a short, segmented lobster tail to guard the back of her neck. But usually her helmet hung down her back or at her side. Mages did not like to wear a lot of armor, but in a pitched fight, the head was simply too vulnerable not to protect it.

Horses or pack animals would give them away too easily and were left behind. They did bring two German shepherd military dogs, trained for use in combat. Each dog had a pair of handlers.

The dogs rotated around the company in a patrol sweep mode to the front, flanks, and rear. The idea was that the keen senses of the dogs might detect danger before it fell upon them, and give them some advance warning. Armored mantles and spiked collars had even been fashioned for the dogs.

After they proceeded ten miles and into the early afternoon, the fragments of the 80/90 toll way mostly disappeared, replaced by rolling patches of hills and the dense, dark forests of Tharanor, as far as the eye could see.

David checked the most up-to-date map he had been given. They were already near the end of most of the charted areas to the west. There were inroads here and there where a few of the scouting teams had gone forward for up to a week and barely made it back. All of them had been attacked by something.

Several red Xs marked where scouting teams had gone in and what direction they had been heading in before all contact with them was lost.

David's chosen path to reach the dragon in the distant mountains did not take them into any previously known areas. In fact, there were at least three red Xs denoting lost patrols all around their current position, before they had even gone an entire day.

Not good.

They had mappers with them who would track and detail their progress, and extra pairs of lightly armed runners to send back with progress reports for their first week out.

"I'm guessing," David said, "that at this rate, it might only take us as little as five days to a week to reach and locate the dragon's lair in the mountains, and as much time to get back. The original estimates factored in all sorts of fighting and trouble along the way."

How long the trip took did, in fact, all depended on whatever trouble they stepped in along the way.

And there was sure to be some kind of trouble. David had no doubts about that.

All of those scout teams sent out this way had gone missing, somehow.

"The dragon hinted at the fact that he had neighbors who were not very friendly," David recalled.

"Then expect the worst," Jerriel said. "Everything in the wilds of Tharanor's New World tries to eat everything else, whenever possible."

Many of the trees and plants were at times similar to Urth vegetation, but wide variation and entirely new species were common.

Jerriel tried to educate them on what she knew about Tharanorian flora as they went along, pointing out which plants, roots, and herbs were helpful or harmful, teaching them the names in her tongue. But in the New World, even her knowledge was spotty and incomplete.

David and most of his people strove to speak Tharanorian to Jerriel, and she tried to speak English to them.

The first day went by quickly and without much incident, other than spotting a few strange animals, birds, insects, and about half of the trees and plants.

Late afternoon came and they still followed their set course along some drifting animal trails. They made attempts to cover and obscure all signs of their passing, including the use of scent and trace odor killers they had, and a few Jerriel had helped develop. They would test them all.

For the time being, their path looked relatively tame enough.

David struck up a casual conversation with his friends, when they weren't on point. There was finally time for him to make an attempt to gather some personal information from Jerriel about herself and her life while they kept marching.

"Jerriel, you've never told me much about your personal life, where you grew up and such. What was it like becoming a wizard among your people?"

Jerriel laughed. "We've been so busy trying to help yoor people stay alive. There really hasn't been much time for us to get to know each other. I have many questions about you and your people, as well."

David grinned. "That's true. We went home exhausted every night. But now we do have some time to talk Tell me something about yourself and you life among your people."

She laughed again, the sound of her voice sweet and lovely.

"Yes, yes," Alejandro said, butting in. "But I'm always especially interested in matters involving love making…"

Jerriel laughed again. "Alejhandro…we weren't talking about love making. Why do you always—"

The Eagle held up one hand. "As I was saying, before I was so rudely interrupted—and you mis-pronounced my name, too, by the way. But I forgive you…just this once. Among people in our world, I have found that most women prefer to make the sweet love at night when it is more dark and romantic. While men often prefer passionate and vigorous loving better in the morning, when they are eager and refreshed, and not so tired. Different preferences such as these cause no end of many problems and disagreements between lovers. The man says he is too tired at night, the woman says she is not awake yet, in the morning."

Al sighed. "As I said, it can be a great problem in the bedroom."

David frowned at his oblivious friend. Great timing, Al. Just when Jerriel was about to actually reveal something about herself and her life. Leave it to that self-obsessed Lothario to bring sex into everything. The guy really had a one-track mind when it came to sex on the brain.

Next, he led them in to the lights on, afternoon loving, or in the dark debate.

"I think men like to see what's going on better," David chimed in, trying to steal a little of the Eagle's thunder. Why let Al dominate and constantly steer the conversation? "Men are simply fixed on the visual aspects of things. That's just the way we are, like it or not. We're visually oriented. We enjoy what we can see–what we want to see. Men usually keep their eyes open, while women often keep their eyes closed during…" Damn it, what was the word he was searching for?

"Intimacy!" he finally blurted out.

Both Jerriel and Alejandro chuckled at him. The latter picked up the thread. "I have noticed that at as well–the thing with women keeping the eyes closed during the actual love-making. Except for those certain times when they pop wide open." He gestured so dramatically with his hands to match the intensity of his suggestive words.

Jerriel shook her head. "It is a well-known fact that men like to look– even to gawk and stare. So, what is there for us poor women, you naughty men, going around all the time, ogling women with your tongues wagging? Women's bodies are indeed works of art. While men's bodies are made more *for* work. And trust me…they are not always…so attractive, no? Honestly, even if they…manage to perform well, they are not always so enjoyable to behold, or experience in total. Perhaps it is because men are such hairy beasts, and it would certainly not hurt them to bathe more often. No wonder most women close their eyes. I daresay many wish they could close their noses as well."

"That isn't fair," David protested. "Men can't control how much hair they have on them. Or that we can be more…pungent."

More laughter. "Obviously," Jerriel said. "Neither the former's location nor its intensity. Just look around at any large gathering of people? Many men lack hair where it is desired, and have no lack of it where it is not. Ugh! Thank goodness women are not so…hirsute."

The Eagle attempted to squeeze in. "Just so that you may know, I pluck out all of my unwanted hairs so that my taut body is smooth and luxurious to the touch. Before the Merge, there were certain electronic devices. And there still are some available creams and lotions that–"

"What do you mean, 'Ugh'?" David said to Jerriel. "Okay, granted, men are hairier than most women, and we can stink more."

"At least I'm glad to hear you admit it."

"Why wouldn't we? That's the way we are. There's no shame in being the way you are. People have to accept who and what they are."

"No, they don't, Daeved. And there are many men who need serious help and guidance on how not be disgusting oafs."

"Don't you think you're being a little hard on us guys?"

"Oh, Daeved. There we must disagree, and most women will side with me, I believe. And don't get me started on male hygiene and the way they can smell. I've been around stinky men and boys my entire life, cursed with a highly sensitive nose."

David laughed. "And Jerriel, if your cute little, highly sensitive nose wasn't stuck up so high in the air…"

"Daeved!"

"…then perhaps you might show a little mercy on us poor hairy, stinking apes. And I've even admitted that guys can be a little more pungent than women."

"A little!"

"But here are the cold hard facts. Not all women are paragons of immaculate beauty, either, and sometimes, they can stink just a bad as anyone else."

Alejandro jumped in again. "I make a habit of smelling like sandalwood, cloves, citrus, and Spanish leather…"

"Of course they can," Jerriel said. "But if men simply took the opportunity to bathe more—"

"Smell me, my lady," Al eagerly offered. "Take a good whiff! Ahhh…am I not intoxicating?"

Both David and Jerriel blinked and stared at their friend for a split second, with their mouths hanging open. Al was clearly lost in his own private moment.

Jerriel picked right up again where she had left off. "Then maybe they wouldn't reek so much!"

Al sighed. "Ahhh…Spanish leather."

David and Jerriel burst out laughing. He liked the way her eyes twinkled with mischief as they circled each other around Alejandro.

"Well," Jerriel said, "perhaps women close their eyes in bed so that they can more easily imagine themselves in the arms of other less hairy, less stinky men."

"I am happy to be of such service," Al noted, with a bow and a sweeping flourish of his plumed hat.

"And you think men don't do the same thing?" David said.

"Imagine themselves in the arms of other less hairy, less stinky men?" Al said.

Jerriel had to hold onto a tree.

"No, no," David said, once he stopped laughing. "I didn't mean it that way."

Al went on. "Well, I suppose some men, such as yourself, apparently, my friend. I had no idea. But then, you never can tell. I am not here to judge you, my friend."

"I meant that I bet some men secretly think about being with other women. Men practically invented that!"

"Yes, I do it all the time, I must admit," Al said.

"And apparently, from what Jerriel tells us, women do the same thing."

"I don't even have to close my eyes to picture myself with other women," Al said.

"Is that what you're telling us, Jerriel?"

"In fact, I'm picturing myself with other women right now, as we speak," Al noted. "And more than one...all at once." He shook himself vigorously. "And yes...more than one...all at once." He shook himself vigorously again. "Yes...it is wonderful!"

"Al, do you need to go off into the trees and be alone for a while?"

"Don't be silly," he said with a grin. "When I go off into the woods, I shall not be alone."

"Daeved," Jerriel said. "If you men must really know, here is the truth. Most women do not close their eyes to fantasize about other men during lovemaking."

Al suddenly looked heartbroken. "They don't? And here I thought they were all thinking about me while they serviced the rest of those hairy, stinky ape buffoons."

"No, it is something more intimate. We close our eyes to become absorbed in the moment, to focus on the pleasure feelings we are sharing with our lovers."

"Well, we'd never know if you were thinking about other guys."

"Oooh! Even when we tell you the truth, you men won't listen to us."

What was he saying that was making her mad?

Alejandro came up behind the two of them and put his arms around them both. "Excuse me, my friends. I couldn't help overhearing your droning little spat. Before this turns into a tedious fight, allow me to be of assistance. I have some expertise in such matters—of the heart and the boudoir. May I be of some service?"

Both of them turned on him flatly.

"No!"

Al stared at them both in shocked, disbelief, mouthing the word 'no,' as if he had heard it for the very first time.

"So," Jerriel said, "I guess you mean that if a man closes his eyes during lovemaking, that means he's imagining being with other women?"

"Well, that's might be one possibility."

"Maybe?" Jerriel fumed. "What do you mean, *might be?*"

Al chimed back in. "That is nothing. As I have already stated, I imagine myself with other women all the time, in any case. I rather enjoy it."

David attempted to cut back in. "Maybe men close their eyes just to enjoy the moment, like you say. To focus on the pleasure they're having."

"That's pleasure feelings!"

"Whatever."

"My friends, my friends," Al said. "Do not argue and become cross, and ruin this lovely day. If it would help in any way, the lovely lady can feel absolutely free to fantasize about being with me whenever she happens to find herself bored to tears and in dire need of genuine excitement."

"Thanks, Al," David said. "Thanks a lot."

"Do not bother to mention it, my friend. I am very generous in such ways. I am only too happy to be of service." He swept his hat off and bowed to Jerriel again, as they marched on.

"My lady, when we have time, I can assume several sensual poses and hold them for a quite a long while, so that you can fully enjoy them. Feel free to happily commit those wonderful images to future memory, for your later use and sensual, fantasy enjoyment, of course."

Jerriel stopped in her tracks and turned slowly around, her teeth clenched together and both fists shoved ramrod straight down at her sides.

"Will you please, just. Shut. Up!"

David laughed. "Al, you'd better back off our cute wizard for a while. She might turn you into a frog or something."

"Ugh! Even on Urth, it's so good to know that men are stupid twits!" Jerriel said.

Alejandro grinned and smoothed his pencil-thin mustache with a flourish of one gloved hand. He stuck out both arms and closed his eyes, chin up. "Go right ahead, beautiful one. Transcombooble me into whatever you like. I might enjoy such a change. I would make a very handsome and dashing frog. Did you know that frogs can make love for days at a time? How amazing is that. Make me a frog. I dare you!"

He turned on his heel and left the two of them staring after him.

Jerriel and David gaped at each other and then burst out laughing once more.

David pointed an accusing finger at her.

"Hey," Jerriel said, holding up both hands in surrender. "Don't blame me for the way your sex-crazed friend is. And I have been meaning to ask you—what is up with that sock that he keeps rolled up in his pants?"

David held up both hands. "Hey, don't ask me. You're the one who started all of this."

"David! I did not. This all started when you asked about me about how I became a wizard," Jerriel said. "You know, I could say the same thing for you. You haven't told me very much about yourself or your family, either. Like that picture you always talk to."

"I guess you're right," David admitted. Neither of them had taken the time during the panic of the Merge to tell their stories.

David just realized.

Both of them were orphans.

That connection between the two of them suddenly struck him like a bolt from the blue.

Both of them had lost their parents.

There wasn't really that much for David to tell her about himself. He did so quickly.

He told Jerriel how his parents had both died in a traffic accident, or as much as she could understand. He took out his picture and showed them to her. David told her their names.

And as with Jerriel and her older brother, David wasn't an only child. He had an older sister named Celine, six years older than him, who lived in Seattle with her family. He seldom saw them anymore, not since the funeral. Who knew how they were dealing with the Merge where they were? He felt a little guilty for not having worried much about them.

He had been too worried about himself.

It was as if the rest of the world had stopped existing outside of Michiana and all of its problems.

David hoped Celine and her family were alive and doing well. But other than them, the only family they had left was an uncle on his dad's side down in Florida, and his mother's sister in northern California. He had only met each of them once. All of his grandparents had been smokers, so they were long gone.

He tried to explain to Jerriel that he wasn't callous about losing his parents. Their sudden loss still saddened him, but he had made his peace most of that grief long ago. That was just the way things were.

Jerriel's loss was much fresher for her, still within a year. But in any case, these days, since the Merge, both of them had bigger things to worry about— like trying to survive and stay alive.

Like journeying through an unknown region to see a dangerous dragon, and keeping himself and Jerriel and all of his friends breathing, so that they could all manage to get back safely with the knowledge they gained.

"It does make me think, though," he said. He looked at Jerriel intently. "For better or for worse, this is our world now. It's up to us what we make of it."

"I agree," Jerriel said. "So much has changed. So much is in the past now."

"So, that's my basic family story, Jerriel. What about you? Where did you come from? What was your life like before the Merge?"

Jerriel's countenance darkened.

7

It was still dark out, barely five in the morning, when Mason donned his plain gray sweatshirt and sweatpants, over shorts and a T-shirt. As soon as he put his socks and athletic shoes on, he would report to the militia training fields for four weeks of militia basic training.

For the next month, he would live and train in a barracks with forty-seven other militia recruits. They'd face physical training, endurance training, and drilling in the morning until lunchtime. More drills and combat training in the afternoons. The first two weeks would be mandatory for him. After that, he could train with Blondie and the mage recruits, and Thulkara and her warrior recruits, if he chose to.

He was the one who had signed up for the militia. This is what he had asked for when he took the oath and became a new militia recruit. He wanted to get to know his fellow troops and make a solid attempt at becoming a regular human being for a change.

Mason was walking past the front of Blondie's magical lab and practice building.

A blinding, blue explosion of magical energy tore a gaping, glowing hole out of the northern side of former warehouse without warning.

The blast knocked Mason on his ass and scared the living hell out of the many militia guards entrenched all around the place.

When the dust and the smoke cleared, Blondie appeared at the open rent, putting out the fires with magical sprays of water. "It's all right, it's all right," he tried to assure everyone as they rushed in to help. "Just a little magical experiment that got out of control. Everything's fine, now. Not to worry."

Mason chuckled. If that was a little one, he'd sure as hell hate to see a big one go out of control.

Blondie's face was blackened and covered with soot from the blast. His eyebrows looked as if they had been singed. But he still managed to spot Mason in the dark.

His friend waved. "Good morning, Mace. Good luck and have fun at your militia training. We'll see you in two weeks, if you can't catch up with Thulkara and I on the weekends, my friend."

Mason called back, "Talk to you when I can, Blondie. Don't blow the whole dang town up while I'm gone."

His friend grinned a wide, sooty grin. "I'll try not to. No promises, Mace."

It was a short walk to the practice fields and the rows of militia barracks that had been set up. About five hundred people, both men and women, waited around outside, some keeping to themselves. Others talked together quietly or joked around in small groups.

Mason didn't see anyone he knew. In a way, that was good.

The youngest recruits had to be at least eighteen, or lie about their age. IDs and school records were checked where they could be. The oldest recruits couldn't be any older than forty-five. This group seemed to run the gambit. Lots of people in their twenties and thirties. Since the militia made little distinction between male and female troops during the war, more than half of this batch were women.

The only thing each of them had been given was a small scrap of paper with a single letter on it.

Mason's had an E.

Others seem to have letters from A to J.

Someone asked out loud, "Anyone know what these letters are for?"

A woman further down shouted, "My brother joined up a month ago. The letters just tell them what company to sort you in. Forty-eight to each company, four teams of twelve. Looks to be about five hundred of us here. That would make ten companies."

"Well, we might as well start sorting out, by the alphabet," someone suggested."

"Hey, screw you, man. I'm not doing nothing until I'm told."

Some people started sorting themselves out anyway.

Mason watched and listened. From what many others said, it seemed as if half of the people were joining the militia just to make sure that they had enough food to eat.

Perhaps that wasn't so odd. Mason hadn't thought about it before.

Without trucks and trains constantly shipping food into Michiana, many people had been running out of food at wherever they called home, since the war ended. The militia had wisely seized all of the grocery stores in town at the start of the Merge, and now had instituted both rationing and vastly expanded food production programs in order to maintain sustainable food supplies.

The authorities also controlled access to clean water. So far, at least, there seemed to be plenty of that.

Finally, about a hundred militia troops showed up and took charge of the mob.

A midsized man in his late twenties with dark hair and sergeant stripes called out, "Echo Company; anyone with an E on their paper. Line up with me, four abreast. There should be forty-eight of you. That will make four twelve-person teams."

It took them a few minutes to shuffle together.

"All right, people. Listen up! You are now Echo Company. I am Sergeant Rivera. I served in the U.S. Army. This is not the army. This is the militia. Our rules are different. Our requirements are different. You must listen to me carefully and follow my orders and directions.

"The clerk will come by and record your names, ages, and what size clothing you wear. The clerk will also confirm any ID you have. ID tags for the militia will be issued to you tomorrow morning, and you will keep them around your neck. From this moment on, until I tell you otherwise, you are now with the militia for the next five weeks. You no longer have the choice to leave from this point forward. If you attempt to leave or escape, you will be arrested and punished for desertion. If you understand my words, say 'Yes, Sergeant.'"

Forty-eight men and women of assorted ages, including Mason himself, said, "Yes, Sergeant." A bit lackluster, but everyone said it.

Once their names were down, all nice and legal, the first thing Sergeant Rivera had them all do was prepare to go for a little run. Hence the sweats they had been given, and the instructions to wear athletic shoes and socks.

They wouldn't get militia gear, weapons, or uniforms until after they completed the five weeks of basic conditioning and training.

"Echo Company, we will proceed to walk one mile double-time, at a fast pace. Then we will run one complete mile. Then we will walk back to cool down. Anyone who cannot keep up with these basic requirements will have three weeks to demonstrate significant improvement, or be kicked out. The militia is not simply a place to flop and get three squares. We expect you to work and perform at certain levels."

They started out. Mason was twenty years old and in pretty decent shape. He didn't have any problems with the militia walking and running requirements. But with the slowpokes in the group, doing the four miles total took them more than two hours that first day.

And even though they had five people in Echo Company who were older than forty, only one of them had trouble finishing. A dozen others in their twenties and thirties struggled with being either overweight or out of shape. Or both.

Sergeant Rivera let them rest and drink some water once they were done. Then they all did calisthenics. A militia corporal named Vickers recorded how many push-ups and sit-ups each of them could do in one minute. After another half hour for a hurried breakfast, they returned to the practice fields and began to learn to drill—to march, turn, and move as a unit.

By then it was lunchtime. They had thirty minutes to eat and wash up. The food they had was basic, bland, but filling—served on mess tin trays. Some kind of chunks of mystery meat in white, creamy gravy on rice with green beans. At least there was plenty of it, along with bread and crackers.

Salt, pepper, hot sauce, soy sauce, ketchup, and mustard became popular in a hurry to add some kind of taste. Canned peaches was the dessert. There was coffee, tea, and some kind of powdered drink mix to slug down.

Sergeant Rivera chided them if they wasted any food. He warned them to only take what they could eat, but eat whatever they took, whether they liked it or not.

They cleaned off their trays, put their tin cups and flatware in racks to be washed, and dunked their trays in big tubs of waiting dishwater.

That first afternoon, Sergeant Rivera keep them hopping. They drilled more, and then had hand-to-hand combat training. They learned basic punches, strikes, kicks, elbows, knees, throws, and grappling techniques. They learn how to defend themselves. Then they paired off and revolved around in brief sparring matches with light padding.

Obviously, some people were going to be better at hand-to-hand than others. Oddly enough, the old guy in their group at forty-two was named Bryan Lister. He had been a boxer in his younger days, and used what remained of his skill to thump almost everyone, including Mason and all of the younger people. Lister only had to tag them once to daze them, and after that, he more or less had them at his mercy.

At the very least, it taught them all how to try to deal with even a partial hit, let alone a full-on punch from someone who knew how to hit.

But fighting all twelve of them in short order pooped Bryan out once more. He needed to work up greater stamina.

Mason was never that good at fighting with his hands. He simply didn't have a lot of practice doing so. Prior to the Merge, most people didn't get into fistfights very often. So most of them were in the same situation.

The experience showed him that he was going to have to get better at that and many other things.

The last two hours of the training day they spent learning the basic concepts of sword and shield, and spear and shield, and they took an archery test.

Mason was only a fair hand with bows and crossbows, and he learned that, for some reason, he could barely hit anything with a crossbow pistol. Go figure.

He liked using spear and shield, and seemed to have knack for it.

Mason was was quickly informed that he would be one of the four spear carriers for Echo Company, Team 3. The other three spears would be Thomas Kelly, twenty-five; Bethany Anderson, twenty-nine; and Lashonda Kincaid, twenty-six.

The quad with the highest archery scores would become their four archers on Team 3:

Ben Yoder, 34.
Francine Owen, 31
Cory Brown, 28
Linda Turner, 36

And their sword and shield quad would be the last four:

Michelle Mitchell, 21
Bryan Lister, 42
Rodell Kim, 20
Caitlyn Reed, 34

None of them had known each other before joining up. They had made some fleeting introductions along the way, but they were never really allowed much time for small talk. Everything they did was performed in a hurry.

After dinner, Sergeant Rivera took them to their barracks and assigned them to their bunks. Their barracks held at least sixty people, the way it was set up. The bunks were divided into two halves.

Bunks for women toward the south end. Bunks for men toward the north end.

Each of them had a locker and trunk for future gear. A clean set of sweats, socks, and regulation underwear were already waiting for them, neatly folded on each of their trunks.

Their names were already taped on their bunks, their trunks, and their equipment lockers. Masking tape written on with markers. Since there was a lower and upper bunk on each bed, there were two trunks side by side in front of each bunk.

It looked as if Mason was sharing a bunk with Rodell Kim, the quiet, mid-sized Korean guy, one of Team 3's sword and shields.

Corporal Vickers came around with Sergeant Rivera and a can full of black markers. Rivera wrote on the chalkboard on the wall.

"We have brought permanent markers to write your name, company letter, and team number on each of your articles of clothing— even both socks. Stretch them out and write it on the inside, if you must. Do it like this: I would be M. Rivera, E-2, if I was in Echo Company, Team 2. Write this on your clean set of clothing first. After that, you will be given twelve minutes to shower as soon as we release you to do so. Use the bath kit, towel, wash cloth, soaps, and hygiene items waiting for you in each of your trunks. Brush your teeth at night and in the morning, for two minutes—part of your twelve.

"Women will use the showers and toilets to the south; men will use the showers and toilets to the north. Anyone found in the wrong place at any time will face discipline.

"Be advised. This is not high school: you are not here to fall in love, and you are only here for five weeks. A little more than one month. During that time you are expected and ordered to keep it in your pants, people—and to yourself, at all times. If you choose to diddle with yourself, I highly advise you to diddle quietly so as not to disturb your comrades. Everyone will need and want their sleep."

Snickering and laughter erupted at that point.

Rivera's eyes bulged in a truly menacing way. He roared at them, "Did I say something amusing to you boys and girls?"

Everyone froze and went silent.

"Did I tell a joke? I ask again, did I say something funny? How do you answer?"

"No, Sergeant!"

51

He paused long enough to pace back over to them. "You're damn right I did not. If I ever do say something hilarious, I will certainly inform you of such. You boys and girls will then laugh hard and long, appropriately. Until that blessed event, you will not have a sense of humor. Do you understand, recruits?"

"Yes, Sergeant."

"Good. Stay where you are, for now. But this will be the protocol from now on when myself or Corporal Vickers, or any other non-commissioned officer or command officer enters these barracks. So listen up!"

All eyes locked on Rivera.

"If anyone in authority enters these barracks, the first person spotting them will yell, 'Attention!' Others thereafter are free to chime in. Once attention is sounded, this means that you will bust ass to stand at attention in front of your bunk, in front of your trunk. You will put your feet and legs together, arms at you side, hands open. You will hold still and look straight ahead, not up, down, or side-to-side.

"You will remain silent in this position until you are given orders, instructions, or addressed directly. You will not continue to dress or do anything else. If you are bare-assed naked, you will stand at attention bare-assed naked. That is why we strongly suggest that you come out of the bathrooms at least in your underwear, to avoid damaging our eyesight. If you choose to dress and undress in front of each other, that is between you and your comrades. Corporal Vickers, let's try this out."

"Yes, Sergeant. Attention!"

Forty-eight people shuffled and scrambled to stand at attention in front of their trunks and bunks.

"Outstanding. Haul ass, people. You have twelve minutes to shower and brush your teeth, starting…now. Once that time is over, we will give you further instructions."

Fortunately for Mason, he had been in ROTC, so he had had a taste of paramilitary/military life. He knew how to hustle and move with a purpose.

He came out of the shower, dressed in his new set of clothes, his hair still wet but his teeth brushed, in about eleven minutes.

His bunkmate Rodell ran back in his underwear and T-shirt several seconds later. What kind of name was Rodell? It sure didn't sound Korean.

But he seemed like a friendly sort of guy, just quiet. Both of them were drying their hair when Corporal Vickers shouted, "Attention!" exactly at the passage of twelve minutes.

Almost a dozen recruits came running back to stand in front of their bunks. Some of them were still dripping wet, but they at least had clothing on.

"Very nice," Sergeant Rivera said. "All of you who just ran up here, drop and give me twenty. If you cannot do twenty pushups, just keep trying until one of us tells you to stop."

Eleven people started doing push-ups.

"Now listen up. Write your name on all of your soiled articles of clothing and toss them in the laundry hamper. They will be returned to you clean by tomorrow night. Each night you will get fresh training clothes and turn in your soiled set. If your clothing gets torn, inform Corporal Vickers to get you a replacement. Do you understand?"

"Yes, Sergeant!"

"Lights out will be at ten p.m., and you are expected to be quiet and go the hell to sleep. Your day will begin again tomorrow at five a.m. You will dress, complete with socks and shoes, and be out in front of your barracks and ready to train at quarter past the hour. No exceptions. If you are still inside after that time, you had better be dead, or in the process of dying. Now, take some time to prepare and turn in your soiled laundry. You have fifteen minutes."

Once the laundry was all turned in, Sergeant Rivera gave them final instructions. "At night, you will not leave your barracks. Anyone who does so unauthorized will be arrested and disciplined, as well as taking the risk of being shot. This area is under heavy guard by the night watch troops on duty.

"After lights out, you will not leave your bunk, unless it is to go to the bathroom. You are not to talk or hold meetings or conversations. No more than one trooper can use the head at one time. Take turns, dammit. Any two troops or more found in the head after that time will be disciplined. The guards will make their rounds and check on the barracks as needed. Even if you are awake, you are not to speak to them unless you are spoken to, by the night watch.

"Keep in mind that if there is any kind of trouble at night, the entire company will be disciplined. There will be no romance, no cuddling, no fights, and especially—no blanket parties. The rest of this evening is now yours to relax and to get to know one another before lights out. Consider yourselves dismissed. As you were, people."

Their sergeant promptly left the barracks. Corporal Vickers pushed out the laundry cart for the laundry wagon to pick up. Then he came back in, sat down at the barracks duty desk, and began to read a book by an oil lantern. There was another oil lantern across from Vickers, and two at the ends of the barracks, by the bathrooms and the doors. They did not provide much light.

In the twilight, some people broke into groups and talked. Some brought out cards or dice. Some just went to sleep. A couple of people even cried.

Mason sprawled in his lower bunk, wondering what Blondie and Thulkara were up to.

Rodell Kim popped his head over the side from up top. "Hey, Mason. Wanna talk a bit? I'm pretty bored."

Mason smiled and sat up. "Sure. Come on down. Tell me about yourself."

One good thing: without his gunslinger outfit, no one had made the connection about him being the Pistolero. Not yet at least.

Now that he was without his powers, maybe that was a good thing.

"Are you from this area, Mason?"

"Naw. Before the Merge, I was a college student from Cleveland. During the war, I spent some time in Elkhart. Now look at me. I'm here in South Bend, joining the militia."

"Me, too. I don't know where my parents and grandparents are. Our house is gone, and I don't have anywhere to go. I haven't been able to find anyone I know. I was starving in Mishawaka, and people said that if you joined the militia in South Bend, at least they'd clothe and feed you."

"Yeah, it's better than nothing. Or becoming a farm hand in the fields. Say, what kind of name is Rodell? That doesn't sound Korean."

"It's not. I'm, like, sixth generation. I'm more or less just an American. Even my parents didn't speak any Korean. I have no idea where my parents got my name. Maybe they just made it up."

"No worries." Mason offered Rodell his hand. His new bunkmate shook it. "Good to meet you, Rodell."

"Good to meet you, Mason. Hey, I got a deck of cards. We could play something to pass the time while we chat."

"Deal 'em. Let's play. You call it."

They spoke together quietly about their lives and families prior to the Merge. The card games they played really didn't matter that much.

A handful of other people from Team 3 and Echo Company came around to introduce themselves. A few went over and tried to talk with Vickers.

After two hours or so of taking it easy, Corporal Vickers looked at the wind-up clock on the duty desk, and then checked his watch. "Lights out!" he yelled. Then he went around and put out the lamps. Even without the moon, there was enough ambient starlight coming through the high windows of the bathrooms to light them and the ends of the barracks.

"See ya in the morning, Mason."

"Get some rest, my friend."

His bunk, with its thin pillow, sheets, and blankets, was barely passable, yet better than nothing. He had slept on worse. By that time, Mason found that he was surprisingly and sufficiently tired.

8

The sky that same afternoon was clear, but the air still remained cool as David and his band continued to march toward the mountains. The land rose quickly, and except for various fir and pine trees, many of the late spring trees still did not show very thick batches of new leaves. Some trees even looked sick, gray, or brown and skeletal.

The Blackhawks tried to move forward quietly, but two hundred marching feet were going to make some noise, no matter what they all did.

As they continued to walk on, Jerriel spoke softly about her life prior to the Merge.

"My mother was a noble woman from Marrandor. My father a powerful wizard from the Sylurrian Royal Family. I have one older brother who is a very powerful Sylurrian sorcerer. We never got along, even as children. I was always running and hiding from him. I have no uncles, aunts, or living grandparents on my father's side."

"You speak of your parents like I do," David said. "In the past tense. How did you lose them?"

"My father led one of the exploration efforts into the interior of the new world. He was very instrumental in founding the Sylurrian colony around

Vaejan. That is the mountainous area you continually refer to as Shee-Kago. It is a very dangerous place.

"The native monsters around that area attacked the colony in great numbers. I can see now that the Dark Khabal must have had a hand in that. Many colonists lost their lives before those creatures could be defeated. Including my father."

"I'm sorry, Jerriel."

"I know. You lost your parents as well. You know how I feel."

"Your mother?"

"She was returning to her kin in Kellendra from a visit to Tornhold by ship, crossing along the Inner Seas."

Tharanorians normally referred to the Great Lakes as the Inner Seas.

"A strong storm came up. Her ship was lost. I never saw her again, either. I stayed with my cousins in Kellendra for a time while I mourned. Then I tried to re-unite with my older brother in Vaejan. That did not go so well. I learned that he and many of the Sylurrians in Vaejan were obsessed with conquest and seizing power in the region, apparently for themselves. He tried to convince me to join them. I refused and fled after my father's untimely death. I was trying to reach Kellendra when the Merge struck."

"Jerriel. Do you think that the Sylurrians in Vaejan had anything to do with causing the Merge?"

"I don't think so; most of them were too busy defending the city there. The Merge upset everyone's plans, I imagine, including theirs. But I did learn that Vaejan was raising armies to try to seize control of the New World as their domain, or as much of it as they could. That and the Merge sound very much like the work of the Dark Khabal. Now that they control Vaejan, I imagine that they'll forge ahead with their plans, while both Urthers and Tharanorians are still reeling and confused here on this continent."

"Perhaps that's why none of our long-range scouting patrols to Vaejan have come back," Jason added.

Jerriel shook her head. "I'm not so sure they got that far. This region can be incredibly dangerous. At first the Sylurrians struggled to control the area near their colony in Vaejan, not the immense wilds all about them. At first they were under siege as much as anyone else, before the Khabal took over."

"Jerriel," David asked, "How do you think the Merge occurred? Did the mages of Tharanor...cause it somehow?"

"It is hard to say. Something like that would be incredibly complex. My brother serves The Supreme Sorcerer of Sylurria, one of the Six

High Mages of Tharanor, who are chosen to help rule and protect our world. My brother did reveal to me, just prior to the Merge, that the High Mages were working feverishly against some kind of grave, interdimensional threat that only they could counter. He said that Tharanor was in great danger of annihilation from—"

David heard both of the guard dogs suddenly yip warnings on the front and left flank.

"Torgs!" their scouts shouted. "We're under attack!"

David snapped back to the present and lifted his crossbow.

Torg arrows whizzed among them.

David shot a torg emerging from behind a tree. It shrieked and fell.

He quickly reloaded.

Troops clustered around David and Jerriel. Arrows thunked into their shields.

"MYVAKKO!" Jerriel cried, lifting both of her glowing blue arms. A spell flashed from her sweeping hands. A sheet of magical blue needles shot out in a huge arc to the side and before of them.

Dozens of torgs charged out of the trees and brush.

The magic, glowing needles cut into them with fierce velocity at face level, checking their advance, wounding or blinding many of them.

"Drop down!" the archers cried. The troops in front crouched down low, just as they had been trained to, taking up defensive positions, weapons set against a charge.

David shot another torg in the belly.

"Fire!"

The archers behind them cut loose. The volley of arrows ripped into the torgs. Another volley hit them as they struggled to recover. David shot another in the throat.

One of the sergeants shouted. "Archers to the rear. Turn and fire!"

More torgs swept in from behind at them. The archers cut them down at the last instant.

David ordered troops on all sides to form up and protect the archers in the center. They prepared to fire again as the horde closed in. He slung his crossbow behind him and drew his long sword and tomahawk.

"BASHAZIL!" Jerriel shouted.

Lightning forked out overhead and blasted the torgs where they raced in at the rear, frying several of them in forefront of the attack.

Arrows tore into the rest. The torgs broke and ran, cut down by more arrows as they retreated.

"They're fleeing," Lieutenant Collier asked. "Do we pursue them, sir?"

"Hold up, Lieutenant," David told him. "They may have more numbers hiding out there, waiting for us to break ranks and thin ourselves out. Let's regroup and go forward carefully. Anyone hurt?"

"Nothing major. A few minor arrow hits. We're good."

"All right. Take out any of their wounded stragglers. Then we move on. I want to get out of this area if they intend to follow us. Leave some large groups of hunters on our flanks and in front and behind. Shoot any spies who try to follow us. Make every effort to conceal our trail and escape."

"Will do, sir."

They retrieved what arrows and bolts they could, left the dead torgs where they lay, and kept going. David was proud of the way the Blackhawks had performed.

They slipped off the main trail, moving fast, and took another direction into the forest.

Twenty minutes later, they stopped for a breather and waited.

After ten more minutes, bow shots rang out on their left flank. David rushed forward to assist the scouts.

By the time he and Jerriel and the troops got to that vantage point, it was over. "Six or seven torgs, sir. We got 'em all. They were tracking us by the looks of it. Probably by scent."

"Put down some more scent killer," he said. "Parties of scouts, make false trails, and piss in a couple of places on purpose and cover it up in part. Then double back to us. Then we try to lose them again. We can't have them harassing us the whole way there, or amassing enough numbers to overwhelm us."

"You got it, Captain."

Jerriel swept the trails around them with wind spells to help ruin any signs.

They sped off in another direction, taking them on an angle back toward their original destination.

Forty minutes later, some of their scouts came running up to them.

"We think we've lost them, sir. A large band of torgs, ka-torgs, and a couple of mor-kahls and gozogs are racing in the other direction where they think we went. The enemy is about forty or fifty strong."

"Good. Keep an eye out. They could still spot us or stumble across our real trail."

"It's going to get dark in a few hours, sir. Any orders?"

"No fires, torches, or lanterns. Jerriel has a spell that will help us see in the dark. We keep moving while we can and find a safe place to camp. Then we post double watches all night."

It appeared that their enemies kept forces posted at the edge of the wilds, ready to intercept their scouting teams. They sent runners back to warn the militia. Dirk would have to send out larger units to protect their scouts. They would need larger units that would rush in once the scouting units made contact. Perhaps entire armies, devoted to clearing the wilds.

This demonstrated to David that they just weren't up against random hordes of mindless monsters. This was a coordinated effort to keep the humans of Michiana isolated and cut off from other human enclaves.

This was an active plot to keep them vulnerable and reduce their numbers over time.

The night grew very cool. They made no fire. They huddled together, hidden in their defensive positions, and kept their watches all night. Lots of weird noises sounded out in the Tharanorian forest. Smaller and larger creatures clearly moved about.

The few hours of sleep they managed were broken and fleeting, yet that night seemed to go on forever.

Jerriel had traveled through these wilds alone? Even with magical protections that concealed her and cloaked her passage, David had a new respect for her courage and her abilities.

He had to admit to himself. Even with a wizard and two hundred well-armed troops around him, he still felt pretty jumpy, and not a little scared.

Fear of the unknown was a powerful thing.

Even fear of the known was pretty intense.

Yet the night finally did pass, and they were glad to see the dawn. Although it was gray and threatened rain.

"Be thankful for the rain," Jerriel told him. "It will help cover our passing and limit any pursuit."

Fog rose up. They walked, miserable, through a cold, damp cloud.

They soon only had compasses to guide their direction for certain.

After several minutes, David suffered odd sensations. He felt weak, almost drained.

They hadn't slept well, but for some reason he now felt worse than just being tired.

Even Jerriel looked sluggish.

"Jerriel. Something's wrong. I feel weak. Like something's sapping my strength."

"I feel it, too." She held up her staff and it glowed. The glow turned gray, and then faded to pulsing black energy.

"Negative energy is at work. It's all around us, feeding on our lifeforce somehow. I've read about something like this before in the wilds of the New World."

David went among the troops.

"What is it, sir?" Lieutenant Collier asked. "The troops all feel weak. Even the dogs are feeling it. What's wrong with us?"

"Keep everyone together," David commanded. "We're going to get out of this."

"Over here!" some of the troops called out, still trying to be quiet.

David stumbled in that direction.

The form of a body lay on the ground, overgrown with vines and moss.

"Two more over here!"

"They're from one of the scouting patrols. Look at their weapons and gear." David tore away the vegetation.

A skeletal face stared up at him, the flesh so dry and desiccated that it pulled away from the skin, still attached to the vines.

Oddly enough, there were no bugs or maggots or anything like that. Not as much as one would expect.

In fact, that part of the forest was strangely quiet—no birds or animals at all.

Not even bugs.

"Here's a deer carcass," one of the troops said. "Same thing."

"What in the hell could do that?" Jason asked. "What kills like this?"

"Something's sucking them dry," David said. "And if we stay here too much longer, it's going to do the same thing to us."

9

Mason continued his basic training with Echo Company. It was difficult at times, but it wasn't the worst thing in the world. The idea, apparently, was to completely exhaust them each day.

For the rest of that first week, rain or shine, they kept up their physical training in the morning, and battle unit training in the afternoon. He and Rodell Kim became friends, along with several others.

There were a few people in Echo and the other companies who didn't seem to like him much in general, but everyone was still being run ragged and given little time to make enemies. And with most of the recruits being older, useless pettiness and aggression was mostly seen as a waste of time and energy. That was a young person's game, for the most part.

At least no one had connected him with the Pistolero yet. So that much was good. Mason could continue his quest to try to become just a normal person—a trooper like the rest of them.

As much as any microcosm of humanity, their company had its types. Braggarts and sad sacks, liars and fools, gamblers and stupid thugs. But most folks in the militia simply wanted to keep their heads down and enjoy the free food and a place to stay busy. After the war, most people really didn't want any more trouble than what they already had.

And being fed three squares each day was plenty enough reason for most. If the war started up again, they'd also face that when it came along.

Everyone hated physical training. But everyone also got something out of PT. Some definitely needed it more than others. It was clearly necessary. A fat, slow militia wasn't going to be much of a threat to the enemy.

Mason was already in pretty good general shape. But he was far from being a soldier. The physical training, and toughening, and the combat practice, would eventually do him good. He still felt that way even at night, when he threw himself into his bunk to pass out and sleep.

The second week was much like the first, but the trainers actually stepped things up a notch. They ran a bit more. They lifted some weights to keep building strength.

In the afternoons, they put on hot, padded cloth gambesons and old football helmets to begin to simulate armor. They used padded practice weapons that were weighted to be more like the real thing.

Even the archers used practice bows, with blunted arrows tipped in foam rubber

They worked on individual fighting techniques against various opponents, and marching, maneuvering, and fighting as part of various units.

Each of them learned to defend and attack against each other. Sword and shield people learned how to fight against spear and shield, or against an archer.

At times, the trainers would surprise them by yanking their shield or their weapon out of their hands and forcing them to use their back-up weapons or improvise.

What if an archer's bowstring was cut, or the bow or crossbow broke? How could a person fight with just arrows, or broken weapons? How could a shield itself be used as a weapon? What about bare hands against a fully armed opponent?

They began to learn the advantages and disadvantages of every type of defense or offense.

A good deal of time was spent on trying not to let oneself get surrounded and cut off, or to gang up on and do that very same thing to others. A strong, disciplined unit could defend itself much better than just a rabble. During the war, this had been proven time and time again against the undisciplined monster hordes.

The twelve troops in Team 3 would fight against the dozen in Team 4. Teams 1 and 2 would take on Teams 3 and 4. One team would try to hold out against two or even three other teams all at once. Terrain and placement became extremely important.

But the facts of combat remained, that larger numbers of troops could degrade and defeat smaller numbers of troops much faster. No big surprise there.

The second weekend brought the first leave times on Saturday and Sunday, starting on Friday night after 8 p.m.

It seemed odd to Mason that he had already been away from his friends and his old unit for twelve days.

Rodell had suggested that a bunch of them from Team 3 see the town and take in a couple of the plays and musicals that had popped up for entertainment. Mason wished his new teammates well and begged off, saying that he wanted to catch up with some old friends.

It wasn't a lie. He just didn't exactly say who his old friends were.

Mason went to Major Bill Avery first. He waited a few minutes before being ushered in.

"Recruit Tyler," Bill said with a ready smile and a warm hand. "I hear you're becoming part of the line. A spear carrier, correct?"

Mason forced himself to smile back. "I am. I'm learning what every militia trooper should learn."

"Good, good."

Sheesh, now that he wasn't the Pistolero any more, this was sure uncomfortable. He hadn't counted on that.

"Have you tried any of your guns, Mace?"

"Nope. Haven't had much time. They're all stowed with my gear. Why? It's not like anything has changed."

Bill reached into a drawer, and put Mason's derringer on the desk. "Do me a favor and just humor me. It's unloaded. Fire it into that trash can."

Mason frowned, grabbed the weapon up, and aimed it into said trash can.

He didn't even bother to look.

Click. Click.

He tossed it back up onto the desk. "There. Happy?"

Bill put the derringer away. "No, Mace. And I don't think you are, either."

"I'm doing my best to move on and be useful, Bill. Maybe you should do the same."

"Don't worry about me, Mace. I'm staying quite busy. So are Blondie and Thulkara. Wanna come and take a peek?"

Mason slapped the arms on his chair. "Sure. Why not? Sounds good."

They went over to Blondie's new magic lab.

From the looks of things, it had been transformed into a heavily guarded military research compound. Even Major Bill had to show clearance papers to enter the compound, and he had to vouch for Mason.

They entered one of the guarded, militia intel observation booths attached to the lab.

Mason guessed that Blondie probably knew that he was constantly under surveillance. Blondie's new enemy "assistants" were hard at work trying to train new Michiana mages—about forty people in all.

"Blondie has accepted a position as the Head Mage of Michiana, Mace. We call him the Mage Captain. These people are all his students, brought here from around the area within the last week or so."

"Impressive," Mason said. "So, after the fake hanging, five of the six captured mages caved and agreed to help us. That's pretty amazing."

Bill frowned. "Yeah, we think so, too. They are under careful watch all the time. All of them know that if any of them make a wrong move, they'll be cut down. We won't take any chances again."

Mason watched them all. Every one of the enemy mages wore some kind of armbands that flashed with magelight every now and then. The armbands were locked on—some kind of shackles.

"What do they all have on their arms?" he asked.

This time, Bill grinned. "Anti-magic suppressors. Certain combinations of metals gems and crystals impede the flow and use of magical energy. Blondie helped develop them to keep our new allies both honest, and not at their full strength."

"You know you can't just trust Blondie?"

"We didn't. The bracers are checked several times each day at random and replaced once a week to assure us that there isn't any tampering. We've checked the bracers on our own people—the Shooting Stars, our other mages. The devices do work. They reduce a mage's powers down to about ten percent of their normal effectiveness. With these things locked on their arms, those mages aren't going anywhere, and they can't hurt anyone. At least not very easily."

"But they can still use magic, and they can still teach others how to use magic. Very clever, Bill. My hat's off to you and the intel people."

Bill nodded.

They watched Blondie and the mages working with the mage recruits for a while without saying anything more.

"So, are they actually helping out, or just pretending to do so?" Mason said.

Bill waggled both hands in the air. "It's hard to tell. Each of them is a different personality. Each of them is holding back to some degree, and yet doing what they think they need to do in order to stay alive. It's only been about ten days, so they're just starting to get over being paranoid."

"What are your gut feelings about them?" Mason asked.

Bill sighed. "Gellonar, Koden, and Tharin show some signs of humanity. How far that actually goes; who knows yet. Ettal and Resh couldn't be more different. Ettal is a smooth talker and seems even friendlier than the others, but there's nothing but sheer contempt in his eyes at times that he can't hide. He'd kill us all if he could. We can't give him that chance. But Resh is the real danger, I believe. He's an introvert, and a possible serial murderer, I believe. One of our psych people says he matches the profile for being a highly dangerous sociopath."

"What does Blondie say?"

"He says Resh is indeed, very troubled–damaged goods. The perfect candidate for becoming a necromancer. But Resh is also super intelligent. He helps out, but he only does what he is told, when he is told to do it. Otherwise, he likes catching insects and torturing them in various ways. He got a hold of a stray cat somehow and almost killed it. It was so bad off, we had to put it down."

"Maybe that one isn't worth the risks," Mason said.

"Maybe. If so, he goes back into the lockup."

"You've got those armbands on the other mages, right? Even the wounded ones?"

"Arms, legs, and even a cap for their heads that prevents telepathy."

Mason shot a glance back at the helper mages. "You've left those five telepathic?" he said. "Isn't that taking a risk?"

"Easy, Mace. They don't know Blondie can listen in on them yet. Nor do they know about the caps. We've kept them away from the other prisoners. Blondie thought it would be interesting to listen in on what they were saying to each other, without them knowing that we could."

"And what have you learned, Bill?"

"About what I've told you. Gellonar, Koden, and Tharin just want to do the minimal to keep breathing. They don't see escape as an option right now. Ettal and Resh are after the others to help them find a way to negate the effects of the armbands and escape. They'll kill if they have to in order to get away, but their main goal now is escape. And Resh just likes to and wants to kill stuff. That's all he fantasizes about."

Mason sighed. "I'll feel a lot better when we have our own telepaths to confirm all that. We still have to trust Blondie for all of that info."

"We know that, too. I trust Blondie, but it would be good to be able to verify that trust."

"Are we gaining any ground on the magic front?"

"On a basic level, yes. We can now sort out new mages and tell where their talents are and what forms they take. We have books of basic spells–in English–for wizards. We can identify budding sorcerers and help them grow their powers, without hurting or killing themselves, or burning their powers out. Our new enchanters–all three of them–are starting to learn how to create basic enchantments. It isn't spectacular, but we're just starting out."

Mason thought a moment. "What's Thulkara up to?"

"Oh, painting and training fighters. That keeps her busy. She has a big abandoned farm called Ravenwood, and a barn that she's converted into training compound and her own art studio. And it's also become kind of a women's shelter and I don't know what else–sort of a women's hippie compound, if you ask me. But they all seem to work hard."

Mason broke out laughing hard for the first time in weeks. "Thulkara? A hippie? No way in hell. Nobody's a hippie anymore, Bill. There's no such thing."

"Well, anyway, she got permission to form an all-female company of militia fighters. They call themselves the Shield Maidens."

"Now that, I can believe."

"Thulkara takes in strays, especially if they and their kids have been beaten up or abused. But once they recover, all of the women and men under her protection and that of the Shield Maidens must agree to learn how to defend themselves and their kids. Any freeloaders, Thulkara kicks them out and sends them down the road."

"Is she still training with the regular recruits and troops?"

Bill smiled. "She sure is. Your group will get the Thul treatment at some point."

"Oh, goody to that," Mason said. "The other recruits haven't made me as the Pistolero yet, Bill. They might not at all. Let's do what we can to keep it that way."

"I agree, and I've given out orders as such. Just remind your friends when you talk to them. You don't want Thulkara rushing up and hugging you and spilling the beans. She's the kind that would forget in the heat of the moment. Both Blondie and Thulkara actually say that they miss you, Mace. To tell you the truth, my friend, I do, too."

"Don't get weepy on me, Bill. I don't think I could take that."

Bill laughed. "No need to worry. I couldn't take it, either. Just remember, you've just joined the militia, and it's not like any of us are dying. As soon as you finish your training, I'll have you assigned to Blondie's guards, protecting our new mages."

"Thanks, Bill. Sounds good. I'm working with some good people in my unit. Could I ask them to join us?"

"Sure thing, Mace. If you think they're good troops, that's good enough for me. Give them a choice, and I'll make the arrangements. Just keep me posted."

Mason looked out at the horizon to the west, at the late night sunset as the early summer continued. He let out a deep breath. "Any more signs of the enemy?"

"Nothing up close. But we think many of them are still out there."

Mason nodded. "I know they are."

10

David saw a bright, blue-green light flare from Jerriel's staff.
The mist and fog dispersed around her as if it were something alive.
She drew her curved short sword and slashed one of the dark trees.
The sap dripped red like blood.

"Shanjegorekal," she said. "Enchanted blood trees. Carnivorous,
vampiric trees. The creepers come from their roots and feed on the
bodies once they drop, too weak to go on. The mist, this vile fog is
exhaled by the trees. It's a magical fog that has the ability to drain
lifeforce energy from the living."

"We have to get out of here!" David said.

"Don't panic. Fleeing in terror will only weaken and confuse us
further. The fog will try to stay with us and mislead our steps. Now that
I know what it is, I can give us some protection. But everyone will have
to stay close. Bunch up around me as we keep going. Light as many
torches as we can. They won't like fire."

"Can these trees attack us openly?" Jason Inada asked.

"Their power is passive, ambient; they'll use the vampiric fog to weaken us until we don't have the strength to move. They are not mobile, except for their slow-moving, smaller creeper roots and vines."

Jerriel cast a protective spell of anti-magic. An aura of light encircled them in an area about sixty feet in diameter. Each trooper lit a torch and brandished the blazing brand around the damp, foggy area.

Outside of that area of protection, the fog seemed to roil. As if it grew angry.

Within the protective dome, in moments, David felt as if he could breathe easier and think more clearly once again. His strength began to return, but not entirely.

They got a good look at the vile trees: tall, with hard, black bark like flint or obsidian. They had long, dark green serrated leaves like daggers, and twisted, gnarled branches and roots like thick veins eating into the earth itself. The militia carefully took some samples.

"We should destroy this entire patch of forest," David said.

"Too many of them," Jerriel told him, shaking her head. "It would take too long, even for us. Their power is collective, and my protective spell will not last forever. We can try to weaken them as we go along, but our main goal needs to be to find our way out. I need to look around."

She pointed her staff at the sky.

"SEVENGA!" She rose up through the trees, and vanished into the mist.

The fog closed in around them once she disappeared.

They did what they could to fend it off, but they started to feel its debilitating effects once more.

After several moments, Jerriel floated back down, bringing her protective aura back, centered around her.

"We're in a deep hollow of a vale where these insidious trees hold sway. If we go another sixty yards to our right, that's the fastest way out."

David and several others took a bearing with their compasses.

Jerriel produced a flame from her staff and scorched a ring all around one of the blood trees. It smelled horrible, like a corpse, seeped blood-red sap, and the tree shuddered. The sound among the leaves was not unlike hissing.

"Shave off the bark on these evil trees, two to four feet all the way around," she instructed. "Everyone do this as we go along and it will greatly weaken and possibly even kill them, in time."

"You heard the wizard-lady," Al Said. "Kill these filthy, bloody trees as we pass through them. They make my skin crawl!"

"They feed off the ambient lifeforce of the area all around them," Jerriel noted. "They are true parasites, but magical in nature as well. Until now, I had only read about their vile kind."

70

David and his commanders continued to spread the word.

They attacked only the trees nearest to them as they made their way. Troops kept moving, but stripped the foul bark off the vampire trees as quickly as they could on either side of their path with their blades and axes.

They passed more bodies of the ill-fated scouting patrol that had wandered that way and become lost within, and those of hapless animals.

By the time they emerged from the fog, eighty yards further out, they gulped fresh air, and a light rain fell, as Jerriel's protective field around them faded away.

The trees changed immediately to more normal, less-lethal varieties.

The mappers made careful notes of where the deadly trees were. David swore to himself to send forces to destroy that patch of vampiric forest and eliminate their threat. Humans would have to look out for others of that kind.

Again, David realized that without Jerriel, they would have never made it out. Like the patrol before them, they would have died before they escaped.

He was very grateful for her knowledge. There was too much about Tharanor that they were still ignorant of.

There was too much out here that could slaughter them, or get them killed.

Exhausted and drained, they rested for a few hours to get their strength back, and had a cold meal. Thankfully, the rain let up, but as they made their way further into the dense hills, the temperature dropped even further.

By evening, all progress stopped, although they only traveled for a few more hours.

It rained. A cold, soaking rain; frigid, clinging, and demoralizing.

With evening approaching, they prepared to endure a very cold, nasty night. Even the wind picked up, and rain even turned to light sleet and wet snow for a short time.

They set up camp part-way up a rocky hillside, and found some natural, shallow caves. The caves sheltered areas beneath huge stretches of massive, fallen trees.

When the Merge struck, half of the land buckled and shifted. There were some natural differences in terrain between the two dimensions. These trees must have toppled over in the resulting chaos.

The Blackhawks set up tents. They put pickets around the camp, sharpened stakes set in the ground. They put down scent killer to obscure their scent in the area. Guard posts were established.

Within the camp and the caves, they set up dome tents. They brought out small backpacking stoves to cook canned and freeze-dried foods. A hot meal would help keep them all going, and the falling rain and the caves would help conceal the scents of cooking.

David had camped in winter before. He found hiking food pasty, starchy, and filling, but the taste just wasn't that great. They also had some military MREs—meals ready to eat—as well, which weren't too bad either. They had food for three weeks total. It was hoped that they might make it back within two.

They huddled down into their sleeping bags and blankets, on their sleeping pads, and shivered together. They tried to sleep again while the wind and the cold rain and wind howled and lashed outside.

Alejandro helped take the first watch. Jerriel stayed up for a while longer in one of the caves, trying to decipher more of her father's journal, and attempting to figure out what else her mother's soulstone was for.

David did his best to rest up and regain his strength.

Just before midnight, the first zombie attacked their camp.

11

Mason spent much of Saturday with Thulkara at her new compound, a nearby group of farmlands that she called: Ravenwood. No one still living seemed to own the lands and the various buildings. At first there hadn't been anyone to manage the lands and their crops, scattered among the sections of dark forest. Then Thulkara took them over and brought her fledgling group there.

Once there was useful work to be done, more industrious people flocked there to be a part of something worthwhile.

Whatever you called it, the old, abandoned farms and its many buildings and assorted dwellings quickly became home to nearly six hundred people. At first, most of them were women and children with no other prospects or places to go.

As their leader, Thulkara more or less became the lady of that growing manor and its fields and woods. She located knowledgeable people and put them in positions of authority where they would be productive and do the most good. That way, Thulkara did not have to do everything herself. She simply had to keep the right people in key positions to keep Ravenwood running well.

Ravenwood even obtained a charter from the city to farm more of the abandoned fields nearby, at the edge of South Bend. They established programs to raise horses, cattle, and whatever livestock they could. Thulkara continued to put smart, capable people in charge to handle all of the growing work. Soon the place was up and running, thriving, and humming along with busy work and industry. She hired several smiths, carpenters, various crafters, plumbers, and even a few engineers and inventors.

Anything they needed, they found someone who could do it, and train others to do also do it.

More labor was required now to work the fields, and any antique farm equipment that could still be used was brought out, repaired, and put back to use behind horses, mules, and oxen, if possible. Advice and know-how from Amish and Mennonite farms and farmers who had survived the initial days of the Merge proved invaluable to the cause of increased food and livestock production.

It would be a race against time to see how much food they could produce before the frosts came, and then the first winter.

Other laborers tinkered with homes, now bereft of central heating and cooling, gas and electric stoves, and modern plumbing.

Teams of mechanics and folks with the know-how were enlisted to go house to house and convert them over to wood burning and coal burning. Lumbering and firewood operations ramped up to process trees. At least the countless, dense, dark patches of woods dotting half of the landscape would prove good sources of fuel that winter, if nothing else. The wood from some of the new varieties of trees proved to burn quite efficiently, while others did not seem to burn at all.

Plumbers and whitesmiths oversaw converting houses back to using cisterns and basic hydraulics to push water through pipes and flush toilets. Anything that could be recycled and made use of was collected and converted for some kind of practical purpose.

But according to Major Bill, many other major problems were brewing. Even with the reduced population they now had, experts and city planners estimated that their current city sewer system would be overwhelmed by human waste and sewage within as little as two or three years. They had to come up with plans to deal with such challenges. Without electricity, the water treatment plants nearby were all practically useless. How would they continue to provide clean water?

Mechanical solutions popped up first. Smaller, localized water towers could be filled with windmill pumps and maintain water pressure in certain areas where that was needed.

They located a few antique well-drilling rigs that operated on smaller, basic steam engines.

Steam power still worked. Its basic, mechanical principles were unaffected by the Merge, and it would rapidly become the basis for society once more. It could not be used to produce electricity, but it could still run and operate almost everything else. Yet boilers and such were fickle and dangerous, and had to be manufactured and operated with great care and an eye toward safety.

Armies of engineers and technicians labored off of old designs and antique pieces in museums to bring that technology back to life with new twists. Steam engines and motors had done much of the work and propelled Urth society once before, and now revised forms of them would again.

If Urth humanity survived long enough to put them back into use.

And because much of South Bend had been burned down during the war, there was a big demand to build new homes and dwellings out of brick, stone, and concrete. All new buildings had to be defensible. And work on fortifications throughout the area expanded on a wide scale in response to the threats they faced.

Again, the key element was time.

Anything solid became building material. Useless chunks of highway, cut off by the Merge, were mined for debris and construction materials. Concrete was even poured over stacked, wrecked cars in a pinch.

Small quarries sprang up and proliferated in several key places, where more building materials could be mined and obtained.

Those who worked hard in the new Urth were well rewarded for their labors and efforts, and shared in the food rationing that needed to be instituted.

Any who could work was expected to join in and contribute some labor that needed to be done. The lazy and the indigent would not last long in such a society bent on survival. If they could not find work on their own, something meaningful would be found for them to do.

When Mason had the time, he read reports sent to Thulkara and her people concerning certain new laws and practices.

In some rare cases, a few individuals refused to do any work at all, or attempted to live as beggars, petty thieves, and other low-level criminals. They and their efforts were hampered greatly by the use of money being suspended and the society relying instead on an economy of barter and trade.

Those who continued to refuse to do any meaningful work were at first given a choice by the town authorities: find a way to work and contribute, or be sent packing. That was it. And banishment outside the borders of town, being sent into the dangerous wilds, usually meant a death sentence.

Yet some stubborn few still chose banishment over doing work that was needed. But banishing people was quickly seen as a mistake.

Such wandering folk, beggars and vagabonds, were also shunned at the borders elsewhere in Michiana. Mishawaka and Elkhart would also not take them in. And it quickly became a law that such folk should not be allowed to have children, or take them into the wilds, either. Since these outcasts refused to do anything to help support such dependents, the children suffered greatly under the care of such fools.

But these outcasts did not go away or die off as hoped. Instead, they quickly turned to banditry, raiding, and robbery on the borders of the wilds. They refused to do any meaningful work on their own, but yet they would go out of their way and spend great amounts of energy robbing and taking from others.

When a few of these bands degenerated into kidnapping, rape, and murder, the militia began to hunt them down and eradicate them with impunity. They were treated as the scourge that they were quickly becoming.

As harsh as it was, under summary justice, all bandits were simply killed wherever they were found.

Once the bandits were eliminated, banishing people from Michiana was halted as a failed policy that simply created more problems. There was no sense creating a class or race of raiders and marauders of their own. The monsters and the enemy had been bad enough.

After that, those small numbers of people who defiantly refused to do any work or help out in any way were taken to a small prison where they could either change their mind and their ways, simply drink water until they starved to death, or had the opportunity each day to take a poison that would put them to sleep and kill them relatively painlessly.

It was a harsh solution for a harsh new world, but stubborn fools and idiots had to be dealt with in some fashion. Career criminals and repeat offenders who were also deemed hopeless cases were given the same three choices at that small prison. A society that was struggling to survive could not coddle or tolerate frivolous stupidity and random human folly for no apparent purpose or reason. The authorities reluctantly agreed that it was more expedient for humanity to cull out such useless attitudes and behaviors.

Such cases were indeed rare, but they still had to be dealt with. The Prison of Last Hope, as it was called, rarely had population of even a hundred persons.

A clear distinction was made between stubborn, able-bodied fools who could work, and yet chose not to, and those in society who were clearly disabled, impaired, or rendered helpless by some kind of condition beyond their control. Such folk were appointed to networks of keepers and care providers were organized to care for such folk, and had the temperament and the training to do. They also supported families and caregivers in the home who struggled to do so.

There were also people who could work, but suffered from various mental conditions and issues, both before and after the Merge. A Department of Mental Health was expanded, and tried to identify persons who had such needs and get them professional assistance. Those who could not function or were violent to themselves or others were sent to the caregivers and keepers to be looked after or controlled.

All of these practices were seen as something very different entirely, as something that a benevolent and moral society should attend to—the needs of the helpless. Such persons had to be registered with the city, and independent inspectors checked on them on a regular basis to make certain that they were being given the proper care they needed. Anyone found to being mistreated or not receiving proper care were placed in situations where they would be treated properly.

Those who abused the helpless could be prosecuted and punished.

Those who were considered helpless or nearly so also included a large number of people who had been severely injured or crippled due to the latest war. Such veterans would need to be well provided and cared for during the rest of their lifetimes. Their families and survivors would also need assistance.

Caregivers who chose to work with such people were provided for. Such work was accepted as their labor, as long as they performed well.

But if Urth humanity was going to survive, everyone had to work together to achieve that goal.

Sheer stupidity and stubbornness were no longer excuses for doing nothing, and would not be tolerated.

Mason saw one other incident occur while he was with Thulkara.

A very large, drunken man appeared at the gates to Ravenwood, raving, cursing, and screaming.

He demanded in no uncertain terms that the lesbian bitches who ran the place release his wife and children to him, and that he wasn't leaving without them. He demanded justice, and he brandished a bloodstained aluminum baseball bat at the guards, who staunchly held him off with quarterstaffs and drawn bows and crossbows.

The Shield Maiden officer on duty told the archers not to fire unless the drunken fool injured someone. Let him scream all he wanted.

Finally, Thulkara brought out the young woman in question; she still had signs of yellowish bruises all over her face and bare arms.

"Name yourself. Who are you and what do you want?" Thulkara asked.

The woman stood on Thulkara's right side. Mace stood on his friend's left.

"I'm Darryl Gunther, and that's my wife, Sherry. Give her over to me and fetch my kids out here, too. They're mine, and they're coming back with me. You had no right to take them, and you have no right to keep them from me!"

"I see. Why did your wife leave you, Darryl? Why did she bring herself and her kids here to Ravenwood?"

"Because she's a no-good, lying bitch. The bitch wouldn't keep those screaming brats quiet…so I could sleep. So now I guess she wants to hide among a bunch of lesbian witches!"

"When the militia brought Sherry and the kids here, Darryl, she and they could hardly walk. Your children almost died from the beatings you inflicted on them. And once you silenced them, as you say, you didn't even go to sleep. You staggered out to find more booze, and left them there, all beaten up. There's a militia warrant out for your arrest, Darryl Gunther."

"What the hell for?"

"Why, any number of crimes. Assault and battery, child abuse, attempted manslaughter of your own wife and two minors You should leave here and go turn yourself in. That would be better for everyone. Get some help, and maybe someday you'll be man enough to be worthy of your family again. They don't need a violent, drunken abuser who almost kills them."

"The lying whore. She's a liar. She made you believe her lies. Give 'em back to me. I'll teach them!"

"What, by beating them all to death?" Thulkara turned to Sherry. "Do you have any desire to go back to this abuser?"

Sherry let her head droop. "No. Never."

"Then stay here, you filthy dyke, like I knew you would once you got among your own kind. But give me my kids. I'm their goddam father!"

"And what a shameful, disgusting creature you are, indeed," Thulkara said. "Your children are staying with us until they recover from you almost beating them to death, Mr. Gunther. With any luck, you will never see them again. Your wife and kids are not your property. They are not slaves. You do not own them. And your violent, drunken actions and behavior have proven that you do not deserve to be around them.

"Once the militia arrests you, you'll be working on a prison gang for many years of hard labor, I would imagine. Farewell and good riddance. This meeting is over. I suggest you run far away somewhere and find a place to hide, like the stinking heap of trash that you are."

Gunther lifted his baseball bat and staggered on his feet. "I ain't afraid of you, you big dyke. I'll mash your head in, too!"

Thulkara took a step forward. "Oh, please, you pathetic piece of shit. Just like you were going to kill your wife and kids?"

He screamed in rage and swung the bat down.

Thulkara reached out and casually caught it in one hand. She jerked it away from him, and then popped him in the face with the end. She finally tossed the weapon behind them into the dirt.

Darryl charged her. Thulkara flicked him in the face with her gauntleted hand, like shooing an insect, and flung him back off his feet with his mouth and nose bleeding even more. He continued to curse and rant.

Thulkara turned to Sherry, who was only about five-foot-two. But she had a quarterstaff in her hands, capped with metal.

"Sherry, this person is never going to hurt you or your kids again. The militia are already on their way to arrest him for his crimes. You need no longer fear him in any way. We've showed you how to defend yourself. Is there anything you want to tell him? Go ahead. I won't let him hurt you."

Sherry stepped forward, holding her staff at the ready. "You leave me and the kids alone, Darryl. You're bad for us, especially when you're drunk. What was between us has been over for a long time. Leave us be. And don't come back."

"You gonna hit me with that stick, Sherry? Pretty brave, aren't you, now that you have all of these lesbians to hide behind. You lying little bitch. I can still take that stick away from you and shove it up your filthy—"

He lunged at her.

Sherry swatted him on the back of the head and knocked him face down.

He got up on his hands and knees, and shook his head like a bull.

"I'll kill you, for that. I'll kill all of you!"

He tried to attack her again.

Sherry rapped him on one side and then the other. Then, with both hands she brought her staff down and bashed him on the head, dropping him face down into the dirt once more. He lay there, wheezing and groaning, too dazed to curse at them anymore.

The guards even cheered.

"Not bad," Thulkara told Sherry.

They had a late dinner that evening.

One good thing about being on a farm with lots of produce and livestock in the summer time. There was plenty to eat for all, and Thulkara liked to eat. She had also found some excellent cooks among her group.

They feasted as Mason hadn't in a long while—not since before the Merge at a family dinner back in Cleveland during the holidays.

Whenever he thought about his missing family, he always felt both sad and helpless. He couldn't control what was happening in distant Cleveland.

He couldn't even control what was happening in South Bend.

"So, how is Blondie doing?" Mason asked Thulkara.

"I go visit him three or four times each week," Thulkara said, gobbling her third chicken. "He comes by once in a while. Mages. Hah! He's just too damn busy with all of his magical crap. Oh, sorry, Mace. No offense."

"None taken. I don't know if I can even call myself a sorcerer any longer."

Sheesh, even as big as Thulkara was—where in the heck did she put it all?

"Is he happy?" Mason asked her.

Thulkara belched, like the great rumbling of an earthquake. Everyone laughed, including herself. "He seems to be happy enough, despite the loss of his best friend. We both miss, you, you know."

Mason nodded. "I know. I miss you both as well. But, I have to do this. For myself."

"Eh, we know that, too. Doesn't make a bit of sense to either of us, but there it is. We're humoring you, anyway. You want to be a soldier now? Fine. There are worse things. But why not be an officer, with your own command? Major Bill would easily make you a lieutenant—even a captain—under his command. But now, for some reason you have to be a mud-marching recruit. Brilliant. And they say Thulls are dense. Those who say that haven't met Urth humans yet. I've met stones smarter than some of your folk, Mace. Like that big turd today. How do some of these people survive from one day to the next?"

"I'm worried about Blondie and these new helpers of his," Mason told her.

"I am, too. I don't trust 'em. But Bill has them under lock and key, I think. They can't turn on Shaeddor in their weakened states. He'd easily murder them all."

"You said 'Shaeddor.'"

"Yes, he only lets his closest friends like us and Bill call him Blondie anymore. Everyone else must use his real name. That is his given name, you know. You can be afraid of that. But he's still Blondie to you and me."

"No, that's not what I'm afraid of," Mason said.

"Then what is it?" she asked.

Mason hesitated. "How much has he recalled? What if he changes his mind? Thulkara, I'm worried he might still go back to the enemy someday."

The big barbarian laughed. "Is that all? Well then, allay your fears, Mace. I've already spoken to him several times—each time we meet. That's no problem."

"Why not?"

"Because he's almost regained all of his memories, and he's still our brother and our ally. And he likes that shrewy, skinny gal of his a lot more than he lets on. Blondie would do anything for her. So stop worrying. He's with us."

Mason said no more, but in his heart of hearts, he was wasn't completely convinced.

He needed to speak with Blondie, in order to be certain.

12

An animated corpse of a ka-torg advanced directly into their camp.

Arrows and crossbow bolts didn't stop it. They held the thing off with spears.

Finally they chopped it apart with swords and axes just as David and Jerriel rushed up.

"It stinks something awful," David said.

Jerriel looked and sounded very worried. "Double the guard. Where there is one, there are probably more. Once animated, they will wander about and attack anything living. As they decay, they become animated, blackened or bleached skeletons. Finally they just fall apart. The dark magic can only keep them going so long. Once the evil spirit imbuing them is released, they will crumble and collapse—usually into dust."

Jason Inada looked down at the beheaded, dismembered pieces of the thing. They still twitched and squirmed on the ground.

He sprinkled some roasted soy beans and holy water over them and murmured some prayers while thumbing his beads.

A hiss of foul, gray black vapor escaped the thing like a small ghost and faded on the wind. The cursed pieces went still.

Troopers brought out their folding camp shovels and buried the pieces quickly. Two more zombies and a skeleton attacked within the hour. Jason helped neutralize and destroy them, both by sword and prayer.

Half of the camp slept while the other half stood watch. The random undead attacks continued throughout the night, all the way until morning.

"When the morning comes, the undead will seek a dark place to hide or bury themselves underground," Jerriel said. "Like many darkspawn, the undead do not like the sunlight. Some even take damage and can be destroyed by it."

"We destroyed almost three dozen of them last night," Al said. "Half of them were human—bodies of Urth people. The rest were monsters. How are these terrible things created?"

"Necromancy is one of the dark arts," Jerriel said. "Some wizards specialize in that skill; higher-level shadow creatures and demons can create undead servants as well. A Ghool Master or Ghool Lord from the Shadow Worlds can command entire armies of undead, giving them greater speed and range of motion. Those advanced undead can wield weapons, obey commands, and even speak with the fell voices of their dark spirits. The evil spirits within them are bolstered and given even greater powers. High-level ghools can even cast spells on their own."

For the first time since they had known him, Alejandro shivered and crossed himself. "These filthy zombie bastards freak me out. I don't hesitate to tell you that, my friends. This is a bad thing. This is very unnatural."

David shuddered as well. One of the undead he had helped cut down looked as though it had once been a young human girl, about thirteen or fourteen, with long black hair.

"Jerriel, we have weird legends about zombies on our world. Would they eat people?"

"I have heard some of your strange lore. Some undead might eat people. Ghools certainly would, but they do so to kill and absorb the lifeforce energy of the living. Or they might be commanded to capture the living and bring them back to their masters as prisoners. Or they could just be sent out to randomly kill anything that lives."

"I'm curious," Jason said. "If a zombie bites or scratches you, do you become infected and turn into a zombie, too?"

Jerriel laughed and covered her mouth with one hand. "That is part of your mythology and lore, not ours. I have never heard of such a thing. A zombie could kill you, but then your corpse would have to be specifically animated and filled with another evil spirit to give it purpose and direction. They are rotting flesh. I suppose you could catch a disease or an infection from them. But they are not like vampires or were-creatures, who can, in fact, affect the living with their disease-like curses."

"Let's hope we don't run into anything like that. Well, we've made it through the night," David said. "Let's pack up and leave this place. Do our best not to leave behind any signs that we've been here."

They departed within the hour.

David and Jerriel went up to point with Lieutenant Collier and one of the scouts. They checked their bearings, making sure they headed in the right direction.

"Looks like we're on track, sir," Collier told him.

"Good," David said. "We should make some progress today. The mountains we need to reach grow closer. We should hit them within another day or two."

David sensed something odd. Something that made his skin tingle.

"Something's wrong," Jerriel said.

He spotted the light, blue-violet glow from the small pool directly ahead of them.

Just as Terry Gallagher, the lead scout, stepped into the water.

The pool rippled.

In less than an instant, the scout vanished. Completely gone. No trace. Lieutenant Rick Collier gasped, even as he kept moving forward.

David reach out to pull him back. Too late.

Jerriel yanked David back.

Collier glanced back at them once, his face in complete terror.

His foot touched the pool. He vanished. Just like Gallagher.

The rest of them gave the pool a wide berth and staked out around its perimeter.

Anything that touched the water vanished. Animate or inanimate. And they did not come back.

David turned to Jerriel. "What is it? Why does that pool do this?"

Jerriel raised her eyebrows and shook her head. "It is obviously magical, and very powerful. But I don't know. I can't study it or examine it without touching it."

"No, don't do that." He couldn't lose her.

"I won't, Daeved. I don't know if our people were disintegrated, or merely transported somewhere else. I hope it's the latter, and that they're still alive…somewhere. But we don't have any time to mess with it any further, so just avoid it. Let's mark it on the maps and move on. We can send wizards to examine it at a later point, if it doesn't dry up."

Two people already gone. Collier and Gallagher, valuable comrades that David knew well. No explanation. They were just gone. Damn it. They faced so much unfairness and uncertainty that didn't make sense.

"They're competent people," David said. "Wherever they are, I hope they're safe."

Their first losses. The bad news shook the entire party. Not a loss from a standup fight. Just something weird beyond their comprehension and control.

"Stay away from any strange pools of water or glowing flowers, plants, or trees," David commanded. "Spread the word. Anything weird, don't touch it. Let Jerriel take a look at it first."

Sergeant Blaylock took point.

The sun came out. The temperature actually rose into the fifties throughout the day. The rain and dew evaporated in the steamy air, but the trails had turned muddy once more.

It grew difficult not to leave tracks.

But they made good progress throughout the day. Scouts spotted a wild boar; it was as big as a rhino. Luckily it did not catch their scent or attack them. It appeared to be carnivorous.

There were many odd and dangerous creatures in the Tharanorian wilds.

As night fell, they reached the rocky foothills of the mountains. With luck they'd find the dragon within the next few days and have their parlay with him. Then they could head home and attempt to get back early.

David and Jerriel snuggled down in their tent, completely exhausted after another day of hard travel.

Before they went to sleep, however, they spoke about the demon they had defeated and its mirrors–and especially about the dark mages who contacted the demon and seemed to have sent it to help conquer South Bend.

"How can a wizard command a demon? David asked."

"It is more dark magic. The wizard helps the demon take physical form in our world, and he can destroy that form. That makes the demon the mage's servant, but it is a very dangerous game to play. Yet it can be done. In this way, high level mages can bind spirits to them as their servants."

"Why do powerful creatures like demons go along with that?"

"They don't entirely. And they're always scheming for an opportunity to break the control part of the arrangement, bust free, and even destroy their human master. They hate humanity. They hate all life. They hate even themselves, and seek the destruction of everything in the universe. They are hatred and destruction incarnate. They only wish to come here to cause mayhem and death."

David still did not understand how it all worked.

"Then why do they do it? Why let mortals control them?"

"Ah, but see, they have no choice. They are forbidden to enter any living world on the Material plane. They cannot come here on their own, no matter how powerful they are. They are evil spirits in nature and must be summoned to a living world. They must be invited, let in, or given a physical material form or avatar, so that they can act and function on the Prime Material plane.

"The mage or person summoning the demon gives them that physical form, and binds them to their service. They can control that physical form, punish and torment it, or even destroy and banish the demon from the Material plane, back into the Void from which it came. The Nine Hells are located in the Abyss and the Void—the dimensions of evil."

"Okay, so the demons need a way to get onto a world like ours?"

"Exactly."

"What if the wizard who summoned them dies?"

"Sometimes the demon is banished automatically. Sometimes it will find a way to remain and still function, if it can. They are amazingly clever, and understand the powers of the universe like few other beings. Even dragons fear their cleverness."

"I imagine they would. I continue to realize that we can't afford to lose you, Jerriel. You're invaluable to us. Without your help, we'd be in deep, deep trouble."

"I think you would have been worse off, but your people are very clever and resourceful. You may have suffered more losses, but you would have found a way. Our enemies underestimated you, and they have paid for that with many defeats."

"I'm still glad we have you." He snuggled up to her in the cold.

Jerriel snuggled back. Both of them drifted off to sleep almost instantly.

All David silently asked for was no attacks on the camp that night.

It rained again the next morning. They awoke to a thunderstorm.

The storm raged for a few hours. After noon, they broke camp and got going. The foothills held some rough, steep terrain. The mountains up ahead looked even worse.

In a forest of dense blue fir and black pine trees, one of their scout teams went out ahead of the main body.

That scout team did not return.

13

Saturday evening, Blondie sent a message for Mason to meet him at a certain tavern for a few drinks at about 10 p.m. The idea was for them to work out how to spend their time together on Sunday, if they only had one day to do so. This would set the standard for their next few weeks, and they didn't want to do anything to blow Mace's cover in the militia.

One idea they had was for Mason to resume his guise as the Pistolero when he was with Blondie or Thulkara, if they went out in public.

That night was short notice for Thulkara, and she begged off for that evening.

She wanted to get some painting done, and said that she would see them on Sunday, in any case.

Her painting time had become very precious to her.

Mason got into his old gear—put on his coat, his hat, and some of his now useless guns. These days, his old persona was nothing more than a disguise.

As far as the public knew, the Pistolero had been on leave, on vacation after the war. No one but a few people, sworn to secrecy, knew that Mace's guns no long fired.

He showed up at the tavern, called the 7-7, partly because it was open from 7 p.m. to 7 a.m. A few militia people noticed him and cheered as he entered. Mason smiled and bartered for a round of drinks with a militia marker from Major Avery. Further cheering erupted from the gathering.

Mason took his own ale and sat at the counter afterwards, listening to the guitar player and a couple of singers who alternated as the evening's entertainment. He tried to relax, but he didn't like living a lie without a reason. Or maybe the reasons just weren't good enough or too convenient, or something.

Bill was right about one thing, however. They had to keep up appearances that the Pistolero was still around and active. That would remain a deterrent to the enemy. And everyone believed that the enemy must have some way of spying on them. Perhaps ways they could not even defend against, involving magic.

By the time Mason nursed down half of his ale, the rest was warm. It was already a quarter or more past ten at night. Where the heck was Blondie?

"Hello, there," a sultry voice said next to him, suddenly.

Mason nearly jumped.

A stunning blond in her early twenties stood next to him at a the bar. He couldn't help glancing down at her equally stunning cleavage, spectacular in a shimmering blouse that barely contained it.

She smiled even wider at his notice, her face very pretty.

Mason looked away. Everyone else kept gawking at the gorgeous young beauty.

She rested a hand on his arm. He flinched and glared at her. She pouted and pulled back. She was a much better actress than he was.

Next she tried humor, in an attempt to disarm him. "I suppose I should have listened to my friends when they told me what a grump the Pistolero was." She laughed very easily.

Mason did his best to ignore her.

"You know, a lot of people, some women included, are of the opinion that the Pistolero is one of the great heroes from the war, who saved us all. And that you've been…greatly unappreciated. In fact, some of us find heroes very, very sexy. If you give one of us gals a chance, we might be…very appreciative. Hell, mister. I think you're pretty hot."

"Thanks, but no thanks, miss."

She blinked and then caught herself. "Really? Think about that. You and I could have a lot of fun, honey. And I am serious. You sure you don't see anything you like?"

He snapped at her. "Not interested."

She jumped, then sighed. They never even got around to her name, if that was of any importance. "All right, honey. I think we're both missing out on this one."

She left. Mason didn't even watch.

Finally he relaxed. Mason slugged down his warm ale and ordered another fresh one. Where the hell was Blondie? Damn it, now he was in a bad mood.

This time he heard clicking footsteps.

Oh, no. Not another one.

He saw her coming in the door. Hell, did someone pick her costume out for her? Long dark hair, gorgeous face and smile, and a body to match. Cowgirl boots, nice legs, cute butt, Daisy Dukes, tied-up red flannel shirt from the boy's department, big, milky-white boobs. All topped off with a straw cowgirl hat.

She worked a deck of cards in her hands.

She bounced over and sat down next to him at the bar.

"Howdy. You wanna play some games, hombre? I likes to play and have me a good old time."

Did she actually call him *hombre*?

"Miss, I appreciate the effort, but like I told the other one: Not. Interested."

"Oh, come on, mister. Why don't you and I saddle up and take a little ride?"

"Please. I don't wanna be nasty about it. I just want to be left alone."

"Hell, sugar. That's no fun at—"

Quick as a snake, he flashed a big, cocked pistol in her cute face. Her pretty gray eyes got real big.

Everyone in the bar froze and went really quiet.

"Get. Away from me." Hell, it wasn't like it was going to go off.

But she didn't know that.

From what most people had heard, on shot from the Pistolero's guns could take down a building.

The young woman screamed and ran in a panic out the door. "Screw this!" she yelled.

Mason chased after her.

Daisy, or whatever her name was, kept running and screamed at his buddy Blondie, standing nearby the bar outside.

"Shae, you dumbass. He nearly killed me. You didn't tell me he was batcrap crazy!"

The first blond with the big chest was already gone. Blondie stood there gaping along with two other scantily clad young women, each of the latter with a different costumed look and frozen with fear like deer in the headlights.

Mason still had his gun in his hand. He sheathed it. "Damn it, Blondie. I told you a long time ago that I didn't need you fixing me up. Especially not now. If you weren't my best, friend, I'd knock your ass down flat!"

The other two cuties quickly fled in terror.

Blondie backed off, holding both hands up in front of himself. "Whoa...okay, Mace. I was just trying to cheer you up a little. You didn't have to scare those gals so much. Forgive a brother for trying."

"Do I look like I need cheering up?"

They glared at each other. "Well, yeah, you messed up, dumb bastard," Blondie told him. "I think it's pretty obvious to everyone but you that you could clearly use a little...release...of some damn kind."

"Well, let's get drunk tonight and talk about what we want to do tomorrow. That will be release enough."

"I sure as hell don't think we want to go back in *that* place."

Mason glanced back. "I guess not."

Mason and Thulkara both finally had time to hang out with Blondie on Sunday, the very next day. Despite the fact that two of them were hungover and the other had paint all of her stained hands.

First, they had to go to breakfast. No small feat with both Mason and Blondie picking at their food, when really all they wanted was some coffee. And then they had to suffer through watching Thulkara hork down her breakfast barbarian-style, without hurling their rumbling guts out.

Then Mason wisely suggested that they go for a walk through part of town that was being rebuilt and out into the country along the St. Joe River. It was, after all, a fantastic, sunny day. And after a while, Mason and Blondie began to feel much better after their debauch from the night before. The fresh air did them good.

Until Thulkara decide to split the morning sky with her thunderous singing, sending all of the birds within four miles fleeing for cover, and driving all of the surviving dogs and cats bonkers—as if Godzilla had suddenly appeared on the horizon, stomping their way.

After she had rattled their teeth around in their heads long enough, the three of them kept walking.

Mason and Blondie pulled the ear plugs out of their tortured ears when she wasn't looking.

But her singing really seemed to get to Thulkara. "My friends, I must apologize. I find that I am quite downhearted."

Mason and Blondie blinked and looked at each other. Thulkara...sad? What the hell were they supposed to do about that? She was almost always the chipper one of their band. In fact, they were the two sad sacks who were usually upset, pissed off, or depressed about something.

This was a terrifying change of events.

"Despite all the good that I have done here, the songs and music of my dear homeland only reminds me of how homesick I am. I yearn for the company of other Thulls, of my own people, who understand and appreciate me. Only a Thul can truly understand the heart of another Thul." She sighed deeply and came about as close to crying as they had ever seen her.

She walked on ahead a bit.

Blondie looked as if he was getting ready to make a break for it, he was so scared.

Mason had to threaten him with great bodily harm. "So help me, Blondie. If you run off and leave me here alone with her, I will hunt you down, tear both of your legs off, and stuff them up your ass!"

Blondie grimaced. "Why, that sounds rather unpleasant, Mace—not to mention unfriendly and unsanitary. Where do you come up with this stuff?"

"Just shut up and help me think of way to cheer up Thulkara. Think, man, think. We owe her that much; she's always been there for both of us, like a rock. She's always giving us a laugh and cheering us up. What cheers up a Thul?"

Blondie's eyes popped. "Now, I'm really scared."

They went on for a bit. Mason an Blondie continued to argue back and forth in a quiet, heated debate. Thulkara hung her head, and kept shaking and sighing, oblivious up ahead of them as she continued to mope.

Blondie finally proposed something drastic.

Now Mason wanted to run away, but Blondie wouldn't let him.

"You said you wanted to cheer her up, Mace. Those were your exact words. I think that would do it. Come on."

"Seriously, Blondie—anything but *that*."

"It's so obvious. You just have to think like a Thul."

"I don't think that's even possible. I don't have the right mindset—or the proper equipment."

"Look, are we going to do this, or not? You said we owe her."

Mason sighed. "All right. What the hell. We are by the river, it is hot, and it's an isolated area. Okay, let's ask her."

He was pretty sure he was going to regret the hell out of this.

"Hey, Thulkara."

"Yeah?" She was obviously still sulking and feeling blue.

"Mace and I were both thinking—since it is pretty hot out—and the river's right here. You wanna go swimming?"

91

Her mouth suddenly dropped open. "You guys mean it? We can go swimming, right now? Like Thulls do?"

"Here we go," Mason muttered.

Blondie grinned. "Sure we can."

"I can get naked and everything, and you guys will join me?"

Mason clenched his eyes shut and stopped himself from saying anything.

Blondie clapped Mace on the shoulder. "You bet we will–naked as jaybirds! Just think of us as your scrawny, wimpy Thul brothers–in spirit, at least."

"I certainly will. And I can laugh at and insult your tiny manhoods to my heart's content?"

"Oh, God…" Mason muttered.

"Laugh at us and insult us all the way. Ridicule our puny manhoods all you could ever wish."

Thulkara lifted and clenched both of her mighty fists. "And I can sing!"

Mason felt his eyes widen. "Oh, God. God help us!"

"Yeah, sure. Sing all you want. Caterwaul until the cows come home."

"And my brothers will sing with me. You must know some of the words by now."

"No way in hell; I couldn't possibly," Mason added. "I don't sing. Never have. Never will."

"Sure we will," Blondie said. "You'll just drown us out anyway. We'll hardly hear the incoherent shit we'll be belting out."

"Damn it all, I am not singing," Mason insisted. "You two stop ignoring me. I'll find a rock and bash myself in the face with it until I pass out or something. I would consider that much more entertaining."

Thulkara looked like a wild woman. "Wahoo! Let's go jump in the river, get naked, and sing like Thulls. Yo-ho!"

"Come on, Mace. Let's catch up to her. She's almost at the river already. What the hell are you doing?"

"Looking for a rock."

Within several minutes, all three of them were Thul skinny-dipping in the river. Thulkara and Blondie sang at the top of their voices.

Mason just sulked near the shore, crouching down in the water so that only his head showed, with a pitiful look on his face. When they called to him to sing out with them, he would only move his mouth mechanically for a while and bob his head to the melody, until they left him the hell alone.

Blondie finally splashed over to him and offered Mace a slug of whiskey from a flask.

Mason stared at him. "Where in the hell were you hiding that? No, on second thought, I don't want to know."

"Come on, Mace. I brought it with me into the water when we ran down. I kept it by a rock near the shore. You didn't seriously expect me to do all of this sober, did you?"

Mason grabbed the flask and choked down half of it in several gulps. "Well, I guess not. Perhaps you have the right idea after all. Drunk would be better. Maybe I'll black out or something, if I'm lucky."

Thulkara continued to sing and laugh.

Blondie laughed. "Well, look at her. At least she's happy now."

Overall, the naked stuff really didn't matter to Mason that much either way, despite the fact that his friend Blondie seemed to be a Clydesdale from the waist down. He'd tried very hard not to look the one day during their bath. But it sure didn't matter now.

Mason didn't want to say anything, but it was hard not to notice, just like the massive, perfectly formed flotation devices Thulkara wore on her chest, under her amazingly pretty skin. Thulkara was perfectly formed–for a giant. Sheesh, could the woman even manage to dive under the surface without being yanked back up by the buoyancy of those things?

And, as noted, Blondie's appeal to the ladies became abundantly clear.

But even with his earplugs in, Thulkara's booming, roaring songs grated on Mason's ears and made him wince. He wondered if her voice could split rocks in half.

Thulls wouldn't even have to fight in battle. An entire army of them only had to sing, and that alone would drive any hapless foe from the field in complete panic and disarray.

Suddenly, he thought he caught movement up among the thick trees along the bank. Was someone watching or spying on them?

They were a sight.

He couldn't be sure. He had only seen it for an instant, and he could have been seeing things.

He had certainly seen enough that day to last him a good long while.

Thulkara shrieked at the sky. "I love being naked!" She swam over to the other bank and began sunning herself, much like a big seal.

Mason and Blondie finally lay back in the water, relaxing and sipping whiskey.

"So, Blondie. I hear you're going by Shaeddor again. You got your head on straight?"

His friend sighed. "That is my name, Mace. And I have regained most of my memories about who I was and what I had done. I gotta say, a lot of that was painful to recall, my friend. As it turns out, I'm more or less a rat bastard."

Mason grunted. "Hell, I could have told you that much. Don't feel too bad. I'm not worth a shit myself, Blondie. So, what else is new? We kinda guessed all of that, didn't we?"

"Well, it's quite another thing to own it all as part of your past self. If I had it all to do over again, perhaps I wouldn't have been such an asshole."

Mason looked at him. "You've been given that chance, Blondie. You're doing it right now. You've had it all along. Losing your memory just gave you time to stop being a dick."

Blondie sighed deeply, and then sighed again. "I guess it's not going to matter too much, my friend. Because I've also remembered a bunch of stuff about our new enemies. I've tried to talk to Thulkara about it, but she won't listen. All she talks about is fighting against incredible odds and dying a glorious, valiant death, like all good Thulls want."

"What are you trying to say, Blondie? I drank that crap of yours too fast. I think I might actually black out here."

"Our foes aren't done with us, Mace. And now I know now what they can throw at us. It's pretty staggering—horrifying, really."

"Seriously, Blondie. I think I have alcohol toxicity here."

"Lie down before you fall down. They're far stronger than us, and they have the resource of an entire magical nation backing them up."

Mason muttered, his head hanging down, "At least if I die I won't hear anymore Thull singing. Oh, god. What if I wake up in Hell and all they have piped in is Thull singing?"

"Mace, you lunatic, are you even still listening to me? Our foes are far too impossibly strong for us to defeat them. They're going to kill us all and drink bloodwine from the goblets they fashion out of our skulls.

Mason smacked his lips, losing it. "Yum. That sounds nice."

Blondie stared at his hands. "I'm serious. There's no way we can win, Mace. Dammit, we're all as good as dead."

14

The dark trees, soggy air, and muddy ground made advancing both dismal and difficult. But this ominous area also grew eerily quiet. Even for the Tharanorian forest, that wasn't usually normal, and presaged something dire.

"The scout team went out on the left flank to the south and simply hasn't come back, sir," Blaylock noted.

"We're going after them," David said. "Spread out. Trackers in front in sight. Everyone look for signs. Jason, I want you and Al on our flanks, along with the dogs. Report anything to me. If our people have been captured, perhaps we can locate and free them. We need to know what happened."

The trail was hard to read. Three well-trained scouts, completely gone.

"Someone's taking great care to sweep the trail," the trackers soon reported. "And they're better than us at doing so; they know this area well."

"Let's hope the Urth areas confuse them." David said. "What do you think happened?"

Sergeant Blaylock hesitated and looked grim. "I think they got jumped, and snapped up pretty quickly. Whatever took them are strong, fast, and smart. Whatever they are, they're tough characters. I'd say heads up or we're next, Dave."

"I know they're hiding their numbers, but how many of them do you think there are?"

"No way to tell. At least as many as us, maybe more."

"Let's take every precaution we can. I don't want them getting the jump on us, and I still want to try to catch up to them and get our people back."

They raced forward. Their quarry tried everything that they could to elude pursuit. False trails, doubling back, moving through streams.

They found the first trap across the main trail a few minutes later. A huge deadfall with spikes. It didn't claim anyone, but the mere appearance of such a trap did slow them down.

How in the hell had their foes had time to get ahead far enough to set it? How fast could these things move?

Sergeant Blaylock came back to him and whispered, "Something moving up ahead, sir. It might be some of them."

"Good. Let's circle around on either side and cut them off. You and Jason circle a platoon to the right, I'll race my platoon around around to the left. Al can lead the third platoon up the middle."

They arrived breathless, barely ahead of their quarry.

Their foes *were* faster than them.

They barely had time to set up their ambush when a dozen large creatures rushed through the target zone single file, on an angle. No sign of the captives among them.

Each of them was almost seven feet tall, well-muscled, and covered in long, sleek, black hair. They bore the heads and large horns of goats. They carried many weapons, and were lightly armored with what looked to be pieces of armor and the tanned hides of their victims—human, animal, and other monsters.

The leader was the biggest and strongest of them. His black horns had been painted red and gold, with strange symbols decorating it. He wielded a javelin and a large, broad-bladed battleax.

He detected something on the wind by sniffing the air, and snorted quietly. He motioned for the others to retreat.

Very clever.

David unleashed the ambush before their quarry melted away.

"They are grun," Jerriel said. There was real fear in her voice. "Grun are fierce fighters—very tough."

David shot the leader in the belly with his crossbow.

Jerriel ensnared their hoofed feet with vines and roots shooting up out of the ground. The troops peppered them with missiles.

All of the creatures got hit with arrows or bolts.

Only two of the twelve dropped. David guessed that these were scouts or skirmishers.

The other ten ignored their wounds, ripped free of their bonds and charged the right flank with amazing ferocity and speed.

They leaped through the air and into the more vulnerable lines of archers, twenty-five feet away. They whirled and fought with weapons in each hand, cutting down troops and flinging them aside. Sergeant Blaylock and Jason Inada cut off the leader.

Blaylock stabbed the leader in the chest with his spear. The leader snapped the haft off like a twig and buried his ax in Blaylock, splitting him open through the head and deep down into the torso. Blood and gore literally sprayed everywhere.

With his other hand, the leader held off Jason's katana with its javelin. No mean feat.

Jason finally slipped under the creature's guard and severed its hand at the wrist.

It grunted and punched Jason in the face with its bleeding stump, and knocked him into the trees with a powerful sweep kick of its muscled legs and hooves.

The grun would have broken through the lines and escaped if Jerriel hadn't exploded the ground under their feet, pelting them with rocks and dirt, knocking them down. She nearly buried them.

That slight delay gave the rest of the ambush time to close in.

As the grun jumped back up, the Blackhawks ringed them in a circle of steel.

Alejandro jumped in and dueled with the leader, methodically slicing him to pieces. But the fierce creature never hesitated once, and fought to the death over several long moments, bashing Al with its stump and even getting in a jab to the leg with a javelin.

There was never any doubt to the outcome. David helped cut down two of the remaining grun. But they went down only after taking several mortal wounds that would have dropped a normal Urth human.

He made a note of it: grun. Jerriel was right. They were incredibly tough, vicious fighters.

By the time the fight ended, David and the Blackhawks up front felt exhausted. They suffered five dead, including Sergeant Blaylock. A few others were hurt or wounded in some way, despite vastly outnumbering their foes over ten to one.

David made a couple of quick field promotions.

Luckily, only one of their people couldn't move under their own power and had to be carried on a stretcher by four people to the rear.

Several, like Al, went forward limping.

"Look," Jerriel said. She pointed ahead of them.

Dark black smoke rose up about a mile ahead.

"Let's move," David said.

"I think these grun are setting the traps," Jason said.

"They're trying to slow us down," Jerriel added. "We may have just take out their rear guard for the main group."

"Well, they succeeded in delaying us," David said.

They went forward, enraged at their losses, ready for battle.

A mile or so ahead of them, among the mountainside covered with dark trees and large rocks, they came upon a horrific scene.

They found the bodies of all three of their missing scouts, clearly dead. Their mutilated bodies were a vile testament to some dark grun ritual.

Each victim lay stripped naked, tied spread-eagled, stretched out painfully across a huge boulder. Each had been pointed head down over a pit fire smoldering with wood and some kind of pitch that produced the thick black smoke.

The faces of the victims were charred black skulls, burned up to the shoulders, faces frozen in scorched screams. But their tongues had also been cut out, nowhere to be seen.

The bodies had been hacked and cut open, the heart and other organs torn out and also missing.

"Grun are a slightly more intelligent race of darkspawn than the other, random monsters," Jerriel noted. "They are said to infest countless worlds that have fallen under the shadow. They devour their victims in such rituals, sacrificing them to their masters–the Dark Ghods. They eat anything that is meat, and relish tormenting their captives–even from other rival tribes of grun. And they do not fear the sun."

"Cut our people down," David commanded. He had trained them, selected each of the three victims personally.

Keifer Saltman, Cassius Nuba, and Sally Rohtstein–all of them good troops.

He remembered how proud and happy they all were to be handpicked for the Blackhawks.

They all knew the risks they took. That was part of the job. That still didn't make any this any easier.

More letters to write when they got back.

"Wait," Jerriel said. "The grun may not have left this area."

"I don't care. I said cut them down."

Troops moved forward to do so.

"This could be a trap, Daeved. They could be hiding nearby, in great numbers. Preparing to attack, even now."

"Good. I hope they are. I hope they try something."

She looked around, pulled her helmet on, and nervously readied a spell. "Be careful what you hope for, Daeved."

15

Mason's arms grew weary from training all afternoon, hour after grueling our with spear and shield on the line.

Today the recruits were part of a mass maneuver.

Alpha, Bravo, Charlie, Delta, and Echo companies squared off against Foxtrot, Golf, Hotel, India, and Jackson companies in a great, mock battle. Five companies versus five companies, two hundred and fifty troops on each side.

The crash and clash of such numbers were stirring and invigorating as the units strained and fought. Despite the fact that they used padded weapons, the contest was real.

And the stakes were also real, in a way.

Whichever side won the contest, won an extra leave that weekend, and the losers would stay in and around their barracks.

For the sake of such training battles, if a trooper received a hard enough blow, he or she dropped and went down, playing dead. Judges roamed the field, calling out to any who refused to drop when they should.

At first, Mason's Side 1 held up very well against Side 2. Both sides punched and dueled at each other, absorbing losses.

Both shieldwalls more or less held up.

Then Side 2 executed a superb sweeping, flanking maneuver on Side 1's exposed and vulnerable right flank.

Side 1's flank began to roll up.

The orders came down. "Echo Company, hold the line!"

The other four companies pulled back to form a protective square.

Echo did their duty, buying the others time.

But Mason and others who had been in actual combat saw what was going on very quickly.

The others weren't forming up fast enough behind them.

And Echo could only hold out so long.

Side 1 needed more time to set their positions.

Mason spotted Sergeant Rivera. "Sergeant, this isn't going to work. Let's attack and press the attack hard."

He glared at Mason. "That's crazy, Tyler. That's suicide!"

"We're dead out here in a few minutes anyway. And, damn it, I want leave this weekend. Don't you?"

Rivera ran over to their lieutenant for the exercise. Both of them nodded and signaled an all-out, explosive attack. "Shark teeth formation!"

Echo formed up into piercing triangles and rushed the surprised frontline forces of Side 2. They penetrated as far as they could. Even the archers joined in. They did as much damage as they could and broke the shield wall at several places.

But within less than a few minutes, all of them were cut down.

Not only did the other companies of Side 1 form into a square, they rotated 180 degrees counterclockwise like diamond, and tore into Side 2's broken lines before they could recover and reform.

Echo company sacrificed themselves to give Side 1 the victory.

Side 2 tried to recover, but the battle ground them up and put them down.

While Mason was lying on the ground in the chaos, waiting for the all-clear to stand up again, two figures suddenly bent over him.

Even heavy blows from padded weapons and kicks still hurt pretty bad. They pounded him quickly and spoke down at him so that he could hear.

"Yeah, we know who you are, you sonovabitch. Where are your pistols now, asswipe?"

"Watch your back, dickhead."

The judges whistled the all-clear signal.

By then, Mason was so dazed he couldn't see what his attackers looked like. They quickly melted back into the crowd of people getting up and moving around.

Rodell found him and offered him a hand up half a minute later. "Shit, Mason. What the hell happened to you?"

Mason groaned. "I think the other side got a little overzealous and was pissed about losing their leaves this weekend."

"Damn, I guess so. Let's get you over to the aid station."

He couldn't tell Rodell who he was or why the two men had beaten him into the dirt while others weren't looking that way. Perhaps it was just those two who had figured out who he was, and now they couldn't let on for fear of exposing what they had done. And they must be in one of the other companies.

This was the first time someone had been able to isolate him in a place where they could attack him without getting caught.

When Mason had a chance, he'd report it to Major Avery. Once he was on leave on the weekends.

But he had to be careful with that also. If he didn't spend time with Rodell and his militia buddies, they would also begin to resent and disrespect him.

Mason decided that the only solution was to divide his weekend leave time between his new friends and his old ones. It wasn't perfect, but it would work for another week or two. Now that he knew he was a target, he would try to watch his back and be more careful.

Major Bill was very pissed off once he found out what had happened that weekend. He offered to launch a full investigation.

That would only make things worse and expose Mason to even more scrutiny and attention. Bill said that it would be better to let the attackers think that they had gotten away with it.

"They did get away with it," Mason noted. "They knocked the snot of me and walked away."

On Saturday night, Mason went out with Team 3 to see a play and hit the pubs. They stayed out late. By one in the morning, twelve of them reduced down to four: Mason, Rodell, Bryan, and Lashonda.

They laughed and poked fun at each other as they stumbled away from one pub and made their way toward another. Bryan and Lashonda knew some of the funniest and filthiest dirty jokes that Mason had ever heard, and the two of them kept trying to top the other.

A night watch patrol stopped them to check them over, asking if they needed any help getting back to their barracks. The four of them laughed and did their best to reassure the watch that they were perfectly fine.

Five minutes later, they got jumped by about twenty people, closing in on them from both sides of an alley they walked down.

The four of them made an attempt to defend themselves, but five-to-one odds quickly left them stomped into the dirty concrete.

Thus far, none of them had been singled out.

In his dazed state, Mason heard the thugs talk amongst themselves.

"So, where are they? These are the ones they wanted us to beat up, right? Do you know which one they're really after?"

"No. They said they'd take care of it. One of the three males, I think. They're close by. They should be here any minute to take over."

"They must want this guy dead pretty bad. Did they say why?"

"No, and I don't care. I might stomp someone, but I'm not offing anybody. I'm splitting as soon as the buyers get here and take over. I'm not going to be part of four murders."

"Damn, do you really think they'll kill all four of them?"

"Do you think they're going to leave any witnesses?"

"I guess not. I'm with you, man. Let's get out of here."

"We just gotta make sure we get what's coming to us. We did what was asked."

"Hey, here the buyers come; those three coming this way."

"Watch it. Two of them have knives and swords. Damn it; one of them even has a spear."

Mason heard other voices negotiating with the thugs. The buyers sounded impatient.

"Let us at them. We need to cut all of their throats, right away."

"Not until we make sure you've given us what you promised—the food, the weapons, the horses, the pigs, and the chickens."

"Already delivered and waiting for you at your place where we hired you. Prime breeding stock. Enough for ten people to make it through the winter and more. Now, get out of our way and let us at the targets."

"They're all yours. We're walking this way. Do us a favor and let us get out of the alley before you kill them. And if we find out that you've crossed us in any way, we'll hunt you down and slaughter you."

"Don't worry. You did your job. Get going, so that we can do ours."

The score of thugs left, walking quickly the opposite way.

Mason tried to move, but he was still too beaten up.

The foremost figure drew a long knife and reached for Rodell.

Mason's friend reached up and grabbed the attackers wrist's. Suddenly, Rodell's hands blazed, first with orange magelight, and then with red flame.

The attacker screamed and pulled back. Rodell looked just as surprised as the other guy, but tried to wrestle, more with his attacker.

Mason heard shouting and thumping. He glanced back and saw Thulkara's familiar shadow moving through the twenty thugs, smashing and bashing them against both sides of the narrow alley, leaving their crumpled forms to fall behind her in her wake.

The second killer, with the spear, tried to stab Rodell in the back but missed. Then he tried to stab Mason.

Mason barely deflected the thrust into the wall next to him.

Then he shot forward and head-butted the spear-wielder in the groin and knocked the wind out of him.

By that time, Blondie appeared behind the three assassins and nailed them all with violet lightning. They screamed and dropped like marionettes with their strings cut.

Rodell was also stunned.

Thulkara whistled and called for the night watch.

Blondie smiled down at him and offered him a hand. "Good thing we decided to tag along with you stupid drunks."

Mason laughed, getting helped back up to his feet. "Good thing. I owe you again, Blondie."

His friend stared at him. "You sure do, Mace. They keep coming at you, don't they?"

"Yeah, they sure seem to."

"Your friend there seems to be a mage. I think we have another sorcerer on our hands."

"I saw that, too. He's a good guy. I can introduce you after he wakes up from you zapping him silly."

"It couldn't be helped. After his basic training, we can recruit him for the mages. You guys don't have much more to go."

"Nah. Hey, here's the night watch. Let's get this sorted out. I'm sure Bill will want these folks questioned."

Blondie smiled viciously. "No doubt about that."

16

"Bastards!" David hissed under his breath.

Even as they cut the bodies down, harsh, croaking laughter erupted and echoed down the mountainside, ringing through the valley below. It rippled through the thick, dark trees. The Blackhawks readied their weapons and looked around uneasily.

Even David had a bad feeling.

"Jerriel's right. As much as I despise it, we must leave our dead. Get the wounded moving around the left side of the mountain as quickly as possible," David commanded. "The rest of us who can travel fast will follow in the rear and hold them off, if need be." The troops guarding the wounded were already moving.

A storm of huge, black-shafted arrows arced out from out of the rocks above.

"Take cover!"

David's troops dropped the corpses and barely made it back into the trees. Large rocks and arrows peppered the area around them.

The fell laughter continued.

Several dozen grun stood up behind the rocks on the mountain side, brazenly displaying their numbers.

Alejandro sounded a bit worried. "David. Ten of those things took on a hundred of us."

"We have to slow them down. Shoot them! Cut down as many as we can. Jerriel. Spells."

Grun raced and leaped down the mountain.

Arrows and crossbow bolts hardly slowed them down.

Then the mountainside exploded up above them. Jerriel's spell struck there. An avalanche of rock and dirt swept down in a huge wave.

"Run!" Jerriel said. "We must leave. That might not be enough to stop them!"

"What?" David said. He didn't believe it. But as he looked back, many of the grun nimbly leapt from rock to rock, even as the mountainside slid down in waves beneath them.

"We're out of here," David said.

They ran full tilt, and nearly caught up to the wounded.

Scouts ran up.

"The grun are pursuing, sir. And they seem royally pissed."

War cries roared in the air behind them. The grun raced after them through the thick trees.

"Damn, and they're faster than we are," he said.

They used every trick they could think of to lose the grun, but they were stuck on a steep trail leading around the southwest quarter of the mountain, with little chance of escape or evasion to either side.

All they could do was run.

Jerriel left a few magical traps for the grun to activate. Hasty efforts at best. Blasts and explosions went off about a half mile behind them.

The grun slowly gained on them. Scouts reported their total numbers at almost three hundred by then.

The trail stretched out and the grun finally caught sight of them, snarled in anger, and increased their speed.

David faced a very tough decision. They could turn and fight and possibly be annihilated, or leave the wounded to fend for themselves, try to scatter, and link up back together with any survivors.

None of those options sounded appealing.

If they were going to die, it was better to die fighting together. Not scattered and being hunted and dragged down.

He resigned himself to that.

There had to be another way.

They sped around a bend where the trail turned less steep and hid them momentarily from the grun.

A large swath of vegetation had been somehow cut down in a huge arc encompassing almost the entire side of one half of the valley that opened up around them and scooped below their position.

The trees were still scattered across the vale. There were numerous exposed rocks and boulders. But the bushes and weeds, thorns and brambles, and choking vegetation had been cut down close to the ground, as if by huge mowing machines.

Not only that, but the ground was pockmarked by hundreds and thousands of weird holes, lips of rock and dirt pushed up around them all.

"What the hell is all that?" David asked.

"It might be cold enough still," Jerriel said with what looked to be a terrified realization. "If so, we might survive. That's our escape route, Daeved! Take us down through there, single file. Everyone must be very quiet."

"Jerriel, I don't under–"

Stray grun arrows fell among them.

"Trust me, Daeved. That is the only way we'll make it without losing half of our forces! Run in between those holes and do not touch them. Don't attack or go near anything that comes out of them. Now run!"

David led the troops down into the vale, just like she said. "You heard our wizard, people. Single file. Keep moving. Don't touch or attack anything. Stay quiet!"

"We'll be caught out in the open!"

"There's no cover, sir!"

"Just do it!" Once again, he hoped Jerriel was right about this. Whatever this was.

They were a third of the way across their weird little corner of the weird open landscape when the grun charged down behind them.

They actually hesitated for a several long moments at the edge, sniffing at the air and gesturing wildly at the holes with their weapons.

Then their leaders tore into them, clubbing, whipping, and flailing at them, cutting some down. They brutally drove the grun down into the valley by force. And the grun took after their quarry once more.

They covered half of the distance in an open sprint across flat ground. Their speed over a short distance was astonishing.

David looked all about them for a place to make a stand. Perhaps that cluster of trees, but he knew they wouldn't last very long against that many grun.

He felt some fear, but he'd faced death too many times before. Going down fighting side by side with people he loved? Not bad a bad way to go—other than at a ripe old age in his sleep, next to Jerriel.

Missing everything leading up to that would be a regret.

Plus, he did not like failing at any mission he took on.

"Jerriel. They going to…overtake us. We need to…make a stand…maybe by those trees."

The ground rumbled.

"No, Daeved! Keep running or we all die!"

He glanced back. He sure didn't see how. The grun were less than a hundred yards away, spreading out to cut them off and slaughter them all. Their hooves thundered over the ground.

Off to the left, something that at first looked like red liquid poured and rushed out of several of the weird holes.

Not liquid.

The red wave was made up of thousands of nasty-looking red bugs. They were beetles of some kind, but each of them the size of a cat.

The fierce grun made the mistake of attacking them, probably out of instinct.

That was definitely a mistake.

The air filled with an acrid, bitter-smelling mist. A terrifying clicking and hissing noise erupted.

"Blood beetles!" Jerriel screamed. "That noise is their attack signal!"

He'd never seen her so terrified before. Not even around the demon.

Within seconds, millions of blood beetles exploded from the holes and swept over the foremost lines of grun—attacking them in a massive, flowing waves.

A terrible crunching and snapping erupted from clouds of dust kicked up by the one-sided battle taking place behind them.

David kept running. When he looked back, the grun fled in full retreat, pursued by what looked to be a flash flood of blood beetles, still dragging them down from behind.

The grun grunted and shrieked in fear. That was perhaps even scarier.

"We're almost to the trees!" Jason shouted.

Only thirty yards away.

A wave of blood beetles caught their scent, detecting them somehow—perhaps from the blood of their wounded—and swept in their direction.

The terrifying clicking and hissing grew in intensity.

17

Mason woke up in a private, sunlit room with a warm breeze flowing in from the wide open windows. He sat up and winced from the bruises, abrasions, and cuts he had endured at the beating the night before.

He guessed it was Sunday morning. All of him was stiff and ached, but he moved anyway. He had endured far worse pain and injury on several occasions, and shuddered at those memories. Simply being beaten and kicked into the ground wasn't going to stop him for very long.

The heavily armed militia guards posted outside his door noticed him groaning, cursing, and moving around. One of them called out. "Major Avery, he's waking up, sir."

More than one wooden door creaked open, and feet came racing across a wooden floor from the sounds. Mason guessed that they were at least up on the second floor somewhere, perhaps even higher. He hadn't had a chance to look out yet. He was still in his shorts and T-shirt, and reached for his clothes.

He had his pants on when Avery's private physician and a nurse came in, and tried to both check him over and get him to go back to bed.

Bill Avery stood at the door right behind them and watched them for a moment, a grim smile on his face. "Tom, Selena, you might as well give up on this ornery galoot. He's more stubborn than the three of us put together. We ought to at least know that much by now. You're dismissed, and thank you. I need to talk with Mace in private."

The doctor and nurse frowned at Mason and departed.

Bill pulled up a chair and sighed, while Mason put his shirt on.

"Good to see you, Bill."

"You as well, Mace. You were pretty beat up last night when they brought you and your friends in on stretchers. You don't remember me trying to talk to you?"

Mason shook his head. "Not really. Between being drunk and getting our asses stomped, the rest of last night remains a bit fuzzy. How are the others doing?"

"Oh, a lot like you. But they'll be fine. We'll send them back to duty with you on Monday, if that's what you want. If I were you, I wouldn't go on any more drunken benders in town where others can get at you."

"There were a dozen of us at first. I figured I was safe among a big group like that. I guess I was wrong once we dwindled down to just four of us."

"It was a good thing that Blondie and Thulkara thought it best to trail after you and your recruit buddies."

Mason nodded. "A very good thing. I'll have to thank them both, again."

"You do that, Mace."

"What have you learned from the attackers?"

Bill shifted in his chair. "We're still in the process of grilling them all."

Mason quickly told Bill what he had overheard them say in the alley.

Bill agreed. "That's about what we know. The first twenty were simply bribed by the others to waylay and beat you four up. They were little more than a gang of local punks and thugs, but they weren't killers. Yet they attacked you all the same, and left you at the mercy of those three who did intend to murder you and your three friends in cold blood. Keep that in mind."

Mason sat up straight suddenly. "What's going to happen to them all?" he asked.

Major Bill didn't hesitate. "We're going to try and hang every one of them according to summary justice."

Mason thought a long moment. "I wish you wouldn't, Bill. That's almost two dozen more people dying on account of me—and I'm not even the Pistolero anymore."

"Most of them didn't know that. And none of them would care."

"The ones who stomped on us didn't kill us. They could have, easily, but they held back. I heard them say so. They didn't want to be a part of murder."

"But that's just the thing, Mace. They were a part of it. They left you all there, helpless. If you hadn't been rescued by Thulkara and Blondie, you would all be corpses by now."

"Bill, please, I'm asking you this as a favor to me. Please don't hang all of those folks. Send them off to hard labor somewhere, but don't take their lives on my account. They were after me. That's what this was all about."

Major Bill Avery sighed again. "I'll do it for you this once, Mace. But never again. We'll convict them of attempted manslaughter and send them away to hard labor in one of the quarries for a long while. That's the best I can do."

"Thanks, Bill. I mean it."

"I know you do. And that's the problem, Mace. You haven't been yourself since you found out that Tori was dead. You're all over the place. What are you trying to do? What is it that you want?"

Mason sat back down on his bed with one shoe still in his hand. "I don't know, Bill. I guess maybe I want to be a human being, somehow. I've never really been much of one. I know that now. I…I didn't deserve Tori. I think that's why she was taken from me."

"Mace, you know that's total bullshit, right?"

"I can't help it. That's how I feel inside. It's all I have left, and that's not much, let me tell you. I just want to be a regular person, and do my duty like everyone else. I'm not asking for any special treatment. If I can just do that much, and be a good friend to a few people, then at least I will have accomplished something. At least then I can hold my head up."

"Mason, you're just feeling sorry for yourself, and in your situation, that's more than understandable. But you are a better man and a better person than you give yourself credit for. I wish you could see that."

Mason shook his head again. "The jury is still out on all of that. That remains to be seen. But I intend to do my best. If Tori is somewhere, still watching me, I don't want her to be ashamed of me for being some kind of asshole."

Bill rested a strong hand on his shoulder. "Mace, when you get there, you'll realize that you never had that far to go. All that any of us can ever do is our best. You've put yourself on this path. So see it through. All of your friends will still be here waiting for you, powers or no, along with your new friends as well. People do respect and admire you, Mace. And it's not just because they fear you as the Pistolero. But the one you really need to prove all that to is yourself. So go right ahead and do it, even if it is the long way around. Like I said before. We'll be here waiting for you."

Mason put the other shoe on. "You know, eventually people are going to figure out that my guns don't work any longer. We'll have to tell them all the truth about my powers going away. I won't be the Pistolero any longer. I'm not right now."

"Damn it to hell, Mace. You hold off on that for now. And I'm not doing that for you. I'm thinking about Michiana. We can't let the enemy know that your powers are gone. We just can't. Like it or not, the Pistolero remains a major deterrent to the enemy. Our long-range scouts have reported at least one massive body of troops or something far out toward Vaejan.

"Another large group of mercenaries has been spotted far to the south, between us and Indianapolis, controlling the farming fields in that region. We need all the time that we can get before they hit us again. We have only just begun to fortify the town and regroup."

"All right. No one will find out from me. Hey, did you hear I have another mage for Blondie to train? My buddy Rodell Kim showed signs of magefire last night on his hands, and burned one of those three, would-be-killers, when they were trying to slit our gizzards."

Bill smiled for once. "Good, good. Blondie mentioned something like that. We can use all of the mages we can get. Send him to us once your basic is over. Blondie will get him squared away. What the hell kind of name is Rodell? It's not Korean, that's for sure."

Mason shrugged. "Dunno. I'm going to the infirmary to check on the other three."

"You do that. Thulkara and Blondie are waiting for you as well. They want to have dinner with you tonight."

"Thanks for everything, Bill. I'll catch you later."

Mason looked down at his friend Rodell, still snoozing on his cot in the nearly empty infirmary. "Hey, Rodell. Wake your ass up, you lazy bum. Dogging it again, eh? Get down and give me twenty. Get your sorry ass up and go run a few—"

Rodell winced, but kept his eyes closed. He snarled back as he tried to roll away on the cot, "Go straight to hell and suck my—" Then his eyes bulged and he gasped for breath.

Mason grinned. "What's wrong, pal?"

"Ugh, I feel like crap, that's what wrong. My head is killing me, and everything else hurts, too! I feel like I've been beat up."

"Uh, Rodell. I've got news for you; you were beat up, dummy. We all got our asses royally stomped. That's why you're sore. But hey, more good news. Don't you remember that spellglow on your hands last night when you scorched that one jerk trying to kill us? That means you're a mage now. After you complete your basic, you can go to mage camp, and learn to play with all of the other little sorcerer and wizard boys and girls."

Rodell continued to groan. "Yippee for me. Too bad right now I wish I was already dead."

"Hey, just take it easy for the rest of the day and recover. These folks will take good care of you and the others. Then we all go back to Echo Company tomorrow. So, enjoy being pampered here while you can."

Lashonda suddenly called out from her cot. "Mason, is that you waking me up and making all that racket?"

"It is."

"Well then you shut the hell up and get on outta here. Cause if I have to get up an' chase you off, I am gonna put one of my big-ass feet right up that skinny white little butt of yours, as far as it will go. And I mean it! Us folks is trying to rest."

Bryan, the fourth of their merry little recovery band, was starting to groan as well.

"I'll check on you and the others later, Rodell," Mason said softly. "I don't want to cause a riot here."

"Okay," Rodell droned. He already sounded as if he drifted off back to sleep again. Mason left the medical tent chuckling to himself.

18

"Get the wounded to safety!" Jerriel shouted. She turned, muttered a spell, and floated into the air about twenty feet up. "Whatever you do, don't fall in their holes. Don't attack them directly. It drives them into an insane rage of bloodlust!"

"We could climb the trees," Alejandro suggested.

"Don't. The grun tried that. Blood beetles also climb very well, and are currently eating the grun up in the trees and pulling them down."

Grun on sticks. Yummy beetle chow.

In fact, in the distance where the grun fled, several large trees toppled over and crashed down. Jerriel spoke another command word and blasted a wide arc of fire in the path of the sweeping insects.

That held them at bay for the moment while David and their troops reached the trees and kept going. David hung back.

"Jerriel, come on. What are you doing?"

"I've cast too much. I can stay up here for a while, but I can't fly."

The blood beetles roiled beneath her and rose up in waves that reached several feet to try to bring her down.

She was slowly sinking closer to them.

"Hold on!" David shouted.

He quickly pulled out a reel of thin but strong fishing line for bow fishing, tied the end to one of his blunted crossbow bolts, and put the reel behind the crotch of a tree where it could spin out. He loaded the bolt, and took aim.

Jerriel misunderstood. "Don't shoot me!" she protested.

"No, no. I'm not going to plug you. Catch the attached line as it reels out and shoots past you. I'll pull you into the trees and you can come down safely where the bugs can't see you land."

"Run, Daeved. There's no time. They will spot you or catch your scent any moment!"

"Just grab the string, damn it. I'm going to fire!"

The bolt shot past her and the fishing line reeled out.

Jerriel flailed with her staff and caught a loop of the line, wrapping it around her hands and wrists.

David didn't bother reeling her in. He turned and ran, flying her behind him like a trailing kite or balloon. Jerriel descended and came down among the trees, out of sight of the lethal swarm of beetles.

Then the cord got caught in some branches.

She had tried to disentangle herself, while David cut her free.

The blood beetles swept into the forest, mowing down everything in sight.

The humans ran, barely able to stay ahead of them.

"Damn it all. Doesn't anything stop these monsters?" David complained.

"Not much," Jerriel said. "They pursue anything in the range of their territory, hibernate when it is cold, and come out as soon as it's warmer."

David stepped in something squishy. Something else crunched and snapped beneath his feet.

A terrible stench erupted.

"What the hell is this...shit?"

Jerriel looked down as they kept running.

She smiled. "Dragon turds, filled with the bones of its food. Look. The offal is everywhere."

Jerriel was right. Dragon crap everywhere, scattered among the trees all up and down that patch of mountainside.

Great. They had run right into Shavalkathar's toilet.

Jerriel waved her hand in front of her nose at the stench. "We're close to the lair, within a mile or two, I would guess. This is the dragon's waste area, the place he flies over and...relieves himself."

It did smell pretty bad, worse with every step.

115

"Sometimes dragons mark their lairs or their territories in such a fashion."

The clicking and hissing suddenly decreased behind them.

"The blood beetles…they've stopped pursuing us."

"I thought so," Jerriel noted. "Even they wouldn't dare to attack a full-grown dragon. Any nest that did so would be set upon, incinerated, and destroyed. They instinctively know what this scent means: death. They understand the grave danger associated with the smell, and actively avoid it."

"Very clever," David noted. "They're no threat to the dragon, but their presence still serves to help protect its lair. Just like the grun."

"Exactly, Daeved."

They caught up to bulk of their their troops. Jason and Alejandro had them catching their breath among some rocks. They were out of the dragon's toilet area, but the stench still clung to them from the mess all over their boots. The odor was horrible.

"I can't stand this," Alejandro complained, stamping and waving his hands like a child. "What do we do? We have sheet all over us!"

David and many others laughed. "Dragon sheet all over us is better than blood beetles."

"I'm not so sure. Please, someone help me. Get this sheet off of me!"

"I agree. Come on, Al. Keep it together, man. Let's find some place to clean up."

A small, oxbow lake, cut off from the main stream, had a heavy yellow white marl around it, sticky and hard to get out of. But at least there was water to clean off in.

They found some rocks and fallen trees that went out into the water.

The troops took turns scraping their boots off with sticks and scrubbing the dragon crap off them with dirt, sand, leaves, and lake water.

Jerriel still looked weak and tired. She was unable to use magic to clean herself off.

David washed off her soft boots while she rested.

Only a few hours remained before nightfall.

"Let's find a defensible area to camp," he said. "We need to rest and take some food, tend our wounded, and get ready to meet with the dragon…tomorrow."

They searched the area and found a rocky cave near the river. Inside, there was room for most of them, except their guards on watch.

They heated up food, treated the wounded, changed bandages and dressings, and checked stitches. Medics gave out painkillers and medicines for comfort.

Stacy Keller was with them as one of their medics. She also showed some budding talent as a magical healer. She just wasn't that advanced at it yet. None of their healers were. Stacy did whatever she could for the wounded, and her efforts helped many who were the worst off.

The next morning dawned warm and sunny, without any further perils in the night, thank goodness.

"The dragon's lair must be on the northern slope of the mountain, the side turned away from us," Jerriel said.

David nodded. "That makes sense. We've seen almost every other angle."

The mountain did look heavily forested on every side. They did find further evidence that the creature marked its territory with its leavings. From the various bones, the dragon appeared to eat almost everything.

"Meat is meat to a dragon," Jerriel said. "They will eat almost everything, no matter how fresh or rotten. Their appetite is huge. The Merge has provided a wealth of dead bodies, no doubt."

Among the bones they saw many skulls–including hundreds of human skulls. Thousands of arm, rib, hip, and leg bones as well.

According to the reports of the scouts, the northern slope of the mountain turned out to be the steepest, and the rockiest. Not too surprising for a flying creature. It would choose an area for its lair that was difficult for other creatures to reach by foot.

Dragons did not normally like much company.

They left their wounded and about sixty guards at the cave. Thus, only a hundred and twenty of them skirted the other side of the mountain, which remained less steep, and then crossed over along mountain trails.

Most of the way was still tough going.

Finally they found the lair, a large cave opening partially concealed in a huge crevice. This was only opening large enough to admit such a creature into the deeper caverns; the entire opening must still lie further within, out of sight from below.

As they neared the primary opening, Jerriel studied several large, brownish-black stains splattered on the rocks, and long strips leading up to the lair itself.

"Dragon blood?" David guessed.

Jerriel nodded. "I believe from these signs that this dragon has been in a terrible fight, and has been horribly wounded. Whether it won or fled the battle, it managed to come back here and drag itself back into its lair to heal up."

"Perhaps we can help it," Jason Inada said.

"Surely you must be joking," Al said. He still limped, but wouldn't remain behind.

"Don't call me Shirley," Jason said with a grin.

"What?" Al said.

Even Jerriel looked perplexed.

"It's a dumb joke," Jason said with a wave of his hand.

Jerriel ignored them and spoke once more. "Wounded dragons—dragons in pain—are often angry and very defensive," she said. "This could be the absolutely worst time to try to contact it. If it is too weak and feels threatened, it could simply fry us. If it is strong enough and too hungry, it might just decide to eat us in order to regain its strength. They are incredible opportunists, and will do what is best for themselves first, before anything else."

"Let's keep that in mind," David said. "Maybe we can use that, if the dragon will speak to us."

"The only way to find out is to go in and meet with it face to face," Jerriel said.

Everyone went silent for a long moment.

David put his hands on his hips. "Most of you stay here to warn the others if something goes wrong. Two of you come with me, Jerriel, Jason, and Al, as our runners if need be. We didn't come here to fight this thing, in any case."

Al nodded. "That's good, right? I mean, we don't want to fight this enormous, deadly creature. What did it ever do to us? Right?"

"Exactly," David said. "I know we're all a little bit scared about possibly being eaten or incinerated, so let's just go in slowly and announce ourselves. Jerriel and I will take the lead."

She smiled and put her hand on his shoulder.

The entrance to the lair stretched high and steep, a dangerous climb with few footholds for small creatures such as themselves.

After about fifteen minutes, they pulled each other up onto the lip of the cave mouth and took a rest.

The hot stench of the dragon permeated the air, with a tinge of ash and sulfur. They had to be close now.

They went forward into the darkness. Their eyes adjusted. Jerriel cast the darksight spell on them all.

It was weird, but in some strange way, David could almost sense the power of the dragon up ahead of them, deep within the cave complex.

More dried dragon blood signs as they went. The injured dragon had dragged itself back into the depths of its lair, bleeding heavily, it seemed, from several major injuries.

David shuddered for a moment, wondering what could have done that to a dragon. And—had the dragon won the battle? Or merely escaped?

"I'm glad dragons have red blood, at least," he said aloud. "The black blood of the shadowspawn always creeps me out."

"Some dragons do have black blood," Jerriel noted. "If they come to serve the darkness and become shadow dragons, tainted by the evil of the negative Material planes. Yet even other dragonkind despise them, and make war upon them."

A deep, rumbling moan ripped through the entire complex. Rocks actually shook loose and fell from the ceiling. "It's still hurt," Jerriel said. "As I told you, this might not be a good idea."

David tossed his hands up into the air. "We came all this way. We can't go back now!"

"No, but perhaps we should wait several days, give it time get better."

"We do have plenty of food, and shelter in the lesser caves," Jason noted.

"Again," David insisted, "the dragon invited us here and we've come a long way. Think of our people who died getting us to this place. Remember all of the dangers we've faced? I have come here to speak with this dragon, and by God, I'm going to speak with it. Not a week from tomorrow. Today! I'll go in myself if I have to. Who's with me?"

"Dave, we're all with you," Jason said. "We're just trying not to die."

"Exactly. Thank you for saying so, my friend," Alejandro said, taking his hand. "I quite agree with you. That death thing is definitely to be avoided."

"I guess we're all a bit worried and jumpy," David said. "Let's just go forward and announce ourselves. Then we'll see what happens."

They crept ahead more, David and Jerriel in the lead. They had no weapons in their hands. Jerriel only walked with her staff in front of her, but prepared no spells.

When he judged that they were close enough, David shouted further out into the cavern, "Hail to you and greetings, Great Shavalkathar. I do not wish to intrude, but we have come far upon your kind invitation. This is Captain David Pritchard of Michiana. I am your friend, remember?"

Several tense moments passed. *Go. Away,* the dragon's voice finally rumbled in their heads.

"We have come far, and faced many dangers to come speak with you, Great Dragon. It is not our intent to bother you in any way."

I am…not receiving visitors at present, the dragon said, into their minds. *Return in a month or two. Trouble me no more until then.*

"He must be gravely hurt," Jerriel whispered. "He sounds weak and labors to speak each word."

"Forgive us, Great Shavalkathar, but that is not possible. We need your counsel now, for our need is urgent. Do you forget that you invited us? We have come in peace and in good faith. I have brought the wizard to speak with you."

Suddenly the dragon roared, and the entire cavern shuddered. *I WILL SHOW HER HOW WEAK I AM! BEGONE I SAY!*

The air suddenly grew thin and stifling hot. "Gather close to me." Jerriel said. "Hurry!" They scurried to her like chicks to a mother hen.

"MILLASHINTAL!" she commanded, and a low, iridescent dome of magical energy, not unlike a big soap bubble, formed over them.

A blinding ball of light grew in intensity down the opposite end of the tunnel. A torrent of greenish-yellow and blue flame blasted through the entire cave.

19

Mason and the rest of Echo Company performed a forced march to the forested wastes in the west, in full gear and with practice weapons, for three hours, rapidly covering eight miles.

This was a grueling test of endurance, one of the final challenges the recruits would face as part of their long, basic training. And it was still torturous for some, who remained mostly out of shape or simply older.

Yet they arrived upon a high, wooded hill and were ordered to prepare a defense.

And were immediately set upon by Delta and Foxtrot Companies, hiding in place nearby.

Even though Echo held the high ground, the other two companies were fresh and waiting to attack.

After a pitched, mock battle, Echo survived, and drove the other two companies off with great losses, mostly with arrows from above. But their own casualties still tallied to over half of their number.

On their way back, Mason heard weak voices calling out to them from the next hill over.

"Help us!"

"Over here. Please!"

Mason finally spotted them, a man and a woman, both in battered armor. They looked to be in a bad way.

Mason called out to Sergeant Rivera and pointed the two people out.

"Don't just stand there, Tyler. You and Team 3 fetch them back. They appear to be in distress. Find out where they have come from."

Mason and Rodell led the sortie. They brought two stretchers and a medic with them, in case they were injured.

The man and woman clung to each other. They appeared to be mostly unhurt, but frightened and exhausted.

"You're going to be all right," Mason told them. "Just relax. Let our medic check you over."

"Where are we?" the man asked. He appeared confused.

"We are militia recruits from South Bend," Mason told them. "We were out here west of town, doing some training."

The woman burst into tears. "Oh, thank goodness. We made it back home!"

At first Mason had somewhat hoped that they had come from some other Urth human enclave. He didn't recognize their gear or their unit symbol, a black circle with the head of hawk set within it.

"So," Mason asked, "you are from South Bend, also?"

"We're from the Blackhawks," she said, as if he should know what unit that was. "Part of a long-range patrol sent out to explore the west."

Mason had heard that some such patrols had gone out, but as yet, none of them had returned.

"My name is Mason Tyler. I'm just a recruit, but I'll take you to our leaders. I'm sure the militia commanders will be glad to hear from you. What are your names?"

"Lieutenant Rick Collier."

"Trooper Terry Gallagher."

Then Mason thought of something. He had to ask. "Is there still a moon where you came from?" he inquired.

Rick and Terry looked at each other and then they both stared at him as if he were mad. "Of course the moon is still there," Terry said.

"Where would the moon go?" Rick added.

Mason caught his breath.

These two people were from South Bend, but they were also from the other side.

"I'm afraid I have some interesting news for you two. Prepare yourselves. It may very well come as quite a shock."

Now he had them worried.

Surprisingly, it took quite a bit of explaining to convince them that they were now on the other side of the Merge.

"Wait a minute," Collier said. "We had two people show up on our side—they emerged out of a lake of Wild Magic during a thunderstorm. Their names were, uh...uh..."

"John and Marie," Terry said. "I got to know both of them."

Mason shouted, "They're alive? John Wolper and Marie Purdy are alive?"

"Yes," Terry said. "They said they were working with someone they called—the Pistolero. Our commander said that he was good friends with the man."

"Who's your commander?" Mason asked.

"Captain David Pritchard," she said.

Mason could only smile. They had been with his best friend, Dave. And they were okay—as okay as any of them could be in a post-Merge warzone.

And this proved that there were definitely ways to cross over, back and forth, from both sides.

The militia and Blondie were going to be very interested in all of these new facts.

Mason now had less than two weeks of his basic to finish up.

One way or another, he had a strong feeling that things were going to get interesting again in their areas.

Even when he had his next leave, Mason was now careful about where he went, especially at night. What happened to them in that alley was played down. As far as the rest of Team 3 knew, a bunch of thugs had simply stomped some of them into the ground. And Rodell wisely decided to keep his mage incident to himself until after his basic training was over. Even Mason agreed that that was a wise decision. Then Rodell could transfer over to the mages. It was funny.

No one in Echo knew that Mason was the Pistolero. They hadn't found any suspects for the other attack on him among the other companies. It was guessed that someone from one of the other units had recognized him on the battlefield at random, during the massed war games.

As long as he didn't run afoul of those jerks again, he might be fine. Recruits in basic could only get around on leave.

The first person Mason went to that weekend was Major Bill Avery. He was very interested in finding out what was up with the crossovers.

"Actually," Bill said, "including these two cases, we have a total of seven reports of people crossing over from one side of the Merge to the other. All of them involved glowing pools of water or glowing lakes of Wild Magic, activated or triggered by the energy of thunderstorms."

"I assume you have people still watching the lake on Allen Street?" Mason said.

"We've never stopped. But from what Rick and Terry have told us, they came here from stepping into a glowing pool. But on their side, our people John and Marie crossed over through the lake here, and into a pond there, near Allen Street. And on both sides, there was a major thunderstorm going on."

Mason frowned. "So, for the lake to work, there has to be a thunderstorm triggering both sides. How are we going to know that?"

"We won't. We can try to find these pools, but they are notorious for drying up and then reappearing somewhere else. We just don't know enough about these phenomena yet to have any control over them."

Mason sighed and shook his head with his lips curled up tight together. All of this was so frustrating.

"Unnh! We're missing something vital here. Some key bit of knowledge. While I bet the enemy knows all about this stuff and more. Blondie has even said that they have several ways to cross over, some more efficient than others."

Bill hesitated. "I hate to keep asking this, but are you sure Blondie is telling us everything he knows? The enemy sent him back and forth to spy on us and gather info to help cause the Merge. Why can't he perform this kind of magic?"

"Because he can't," Mason said. "It takes a special kind of mage, with special abilities. They call them Travelers, and they are very rare. He says dragons are also Travelers, and some other beings. Very high level mages, like Blondie's old master, could manipulate such magic. But we haven't found anyone on our side who can use travel and transport magic."

Now it was Major Bill who frowned. "So, once again, we're stuck."

"I'm afraid so."

"Damn it to hell. Our enemies have every advantage over us, and we have nothing to go on!"

Next, Mason went to his friend Blondie, who was up to his neck in dealing with and trying to train the new mages.

It was clear that Blondie was under a great deal of stress and was working many long hours. The lines in his face were very clear and tight. His color wasn't that great, and he simply looked exhausted.

"Sheesh, Blondie. Get some more rest. You look terrible."

Blondie snorted and tried to force a grin. "I can't, Mace. There's too much to do, and I'm the only one who can do it all. And when I do manage to go home, Jennifer either wants to fight, screw, or both—in whatever order.

She's not happy, I'm not happy, Bill's not happy—nobody's happy. And I know you, of course; you're never happy."

"I suppose that's about right. I'll get Winger and Ginger saddled, my friend. Let's take a ride out to see Thulkara."

"Mace, I just said that I can't."

Mason simply stared at him.

"Sorry, Mace. I'm sorry I snapped at you."

"Let's take a ride, my brother. All of this crap will still be here when you come back."

Blondie grunted. "Sure it will. That's what I'm afraid of."

"I'll bet Ginger misses you."

"Hah. She probably wants to scream at me, too."

"No, she doesn't. Not that sweetie. You'll see. She'll be tickled to see you."

"Then...I'd better bring her some of her favorite treats. Give me a sec, as you Urthers say."

They took a nice easy ride to Thulkara's compound. They only cantered and ran a little bit, because the horses seemed to need it. They even walked their horses for a long while.

Ginger kept nuzzling and loving Blondie, she was so happy to be with him. And in turn, Blondie petted and spoiled her something awful.

"You seem like you're under a great deal of pressure, Blondie. Anything you wanna talk about?"

Blondie sighed pretty heavily. "It is what it is, and in the end, it probably won't even matter."

"You still think the enemy is going to swoop down and crush us?"

"Whenever they get around to it. Yes, I know they will. It's just a question of when. They could be busy right now with much larger concerns. But they won't forget about us here. And it's not like we're going anywhere. They can wait to deal with us, whenever they're good and ready."

"That doesn't sound very promising."

"No, it does not."

Their friend Thulkara was in her studio painting, with several live-in instructors who had moved in with her in order to have support and a place to live. The Thul was their patron.

Except for the usual Thul choices of subject matter—gory battle scenes—the techniques used in each painting showed great improvement. Thulkara was actually becoming quite the accomplished artist. And from what they heard, she worked hard at it for hours each day.

"My friends!" Thulkara yelled. "My scrawny Thul brothers! Ready for another bath day?"

Mason felt the color drain out of his face. "God, no…please help me," he muttered.

She charged them as if she meant to scoop them up in her arms and yank them off their horses.

Blondie held out both his hands defiantly. "No, Thulkara. No! You'll get paint all over us again!"

She stopped and chuckled. "Very well. I'll clean up and then I can squeeze the air out of my favorite wimpy little mages. Come, join us for lunch!"

They ate, and talked, and laughed together for a long while that afternoon. Mason and Blondie ate until they were near to bursting.

With the rationing going on, it was a rare treat to feast the way they did.

But Thulkara's farm and holdings were a mecca of food production, and all of her people seemed happy and in excellent health.

She spoke about the Amish who were now under her protection, and her own militia units had swelled to more than three thousand troops now, who mostly guarded the crops and livestock.

"I'm worried," Thulkara said. "If the enemy is going to hit us again, they'll do so this fall, right at harvest and before winter when we're most vulnerable. They'll either seize our crops or destroy them, and starve us out over the winter. Then there won't be that many of us to crush in the spring."

Mason and Blondie both nodded in general agreement.

"Yep," Mason said. "We think the same thing, and so does Major Bill and the militia. Protecting this year's harvest is going to be a key factor to our overall survival."

Blondie didn't say anything at all, but he looked grim.

"What more can we do?" Thulkara asked.

"Nothing," Blondie said. "That's the problem. We're already doing everything that we can. There really isn't any more that we can do. And it's still not going to be enough against all of the dire threats we might face."

20

Only Jerriel's magic force field bubble protected them from the dragonfire that shot through the cave.

She maintained it for several long moments after the actual flame dissipated and the chamber went dark again.

"Stay close," she said. "The air in the cavern has burned up. If I put the shield down too soon, we could all suffocate. Watch the dust and debris in the cavern's natural air currents. Let the air replenish itself. Then we'll have enough to breathe in here, in just another few minutes."

Once Jerriel did drop her defensive shield, the air of the cavern still felt hot and close, but at least it was breathable, and growing better by the moment.

David called out again.

"Come now, great dragon. We have journeyed here in peace—at your request, even—and now you attack us. How very rude. We are your friends, you're honored guests. We wish you no harm. All we want to do is speak with you. If you are—"

Jerriel waved her hands in the air to stop him.

"Not…that a dragon such as yourself would ever need help from humans. Perish the thought. But if you ever did happen to, as your friends, we would be glad to give it, in exchange for your invaluable information. And, perhaps, some of your wisdom."

Another long pause.

At least the dragon did not try to cook them again. Then there came a great rumbling.

Laughter. The dragon actually chortled.

Well…you are persistent, and incredibly and inventively polite. I will say that much. What sort of…information do you seek…my friends? Perhaps we should test the extent of thy friendship.

"Oh, nothing much. Whatever you know about the Merge, what's happening in the region, how we might defeat the Dragon Cult in Elkhart—"

The dragon snarled and cut him off. *You make war against the Dragon Cult?* he said. Pure hatred in the tone of his thoughts.

"We may be forced to it, but only if we have the right advice and information on how best to deal with them."

The dragon laughed. *Come ahead, then. Enter my lair with my provisional protection, and let us speak of these and many other things.*

"Do we have your word, then, that you will not harm or kill or eat us?"

I said provisionally, did I not? I haven't decided yet just how famished I am. If it comes to that, I may only need to devour one or two of you. The rest will be relatively safe for a time. You can all draw lots if you like. It matters not to me.

The two runners elected to stay back.

Jason and Al went in with David and Jerriel.

In the hot chamber, the great form of the dragon gave off a slight green glow. So did many of the rocks about him, still glowing hot from dragonfire.

The beast lay shifted on one side, with its wings curled as the rest of its body sprawled. Its long tail and neck curved to somewhat encircle anyone who stepped into the chamber.

David half-expected the dragon to sleep on top a mound of coins or other such treasure. But where would a dragon find something like that? Or move it around?

Probably just another myth.

What would dragons do with such treasure anyway?

As they drew closer, it became apparent just how messed-up the dragon was. Shavalkathar had indeed been through some kind of terrible battle. David found it amazing that any creature—even a dragon—could take that kind of punishment and survive.

It looked wounded, almost everywhere. Broken horns and spines. Rents in its wings, deep claw scratches, and huge bite marks. The end of its tail had even been bitten or torn off. It was also blistered and scorched in several places, and missing huge patches of its thick, armored scales.

David noticed something else.

Fresh dragon blood glowed brightly and steamed in the open air. Shavalkathar's blood was red, but glittered somehow with a bright green aura; probably infused with dragon magic, no doubt.

"Who or what could have done this to you, Great Shavalkathar?" David asked.

Jerriel cautioned him. "David, that's rude."

Shavalkathar chortled weakly. *Indeed. I have seen…*He coughed and belched smoke. *…better days, I am forced to admit. Do not fear, wizard girl. I am almost accustomed to Captain Pritchard's inconsistent impertinence. What happened to me? We shall speak of that anon. First, introduce yourselves. The pleasantries of accepting guests in my presence must be strictly observed—even if I am forced to eat a few of you later on.*

Jerriel stepped forward, bowed low and gracefully, and saluted the dragon with her staff. "I am Jerriel Andelora Holleth, daughter of—"

Prince Manathorran Holleth of Sylurria? A worthy mage, indeed. And extremely valiant to the very end. A great loss, my little one. I join you in mourning the loss of one so wise and mighty.

She bowed again. "My house and I thank you for your kind and gracious words, great Shavalkathar the Fantastic."

See, now, David Pritchard. Listen to such words of courtesy as these, Shavalkathar said. *And your mother, my fair and glorious gem?*

"Princess Yinnaerra Imenda of Kellendra, of the Royal Ruling House Darrando of Marrandor."

The dragon's eyes actually widened. Your mother was a princess, of the House Royal of Marrandor?

"Yes, but not in line of ascent, great dragon. My direct line are merely close cousins. I regret to say that my mother was also lost to us, less than two years ago as well, in a shipwreck on the inner seas."

Again, I mourn your loss, Princess Jerriel.

"Thank you, kind dragon. I do not use my purely figurative title. Jerriel will suffice, if you would be so kind."

Not at all. Of course. Do let us be on familiar terms with each other.

David was still stunned. Jerriel. A princess.

The dragon's gleaming eyes roved to the others.

David Pritchard I know. These other two swordsmen? One an Urther priest of some kind? Their various odd faiths confuse me.

Jason Inada stepped forward and bowed.

"Greetings, O great and honorable dragon. It is wonderful to meet and speak with a mighty and celestial being such as yourself. It is a great honor. I am indeed a follower of the Buddha and his wisdom. I would be happy to share that wisdom with you."

Perhaps we can speak together about your ways. Your mind is somewhat disciplined, I sense. Usually priests are like that. Wizards even more so, but in a different way. And the last of your small band, not to mention the two skulkers outside in the cavern, and the many other troops around the mountainside?

Al stepped forward with a flourish of his feathered hat and did his thing. "I am Alejandro Maximillian Aguilar. Eagle of the Southwest. Three time Champion of the Combat Sport Fencing Association. Fencing instructor and sparring master for what would have been the next Olympic Team."

Your flair for the dramatic suits your conceited nature. You would make a good dragon were you one of my kind. Forgive me, good guests, but I am famished and find myself at quite a loss here, I am afraid.

"Why is that, noble dragon?" Jerriel asked.

My hunger demands that I must eat two of you, but it is so difficult to choose. I could have good conversation and banter with each of you. What to do, what to do.

"That sounds somewhat...unpleasant," Al said.

Not for me, Shavalkathar said.

"Perhaps you should not eat any of us," Jerriel said.

I don't see how that would work. What do you propose?

David stepped forward. "Let my people and I hunt for you. We can bring you sustenance in the form of fresh game. It is a small price to pay for the wisdom and information that we seek."

Let you all back out of here? I think not. What guarantee would I have that any of you would ever come back?

"You don't," Jerriel said. "But Alejandro and I will remain with you while the others bring you sustenance."

Al blinked. "We will?"

"Yes, they will," David said. "So that you will know that we will return, according to our word."

Hmm...I wouldn't take too long, if I were you, Shavalkathar said.

Jerriel turned to David. "Hurry. Send word to the others to get hunting as well. Bring as much meat as soon as you can."

"Jerriel, I—"

"Just go. We'll keep him busy talking as long as we can."

"Great Shavalkathar," David said. "We shall return as quickly as we are able, according to our word."

Shavalkathar laughed. *I hope so...for the sake of your friends.*

21

Mason finished his basic training at the end of the following week. That week had been hot, muggy, and unpleasant to train in.

Just the way to wrap things up—sweaty, exhausted, and miserable.

But he was a trooper now, and in the militia proper.

Once they were released to serve in their actual units, Mason and Rodell would continue their training. They held a confab with the other ten people of Team 3 in one of the mess tents.

He didn't tell any of them that he was the Pistolero yet. Perhaps he wouldn't have to for a while.

But he did explain that Rodell had showed signs of becoming a mage, and would now start training with them.

Everyone looked surprised, and congratulated Rodell.

"Who would have thought it," Michelle Mitchell said. "Our own Rody, going off now to be a mage."

Bryan Lister shook him by the arm. "You're still sword and shield to us, buddy. Even if you do learn to sling spells."

Rodell laughed. "Hey, I'm a sorcerer. I have powers that I manipulate and put forth. I don't cast spells. That's a wizard."

"Ooh, listen to him now," Caitlyn Reed added.

"My friends," Mason said. "I will also be transferring to the militia unit that guards the mages like Rodell. I know some of the officers of that unit personally, and I have many close personal friends there. If any of you would like, I might be able to bring you along with me, if you're interested."

"Sounds good to me," Tom Kelly said. "Let's keep Team 3 together, I say."

Beth Anderson asked, "Is their food any better than ours? I would think they'd serve the mages better food."

Mason shook his head. "I think some of the cooks might be a little better, but the mages more or less eat and drink the same stuff as the troops."

"What if there's another war," Lashonda Kincaid asked. "Mages and wizards are real important. Would we be any safer with them?"

Mason made a face. "Hmmm, I kinda doubt that. They'll be right in the thick of things, and we'll be there with them, trying to keep them safe. Our mages will be able to inflict a lot of damage on the enemy, and that will also make them prime targets during any battle."

Lashonda grinned, ear-to-ear. "Who wouldn't want to be a part of all that. Count me in. I wanna see some of that magic stuff close-up."

"Me, too," Ben Yoder said.

"Me, three," Francine Owen added.

Mason held up his hands. "Now, you do understand, that guarding the mages—especially during wartime—could even be more hazardous than regular militia duty on the front lines, right?"

Cory Brown laughed, "Hey, some of those mages might be kinda cute."

Linda Turner laughed with her. "One of them might even be my age."

Mason frowned. "Guys, I wouldn't expect it to be like, a dating service or anything."

Cory and Linda stuck their tongues out and gave him raspberries.

He gave all the others a chance to transfer in, as well.

In the end—all ten—everyone from Team 3 asked to join up, whatever came their way. Most of them said that if the war did return, serving with the mages would be a way that they could do the most damage to the enemy.

Everyone in Michiana had some kind of score to settle.

Later While Rodell Kim was introduced to the other mages, and especially the other sorcerers, Mason took the time to get to know the five "former" enemies, now working as mage teaching assistants thanks to Blondie's magic-suppressing armbands.

The very first day, the militia guards had to break up some kind of heated discussion between Koden and Resh. It actually seemed to be about a girl—Sharon Weekes, one of the workers in the mess hall.

As strange as it sounded, Koden and Sharon had some kind of thing going, relatively harmless. Koden was under watch 24/7. It was mostly flirting, but they had begun to seek each other out to talk. An actual friendship–a human relationship–was starting to form between the two.

Apparently every possible aspect of this relationship infuriated Resh to no end. And over the past three weeks, Resh had never missed an opportunity to chide and insult first Koden, and then Sharon, also, concerning the situation.

Resh was clearly incensed and practically driven mad by the fact that one of his former mage comrades was for some reason talking to a cute enemy girl. Imagine that.

Part of Resh's pathology of his profile included the inability to form close relationships–especially with females. He was seriously repressed to the point of outbursts of rage and violence.

As with many sociopaths, he had also been caught keeping small animals hidden for the purpose of tormenting and killing them slowly: a mouse, a rat, a bird–even a squirrel. He would snare them and torture them in hideous ways, and was incredibly clever at keeping them hidden.

Only random searches of his living quarters turned them up. Some had been found nailed to floor boards, or glued to ceiling panels.

In another instance, a pet cat of an officer had been found with all four of its legs and tail broken. The cat had been throttled to death, and its head nearly twisted off, found near the showers and latrine that Resh was allowed to use.

Resh hated women, and spoke even less to them than he did to the males around him. Yet he glared at them with even more seething hatred, and watched them with a concentrated intensity that was anything but normal.

Children, especially female children, seemed to agitate him and throw him into a special tizzy. Fortunately, they were usually kept away from the captives. Everyone considered that to be for the best.

Physically, Resh was about twenty-one, five-foot-nine, and of medium build. Not an unattractive fellow, if you didn't account for his crazy glare and a penchant for jumping, twitching, and snapping his head around with his face twisted into an insane scowl. Quite the charmer, really.

Yep, a real piece of work and just a darling, Resh was. He had medium brown hair, blue eyes, a smallish nose, and a round chin. His hands and forearms seemed abnormally strong for his size and musculature.

Mason tried on several occasions to engage him in conversation.

Resh avoided shaking hands or even touching others. He also spent a good deal of time washing his hands.

"So, you're the one they call Resh?" Mason asked.

"Yes."

He normally tried to keep his affect and his tone flat—a real monotone. When he started to get upset, he would suck in his breath and hiss somewhat. At times his lips might twitch or begin to curl up.

"You're a Sylurrian mage."

"So?"

"Oh, that's right. You're all Sylurrians."

No response to that. Resh just stared straight ahead without any other reaction but open contempt.

"How do you like it here, Resh?"

"Fine."

"Better than being chained up and hooded in a cell, right?"

Resh shrugged. No audible response.

"See, Urth humans aren't so bad, are they? If it was the other way around, and we were your prisoners, the Dark Khabal would simply murder us all, or sacrifice us to the Dark Ghods, wouldn't they?"

For the first time, Resh's glazed eyes brightened. He tried very hard to suppress a sly smile.

"See, at least we didn't kill you outright?" Mason Persisted. "Not only have you been allowed to live, you can even perform meaningful work, helping new mages develop their abilities. You even have relative freedom, thanks to the anti-magic bracers."

Without looking at them, Resh absently rubbed and clutched at the devices locked to his wrists and forearms. He grunted slightly, and his lip twitched just a little.

"You can move around, talk to others—within reason. You can look at the sky, the stars, feel the wind in the trees, listen to the birds sing.

Resh's hands suddenly clenched into fists.

"You're not just trapped in a prison cell for the rest of your days. You can make friends, talk to a pretty girl, even, make her laugh and smile."

Resh wrung his hands, and then started rubbing the tops of his thighs nervously. He sucked in his breath in ragged snatches.

"You do like girls, don't you, Resh?"

"No."

"Oh, no girls, huh? Hmmm…Well, I'm not here to judge. To each their own. So…you like boys, huh?"

"No!" Resh snapped his head, sneering. "I don't like anyone. And I especially don't like you—*Pistolero*. Yeah, that's right. I know exactly who and what you are. I remember everything. So wear whatever clothes or uniform you want."

"Sheesh, Resh. Don't get mad. I was just trying to be friendly. Come on, let's be pals."

"No! I'm done talking to you. Leave me to my work!"

Blondie wandered over to them.

Resh's eyes widened and the blood drained from his face. It seemed that he was terrified enough of Blondie, but the hatred and contempt behind that fear also soared.

"Resh isn't giving you any trouble, is he, Mace?"

"No, not at all, Blondie. In fact, we were chatting about pretty girls and how to talk to them."

Resh turned bright red and gritted his teeth.

Blondie burst out laughing. "Yeah...that'll be the day."

A while later, Mason dropped over by the wizard and the enchanter Ettal.

Ettal was short and a little chubby, about five-foot-six with curly red hair and freckles. He had an affable, disarming smile, and spoke easily with whoever he was working with. He worked calmly, quietly, and efficiently with Blondie, some of the other new mages, and the wizard Gellonar.

He acted like he was a kid brother—a very smart kid brother.

Mason offered him his hand.

Ettal shook it warmly. "Hey, Mace. I was wondering when we would get to talk. Good to meet you."

"Glad to meet you, Ettal. So, you're a wizard."

"And you're a sorcerer, and a very unique one at that. I'm very intrigued about how your pizzles work. If you could let me examine—"

"Pistols. They're called pistols—not pizzles. *Pizzles* in Urth English are bull penises."

"Oh...well, I guess you wouldn't shoot much magic out of those."

"No, gosh, I hope not. And I'm sorry, but my pistols and all of my gear are off-limits to you and the other helpers. Sorry about that, but I'm sure you'll understand."

"Certainly, of course. You know, I'm glad to get a chance to talk with you. I want to be more like Shaeddor and really join up with you people. You need an experienced wizard training your new wizards. I could be your top wizard, just like Shaeddor is your top sorcerer. Think about it. Just give me a week without these arm bands off. Let me prove to you what I can do, and how I can help you."

"I'll send that up the chain of command, Ettal."

"Good, good. That's all I ask. You can give me the same deal you've given Shaeddor. Whores, booze, a place of my own, a lab to work in—the works."

Mason forced a smile. "Sure thing." He checked with some of the other guards and exchanged some info for the day. Nothing much.

Blondie walked over. "Hey, Mace. Let's take a walk, and get some fresh air."

135

"Sure."

It was a nice day outside, albeit a little hot. They walked under the shade of some oak, willow, and cottonwood trees.

"Mace, I could read Ettal's mind the entire time that you were talking with him. Do you want to know what he was really thinking?"

"Sure. Hit me. He sure can sound sincere."

"Well, don't believe any of it. He's a very clever actor. And that's all that it is—an act. The whole time he was plotting on various ways to murder and torture us all, once he has us at his mercy. He doesn't know that I can read all of their minds without them detecting me. He's more dangerous than Resh, for the very reason that he appears to be harmless and sincere. At least Resh appears to be exactly what he is: a messed up, homicidal killer. While Ettal is the kind who can fool people and get them to let their guard down. Don't ever do that. Never turn your back on that one."

"You warned me before that it was that way, Blondie. I just wanted to see for myself how good he was. If it wasn't for your telepathy, he might be able to convince us to give him a chance, after a while."

Blondie shook his head. "Don't ever do that. Ettal wants to kill all of us, just as badly as Resh does."

"So, any change in the other three?"

"I'm not sure about Gellonar and Tharin. I think they're still on the fence and could really go either way. The person we should give a chance to is Koden. He's young, decent, and he only went along with the Khabal out of fear of being killed by them. He hated being a battlemage for them, but he wasn't given any choice. He either fought for them, or they killed him. It was that simple."

"You really think that he would join us?"

"I know he doesn't want to go back to the Khabal. He'd love to get back to the Old World, but that's not an option. And now he has this relationship with the girl in the mess tent. He sees Urth humans as people now, and in her he sees a lot more. Koden is also a wizard, and a pretty decent one. If he came over to our side, it would be a big help."

"Would it take some of the heat off of you, Blondie?"

Blondie sighed. "I hate to admit it, but it sure would. As a prisoner, he's still held back. But I think you should talk it over with Bill and intel, and make an offer to Koden by the end of this week. Consider it."

"I will, Blondie. Why don't we both talk to Bill about this?"

"I will if I have to, Mace. But you see how it is around here. I'm swamped. That's why I need Koden so badly. We could work with the mages in shifts, and it wouldn't be so overwhelming."

Mason laughed. "You mean you'd be able to go back to screwing around and enjoying yourself more."

Blondie smiled. "Well, yeah… Who in the hell wants to work like this all the time without at least having a little fun? Doesn't everyone want a normal life?"

Mason smiled. "Depends on what you call 'normal,' Blondie. But I suppose Jennifer would be less bitchy if you spent a little more time with her without falling asleep…on top of her."

"How did you find out—"

Mason rolled his eyes. "Come on, my brother. She only shouted it to the entire city, Blondie. Everyone heard."

"She is kinda loud when she gets worked up."

"Yeah, and then she practically took my head off later that same day—to my face, in person. As if I have some control over your schedule. I tried to tell her, but she wouldn't listen. I practically had to jump on Winger and ride fast and hard to get away from her."

Blondie sighed. "She just needs me to get her drunk and keep her awake for a couple of nights—or, as she says, to make the lights flash on and off inside her head. She actually likes it better when she sleeps through most of the day."

Mason picked at one of his ears. "She's a bit loud, but that gal's good for you, Blondie."

His friend nodded with a sad smile. "I know she is, Mace. I wanna be good for her, as well."

Blondie sighed, perhaps the deepest, heaviest sigh Mason had ever heard anyone release. "I just wish that I could find some way to save us all from what's coming. But I haven't found it yet."

Mason rested a hand on Blondie's shoulder. "It's not your job to save us, Blondie."

His friend held his eyes for a moment. "If things go wrong, Mace. I mean really bad. Would you and Thulkara try to get Jen away for me, and keep her safe?"

"You have my word, Blondie. You know we'd both die trying, if it came to that."

Blondie looked down and nodded. "Thanks, Mace. It just might."

22

Even with several teams of experienced hunters, it took a lot longer than David wanted to go out, round up their forces, find and bring down game, and haul it back up to the dragon's lair.

More than four hours.

They bagged three big lizards with long tails, four deer, a lesser wild pig, and an elk-like creature with a nest of black horns.

Exhausted and sweating, they dragged the carcasses back through the caverns or carried them strung up on poles as soon as they could.

He sent other hunting parties out at the same time.

David announced himself and strode back into the lair ahead of the parade of meat.

He saw Jerriel and the dragon, but grew worried when he did not spot Al right away.

"Alejandro?" he asked.

The dragon laughed and coughed.

Jerriel put a hand on his arm and smiled. "He'll be back. I stayed here so that he could go out and relieve himself. He did the same for me."

Shavalkathar sniffed the air. *Ah, it took you long enough. But you must have had some luck. I love the smell of fresh blood. Mmm...what did you bring me? Reptile, deer, elk, oh, and pig. I love pig! Several of each I hope.*

Several? Of each?

"Uh, I'm afraid not," David said. "We wanted to hurry back, so we managed as best we could with a short hunt."

Al came back to them. "Hello, it's very good to see you, amigo."

Troops brought the game in and piled it up right in front of Shavalkathar. They backed off quickly.

Shavalkathar frowned as only a hungry dragon could.

That's it? He snapped up two of the deer in one bite, chewed, and gulped them down–hooves, antlers, and all.

But that was still more meat than two puny humans could have provided.

I suppose it will have to do. Next went the big lizards, tails and all– slurped down like spaghetti. Then the elk creature, which, being larger, sounded somewhat crunchier.

The cracking, snapping, and crunching of bones and horns actually sounded pretty grim to David.

Al looked on, pretty pale, as well as some of the troops.

The other deer, and then the pig, went last.

Ah, excellent hog. What a toothsome morsel. He relished it for several long minutes, chomping on it carefully until finally it slipped down with the rest.

Ahhh... Shavalkathar made happy noises and licked his mouth and teeth with a long tongue.

His hot breath blasted out in a loud dragon belch, stupefying and incredibly hot.

Well, I do feel...somewhat better. Now. What shall we discuss next?

Jerriel still managed to step forward before anyone else.

"Dragons are magic and can read magic signs almost better than anyone–perhaps even better than the Six High Mages who ruled Tharanor."

There is no 'perhaps' about it. Of course we can. He belched loud and long until the caverns echoed.

"Then I would like to know what you know about the Merge. How and why it happened."

I would think that that would be pretty obvious. The interdimensional cataclysm being referred to as the 'Merge' resulted from a highly secret attempt by the Six to save Tharanor from total destruction.

"I never heard anything about that, nor did my brother mention it when I saw him, and he is one of the apprentices to High Magus Gorrial

Lankorro of Sylurria, once one of our father's closest friends and allies. And one of the Six High Mages of our world."

David noted that Jerriel did not make any mention yet about Gorrial being the secret leader of the Dark Khabal.

The dragon thought for a moment. *I can only tell you what I know for certain, but did it ever occur to any of you that this matter was so important and so sensitive that the Six failed to share it with anyone but themselves? There have been many such matters, if you would like to know. Why do you think the Six High Mages are always so busy? They hardly have time to talk decently with anyone these days—even dragons.*

Why, let me tell you, when I was in Vaejan just a few months ago, Gorrial acted very closed-mouth and would not divulge much of anything about what was going on. He said their hands were far too full trying to maintain their own colony stronghold and stay alive themselves. I did not happen to see or meet your brother.

Jerriel gasped. "I can't believe it. The Six caused the Merge? Why would they ever do such a thing?"

Shavalkathar shook his head. *I suppose I wouldn't say they caused it. Perhaps it is more the fact that they did what they could do to control it. Tharanor and Earth are merely the two closest of many parallel worlds.*

Thanks to the scheming of a veritable army of mages from the Dark Khabal, and the assistance of many demons and perhaps one or more of the Dark Ghods themselves, Tharanor was on the brink of total annihilation. About to be chewed up by celestial forces beyond its control and sucked into the Void. Perhaps Urth and many of the other linked worlds would have been destroyed or damaged as well. I honestly believe that the Six did what they could, and barely in the nick of time, as it would appear. Despite one of them being the leader of the Dark Khabal itself.

Jerriel paced while she listened, and suddenly stopped when the dragon took a breath.

"So, the result was the Merge. They could save Tharanor and Urth, but not keep them from getting jumbled up with each other."

Yes, I suppose that's a rather simplistic way of putting it. All of the Six were severely damaged by the attempt and are still recovering in seclusion. The Spectral Keys and their spirit guardians are on the loose now. But at least the two worlds were saved from being destroyed outright.

"At the cost of millions of lives and all of this chaos?" David said.

The dragon looked at him directly. *And if they had done nothing, both worlds would have most certainly been obliterated in a twinkling, and perhaps others sucked into the chaos and destroyed as well. Think about everyone dying as an alternative.*

Shavalkathar sniffed. *Humans. Humph! Never satisfied.*

The dragon was one to talk.

"Well," Jerriel said, "it is nice to fill in some of the details. So. Tharanor and Urth are now linked, due to the Merge—more or less just as we thought.

In Tharanor's dimension, half of it is linked to half of Urth. And in Urth's dimension, the other half of it is mixed up with the other half of Tharanor."

Precisely, so.

"That's what we guessed. Then it stands to reason that there must be links, ways to get back and forth from one dimension to the next."

Shavalkathar nodded. *It should be so, but I haven't found where any of those links are, and I have searched. But it would be difficult to find one that is dragon-sized.*

"Another puzzle we must unravel, on top of everything else."

It would appear so. Amidst the chaos, it also appears that the Dark Khabal of Sylurria is also making a power grab—especially with the Six sidelined, and all of the Spectral Keys in play on both worlds. The Khabal normally does trust in a good offense rather than a good defense.

Jerriel rolled her eyes. "I know. My older, stuck-up brother used to say things like that all the time! We argued about thing constantly—how the world would be better off if the Sylurrians were in charge. If everyone simply let them establish order everywhere. Right! With their heavy-handed mercenaries, and their conjured monsters, and by blasting anyone who disagrees with or opposes them. Then I learned that the Dark Khabal was now in charge of Vaejan and were behind the deaths of my parents. That's when I became both angry and frightened, and I left. Then they tried to keep me there against my will, and I think my own brother was helping them!"

"There will always be opportunists," Jason Inada pointed out.

"That is very true," Alejandro said.

"So, tell us," David said. "What is going on in the wide world in this region and beyond? You probably know better than any of us. It takes us weeks and months to get anywhere and get back, if we get back at all because of the wilds and the many threats out there. Tell us, please."

Shavalkathar belched again. *The hordes in the wilds did not take long to realize that the colonists were in chaos and confusion. Without their wizards at full strength, they are vulnerable. And Urthers didn't even seem to have wizards.*

"They do. They have the ability, they're just not trained," Jerriel said.

Well, be that as it may, talk about opportunists. The many and various wild hordes see their opportunities and won't hesitate to capitalize on them. Everything is up for grabs in both dimensions, and here in the New World, the hordes are grabbing all they can get their hands on each day. They view helpless groups of Urthers as little more than a new food source.

141

Only the strongest and most numerous bands of humans, like your group here—before they fragmented—have the power to defeat them. If the hordes stop fighting each other as much as they fight everyone else, and really band together, then watch out. With their vast numbers, they'll be almost unstoppable.

"As you said," Jerriel noted. "The hordes war with each other as much as anyone else. We can only hope that continues. The colonies of the New World are therefore in disarray. What news from the rest of Tharanor and Urth? They do not have the hordes to deal with, as we do here in the New World. That the Six High Mages were all gravely injured is terrible news, indeed."

All the nations have been shaken," Shavalkathar said. *"Both worlds are a chaotic mess, which only fuels the normal rivalries and hatreds, and creates new ones. Language problems between billions of confused Urthers and Tharanorians. Many are facing starvation and subjugation by outsiders or internal thugs and despots, who pop up like petty warlords overnight. You have seen it yourselves in your own area. Magnify that worldwide.*

"I can only imagine," David said. "Our world had its own serious divisions and conflicts already. Everything has been totally disrupted."

Urthers are vulnerable, Shavalkathar said. *Their reliance on their magic technology made them too dependent on it. Now that that is gone, they are placed at a grave disadvantage.*

"That is a fact," David said. "But who could guess that such a thing would take place? And how exactly did that happen? It is very weird."

Tharanorian magic has been somewhat disrupted as well, but they are trying to recover. At least they are grounded in magical systems and can adjust much more quickly. Whether Urthers can find a way to make a similar adjustment remains to be seen. When such a dimensional event occurs, the natural laws of the very universe are disrupted on a cosmic level, and on many basic levels. The Six did all that they could to keep both worlds from being destroyed—and mostly, they succeeded. But at a price. Many changes have been wrought on the Prime Material planes of both worlds in the places which they exist.

Jason Inada chimed in. "Can it be reversed? Could it ever go back to the way things were before the Merge?"

I suppose, the dragon said. *Such a thing may be possible. But that would require regaining control over all of the Spectral Keys, of both world, and another interdimensional event, perhaps just as disruptive as the last or potentially more so. They would have to study each world and get everything almost exactly right to reverse the effects on the two worlds, separate the pieces, and put them back together—exactly correct.*

"You make it sound impossible," Jerriel said. "I can only imagine all of the variables that would have to be taken into consideration."

Shavalkathar laughed. *Not impossible, but certainly extremely difficult. Especially with the Keys disrupted as they are now.*

Jerriel gasped. David watched the blood drain from her face. "What? The Spectral Keys have been damaged? How?"

"I am not a mage, and I am still confused. What in the heck are these Spectral Keys that you keep mentioning?" Alejandro asked.

23

Mason sat in a conference room with Rick Collier, Terry Gallagher, and a handful of other Urth people who had crossed over from the other side—all of them by accident.

Blondie probably would have been very interested, but he was still too busy to attend.

Mason was glad to hear about his old friend David Pritchard. It did his heart good to hear that his best buddy Dave was now a famous commander of an elite force of fighters known as the Blackhawks.

Way to go, Dave.

And that David was also apparently smitten with a pretty Tharanorian wizard girl who had somehow wandered into Dave's half of Michiana after the Merge. Well, good for them, and he meant it. He wished them well and was happy for them. Mason hoped to meet with them some day, and possibly even celebrate with them.

He still felt a stab of pain as he thought of losing Tori. But at least things seemed to be getting better for someone.

More than ever now, they were certain that it was possible to cross over to and from both sides of the Merge.

They had to find a way to at least communicate and send word back and forth, even if they could not find a way to send people. They could exchange ideas, information, and knowledge, especially about magic and what their enemies were doing.

"But this part is worse," Major Bill Avery said. "We know that the enemy is attacking Michiana on both sides, and not only that, but they have some reliable way or ways of crossing over, which we do not. They possess a terrible advantage. It is likely that they can send as many troops and reinforcements to either side as needed. That is a superior force multiplier that we cannot match or reckon with. Just the concept alone is devastating to consider."

"I agree," Mason added. "They can attack us on either side with overwhelming numbers that we cannot match, and we do not even have the power to go out into the dangerous wilds and attack them. We can only wait for them to sweep over us and destroy us. That is a grim situation to be in."

Bill held up his hands in frustration. "We don't have much to go on, either. Pools of Wild Magic that come and go without any rhyme or reason. Rumors about a magic, enemy cave, weeks away from us in the wilds, and in the heart of their power, that we could never hope to fight our way to.

"Without a Traveler, or a mage who can manipulate transport and teleport magic, we have no hope of constructing a method or pathway of our own."

Lieutenant Rick Collier from the Blackhawks suddenly broke in. "We have a Traveler on our side, but like most of our mages, he's just learning to use and control his abilities. He can only spot-teleport twenty or thirty feet by line of sight or by memory, but I heard he was getting stronger each day. If we can get word to them, and impress upon the other side how urgent this is, perhaps we can find a way."

Major Bill sighed. "Well, at least they have a Traveler on the other side. That is some hope. But I seriously doubt that our foes are going to hold back and give us time do all of that: train our own mages and fortify the town. We think that the enemy will attack toward the end of the summer at the very least. Probably during the crucial time right before our harvest and the coming of winter. Strategically, that would be the perfect time to launch a campaign to take us down. And we can only guess that they are going to hit us extremely hard."

Mason stood up, still just in his trooper's uniform. "Major, I think we have someone who can shed some new light on what the enemy is planning and what their strengths truly are. He can tell us what we can expect, give us information and intel that we could never acquire on our own."

"Who?" Avery said. "Who is this person, and where has he been hiding? Even Mage Captain Shaeddor does not know these things."

"Koden, one of the enemy mages. He wants to join us, sir. He was never part of the Dark Khabal, and he only chose to fight with them as one of their battlemages because they gave him the choice between that or death. He wants to get away from them and the rulers of Vaejan. He hopes to return to his Sylurrian people back in the Old World someday. Most of his people would be horrified to learn what the Khabal has done and is doing. With the Merge, the other Sylurrians don't even know yet that the Khabal has hijacked and usurped their colonies on this side of the New World."

Bill knitted his hands together. "I see. I know that we have spoken at length about this individual before, Mace. We still have grave doubts about any of those captive mages actually switching sides. It is a great risk for us to even consider doing so. But frankly, I don't see that we have any choice in the matter any longer. At some point, we must take some chances."

Mason nodded. "I feel the same way, sir."

Bill smiled. "And let me guess. You and that golden-haired enemy demon of yours that we call friend has this guy waiting outside our door right now, ready to spill his guts to us. If we free him and accept him as one of our new allies."

Mason smiled. "You know us too well, Bill. But as long as he's here, why don't we bring him in and at least listen to what he has to say? He's willing to talk."

"And how do we know he isn't just filling us up with misinformation so that his people can destroy us?"

With a shrug, Mason went over to the door. "Hell, Bill. We know they're going to do that anyway. No matter what we do. We think Koden is on the level and that he means what he says. His offer to join and help us is legitimate. Both Blondie and I are sure of it."

Silence passed for the length of a few breaths. "Very well," Bill said finally. "Let him come before us and speak."

Mason let Koden enter through the side door to the conference room. He came in with his four armed guards behind him.

He still wore the anti-magic shackles that suppressed his powers.

Koden was about Mace's age, either nineteen or twenty, about five-foot-ten, with longish, dark brown straight hair similar to Blondie's fashion, a distinctive Sylurrian style. He had sharp gray eyes, a rugged face, and was slightly stocky for a mage. He looked proud, but also a bit nervous.

"Mage Koden," Major Bill told him. "We have been told that you wish to join us and help us in our cause here in Michiana. State your full name for the record, and explain why you wish to do so."

"My name is Koden Unithera of Gallava, back in the Old World. I was of noble birth, but I was a fourth son of six, without land or title or inheritance. I came with the colonists to the New World to make my fortune.

I did not come here to join the Khabal and become part of their evils. They only wish to destroy all around them that they have sought to touch and subjugate beneath their will.

"I saw it in Vaejan when they took over. They are transforming it into an outpost of the Nine Hells themselves. After enough of the rest of us had died, defending the city against the monster and zombie hordes, then we quickly learned that it was the Khabal itself that was controlling our attackers. Once they seized power, the attacks ceased. And they gave all of the remaining Sylurrians a grim choice: serve them, or die."

Koden took a deep breath and looked down at the floor. "Some few chose death, and it was readily given to them in vile ways of which I still shall not speak of. Some tried to break out and escape, and found death in battle. Many who still wished to live joined the Khabal's armies when there was no other way. I speak true when I tell you that I have no wish to go back to them. The Dark Khabal is the true enemy of all light and life on both of our worlds, and we must all join together to defeat them, before it is too late."

Another long moment of silence passed.

"Mace," Major Avery said, "make a gesture of good faith to our new ally. Take the keys and remove Koden's anti-magic shackles."

Mason grinned, took up the keys, and unlocked Koden's bonds, completely removing them.

Koden let out a deep sigh and rubbed his pale forearms. Emotion seemed to play across his face. He looked from Mason to Major Avery, and suddenly stood a little taller.

"Ask me any question you wish," Koden said. "I will answer to the best of my knowledge and ability."

Several intel people and recorders leaned in eagerly to listen and record what was said.

Questions and papers flashed back and forth from various officers, intel people, and the major.

"How many Sylurrians hold Vaejan?"

"Over one hundred thousand," Koden said. "Before the fierce wars of Vaejan against the wild hordes and the undead–"

Everyone paled and seemed to jump at that. Fear struck everyone.

Undead? They actually had to war against undead now?

Bill was a rock. "Steady, everyone. We'll get to it. Go on, Koden."

"As I was saying, there were almost two hundred thousand of us who came to Vaejan, the strategic northern anchor on the inner seas. Many of us fell valiantly during the great wars than ensued. What we did not know, until it was too late, was that the Dark Khabal, its allies, and sympathizers were secretly in control of both sides of that costly war. They used it to wear us down and destroy our leaders–including Shaeddor's parents–until the Khabal

147

could seize complete power after the Merge. Then they gave everyone who was not of them a choice: join their armies, or face death at their hands."

"How many of this hundred thousand are mages?" Major Bill asked.

"About eighty to ninety percent."

That much was hard to take in itself. Eighty or ninety thousand mages of various kinds.

"How many of these mages would be useful in war?"

"About half, I would say. Not every mage is suitable for combat, just as every person is not fit to be a soldier."

That still left a very large number of enemy mages that the Khabal could hurl at them, if it so wished to send them forth against little Michiana.

Then the next blow.

"How many mercenaries has the Khabal hired?"

"Last I heard, the number was about another hundred thousand sellswords and additional battlemages, mostly from Khairun. And yet a hundred thousand more were still on the way, from now throughout next spring. They continue to come up from the southern port of Jashakal, and past Kavendo to Vaejan by ship and troop barge, via the inner seas and finally to Vaejan."

Their primary enemy in Vaejan was going to be over a quarter million strong—against Michiana's total population of less than two hundred thousand.

"The Sylurrians also hold Kavendo/St. Louis and Jashakal/New Orleans," Major Avery said. "How many persons are there, and does the Khabal openly control those colonial cities as well?"

Koden shook his head. "As far as I know, my people in those cities are not completely aware of what is going on in Vaejan since the Merge. But I'm guessing that the Khabal, as it often does, has key people secretly established in important positions of power in those other cities. And they also control, more or less, who goes north to Vaejan. Anyone who decides to resist them could easily be gotten rid of, and even sent north for that express purpose."

"We have to get word to those cities somehow about the Khabal," Mason said. "They could cut off further reinforcements to Vaejan."

Koden readily admitted, "The Khabal is already entrenched there and could easily form their own nation. And now they control the monster hordes in this region, and an army of millions of undead."

Everyone grew silent at that, taking in the ramifications.

Millions. Millions of undead.

"Getting back to answering your questions," Koden said. "There are about forty-five thousand Sylurrians and about the same number of mercenaries settled around Kavendo. And about twice those numbers settled around the city state of Jashakal."

"At least," Major Avery said, "the people of those two cities are not directly our enemies. And might yet become our allies once the Khabal is exposed. But we can't even safely travel fifty or sixty miles outside of Michiana, let alone reach these other regions."

Mason jumped in. "And keep in mind, those colony cities are also dealing with the Urth human populations around those areas, as well. Koden, what have you heard has happened to most of the Urth humans around Vaejan?"

Koden looked down for a moment. "We heard many rumors, but we were told that most of the Urth humans around Vaejan—eighty to ninety percent of them—perished during the first few months after the Merge. It was awful. They ran out of food within days, fell to monsters, and even turned on each other. The remaining remnant have been enslaved by the Dark Khabal."

"You say that there are millions of undead around Vaejan," Bill said, arranged into armies. Explain that. How did they become undead?"

"Special necromancer mages specialize in raising undead. They are called zombiemasters or zombielords."

"How is a zombie created?" Mason asked.

"A necromancer summons an evil spirit to take command of a dead body and animate it. They can be directed to attack and kill others, and left to themselves, such zombies will attack anything living. If they decay enough, the remnants of their flesh sometimes forms a vile, black crust around their skeletons. But this process can take years. The dark magic that binds them also preserves them by force, but eventually, they will crumble to dust.

"The only way to destroy them before that happens is with destructive magic, or by physically busting or chopping them up. The pieces will burn and be consumed, and the evil spirits binding them released."

Lots of questions followed about zombies or skeletons biting people.

Koden explained that such concerns, other than infection or disease, were not an issue. "A living person or other physical creature cannot be transformed into one of the undead, by a bite or anything else. A dead body can only be animated by dark magic, and controlled by an evil spirit placed within the host body, or by mages who can control such creatures."

"Does the enemy have ways to travel back and forth between the two sides of the Merge?" Bill asked.

"I have heard that the Khabal includes a few Travelers, and a special cave that leads back and forth between the two sides. This cave is somewhere northwest of here, in the mountains about half-way in between Michiana and Vaejan. But as a lowly battlemage, I marched here with the mercenaries. I have never seen this cave, and I do not know its exact location. I would guess that it would be heavily guarded and protected."

"Do you know of any other ways that the Khabal can travel between the two sides?"

Koden shrugged. "There have always been rumors that they were trying to construct portable gateways that their armies could take with them, but no one I know has even seen anything like that in use. As far as I know, those are still just rumors."

"How can you help us more, as a wizard?"

"Now that I'm no longer a prisoner, as an ally, I can translate all of the wizard spells I know into your language. I can help test and sort your new mages and take over training the wizards. That will free up Shaeddor from having to do all of that on his own, especially when he is not a wizard. He can focus more on the sorcerers. I would also warn you against trusting either Ettal or Resh, but Shaeddor said that you have already figured that much out. I would also say that you are woefully lacking in trained healers and mages that specialize in healing magic. A program must be started for that, as well, even though we do not currently have anyone to lead such a program."

Major Bill leaned in and asked, "And what do you expect in return?"

"My freedom, most of all. And the freedom to return to my nation, if that ever becomes possible. Treat me the same way you treat Shaeddor, and I think we'll do fine. I don't want to be counted among the Dark Khabal, and I'm sick of being treated like a prisoner by both sides. So, do we have a deal?"

Koden put out his hand, just like a good Urth human.

Major Bill glanced over at Mason, who raised his bottom lip and nodded.

Bill shook Koden's hand. "Granted. From now on, Koden Unithera of Gallava, we are allies, and we will defend each other from our common foes. Michiana agrees to your terms, and grants you your freedom. We welcome you support and assistance, attached directly to the militia under my command."

Koden nodded. "I accept your terms, as you have accepted mine. I'm ready to get to work."

Mason supplied Koden with a militia mage uniform, the pending rank of second lieutenant, and wizard robes similar to the black mage robes that Blondie wore.

Koden cast a slight spell and changed the color of his robes to dark blue.

"Only sorcerers and necromancers wear all black," he said. "Other mages usually mix it up with other colors, or by their preference. This is just mine."

Gellonar and Tharin smiled slightly and nodded to Koden as he re-entered Blondie's workshop as an ally and no longer a prisoner. Ettal froze for a moment and then painted on a smile full of congratulations. Resh sneered in suppressed rage until his face twitched and his eyes almost popped out in pure hate. He shuddered, almost convulsing violently. But he did not speak a word.

Blondie nodded and quickly put Koden in charge of the wizards.

And promptly took the rest of that day off to go home to his Jennifer and celebrate.

Mason walked with his friend. Both of them seemed happy.

"Mace, you should have felt the hatred coming from Ettal. It was something. Far worse than what you could see from Resh. I gotta hand it to Ettal. He is some actor."

"I think those two are going to try something at some point."

"I think so, too. But now that we have Koden, and his telepathy working for us, the two of us should be able to head them off. We'll lock them back up for a while if they don't continue to cooperate. But I think we have other concerns."

Mason blinked. "Oh? Where did the list end? I think anything new will have to get in line."

"There's something strange about you friend, Rodell. I can't read his mind, Mace. And he seems a little more advanced in some ways that I would not expect in a new sorcerer."

"And why is all of that strange?"

"I can't prove it. I have no proof. But something is off with him. I just know it. I'm watching him."

"Has he done anything wrong?"

"No—in fact, I like the guy. He's focused and he studies hard and learns quickly. I just can't say what it is."

"Maybe he had a head injury at some point like you did, Blondie. Maybe that's why you can't read his thoughts."

"Maybe. If I figure out anything, I'll be sure to let you and Bill know about it."

Mason laughed. "You do that, Blondie. Hey, give Jen my love."

Blondie smirked. "To hell with that. She's gonna be too busy with mine."

24

Shavalkathar rolled his eyes. He shifted his weight until he was more comfortable, and braced himself against the side of the cavern.

Urthers. Annoyingly ignorant at times. The six Spectral Keys were each controlled and utilized by one of the Six High Mages of Tharanor to maintain both magical and dimensional stability. Each key helps stabilize reality, and maintain the interdimensional nodes of power which cover the surface of all living worlds. There is a web of Spectral and lifeforce energy exuded by all things. In theory, such nodes of energy, and their connecting ley lines should exist on and crisscross over the surface of every known world. At least they did on the world of Tharanor, prior to the Merge. There should be many similar major and minor nodes of power on Urth as well, but it is unknown how badly the Merge has disrupted them all on both worlds. Just that it has.

David shook his head. "I'm with Al, great dragon Shavalkathar. None of us are wizards. You're still losing us," he said.

"I do not understand either," Jason admitted, "and I'm pretty open to this kind of stuff."

Jerriel turned to them for a moment.

"Each world is crisscrossed with a pattern of ley lines and intersection points—various major and minor nodes of power. This confluence of energy sustains and stabilizes worlds and the entire Prime Material plane. Part of that energy is Spectral or Cosmic, part of it is Nature based and elemental, and part of it is Dimensional energy. Some wizards believe that these three modes, bound and working together, are the true source of all magic and life that we know of. They comprise up the universe and all of its structures and forces."

"What are these nodes, then?" David said. "What are the keys and what do they unlock or control?"

Jerriel continued, "There are six primary nodes of power that tap into and can be used to stabilize and control the flows of energy for any world. But if they are destabilized, or wild, as they are now, they can fluctuate and appear at random locations for various periods of time. This can leads to a dangerous excess of Wild Magic. The keys to these Primary Nodes are not what you might think. They are not actual keys, like those for a lock."

"Oh, of course not," Alejandro said, holding up his hands. "That would be far too simple."

They are called keys, Shavalkathar said, *but in reality, they are far more complex. They are constructs, links to the power nodes that they serve and tap into. They take the form of both an entity and a power. At times the six entities can be summoned, spoken with, and actually take physical form—similar to that of a familiar or spirit-being who serves each of the Six High Mages they are attach to. Working together, in harmony, they help control and protect their world. But when they are disrupted and out of control, as they are now, Wild Magic can escalate exponentially, causing dimensional problems such as the Merge, or even destroy worlds entirely. When control of the Six Primary Nodes and their energy flows have been damaged or radically altered—as you have seen—chaos, destruction, or both are often the direct result.*

"Very intriguing," Jerriel said. "So, how were the Spectral Keys and the rest all disrupted? In what ways? It would require an immense amount of power."

From what I can sense, the Six High Mages and their powers have been greatly diminished, and the damage to both worlds and their power structures has been severe. This was part of the high price they paid to save both worlds and keep everything from being sucked into the Void and lost. At least temporarily, the keys have been lost or dispersed, and cannot be re-summoned or directly controlled any longer—even by the Six. Control over all Six Keys and over their corresponding, Primary Nodes would need to be reestablished and fully stabilized—before there could be any hope of ever perceiving and reversing the complex effects of the Merge.

"That could take years," Jerriel said. "Possibly even generations."

No one knows, Shavalkathar said. *Under the right conditions, with the High Mages healed and restored to their full strength and ability, it might only take days, or it could take eons. Perhaps it will never be possible again.*

"I don't get this," David said. "You say every world has these nodes and these keys, and some kind of guardian spirit beings protecting them. But we didn't have any mages like that on Earth before, controlling these nodes, or any kind of keys or spirits. How did our world still function?"

"I simply don't know what your world was like before, Daeved," Jerriel said. "I don't know."

The dragon sighed. *Captain, some worlds are naturally more stable than others and maintain their equilibriums automatically on their own. In essence, all magic is to a certain degree, Wild Magic. Worlds which are more stable than others make magic less powerful and possible. With the Six Mages maintaining the harmonic equilibrium, Tharanor did not require much effort to sustain itself, either, until the crisis arose—brought on by outside forces trying to deliberately destroy things.*

"What will keep those outside forces from trying again?" David asked.

The Prime Material plane is normally very well-protected, but the agents of destruction are always looking for an opportunity. They keep trying. Sometimes they manage to succeed here and there.

"Great. Supernatural terrorists. That is just wonderful," Alejandro said. "So, they just happened to get lucky with our two worlds?"

Once again, Shavalkathar said. *Simplistic, but I suppose your logic will have to suffice, for your limited minds.*

At the moment, David felt pretty limited.

"So, as the Urthers say," Jerriel noted with a grin. "what the heck do we do now?"

I would continue as you have been doing, if I were you, Shavalkathar said. *Which thankfully I am not.*

"Pardon me for noticing," David said. "But it appears that even you, mighty dragon, have seen better days yourself. Please tell us. What happened to you? Were you in some kind of terrible battle?"

Shavalkathar huffed. *Take care, human. I like you, but there are limits.*

"My apologies, but you did mention that you would speak of it. If there is something out there that can injure a dragon in this fashion, we need to know about it."

Nothing so mysterious, Captain Pritchard. One of the few threats capable of harming an adult dragon—is comprised of two or more other dragons, working together. I was traveling southeast of your area—looking for a potential mate actually—if you must know, when quite by accident, I stumbled into the extended hunting area—poorly marked by the way—of an already mated pair of young, but quite powerful and adult dragons.

"What? You dragons don't get along with each other?" Al asked.

154

Not always. The female was near her time to clutch...to lay her eggs. During such times, mated dragons can become extremely aggressive. I tried to explain to them that I was only passing through, as quickly as I could. But they became enraged at having their territory invaded by any potential competitor.

"It looks as if they tried to kill you," Jerriel said.

That they did, and I must say, I have never fought harder for my own life. I must also readily admit, that with two adult dragons against one, it was a very near thing. They clearly planned on eating my carcass over a period of several days. In some ways, it was logical. I would have provided great sustenance to the female at her crucial clutching time. Even they had grown very tired of human sacrifices and had ventured out together for some real hunting in the wilds.

"How did you manage to escape?" Jason asked.

I clearly could not defeat or kill them. My only chance was to wound one or both of them badly enough, so that they decided to let me flee. I damaged the female's wings as much as I possibly could, knowing that the male would never leave her side, once she was grounded and made vulnerable.

"You mentioned human sacrifices," Jason Inada said. "Were these dragons by chance red and blue–part of the Dragon Cult from Elkhart that we have heard of?"

Indeed, one and the same. They are, in fact, the primary source of that cult. They will only allow their offspring to help expand and spread such a vile cult elsewhere. The worshippers of the cult are forced to view and treat them as gods– protectors and sources of knowledge. But nothing protects the worshippers from the dragons' whims and rages. Worshippers provide sacrifices and other gifts to the dragons in an attempt to appease them and get them to do certain things. But the dragons merely see the fools as little more than a secure, and sustainable food source. The sad thing is, that some of the cultists actually begin to adore the dragons and seek to protect and serve them as actual gods, becoming their minions. Even the dragons begin to think of themselves as deities. Pathetic.

David laughed. "You speak of it with such disgust. I would think that being worshiped as gods would appeal to the vanity of dragons."

Some dragons are weak enough to fall for that allure. But trust me–tis far better to be a dragon than a god. Who wants to be burdened with playing a false god to a pack of sniveling fools? Bah! Much too tedious. Too much responsibility. Much better and far freer to be a dragon. Real dragons don't have worshipers! Cults like this are an abomination to both man and dragon. They need to be destroyed.

"That and the fact that they ganged up on you, attacked, and tried to kill and eat you," David noted.

Well, there is that as well, Shavalkathar said. *That would pretty much make anyone their personal enemy, I suppose. My vengeance will be poured out on them in time. Your people will have many reasons to make war against them also.*

"What can you tell us about them that could help us in that event?" David said. "We would be happy to be your allies in this matter. Perhaps we can even work together."

Don't get ahead of yourself, human. The dragon yawned. *"I think that I must rest for a time after that meager meal you brought me. Let us retire until the dawn. I hope the food you bring me then will be better and in greater quantity. You should be safe in my cavern if you aren't out hunting. By now you should be able to avoid the grun and the ak-kla. What you call blood beetles.*

David rubbed his neck, happy he still had their troops out hunting. "I wasn't exactly sure if it was going to be up to us to provide breakfast."

Shavalkathar grinned.

Why of course you will...either way.

25

Mason watched the pace of progress pick up dramatically when Koden worked full time with the wizards and other mages. Between the two of them, Blondie and Koden shifted the mage training project into high gear.

After the first week, Major Bill started preparing another mage workshop next to Blondie's in an adjacent old warehouse. This one would be for the wizards, and Blondie would continue working with the sorcerers.

They would divide working with any other mages between them, and switch back and forth as needed.

And with his new found freedom, Koden immediately started seeing a lot of cute little Sharon Weekes, in his free time.

By the end of the second week, Koden's bodyguards quietly reported that Ms. Weekes had spent her first night in Koden's new quarters.

The pair seemed very happy together. Mason himself always felt a twinge of his own sorrow at the romantic joy of other couples, but he never let it get in the way of feeling glad for his friends, new or old.

Life after the Merge was obviously pretty rugged for everybody. Good people and everyone deserved whatever happiness, love, and joy they could find together. Who knew what could happen each day?

Their new friend and ally Koden was no exception to that rule.

And Koden was right in other ways about their mages. About half of them would be unsuited to be battlemages in combat who needed to use their powers to fight and aid the militia. Some of their mage prospects simply weren't fighters. Some were too old and out of shape, and would not do well in battle. Some were still young kids, just getting their powers.

Word reached them that Elkhart and Mishawaka were starting to discover mages also, and wanted to send people over to be both tested and trained.

Mason took it upon himself to watch Rodell closely, to see if there was anything to Blondie's suspicions. Blondie must have said something to Thulkara as well. She came by much more often that usual, and sometimes Mason caught her squeezing into or out of the intel observation booths for watching the mages and their progress.

With all of their new mages, and a new ally to watch, it was becoming a tall order to keep track of everyone.

His friend Rodell seemed to be primarily a fire sorcerer. Most of his abilities revolved around fire. He did seem to be extremely talented, and his powers did appear to grow in both variety and power very quickly. But who was to say?

Why was that so unnatural? Perhaps Rodell was just a fast learner.

Then Mason took up Blondie's line of thought. What if Rodell was a ringer, just pretending to be a new mage to infiltrate their ranks?

If that was the case, who had sent him? Who was he working for? If he was a Tharanorian, what was he planning?

Yet after much observation, Rodell didn't seem to do anything suspicious. He seemed proud of his growing abilities and happy to be a mage for the militia.

Then one day, Rodell suffered a setback that about half of the young sorcerers experienced. He simply pushed himself too hard and experienced a flare-out.

He had been working with Blondie, when his powers erupted out of control, and he fell back, slightly scorched and pretty scared. Such events were always scary, but the training group saw them on a semi-regular basis.

For sorcerers just learning to control their powers—unlike wizards, who cast finite spells and put finite powers into them—flare-outs and even burnouts could occur.

Blondie reacted properly and shielded everyone from Rodell's flare-out in time, containing it. The whole place was warded against magic by now, and did not burst into flame as it once might have.

Rodell suffered a serious scare and slight injury, but after a few days of rest and focused meditation, he would most likely return even stronger. That was usually the case after flare-outs. Burnouts were much more dangerous, and could even kill. After a burnout, a sorcerer could take months or years to get some or all of their abilities to return. Or, in the worst cases, they might never return at all.

Mason sometimes wondered what he would have done if something like that had happened to him. But he had never had an actual burnout. With him, his power simply seemed to have vanished after the knowledge of Tori's death.

His friend Blondie still believe that the problem was basically psychological—meaning that it was all in Mason's head. But even if that was the case, it did not make the problem any less real.

Mason was surprised when he got promoted to corporal, and then acting sergeant within his unit, when Sergeant Schilling took a medical leave to help his young wife with a new, colicky baby. Mason wasn't the greatest soldier there ever was, but he could still manage his duties well enough.

He found time for his friends, and made extra time to spend playing cards and chatting with his buddy Rodell, who was stuck in recovery and lonely for those three days.

Mason got with their old Team 3 pals from Echo Company and made it possible for others to spend time with their old teammate. Mason felt justified in dropping his suspicions, and informed Blondie and Major Bill about his decision.

Thulkara, for some weird reason, seemed not to like Rodell, and became even more suspicious of him than Blondie. None of that made any sense.

Rodell wasn't even doing anything. Mason decided to concern himself with a host of other issues that were far more pressing.

Intel continued to watch everyone, in any case. They didn't trust anyone—not even each other. But such was apparently their job.

Out beyond Michiana remained a mystery. Rumors and sightings from long-range scouts and patrols continued to be ominous. The militia quietly moved up more units for training along the outer lines. A number of border patrols continued to vanish, and nothing was ever heard from them again. The size of the patrols were increased, and special runners and messengers were sent with them.

There was one odd thing. Mason knew Blondie better than anyone. Something was still wrong with his friend; he could sense it. Blondie was being stoic, as usual, and did his best to hide it, but something was definitely eating at him.

With Koden working for them now, Blondie wasn't as tired. He had more time to keep Jen and himself sated, and he even took relaxing rides on Ginger with Mason and Thulkara, and even by himself. His bodyguards would follow from behind and keep their distance. The pressure on Blondie should have decreased. But somehow, Blondie seemed more melancholy, even depressed at times. He was very thoughtful, and that usually meant that he was deeply troubled by something.

When Mason asked him what the trouble was, Blondie simply stated that he was still really worried about their future.

Mason would laugh and say that everyone was worried after all that they had learned. But Blondie wouldn't laugh about it. Mason tried to tell his friend to shake it off and not let it wear at him so much.

Sometimes Blondie would come close to snapping at him, and then sigh and apologize. "Sorry, Mace. I just know too much not to worry. I know what they can do to us, and right now, we can't stop them."

Mason would come right out and ask his friend, "You worked so hard for them once. You helped them bring about the Merge. What made you stop? Why aren't you with them, on their side anymore? Especially if we're so outgunned?"

Blondie met his eye and stared at him sadly. "Mace, they want to destroy or enslave everyone and everything. I don't want that anymore. I don't know if I ever really did want that. I was raised to be obedient to my masters. I was just following orders. Losing my memory for a time gave me a chance to question all of that, and make a choice for myself. What they want is both horrific and insane."

Mason had to ask, "And what do you want, my brother?"

Blondie sighed and patted Ginger's neck. She tossed her head and he smiled slightly. "I want to protect and save the people I've come to care about, Mace. We all have something worth saving."

"That's natural, Blondie. I'm sure everyone feels that way."

His friend glared at him again, obviously in pain. "I can't find a way to save us, Mace. If I could find a way to do so, even at the cost of myself, I would take it. But there isn't such a way. And I would have to go back in, and get pretty dark and dirty just to make the attempt–and in the end, all of that would still be futile as well."

"Blondie, I'm not sure what it is that we're talking about here. You seem to talk in riddles at times. But once again, you're starting to scare me a bit. Whatever you are thinking in that machine-like head of yours, don't go and do anything crazy without talking it over with me, first. All right?"

"Sure, Mace. Like I said, it wouldn't work, anyway. I'm not going to sacrifice myself like an idiot for nothing. That won't help anyone."

"Blondie. Don't sacrifice yourself at all, either way. No one is asking you to do anything like that."

His friend clammed up and wouldn't say anything more. They rode back quietly and took care of their horses. Mason was worried about his brother.

Blondie was obviously taking on too much and blaming himself for their situation. There was only so much that any of them could do.

Mason kept his derringer on him to humor Major Bill, and took it out once each week and tried to fire it. Every time he did so, it still clicked and nothing happened. He came to accept the fact that his powers could be gone for good.

By all appearances, the days of the Pistolero seemed to be over.

But Mason had taken time to make peace with himself and his ghosts, as much as he could. He was a trooper in the militia now, just like so many others, and he was a soldier, who did his duty with at least some pride.

He had also forced himself to more or less become a human being, and that was also a good thing. Perhaps he had just grown up and matured, from being a selfish college brat chasing his own interests and pleasures, to being a weapon for a time, and then a simple soldier and a young man who cared about others, and had a sense of duty and real commitment.

Whatever the future brought, he had made progress, according to his own yardstick. And that was all good enough for him. No one could control whatever was going to happen next.

26

The green forest dragon stretched and grinned its toothy grin. He glowed a little brighter, waving them off so that he could rest.

At least he did not demand hostages any longer.

"Great dragon," Jerriel said. "We have a young healer with us. Would you allow her and myself to look over some of your injuries? We might be able to help you recover more quickly. Then you can hunt for yourself, and I know how much dragons enjoy the hunt. Allow us to do this favor for you."

I will allow it, since you offer so kindly. I will still be stiff and sore tomorrow. It will also make me very cranky to be forced to fly out and hunt some of you down. And that will also end our pleasant little parlay, which I have grudgingly enjoyed...at times.

David clapped his hands together. "Well then, off to help with the hunting it is."

There is a wealth of game in the area at night, David Pritchard. Beware that some of it does not eat you instead. That would ruin my breakfast plans. And, oh, yes, remind me to advise you on a safer path back to your people. There's no reason to go back the same way you came.

David shook his head on the way out.

Thus they spent a good part of the night hunting and ambushing game.

Four troops got mauled somewhat by a rather large hill bear who tried to take one of their lizard carcasses from them and got added to the breakfast menu for his trouble.

After they filled the creature full of arrows and spears, of course.

David had never killed a bear before. Or helped kill one that large. He'd killed lots of other things thus far, but not a bear. He had been both a Cubs and a Bears fan and had always liked the bears at the zoo.

Who knew they smelled so bad up close and personal.

It still kind of made him sad. Bears had a right to live, too. They wouldn't have killed the bear if it hadn't attacked them first. But once it was dead, they couldn't pass up using it for the dragon's breakfast the next day.

After three or four hours sleep, they dragged their game deeper into the lair and piled it up for Shavalkathar's breakfast.

Despite the fact that they provided almost twice as much meat as they had the day before, the dragon's lack of gratitude was predictable.

Well, all right, I suppose it will have to do. I will definitely need to fly out tomorrow and have a proper hunt.

You just do that. By then David and his people would be heading for home with a wealth of valuable new information.

Then Shavalkathar devoured the meat pile–in minutes.

He did appear to be quite famished.

But the dragon remained true to his word in many respects. He had answered all of their questions and provided them with key information they could not have obtained anywhere else. He also gave them excellent advice concerning their trip back, various threats in the wilds that they marked on their maps, and detailed information about the two Dragon Cult dragons, their territory, and the wounds that he had given them both.

Jerriel had even gained permission from Shavalkathar to allow her and Stacy to treat his wounds with some of their new healing salve, and help sew up the rents in his wings. All the while, they kept the dragon talking, and pumped him for more and more information about the Merge and what was going on among the colonists and the other nations.

Before long, it neared evening again. The dragon advised that they spend the night in his cavern once more. Traveling at night in the wilds? Not a good idea.

Jerriel sang for them all that night. Even the dragon, who smiled as he dozed, appeared to enjoy the entertainment.

She sang songs for them, Tharanorian songs that she had learned among her mother's people, the Marrandorians.

No one except for perhaps the dragon understood the songs, but they were still beautiful. And so was Jerriel.

She and David found a secluded spot under the stars and moonlight, on the dragon's mountain. Nothing in all their crazy, mixed-up world could match his wizard girl lying next to him—starlight mirrored in her eyes.

Although not much of an astronomer, as they lay back together, even David realized that the stars above them were still the stars of Urth. Were the stars on the other side the stars of Tharanor?

Perhaps one day they would see them.

There was a flash of magic, and both David and Jerriel sat up.

Rabbi Bergman, the Traveler, stood before them with his back turned. He looked over his shoulder to find them, and smiled as if him popping in on them was the most natural thing in the world.

"Jerriel, Captain Pritchard. I was looking for you. I was flexing my Traveler muscles and contemplating a leap to the other side. But I didn't want to risk it yet, without first talking to Jerriel. Do you have a moment?"

"Of course," Jerriel said.

They held a short confab and spoke rapidly back and forth for several minutes.

"You will be happy to know," Bergman told them, "that I'm pretty sure that I know where the enemy transport cave is in the distant mountains. I plan to go there in astral form, and study its function and basic principles. If I can understand and learn them well enough, perhaps we can find a way to apply them for our own use."

"Watch out for the enemy," David warned. "We can't risk losing you, Josef."

Bergman smiled. "As a devout coward, I will be the very embodiment of caution. But I might just slip over to the other side and back, if I can manage it."

"You, a coward? Never." Jerriel wished him good luck and kissed him on both cheeks.

With that, their roving Traveler was gone once more.

Shavalkathar swept out of his den early the next morning, rising up into the dark sky. His newly healed wings worked a little stiffly but he looked incredibly powerful, and appeared to have healed very quickly.

I go forth to hunt. Our little visit is now concluded. Perhaps we shall meet again one day. You know where I reside, and I you. Just don't bother me too often, or I might be forced to eat you. Of course, any important news you discover is always welcome. Farewell, little friends.

In seconds, his great speed carried him out of sight.

David turned to his fellow little friends.

"Time to head home."

They used all the information the dragon gave them. They took the paths he advised and avoided certain places if they could.

But three hours later, the wilds still proved dangerous.

And immense striped snake attacked the entire party, racing out of a hidden, cave-like hole.

The snake was four feet in diameter at the widest and almost a hundred and thirty feet long.

In seconds, it knocked down half of the party and constricted several people in its massive coils.

"RASHARROK!" Jerriel commanded.

Green flames poured out of her staff and scorched the snake's massive head and throat as it reared up to swallow a trooper. David and Alejandro managed to pull the hapless man free, getting only lightly singed while doing so.

A massive shadow swooped down.

Shavalkathar grasped the enormous serpent and sank his razor-sharp talons into its length like so many swords. With a shake, he flung the humans free and rose up into the air with his prize.

As the serpent tried to attack the dragon, it was quickly cooked by dragonfire and went limp.

Thanks for the additional meat, he said. *Good journey!*

David waved weakly. But they were grateful for the assistance.

That huge snake would have been bad news for them on their own.

After resting and tending wounds for a few hours, they went on their way once more.

It cost them a few more hours to skirt a wide swamp that Shavalkathar said teemed with mor-kahls, who apparently loved swamps.

They made camp that night in a dark grove of huge, black bamboo-like plants. The only things they had to fight off were the biting flies and insects that seemed to rule the warmer nights in the wilds.

The next day, they rose early and skirted the wooded ridge lines to stay out of sight and cover a lot of ground. By well after nightfall, they kept a cold camp among some large stones and loose shale in a deep, narrow valley.

On the third night, David estimated that they were less than two days away from South Bend. They had traveled fast and made good time, again, thanks to Shavalkathar's excellent advice.

Hours later, about three hundred torgs, ka-torgs, mor-kahls, and even a few gozogs tried to cut them off, and chased them through the wilderness the rest of the night.

With Jerriel's help, they managed to elude and lose the large enemy band a few hours before dawn.

They dropped down, hidden under a river bank, and huddled together exhausted, to catch a little sleep.

An older woman in her fifties, drenched to the skin in her flannel nightgown, suddenly stumbled upon them after dawn, complete with muddy bedroom slippers.

She wept openly, nearly hysterical.

"Oh, thank God. Thank God!" she stammered. "Help me. Please help me! I don't know how I got out here. I don't know where I am!"

"It's all right. Calm down," David said. "We're with the militia. We'll help you."

"Oh, praise God. Thank you. Thank God you weren't…those things. Where are we? Where the hell are we?"

"We're a day out of South Bend. We should be back there by nightfall. How did you get way out here?"

"I don't know. I don't know."

What was wrong with the woman? It was weird to find her in the middle of nowhere out here by herself. Not a good thing for anyone.

She shook badly and went into shock. Stacy gave her a sedative to calm her down. Troops carried the older woman on a stretcher wrapped in blankets.

A striker team of two hundred militia met them six hours later.

The Blackhawks handed the woman off, made a note to check on her later when she felt better, and warned the troops about the monsters they had bypassed. More troops would be called up to hunt the monsters down.

After a quick meal, they were on their way to make a full report to Dirk and some of the town council members.

That took hours. By then, they nodded off and fell asleep in their chairs, too tired to go home.

Dirk allowed them to rest right there in the auditorium that night, safely under guard, off to the side. Nice and warm and dark.

They finished their debriefing early the next day.

A short while later, a messenger rushed in, breathless, clutching a piece of paper.

"Well, what is it now?" Dirk asked.

Still breathless, the messenger handed Dirk the note. He read it quickly.

"The Council must hear this. Gay Town asks for our immediate assistance. A large, armored human, heavily armed and an expert fighter—speaking in an unknown language, has taken up residence in one of their taverns. He brawled with the locals and their town watch briefly. He hasn't killed anyone yet, but seems content for the moment to eat and drink everything in sight. He busted some heads whenever they tried to move him."

Jerriel read the report. "Gay Town's leaders are smart enough to recognize that he could very well be a traveling Tharanorian. Most likely a Thul from the descriptions given. That's one reason why they haven't tried to arrest him or fill him full of arrows."

"We must go at once!" Jerriel added.

Dirk nodded. "I agree. David. You and Jerriel take a detail of your troops to locate this…individual. Determine who he is and where he's from, and invite him to speak before the council if need be."

David rose up. "We're on it, Dirk. We'll report back as soon as we can."

Within ten minutes, they had forty Blackhawks speeding through town on bikes with them at the lead. Jason Inada and Alejandro the Eagle accompanied them.

All of them were extremely curious to meet the new visitor.

27

Mason and all of Michiana grew more than just worried when the enemy started to show their hand and put their new plans in motion.

Whatever they were.

By all reports, the enemy was carefully surrounding Michiana from about sixty miles out. They weren't closing in yet.

They were just roving out there on the horizon, and in very large numbers.

Larger numbers than scouts had ever reported. And the mercs and mages did not come alone. At night, there were the regular monster hordes roaming the outlying areas. Then, at other times, there were sightings of undead, both zombies and skeletons. And entire units of humanoid creatures that looked to be both half goat, and others that were half reptile.

All of these reports were starting to frighten the general population. But the militia thought it best if everyone knew what they were up against.

Thulkara said that the goatmen were called grun, and were exceedingly violent and militaristic, and more cunning and clever than your average monsters. The reptilians were called slurgs, and were incredibly stealthy and often used as assassins, to slip in behind enemy lines and kill important leaders. They could leap high and far on their strong legs.

"We must now be doubly on our guard, and protect our mages and our leaders," Thulkara warned.

All of the watches were doubled. The defenders stepped up their attempts to fortify key positions and defensive walls and lines. There was still far too much to do.

Another major problem arose for the defenders, to add to their growing list.

They did not possess enough forces to guard the entire perimeter of Michiana.

When the enemy did choose to attack, they could simply have their choice of weak points to exploit.

Mason spent his share of time on the line, on guard duty, and with patrols.

And because of his penchant for staying up at night, he was also restless, and would take walks to check on positions on his own, or with Blondie, Thulkara, or Rodell and others. Everyone continued to grow paranoid, jumpy, and nervous.

The enemy mage prisoners were also pulled back and kept hidden, in case the enemy tried to sneak in and free them.

Then Blondie warned Mason, Bill, and intel that something was up with Ettal and Resh, and the enemy mages still being locked up.

They now had developed some way to block his telepathy, even though he thought they weren't aware of it. Koden confirmed it.

Bill asked Blondie if he wanted the two wild cards locked up, just to be sure. Blondie said not yet. He wanted a chance to try to crack through however they were blocking him, and not to do anything to tip them off. Just increase the watch and security on them and the compound. That would be understandable to everyone, considering the enemy threat.

All of their new mages were training as hard as they could, around the clock, struggling to learn as much as they could. If hostilities did break out, they would all be attached to military units along the line.

And it would quickly become painfully obvious to everyone that the Pistolero was no longer in business, helping defend Michiana.

Mason was surprised one night to spot a shadowy figure moving across the top of Blondie's magic compound building.

He told Thulkara, who could move quite quietly when she took the time to do so. She went up from one side.

Mason went up on top from the other.

They met somewhere near the middle with drawn weapons. Mason had his spear and shield. Thulkara had a throwing knife and one of her axes out.

169

"Show yourself," Mason ordered.

Rodell stepped out of the shadows. "Something's wrong, my friends," he told them. "I can sense it. The air is too still, too quiet. I came up to try to see what was amiss from this high vantage point. Can you not smell it, on the rising heat?"

Thulkara sniffed. Even Mason could detect that sweet coppery tang on the wind. Anyone who had been in battle before knew what that scent was.

"Human blood," Mason said.

Thulkara glared at Rodell. "I still don't trust this lurker in the shades, but damn it, he's right. Blood is being spilled while we speak."

Rodell gasped and then pointed northwest, speaking quietly. "Look...over that way."

Several silent creatures quickly sped over the rooftops, leaping with agile precision over them, and even alighting on old telephone poles, lampposts, and trees, not unlike monkeys or apes. They mostly kept to the shadows. Only brief flashes of movement gave anything away, and even those fleeting glimpses were difficult to make out.

They had long, agile tails that seemed to assist them in climbing, running, and leaping, but they were not like monkeys or apes at all.

They were clearly reptilian, and half of them went for Blondie's compound and the other half sped for the garrison keep where Major Bill and the bulk of the officers were.

"Slurg assassins," Thulkara noted.

"We should raise the alarm," Rodell said, his voice shaking with terror.

"No, not yet," Mason insisted. "If we sing out now, they will only melt away. Let's draw them in to where our defenses are the heaviest. Then they will not escape. The guards on duty have ways of alerting each other."

He reached into a certain pouch and took out a handful of red stones.

"Here," Mason advised. "Start flinging these small, red stones at the guard and watch stations down there. It's an old silent warning trick we used on the lines during the war. They'll figure it out. We've trained for this."

Shielded from the approaching foes by a supply shack up on the magic compound, they hurled the rocks at several guard posts. Some of the guards came out into the open and yawned or stretched and did similar casual things.

More guards started to move. Some even slipped into darkened barracks.

With seconds, as the enemy approached, Mason saw more archers and troops hiding behind cover and assuming defensive positions on the high points to defend the entire area.

Rodell gasped again. "On the ground. Look, something else. The slurgs are not alone."

Thulkara sniffed the air. "Grun goatmen. I can smell their stink from here."

170

Mason tried, but he couldn't smell anything but the blood on the air still. He went over to a certain air vent and tossed some of the red stones down the pipe. They rattled quietly through the building. That signal should alert the guards and get the mages up. Too bad Blondie wasn't here to—

Damn it to hell.

If the enemy had scoped out the mage compound and the officers' quarters, they knew where to find Blondie and Jennifer in the couple's private digs.

That area was well-defended, also, but would they have advance warning there, as they would here?

That doubt troubled him greatly. Even Blondie, with all of his powers returned, could be caught in a bad way against large enemy numbers.

And what if they somehow knew where the mage prisoners were being kept?

One problem at a time. "Thulkara, Rodell. I think our forces can spring the trap on them here. Let's hustle over to warn Blondie. They might not have any warning over his way."

"Are you insane?" Rodell asked.

"He's right, Mace. Leave, right at the beginning of a major attack? Blondie can handle himself."

"Please," Mason said, following his gut, "just trust me in this."

Even as they spoke, squads of heavily armed militia and archers spread out on top of the compound. They were well-led by tough Lieutenant Neil McCallister, a veteran fighter from the wars. "Neil, I'm just an acting sergeant. You're a good field officer. Can you please take over here? We're going to secure Blondie."

Neil nodded to him. "You got it, Mace. Keep him safe."

Even as they climbed down through the building, the insides were still dark, but everyone within was quietly preparing to defend it against an attack.

They broke out the back of the compound through an exit door at a full run. Thulkara pulled ahead of them with her amazing speed.

"I can get there first," she told them.

"Get there alive," Mason said. It was good to have Thulkara jetting there as fast as she could. But now Mason and Rodell were on their own.

The attack and the battle behind them erupted even as they ran.

They had gone two blocks, with two left to go to reach the garrison where Blondie and Jennifer kept their place. It was a third floor apartment in a building where the militia kept troops on the roof and all throughout the building as a major garrison and observation post.

That building and its strategic location had a wide view of the entire area, and the many militia training areas, supply buildings, and additional barracks for troops.

171

As the two of them ran, militia troops at the intersection swept out and surrounded them with spears. "Halt, and identify yourselves!"

"Sergeant Mason Tyler and mage Rodell Kim. We've come from the mage compound, which is already under attack. Sound the alarm and defend Mage Captain Shaeddor and his lady. The enemy may strike directly at them!"

Even as they spoke, heavy attacks struck the garrison from above and below, two blocks in front of them.

"I'm Corporal Kajewski," the commander said. "We'll have reinforcements here in about a minute to secure this intersection. Team 2, go with Sergeant Tyler here and help defend the garrison against whatever foes you find there."

Mason nodded and hefted his spear. "Thanks, Corporal. Good luck here. Let's go, troops. Form an attack V to either side of me. We've got a mage with us." The additional dozen troops made them a group of fourteen. The troopers spread out with easy precision, and they covered the two blocks together on the run.

When they reached the garrison, about two dozen troops fought in the street against about thirty of the grun goatmen, who had slipped in close under the cover of darkness. They had seized the area around the front of the garrison and were holding it with great ferocity. Several militia guards and troops were already down, dead or wounded.

Mason assessed the situation. What bothered him more were the three dozen slurgs crawling rapidly across the sheer face of the garrison building itself, all of them converging on the balcony and windows of Blondie and Jennifer's third floor apartment.

The grun on the ground would fight to the death, buying time for the slurgs to try to kill Blondie and anyone around him.

Despite the pitched battle on the ground, the real thrust of the enemy attack was focused on taking out Blondie.

More reinforcements flooded in, all focused on the grun.

"Shield wall!" Mason yelled. "Shield wall. Form up. Hem them in with steel and spears. They're not going anywhere. Every archer, take up a position and shoot the assassins climbing the building. Take them down! All archers, fire at will! Take the high ground if you can."

Under concentrated archer fire, a third of the slurgs plummeted shrieking and hissing to the ground, riddled with arrows.

The grun saw this and immediately charged out, trying to smash through the shield wall. Some of their berserkers, fighting two handed, leaped over the shield wall and tried to attack the archers.

Grun were tough fighters, it appeared, but ten or twelve spears and swords shoved through their thick bodies slowed them down or dropped them in their tracks.

The militia archers continued to fire. More slurgs fell from the building.

A gout of red-violet lighting ripped out of Blondie's balcony and blasted the burning bodies of half a dozen slurgs out across the street to smash into the building next to them and fall to the ground. None of them got back up or even twitched. They fell and continued to burn.

Enemy arrows cut down militia archers behind them and to their left, in the street.

A mixed team of about two dozen additional grun and slurgs poured at them from another angle.

Rodell stepped in front of them as they turned, and lifted his red-glowing hands. Gouts of scarlet, orange, and yellow flame engulfed the foremost several foes, and they became shrieking torches from the waist up.

Thulkara led a knot of militia on the left. Mason called his borrowed team to him on the right, backed by others. The confused archers tried to regroup and keep firing up at the building.

"Set spears for charge," Mason commanded. He snapped his set spear out in front of them. "Shields up, and charge! Swords, gut any of them left in the belly and groin. If they fall, make sure of them!"

They surged into the enemy attackers.

Rodell flung a cloud of burning sparks and popping cinders into their foe's faces to blind and distract them.

On the left, the enemy learned the terror of facing a Thul warrior goddess as her battle axes whirled and sliced through them, dancing her spinning dance of death.

Like the other darkspawn, slurgs and grun also appeared to have the same black blood.

Mason shoved a spear right down the open maw of the foremost slurg as it sprang at him with its two weapons, a javelin and a curved scimitar. His spear choked it and then pierced through its torso and fully out of the monster's back.

Up close, he could only describe the slurgs as something between a humanoid and small velociraptor, with a striped, whip-like tail. They wore no armor because of their tough hides, and their teeth and claws looked lethal. Especially their large back claws.

It collapsed dead on his shield, and he had trouble yanking his spear back because of the corpse's weight.

That was the only foe he managed to engage and take down.

The militia clashed with the enemy, suffered a few casualties, but quickly overwhelmed them with superior numbers and discipline. Once the enemy lost the element of surprise, the militia took them down. Each foe was pierced and hacked numerous times. Most of them lay hewn into pieces.

The slurg hind claws tore through metal shields and armor like big can openers. That was something to watch out for.

Mason would hate to fight an entire army of these things; they and the grun could outleap humans with ease. That would have to be taken into consideration when fighting masses of them.

These foes could leap over a shield wall in great numbers. New formations would have to be devised to counter such abilities.

Mason, Thulkara, and Rodell charged up into the garrison to reach Blondie's apartment.

A militia captain and his troops guarded the stairs and the hallways leading in. Mason didn't know the officer in charge. Troops carried out several dead slurgs, most of them horribly mutilated. Some were almost unrecognizable. Just hunks of scorched, mangled flesh.

"Let us through," Mason yelled. "I'm Sergeant Tyler, this is Lieutenant Rajan, and Mage Kim from the compound."

The captain stepped in front of them. "Stand down, troops. I'm Captain Soderberg. This area is secure. What's your business here?"

"We've been sent by Major Avery to make certain Mage Captain Shaeddor is safe and sound. Those are our orders," Mason lied.

"Tell the major that the enemy attack is over, and it failed. Everything's under control. You don't need to go in there right now. The medics and my physician are seeing to the injured."

Mason stared at the guy, not knowing him. "Captain, I'm the Pistolero. Blondie and I are good friends, as you have probably heard. I'm asking you to let the three of us in there, as a favor to myself and Major Avery."

Captain Soderberg stared back at Mason, frowned, and then bit his lower lip. "Well, I guess it's all right. Just don't get in the way of my people or the medical teams."

"Thank you, sir. We won't." Mason didn't know what he would have done if the guy said no. He guessed that his Pistolero status probably wouldn't open doors for him much longer.

From the look on Thulkara's face, she was about ready to chuck anyone blocking her path out the nearest window.

Inside, the place was pretty much a disaster.

More of the slurgs had slipped inside than Mason had guessed, based on the piles of enemy corpses.

Mason counted several splattered around the balcony alone.

He didn't see Blondie. A knot of troops and medical people were gathered around someone lying on the blood soaked carpeting, working over that person rapidly and talking low to each other.

There was a lot of red blood from someone human.

Several militia troops stared at the other parts of the apartment, dark now except for some strange red lights sparking deeper within the shadowy depths.

Those troops looked scared shitless.

Mason and his two companions skirted around and saw Jennifer Gilbert's pale hand, a bloody mace spilled from the hand and a dead slurg with its face bashed in a few feet away.

"They poured in from the balcony and the windows," Thulkara said.

Blondie and Jen had met the enemy attack as best they could, most likely back to back.

From another angle, five different medics, and the doctor were trying to close serious wounds and cuts on both legs on her arms, as well as a deep gash down her abdomen. They kept calling for blood or plasma, but the equipment hadn't come up to them yet.

Jen had lost quite a bit of blood from her many, deep wounds.

Mason quietly asked one of the troops, "Where's Mage Captain Shaeddor?"

The woman stammered and looked scared. "H-he l-left the woman to the medics when she lost consciousness. Several of those wounded lizard people dragged themselves back further within the apartment. The sorcerer seemed to go mad at first, and then he got real quiet. Some kind of power surrounded him. It took the form of something like spinning blades of scarlet lightning.

"I've never seen anything like that. Our people pulled back. Everyone stayed the hell away from him. He went after those trapped lizard-things, slicing right through the walls and even some of the iron building supports to get at them. Then those things started screaming and shrieking, like devils in hell ripping people apart piece by piece. He hasn't come out yet, and nobody is going to dare to go in there after him."

Mason walked straight into the darkness.

These creatures had nearly killed Jen.

Mason had witnessed both the intensity and the ferocity of Blondie's wrath. No doubt these assassins had paid a high and heavy price. There was no doubt that his friend would make sure of that.

"Blondie," Mason called out into the darkness, "it's Mace, Thulkara, and Rodell. You okay, brother?"

The blood-red glow preceded Blondie. He merged from what looked to be the shattered back rooms of the apartment, everything painted and splattered almost completely black. The walls were steaming with smoking black goo and bits of bloody meat.

175

Scores of red electric blades of lightning buzzed around Blondie still, and he was drenched and dripping in black blood and gore as if he had been inside a gigantic blender with the creatures.

The blades still buzzed and burned through anything they touched.

Blondie caused the lethal blades to vanish before they could harm his friends.

His grim face suddenly filled with fear as he looked over toward Jen. "I took care of the rest," he said flatly. "How is she, Mace? They hurt her pretty bad. Jen saved me from getting stabbed in the back, but they dragged her down screaming. There were simply too many of them. I couldn't slay them fast enough."

"It's not your fault, Blondie. I don't know how Jen is. They're working on her as best they can. She's in good hands. Rodell, will you take word back to Major Avery and tell him that the Mage Captain and the rest of us are okay? Take a few troops with you, just in case."

"Sure, that's all a good idea. I'll leave right now. Shaeddor, I hope Jennifer is going to be all right." Rodell ducked out.

Blondie closed his eyes and nodded.

"Come on, Blondie," Mason said. "Let's find some way to get you cleaned up a bit. You look like hell itself. You're not hurt anywhere, are you?"

"No, just a few cuts and bruises. But I'm not doing anything until I know she's out of danger."

Mason and Thulkara waited with him to find that out.

"They attacked us in our home," Blondie said flatly, clenching both fists. "I will not forget that. The slurgs asked me who I was. I told them I am the Black Prince. Then I showed the vermin what that means."

28

When David and his group reached the Eight Ball Tavern, a large group of bikes and horses were already clustered about the area, including a contingent from Black Town.

The Gay Town militia wore head scarfs, helmet bands, or sashes of pink or purple. The Black Town troops wore black. One group of them looked to be no more than street thugs, in full gang regalia.

David recognized K-J right away, the ambitious thug the demon had been coaching. Now that the demon was gone, it looked as if K-J was reduced to just being a soldier.

The thugs also noticed their arrival, and looked the other way. K-J just glared at David and Jerriel; he'd obviously been demoted to flunky status. He and his boys were just grunts now.

Three Gay Town people approached David and Jerriel, two armed men and a civilian woman.

"I'm Madison Wycliffe," the woman said. Thirtyish, with glasses, steel-blue eyes, and a sleek brown pony tail. "I'm the Block Leader here. We're glad to see you and your people. The Black Town troops got here first. We asked for their help, too. Despite our advice not to do so, they tried to carry the big guy off–back to Black Town–while he slept off the drunk he put on last night."

"What happened?" Now that they were closer, David could see several members of the Black Town militia being carried out of the tavern, limp and unconscious on stretchers. They looked badly battered, bruised, and bleeding.

Madison Wycliffe shook her head again.

"Our new guest woke up before they could get him to the door. He got angry and proceeded to wipe the floor with them. Then he crashed behind the bar and started to snore again. Nobody wants to go near him now."

"Has he drawn any weapons?" David asked. "Has he killed anyone?"

"Not yet; he hasn't had to. So far he's just used his fists and feet, but that's been enough.

One of Madison's guards chimed in, "We've never seen *anyone* so big and tough as this guy. And he's heavily armored and bristling with weapons. I shudder to think about what damage he might do if he decided to use any of them."

"Let's go in," Jerriel said. "He's must be a Thul."

K-J and some of his people tried to block their way.

"Go on home," K-J said. "The queers asked for help, and it's here."

"I happen to be straight," Madison noted.

K-J shrugged. "Whatever. Black Town has it all under control. You feelin' me? You all got your pet." He nodded at Jerriel. "This one belongs to us. He's goin' back to Black Town."

Frank Jackson, one of the actual Black Town Militia Commanders stepped in and waved K-J off. David knew Commander Jackson from the battles with the monsters.

"You're not in charge of anything, K-J. You and your crew stand down and back off. I didn't see any of your people go in and try to carry the big guy out. That's Captain David and the wizard girl. They lead the Blackhawks. You don't want to be in their way."

K-J fumed and stalked away. His crew swarmed behind him, casting off a lot of anger and attitude.

David ignored them and shook Commander Jackson's hand. "Thank you, sir." He talked to him briefly about K-J's connection with the demon. Jackson seemed well aware of the issue.

Madison breathed a sigh of relief when David came back to her. "We don't want any trouble; we just want someone to deal with this guy."

"Our turn," David said.

He went in first, Jerriel and some of the others close behind him.

The inside of the tavern looked like a cyclone had hit it–several times.

Loud snoring, like that of a monster, roared from behind the bar. The heavy wood and metal bar itself stood shattered and knocked out of place.

They peered over the ruined bar.

David looked upon a giant of a man, well over seven feet tall, bigger than Pastor Bryan Doran, even. This warrior was muscled like an ancient warrior god. He was also armed and armored from head to foot. Long blond braids, beaded beard, and long mustachios completed his look.

"That's a Thul all right," Jerriel said. "And one of their champions, by his markings and decorations. This guy is an elite expert in every form of combat, a master of weapons and tactics unlike anything you have ever seen before. A warrior supreme from a race of mighty warriors."

"Yeah, and he's passed out drunk on the floor." David waved in front of his face. "Ugh...he stinks worse than a dead gozog."

"When he wakes up, we can offer him a bath," Jerriel said. "He's obviously been traveling for many days."

"So, how do we wake him up, make friends with him, and get him out of here?" Jason Inada asked.

"Do *you* want to wake him up?" Al asked, looking around at the damage.

"Not particularly," Jason noted. "You saw what he did to a dozen of those Black Town guys."

"Wise decision," Jerriel said. "On Tharanor, it is not known what's worse: waking a sleeping dragon or a hungover Thul."

David chuckled. Jason and Al joined them.

"So, what do we do?" David asked her.

She grabbed an apron from the bar and nodded toward the kitchen.

"We make breakfast. If it smells good enough, he might wake up and join us. He'll probably eat enough for ten or twenty people. Just let him go. After he eats, if the food's good, he might talk to us then, or he might just get drunk again, or go back to sleep. We need to be hospitable and wait him out. When he's fed and rested, he'll be ready to talk to us."

David grabbed a skillet. "I spotted a small smokehouse out in back with the chicken coop. I can make bacon and eggs if they have some. The secret to bacon is to slow cook it on medium heat and get the grease just right, and keep turning it."

He looked at his friends.

Jason Inada shrugged. "I can make juice. I see some citrus juice and concentrate in cans."

Alejandro bowed. "Never fear, my friends. I just happen to be the world's foremost expert on making...toast."

David wrinkled his nose. "Toast? That's the best you got, Al?"

"But it is very good toast. Oh, you're not buying that?"

"Al. Anyone can make toast. Sheesh!"

"I beg to differ. And in any case…mastering swordplay and attending to the many willing and nubile young ladies out there leaves very little time for acquiring other culinary skills."

Jerriel waved her hands and rolled her eyes. "All right, let Al make the toast, Daeved. Three or four loaves should do."

Alejandro gaped. "Three or four…loaves?"

"Unless we want to eat, too. Then you'll need more."

"How much bacon, then?" David asked. "A pound or two?"

"Thulls are legendary for their battle prowess. And their eating skills. Try six or seven pounds."

"Eggs?"

"Four or five dozen." She looked at them staring at her. "I don't think any of you believe me." She pointed at the big Thul.

"Just wait until that big oaf rises up and starts stuffing his gullet. You *don't* want him to run out of food. Thulls don't get that big by having a tiny bowl of that stuff you call cereal to start their day."

David looked around in the sparsely supplied pantry. "Then we have a definite problem, Jerriel."

"What is that?"

"There's not enough food to cook here."

Jerriel's eyes got big and worried. "That is a problem. You think Thulls get cranky when someone wakes them up with a hangover? Wait until he wakes up and there isn't enough to eat. He'll tear this whole place down."

Alejandro lifted his hand. "Excuse me, lovely one, but have you seen this place? It is already mostly torn down."

Jerriel turned to David. "This is serious. Get with your militia friends out there and have them bring us some more damn food. Before that bloody Thul wakes up!" David ran outside to Madison and explained the situation. Runners ran off to both camps for assistance.

Jerriel stuck her head out the door. "And meat. Ham. Sausage. Big hunks of beef if we can get it. Hurry!"

Madison and her people quickly scurried to comply.

Within thirty minutes the kitchen and four propane grills out back were firing on all cylinders.

Scrambled eggs, fried eggs. Al's world famous toast, Jason's pitchers of juice, fresh milk, coffee. Sausages, thick slices of ham, even several steaks marinating and getting ready to grill.

Minutes later, just as they put the steaks on, the big Thul yawned and sat up.

No one stood in his way as he staggered outside, rubbing his eyes, and relieved himself in a nearby patch of bushes for several long moments.

Then he fell upon the serving platters heaped with food that they set out on the picnic table. The big metal table nearly buckled when he plunked down in the middle of it, taking up one entire side. He used the serving spoons and his grimy hands to shovel the food into his maw.

Jerriel smiled and motioned to her friends. "Just leave him alone. Let him eat his fill."

"That might take a while." Al noted.

All of them stared for a moment. Professional eaters couldn't keep up with this guy.

David stood at a blazing grill nearby and flipped the nearly raw steaks. They smelled great.

"Jerriel, how do Thulls like their meat cooked?"

Before she could even answer, the huge Thul reached over and swept four still sizzling steaks off the hot grill and devoured them in seconds, red blood dripping down his beard. He threw the bones to the dogs waiting nearby. None of them ventured too near the fearsome giant.

David guessed that that dogs were probably afraid of being snatched up and devoured alive by the eating machine just like those steaks. If they got in too close.

The Thul slurped down pitchers of juice, pushed back the milk, and seemed to enjoy the coffee quite a bit. But he pounded the table with an empty metal pitcher.

"Agga! Agga. Boro. Tregg mar Boro!"

Jerriel clapped her hands. "Bring ale, beer, mead, anything like that!"

"He drinks in the morning?"

"Just do it. Hurry!"

They emptied bottles into pitchers and poured tankards. The Thul repeatedly scooped up eggs in a slice of toast and sucked them down in one gulp. The same way that anyone normal would eat a cracker.

David continued to be astounded. "Is he even chewing, or just swallowing it all?"

"He's probably been traveling hard and fast," Jerriel said. "Thulls can go days, even weeks, without food if need be, but once they do start to eat–look out."

"We might not be able to afford an alliance with these guys," David said. "We couldn't afford to feed them!"

The big Thul belched like a roar of thunder and laughed, deep and hearty.

"*Heru gohn denda!*" he said repeatedly.

Jerriel's eyes widened.

"What is it?" David said. "What does that mean?"

Jerriel blinked. "He keeps saying…'very good toast.'"

Alejandro beamed with pride.

29

Mason worked with his militia unit the day after the assassin attacks. Like the monsters before them, the militia and intel wanted to study the anatomy of the slurgs and the grun, in order to figure out their physical strengths and weaknesses.

And, of course, the best ways to kill them.

They would share all of their findings with Mishawaka and Elkhart.

Koden took over the mage training the next day while Blondie stayed at the field hospital with Jennifer. She was still in serious condition, but barring infection, she should make a full recovery.

The early warning allowed the mages and the officers to survive the initial attacks and even help defeat them.

For once, Mason felt that they had been lucky, and that it was a good thing that Rodell had been suspicious and gone up onto the rooftop, unauthorized, to check out his hunches.

They had suffered almost three hundred dead and wounded from the attack, spread out over several key locations. Their count had the dead attackers at about four hundred. Not many of the enemy had gotten away, if any. It had seemed to be a suicide mission from the very beginning, bent on killing key personnel. The slurgs and the grun fought ferociously to the death.

But Mason and Major Bill assessed the aftermath, and between them, they felt as if the enemy had them bottled up and could fling such attacks at them with impunity.

It was clear to anyone with any kind of a military mind that their foes were testing and softening them up for bigger and better things.

Thulkara was extremely curious as well. "If they have all of this overwhelming might to throw at us," she asked, "then what are they waiting for? Why aren't they attacking?"

Major Bill Avery sighed. "I think they want to be sure. We've surprised and beaten them back several times before when they least expected us to. I'm sure they have a plan, and they want to be very certain that it is going to work this time. We just don't know what that plan is, and we probably won't know until it is too late."

A messenger ran up to see them both.

Both of them stood up. "What is it?" Bill said.

The messenger girl, a runner, was nearly breathless. "Sir, the Mage Captain is urgently requesting your presence, and Sergeant Tyler's. Something is seriously wrong with Ms. Gilbert, the Mage Captain's girlfriend. He requests that you come at once, with all speed."

Mason and Bill grabbed two post horses that were handy and rode over to the heavily guarded field hospital.

After the attacks from the night before, the enemy had proven that it could strike anywhere within their cities. All of their key points and people were now heavily guarded.

Mason and Bill rushed into Jennifer's airy recovery room. She looked to be unconscious still, and Blondie was nervously waiting for them.

"Glad you two could get over here so fast," Blondie said. He glanced down at Jennifer. "Say again what you just told me."

Jennifer's eyes were closed, but her lips moved, even though the last they had heard, she was being kept sedated due to her many injuries.

But when she spoke, it did not sound like her voice at all.

"My name is Rabbi Josef Bergman. I am a Traveler mage from the other side. I came here in astral form to try to find the cave in the mountains to the northwest of Michiana. The same cave that the enemy is using to transfer troops and supplies from one side to the next."

Mason and Bill pulled up chairs. Bill spoke first. "How do we know that this is not just some trick of the enemy, to confuse us and feed us misinformation? How do we know you are who you say you are?"

"I understand your suspicion and reluctance," the Traveler said. "I came here to the hospital, hoping that I could find someone unconscious. While I am in astral form, I am like a disembodied spirit, and I can speak through others if they are not awake enough to block me. I saw this injured woman lying here with an important mage watching over her.

"How about this for proof? Two people from your side crossed over to us accidentally. I can tell you their names, and I have spoken with them several times. They are John Wolper and Marie Purdy. They came through a magic lake during a thunderstorm. They worked for someone they call the Pistolero. His name is Mason Tyler, and he is a good friend of one of our elite militia officers, Captain David Pritchard of the Blackhawks. The enemy would not know all of that, I don't think."

"Perhaps," Mason said. "I'm Tyler. Can you relay a message to Captain Pritchard for me?"

"I can when I get back, but right now I am out of my body. And before I left to make this test run, Captain Pritchard left on a long-range exploration mission into the wilds."

"Tell David and the defenders there that the portal through the lake might work if there are thunderstorms on both sides at the same time. We think that is how John and Marie accidentally crossed over. We haven't found anyone on this side among us who is a Traveler, yet."

"I will pass that message along."

"Are you the only Traveler mage that they currently have?" Major Bill asked.

"I am. I'm currently exploring my powers through astral travel to begin with. I have been told that in many ways, that is safer, and that I cannot be physically harmed while doing so in this form. First, I'm going to see if I can return to my own body and transport between the two sides that way. Once I make the connection, I should be able to retrace the threads and repeat the process and return, either in my astral or physical form, once more. Or, possibly, by using my powers to transport directly back and forth between locations that I have familiarized myself with and anchored myself to on both ends."

"Interesting," Blondie finally said. "I've only met one other Traveler in my entire lifetime, and she was very old and soon passed away. They are exceedingly rare among all of the different kinds of mages. That is a tall order. What if you cannot transport back directly?"

"Then I will return the same way I came, by returning to the enemy's fixed cave gateway and passing my astral form back through it. There is little chance that they will detect me."

"Tell us," Avery said. "What are the enemy defenses around that cave like? Could it be attacked and seized by force?"

"Unlikely," Bergman said. "They have the entire mountain fastness fortified and surround by several armies. It would take several more rival

185

armies just to attack it, let alone have any hope of taking the cave by force. But I've been studying the magical properties of the cave itself, as they can be seen and studied while I am in astral form if one knows how to look."

"What have you found?" Blondie asked.

"I'm no enchanter or theorist, but I don't see why the basic magical design and the structure of the portal itself could not be duplicated. I can see what the connections and magical flows are, but I have no idea how to replicate them or how they could be put into practice. I think a wizard or an enchanter might have to work out that part."

Blondie sucked in a breath. "Traveler Bergman—this could be the breakthrough we have been waiting for. It could spell our survival, and the survival of both sides of two entire worlds. You must take every precaution, and record and remember all that you can about its construction, and its magical energy flows.

"When there is time, you must write down and describe what you have seen about the magical principles and connections, and how the crucial ends of such a portal are created, energized, linked, and sustained. That is all paramount to understanding and controlling this knowledge and implementing any kind of transport portal. So much is riding on what you do next."

"I shall do my best. I have a notebook and a pen with me, even in astral form. I have already made many notes, and will record all that I can."

"Good. Get them to your mages on the other side. Get copies of those notes to us, if you can. Please, try to find a safe way back to us."

Mason knew that Blondie considered himself an atheist and was not a praying man. But he saw his friend clench his hands together, bow his head, and shudder with deep emotion while he muttered to himself.

"It just might work now. It's a slim chance at best, but it just might actually work now."

Bergman continued. "I should most likely prepare my astral form for the attempt to get back. Is there anything more that you wish to tell my leaders here on this side?"

"The enemy has us surrounded with superior forces on our side," Major Bill said. "We are training mages as quickly as we can, but our resources and numbers of defenders are finite. A massive enemy attack could hit us at any moment. We could use help and any information. If a way could be found to link both our sides, we could travel back and forth and support each other, just as the enemy is doing."

"I see. I will convey all that. If I can cross over with my physical body next time, I will be able to bring you a host of information from our side and our leaders and thinkers. I suggest that you prepare to send us similar knowledge and communications from your side."

"Good. An information swap. Then you can take back much of the knowledge that we have gained," Mason added. "And we can see where both sides are. Oh, one more thing. We have two troops from the Blackhawks who stepped into a magic pool and crossed over. Lieutenant Rick Collier and Trooper Terry Gallagher. Leave that word for David and his unit. Those two troopers of his are safe and with us on this side."

"I will be most happy to work as such a courier, relaying all and any important news," Bergman noted.

Blondie insisted. "It is vital that you get that transport portal information to your mages and enchanters and have them start working on constructing such a gateway, immediately. That is of primary importance right now. If you can get the information back to us, perhaps we can even start constructing the other end of the gateway on this side. Again, this could very well save us all!"

"If I am able and a way can be found, I will do so. But first I must find my way back. I must go now. Farewell, my new friends. I hope to see you again."

Mason didn't like the sly, wild look he saw in Blondie's eyes now. It was almost maniacal, like that of a mad genius. His friend no longer seemed defeated and depressed, as he had been before. In fact, his highly intelligent mind seemed to be racing a mile a minute, calculating the use of such transport gates and the tactical advantages they might provide.

Not to be outdone, Major Bill had a similar look on his face.

But such gates were still just pipe dreams for the present, and they remained in a very tight spot. For now, they had to find a way to hang on against all of the odds stacked against them and merely survive.

Blondie kissed Jen on the lips and her forehead, and then whispered something to her. He caressed her face tenderly with his hands.

Then he rose up and demanded that Bill place a guard contingent on her greater than his own. Bill agreed to do so.

"I want to be updated ever hour on her condition. I have a great deal of work to attend to," Blondie said.

30

The later morning sunlight shone beautifully. The birds sang in the trees. They heard and saw spring robins here and there among them while the Thul continued to stuff himself.

"Good," Jerriel noted. "Our guest sounds happy."

"He'd better be," Jason said. "He's eaten forty-five pounds of food and drink or more. And he's still going!"

"Thulls are like wolves. Some of them can stuff themselves with up to fifty pounds of food if need be. All in one sitting."

Half an hour later, every scrap of food was gone, along with four more pitchers of beer.

Their ravenous guest walked back into the bar, inhaled another pitcher of beer, and proceeded to go back to sleep behind the bar.

He waved to them and smiled before he dropped back down to his favorite spot. He snored again in minutes.

David sat down with Jerriel and their friends, all of them stunned and exhausted. It was almost noon by then.

Now they were hungry. And there was nothing for anyone else to eat. The Thul had inhaled everything.

"We're no closer to resolving this than we were hours ago," David said.

The militia from Black Town got bored and left, except for a couple of messengers and spies hanging around to keep them informed. After that display of eating prowess, nobody was going to want to keep the Thul fed. Not with a food shortage looming over everyone.

"What are we going to tell Dirk and the council?" Jerriel asked.

"To hell with that," Alejandro said. "What do we do when that big bastard wakes up and wants lunch?"

They all shuddered just thinking about it.

"We fed him pretty well, we didn't interrupt him," Jerriel said, "and we let him go back to sleep. I think he'll be in a better frame of mind when he wakes up."

"Whenever that is," Jason said.

A new commotion followed along when the Blackhawk messengers returned. David and the others stood up and walked forward to see what was coming their way this time.

The messengers had a young woman with them, dressed in some kind of makeshift armor, carrying a spear and shield, and wearing a battered lacrosse helmet.

She stumbled along as if she were exhausted.

David couldn't see her face, even as she spotted him and rushed up to him. She threw her arms around him. She was crying and breathing hard by then.

Even Jerriel looked on, a bit surprised.

From this new woman's actions, David had the distinct feeling that he should know her, somehow. She definitely seemed to know him, whoever she was.

She also seemed so upset and exhausted that she could not speak. David held her still for a moment and tried to comfort her. Perhaps he could get her to talk once she calmed down and stopped sobbing and shaking.

"Relax. You're safe here," Dave told her. "Can you tell me what this is all about? Why did you come looking for me?"

She pulled back slightly and yanked her helmet off. Big brown eyes and freckles. A wealth of red hair spilled out.

"Tori!" he yelled, ecstatic to have found her at last.

Or rather, she had found him. Tori Nelson, his best friend Mason Tyler's cute girlfriend from Elkhart.

They hugged again.

"It's so good to see you, Tori. The last I heard, Mace said you were in Elkhart with your family. You came all this way?" His head was in a whirl. Did she even know Mason was missing?

Tori held him at the elbows with both of her hands, and her face grew very serious and riddled with worry.

"Mason's on the other side, David. We have to find a way to reach him or send him a message. We're all in great danger. We have to warn him–help him and the people there."

David tried to laugh. "Calm down and let's talk. We're all in some kind of danger these days."

She pulled away from him. "This isn't a joke, Dave. There's this seer in Elkhart now who has been having visions about the future. Our enemies are planning to bring more of their forces from Chicago out this way and kill us all. They underestimated us once. They won't make that mistake again."

David shook his head. "Tori, if you've come all the way here from Elkhart, you know for a fact that the enemy has been a major problem on this side as well. And we've been actively looking for ways to contact or reach the other side, but we haven't found one yet that works. I hope Mace and the others are all right, but we kind of have our hands full here on this side as it is. What else do you expect us to do?"

Tori shook her head. "I don't know, but the enemy has at least one or more ways back and forth that they control. The seer saw it all in one of her visions. The enemy is going to use them to combine more of their forces from both sides into one massive army, and obliterate Mace and everyone else on the other side who stands against them. Then they'll come here and do the same thing to us."

Divide, combine, and conquer.

David looked away for a moment, his mind racing. No one could stand before the sheer might of an enemy force that huge.

Tori grabbed him again. "Don't you understand, Dave? If we can't find a way to stop them–all of us on both sides are as good as dead!"

Tori's head drooped back and her eyes rolled up white in her head.

"Is she hurt?" David asked.

The messengers shook their heads. "She's exhausted. She told us that she's been traveling nonstop for three days from Elkhart to find you. She insisted on it, despite her fatigue."

"She is very brave," Jerriel said, "and also very pretty."

"She's Mason sweetheart," David said. "She is one of us now, and will stay among us. David recognized one of the troops with her. "Sergeant Caufield?"

"Yes, sir?"

"Put her on a stretcher and bring her to our unit medical station. See that she is given the best care possible. Keep runners nearby to alert us when her condition improves. Guard her carefully and keep her safe."

"Yes, sir. It will be done, Captain."

David muttered to Jerriel. "I bet Mason is worried sick about her. We must find a way to contact him and send word. When Tori feels better, perhaps she can send him a letter with the dispatches we want to send over."

Jerriel nodded. "I will speak to our Traveler," she said. "We will find a way to reach your good friend, Daeved. But we must remain here for now. An alliance with the Thulls of Tornhold would be a major accomplishment. If you have ever seen an army of Thulls in combat, it is a stirring sight indeed. We need to do all that we can to make this champion and his people our ally and friend."

But right now, that meant letting the big Thul sleep it off again.

They held a light weapons practice with their troops and the Gay Town militia to pass the time that afternoon.

Alejandro, always a more of peacock than he namesake eagle, made a big impression among the locals. That garnered romantic overtures from several interested parties, all of them male. Gracious and flattered, but not being gay, Al declined the opportunity to spend a few days there. With great regret, of course.

The Gay Town militia had a few of their people who knew their way around a blade or some other such weapon. They also had several good archers and crossbow shooters. Two lesbians were experts with spears and quarterstaffs.

Even David and Jerriel had their hands full sparring with them.

People learned quickly to defend themselves with hordes of monsters trying to kill and eat them. And many people found that they had a natural aptitude for one weapon or fighting style or another. In the downtime from guard duty and work details, there was usually time to practice.

There was something to learn from everyone.

Around dusk, the big Thul actually woke up.

He stretched and went out to one of the public latrines to unload a bit. He barely squeezed into it.

Everyone backed away from all that.

"My friends," Al said, pointing at the porta-john, "I'm never going to go into that one. I suggest we have it taken out, burned, and then the remains buried."

After another half hour of humming and whistling inside the porta-john, their new guest emerged, happy and refreshed. He walked right up to Jerriel and started talking to her in rapid-fire Tharanorian, as if they were old friends.

David picked out some words, but even he couldn't keep up. And he thought that he could speak Tharanorian with Jerriel pretty well.

He found the Thul's accent very strange. It threw him off. Jerriel told them that Thulls had their own language, simply called 'Thuldoran.'

Regular, Tharanorian was actually a common or trade language that most of the nations used.

Jerriel finally raised a hand and turned to David and their friends, but the Thul kept rambling on, and gesturing broadly with great sweeps of his huge arms and hands.

"He says that he thanks us warmly for our wonderful hospitality. He hasn't always been welcomed and treated so well among the people of Urth, as he calls you. "Urthers," to be exact. His name is ThulKazar and he is one of the princes. As I guessed, he is also great champion and explorer among his people, and has traveled far and wide and faced many dangers to reach this place of the White Waters and the southern river bends of the Great River Jo. He says he has much news of the Merge and from the surrounding wide world to tell us.

"He does not speak much Urther, and only knows a few of your words. We will have to speak to him in Tharanorian, and translate anything he says to us. I do not speak much Thuldoran. I could lend him use my damaged mindstone. That might help speed things along."

David nodded. "Let's introduce ourselves and bring him before the council. That way he won't have to repeat himself much. Make him understand that he needs to go with us to speak to our leaders."

Jerriel spoke rapidly with ThulKazar, both of them gesturing and bantering back and forth. They looked very serious, but at last the big visitor smiled again, and even laughed.

"Yo, ho!" he roared, without warning.

Unexpectedly, he scooped Jerriel up into the air, his enormous hands encircling her slender waist, hugged her several times, and set her back down.

David blinked and grinned.

"I'd say you've made a new friend," he told her.

Jerriel only rolled her eyes.

"Either that or we are now engaged."

David felt himself pale. He wasn't too happy with that.

Jerriel grinned. "I was kidding, Daeved. Remember, we definitely want the Thulls on our side. You would not want them for enemies."

"Good enough," David said. "I think we're doing all we can."

"Daeved, the Thulls northeast of here would make tremendous allies. As much as ThulKazar didn't want to admit it, they're in trouble, too, along with everyone else. The Merge has left everyone confused, reeling, divided, and vulnerable to every enemy out there."

ThulKazar had no mount and did not know how to ride a bike, even if they had one big enough for him. Therefore they walked with him back across town, their bikes at their sides.

The Thul champion continued to speak at them the entire time. Jerriel translated as best she could.

"Daeved, he says that his people have heard about the Urthers here and in other places. The Thulls have heard about their bravery in battle against the monster hordes. That is why he and others from his people have been sent out as messengers to offer alliances with the Thulls."

"Thank him for his valor and the many hardships he has overcome in the wilds to reach us with this wealth of information and the good will of his people."

ThulKazar laughed and rattled off something briefly.

Jerriel laughed as well. "He says it was nothing. And well worth the bountiful food and drink we fed him. Especially the toast. He looks forward to fighting beside us, feasting, and getting drunk with us. For a puny people who eat and drink like birds, we seem amazingly tough and fit for battle, despite our size. At least to him."

"Hmmm...well, thank him again for such a compliment, I guess."

"That's about all the praise you're going to get from a Thul, until he sees you split some skulls. Oh, and don't go bathing with him, if he asks you to. I'll explain, later."

ThulKazar went on again for a good long while as they continued walking through the town on a fine, but cool late spring evening.

"He says that the Urthers to the east, north, and south of us are in grave danger, and that we should consider rushing to their aid."

"Elkhart?" David said. "We know about some of the troubles there. What news does he have?"

"He came through that way during his travels."

They went up Angela and reached the intersection with 933. Horns blew wildly, drums pounded, and the militia held people back along both sides of the road.

"What is it?" Jason Inada asked. "It's almost sunset. Are they having some weird type of parade?"

"There's nothing like that scheduled," David said. "Let's get up there."

31

A few days later, Mason returned from a patrol duty shift and learned from Blondie and the other mages that Rabbi Bergman, the Traveler mage from the other side, had popped in on them again.

This time Bergman came to them in person–in the flesh–via a transport spell that he himself had helped devise, in conjunction with the mages on his side of Michiana.

This new spell opened a temporary portal that the mage could pass through, but it did not last very long, and they were unsure whether it would work both ways, or have to be cast again from the other side. They also weren't sure if it was safe for anyone besides the mage casting it, to attempt to use it.

Apparently there had been some kind of prior, serious injury to another mage during an ill-fated, experimental attempt.

Bergman couldn't stay long, but as promised, he brought a wealth of information with him from the other side–including lots of magic data and research. The backpack he carried held many items. Several letters of introduction were included from various leaders on the other side, including offers and proposals of an obvious alliance. There were several, partial spell books in English, with various types of magical research and instruction, including basic transport magic and enchanting.

There were technical details and treatises, outlining what was working for the other side and what wasn't.

There were also numerous copies of their newspapers, detailing certain events as they had unfolded. Military accounts of certain battles and exploration attempts. Future plans for modifying dwellings, raising food, fortifying the town, using steam power once more, and seeking solutions to various problems the city faced. And finally, a copy of a working map up to that point.

Blondie said that he had quickly looked through the stuff, and then had Mason take it over to Major Bill for him and intel to sort it out further, and finish arranging a packet of similar answers and information in response.

"I don't have time for most of this diplomatic crap," Blondie said. "Tell Bill I'll pass along the spell books and magic books, after we have a chance to study and copy over anything we don't already have. We'll send the other side what we know that they don't, and that can go back over with the response. But most of this is political and development junk that I don't even work with. So it's better off going to Major Bill and the other leaders."

Now the leaders on their side could examine everything and finalize a response of their own, detailing where they were in many of the same fields. Perhaps by comparing notes, they could learn a few things, and pass on data, info, and breakthroughs, saving each other a great deal of time, which otherwise would end up being wasted doing much of the same things on both sides.

If only a reliable way of sending information and persons back and forth could be devised that did not simply rely on one person being the only courier.

This trip, Bergman had dropped off a backpack of stuff, spoken for a few fleeting seconds, and then popped back through his spell before it faded. He would try to return again later that same day or the next, to pick up their responses and bring them back.

A decision had been made to not inform the public about these fledging crossover attempts until later. The public outcry might be huge on both sides. They could imagine individual cries from people wanting to go from one side to the other for various reasons. Or the sheer danger that could awake during thunderstorms, with people jumping into pools of Wild Magic in the hopes that they would cross over. While the facts indicated that the random effects of such pools could vary and be quite dangerous.

But even among those in the know, the visits awoke no small amount of buzz and speculation.

Then ominous reports from the scouts and spotters clearly noted that large bands of the enemy were on the move, shuffling around the perimeter of Michiana in the far distance.

The militia went on high alert.

The mages and their students were busy that day, going over much of the new information from the other side and preparing a response to send back, at the next opportunity.

Blondie and Koden both agreed that such information should be kept from the other four helper mages, for now. They were all kept out of the loop and given other duties elsewhere.

Later than evening, Bergman came and went in seconds, as promised. He only took time enough to pick up their backpack of responses. He merely reported that the process was exhausting for him, and that he might require a day's rest between trips. He was adjusting to the process, as well.

With all of the excitement, another busy day passed quickly. All of them had plans for dinner. The four remaining helper mages returned to their quarters under guard where they were usually held, in comfort, but locked in and confined to those quarters.

The mages in training stuck together and usually went to the same mess hall, where they had a special time to eat and were served separately. Intel wanted to control what and how they were fed as a security precaution, due to the fact that mages were now so valuable.

Koden smiled like a newlywed and couldn't wait to get home to his new, little guarded house nearby. He and Sharon had just picked it out and moved in together. They were busily painting rooms, picking out furnishings, and actually talking about getting married very soon. Much like Blondie, Koden seemed both happy, and very worried about the future at the same time.

Sharon was also a pretty good cook, from the way Koden boasted. And she enjoyed having a nice, simple supper ready for the two of them to sit down to when Koden came home.

The enemy troop movements outside of Michiana also kept everyone on edge.

Mason, Thulkara, and Rodell waited for Blondie to go to dinner with them at another place. But as usual, the Mage Captain begged off, and insisted that he would join them later, once he was finished. He also warned them that he might bring Jen with him. She was apparently on the mend, and doing much better.

They had heard all of that before and merely groaned as they left. Many times Blondie wouldn't show up at all, and worked through the night on some project he was obsessed with. Sometimes he would show, famished and ready to get good and drunk to relieve some of the pressure he was under.

And then there were the times he actually did bring Jen. She was always a hoot, that wild gal. Anything could happen with her around.

Mason and his two companions went past the mages in training as the latter were dining at the appointed mess tent. To Mason's surprise, the mages were singing a song together and appeared to be drinking something they passed around in several bottles, that looked to be champagne. Some of the mage recruits poured it into their cups and sucked it down like water. That was all very odd to Mason.

"Where's the duty officer and the intel people?" Mason muttered to his friends. "Drinking isn't allowed in the mess tents. Only in the taverns and bars. We should check this out."

Thulkara and Rodell shrugged and followed his lead.

The new mages spotted them, and called to them to join them in their celebration.

Mason smiled and put them off, going to the mess tent service leader instead. "What's going on here? These people aren't supposed to bring in outside drink, let alone alcohol. Where's the duty officer, and the intel people?"

"I don't know, Sergeant. These people brought the stuff with them and started opening it and sucking it down. We just run the line; we don't have any authority to tell them what to do. They brought it with them, so we guessed it must be all right. From the look of things, I'd say it's too late now."

That's what he was afraid of. Mason turned to his friends. "There's something not right about this," he insisted. "I don't like it."

They went to the mages themselves, who by then were happy and sassy from passing the dozen or so bottles around.

"Where'd all of this champagne come from?" Mason demanded. "Who gave you guys this stuff? You're not supposed to drink booze in the mess halls."

One of the mage recruits answered, "Relax, Sarge. It was a gift from our instructors, for all of our hard work," she said. "We think it must have been Koden. Because he doesn't have a stick up his ass like the Mage Captain does. That slave driver!"

Then the mages started to pass out and drop wherever they were—every one of them. Mason quickly checked their pulse and breathing with Thulkara.

Rodell examined the bottles and then some of the cups some of them drank out of. He tasted something odd and spit it back out upon the ground. "Mace, we've got a problem. I could be wrong, but I think they've been poisoned. Both the booze, and the cups they used have been tainted with something. Whoever did this, wanted to make sure they got them all."

Thulkara looked even more worried. "I think…they're all dying."

Mason whistled for the guards and the night watch. They sent for a full battlefield stretcher team and medics from the infirmary. All the while, the condition of the mages appeared to worsen. Rodell sent several cups and bottles to the medical people to try to identify what the poison could be.

Messengers ran to inform Major Avery and Blondie.

Horns and drums suddenly awoke in the darkness, close up to the defenses.

Then the sounds of battle erupted.

Word swept through the city quickly. The monsters were making an all-out night attack on the outer lines.

"None of this is an accident," Mason said as the militia force and medical teams took over. They would get the stricken mages to the infirmary and do whatever could be done for them. "Come with me, my friends. I have a bad feeling about this. And if Koden did have a hand in this, we need to determine that as well."

First, Mason led them to the quarters of the four remaining enemy helper mages. At a glance, everything looked all right. The guards were at their posts. All four of the quarters appeared to be quiet.

Then Mason called out to the guards to look in on the mages.

No response.

They rushed up. "Are they asleep?" Thulkara asked.

"They're still alive, but they're propped up," Mason said. "Check on the mages."

"This is the work of magic," Rodell said. "They've all been stunned."

Thulkara peeked in at the quarters. "These two are gone."

Mason checked the other pair. "Yeah, just like I feared. Ettal and Resh are both gone, too. We'd better get over to Koden's place to see if he's a part of this."

"They had to have some kind of inside help to pull this off," Rodell noted.

"I know that," Mason said. "I just can't believe that Koden would do it. He's so happy. But we can't take any chances. Thulkara, I need you to get to the front and talk to Major Bill. He's going to have his hands full and be distracted, but let him know what's going on here, behind the lines. Then meet us back at the compound to help protect Blondie. Our guests might simply use the attack as cover to escape, or they might try to do some more damage to us before they bug out. Go and get back as fast as you can."

Thulkara nodded. "You can count on me, Mace." She gave Rodell a weird glance. "Watch yourselves."

Mason and Rodell carefully sped over to Koden's house.

The small home was mostly dark and quiet in the early part of the night. Nothing seemed wrong at first. The lights inside seemed to come from the back part of the house, in the kitchen area.

"No guards," Mason noted once again. "There are supposed to be several guards stationed here, watching this place."

"They've been neutralized and hidden somewhere, either stunned or killed," Rodell added.

"Let's sneak around back where the lights are. Maybe we can look inside through one of the windows."

As they made their way around back, the small house seemed to be buttoned up tight, the curtains drawn.

But around back, the windows were open for the summer, and Mason could hear low voices talking.

They peeked in over the kitchen sink, spotting movement. The only lamp that was lit seemed to be in the nearby dining room, not the kitchen

Koden was bound to a chair at his ankles and wrists. A gag was in his mouth, and Ettal and Tharin were punching and slapping him. But despite their abuse, Koden kept straining to look into the kitchen.

Mason went up on his tiptoes and looked down.

Resh had Sharon down on the kitchen floor, sitting across her stomach. Sharon was tied up and gagged also. Resh was staring down at her, and his face twitched as if there were snakes and bugs under his skin.

A block of kitchen knives was next to Sharon's bruised and battered face.

Resh selected a knife from the block and moved down lower. He slowly began cutting Sharon's pants and blouse off of her, indifferent as to whether he made her bleed along the way.

Koden could see the whole thing, and strained against his bonds, trying to break free. Ettal grabbed a steak knife from the table and plunged it into Koden's right thigh to get his attention. Koden snapped his head back in pain.

Tharin seemed to enjoy that, and plunged another steak knife in Koden's other leg, and then one in the upper left arm.

"They're going to kill them both," Mason said. "You use magic and blast in the front door. Take those two bastards down any way you can, but try not to hurt Koden any further, or set the place on fire."

"No promises," Rodell said. "That's two against one. What about Resh?"

"Let me worry about Resh. I'll come in from the back. You're the distraction. I'll move when you strike."

They didn't see Gellonar. Where was he? That wasn't good.

199

Mason got ready, and waited by the back door where the laundry room was. That door was already broken in. Maybe one or more of them had come in that way at first. But that also made it easier and quieter for Mason.

He slipped in, and could hear Resh softly cackling to Sharon as he continued to work on her with those knives.

Rodell blew the front door off its hinges and sent it crashing into the wall. So much happened all at once after that.

Mason charged into the kitchen just as Resh rose up to look out.

The haft of Mason's spear rammed into Resh's guts, winding him and driving him back off the young woman.

Out in the dining room, Tharin panicked and dove out a window, crashing through the glass to get away.

Ettal had magefire on his hands and halfway up his arms, as he and Rodell squared off.

Resh's hands also began to glow. He recognized Mason and smiled. "Die!" he shouted.

Mason whipped his spear around and shoved the point past Resh's teeth and out the back of his head and neck, pinning him to the door of the kitchen pantry.

Resh hung there, and sat back, twitching and convulsing, choking on his own blood until he went still. The glow from his hands quickly faded. Mason yanked his spear back out.

Sharon looked okay for the moment. Mason had to help Rodell. And Koden was stuck in their crossfire.

Ettal got his spell off first and swept a wave of razor-sharp ice blades at Rodell, who dove behind a sofa. It got shredded instead of him.

Rodell cast a spell that either looked like spreading roots or snakes, writhing across the floor to try to ensnare Ettal.

Mason just missed gigging Ettal on his spear, but the bugger was already dashing to his right, and dove out the same window that Tharin had used.

"You check on Koden," Mason said. "I'll get Sharon." Mason blew his sergeant's whistle repeatedly, hoping that neighbors or the night watch or someone would come to help.

It bothered him greatly that Ettal, Tharin, and possibly Gellonar, were all three still on the loose. They could even double back and attack them with magic. But most likely, they'd clear out.

Blondie. After they secured Koden and Sharon, they had to get to him next. Blondie was the next one in danger now, especially if the escape mages could locate the other five prisoners, including the dangerous necromancer. Luckily, those five enemy mages were all hidden in separate, isolated locations. And only a few people knew where they were.

Finally, a few neighbors wandered over to help. Then the local night watch arrived. Koden was worse off than Sharon, but both of them had been beaten badly and need to go to the aid station for treatment of their injuries.

Once they had the pair stabilized, Mason took off their gags. He asked Koden, who looked a bit dizzy, "Hey, Koden, it's me, Mace. Did you send a case of champagne–booze–to the other mages to celebrate with?"

"No...what booze? It wasn't me. Sharon...how is she?"

"She's fine, just a few cuts. You're injured more than she is." So, if Koden hadn't send the poisoned booze to the mages, who did? Perhaps anyone who knew where the mage recruits ate could have done so, and also tainted the cups.

Sharon started calling out for Koden.

Mason tried to reassure them both. "You two are safe now. Resh is dead. We have to go out and track down Ettal and Tharin. We think they might be going after Blondie next."

Mason ran out the wrecked front door opening. "Come on, Rodell."

Rodell ran with him. "Mace, I don't know if this is a good time or not, but I have a slight confession to make."

"Sheesh, Rodell. You've got some dire surprise for me, too?"

"I'm still on your side; don't worry. But Prince Shaeddor was kind of right about me. I'm not Korean, or even an Urther. I'm a Darshian agent and sorcerer from Dorundia, sent to spy on the Khabal. I'm already a full mage."

"Damn it, Rodell. You're from Cleveland and you didn't tell me?"

"I couldn't. That was my cover. I came here, using magic right before the Merge hit. Then my powers were messed up for a while, until I figured out how to use them again. I'm and agent of Darshia, and I was on my way to Vaejan to spy on them. We had suspicions that the Dark Khabal was trying to take over the Sylurrian colonies."

"Well, I'd say those suspicions are confirmed by now."

"And Mace, there's something else you need to know. It gets worse."

"Great. Now what?"

"I'm pretty sure your friend Shaeddor is the traitor behind all of this. It's the only thing that makes sense."

32

David and his group made their way through the crowd lining the highway up toward Roseland. Everyone stared at ThulKazar like the gigantic figure he was, and made way for them all.

The crowd continued to thicken at the intersection of Douglas and 933 near St. Mary's and the Inn. In the near twilight, the last rays of the sunset fell upon the stirring sight of well-ordered military units marching down the broad street in formation. Banners and pennants waved, drums boomed, and battle horns blared.

About three thousand troops in all, and from the looks of things, they had seen combat along the way.

First came sixty scouts or skirmishers, lightly armed and armored to be able the move quickly, short horse bows across their chests, long swords and fighting daggers at their sides on wide armored belts. Their soft boots and high leggings were dusty with mud and travel. They wore mottled, hooded cloaks of green and brown to hide them in the wilderness. Some carried short fighting spears. Several at the rear of their unit rode smaller, powerful horses that looked both fast, compact, and strong.

"Who are they?" David asked Jerriel as the newcomers filed past.

She turned to him and smiled.

ThulKazar roared something at them that sounded like half an insult, but the skirmishers merely grinned and laughed. They spotted the big Thul and pointed at him in surprise.

"They're emissaries from the Marrandorians!" Jerriel said. "From Kellendra, due east. Where your Toledoo was."

"That's Toledo."

"That's where I was going when the Merge hit. I was trying to reach my mother's people to ask for their help."

Another fanfare. Two hundred pikes. Then four hundred infantry troops marching with bright, drawn longswords and lozenge-shaped shields. All in livery of green, white, and orange, a fierce, rampant tiger emblazoned on every breast, shield, pennant, and banner.

"Has the Great Lord of Kellendra come himself?" Jerriel said. "I've yet to see the main herald and the primary banner."

David craned his neck to see what could fill even Jerriel with such awe and wonder. It was, in fact, a very stirring sight, and the sound of many armored horses came their way as well. But they could not see them yet for the crowd.

Cheering erupted ahead of their approach.

First came a flight of three hundred longbow archers.

Then fifty Marrandorian wizards and mages in shimmering, elaborate robes. Some of their staffs of power in their hands sprayed light and color into the sky around them like fireworks as they rode past on their mounts.

"Excellent," Jerriel said. "More wizards. They can help me with my students. I think I know some of those mages."

ThulKazar laughed and said something disparaging about wizards.

Jerriel giggled, shoved him, and told him to shut up in Tharanorian.

After the wizards, finally, in full blazing color and panoply of war, marched two hundred knights, their enormous horses fully armored, stepping in time to the music of the drummers and minstrels surrounding them. Magnificent.

The knights paraded forward in two long lines. Colorful heralds rode before them. The two most glorious knights at the head of both columns wore silver crowns on their helms and had squires on palfreys on either side of them bearing their bright banners.

Jerriel gasped and looked slightly worried. "See the cadence marks on those banners? They are not those of the king, but of his valiant sons—the royal princes. His twins: Crown Prince Valandin and his younger brother, Prince Alendel."

"You don't seem completely happy that they're here," David said. "What is it you're not telling me, Jerriel? What's wrong?"

She lowered her gaze and shook her head. "It's nothing, really. I am glad to see them. They're my friends. I know their family well, for we are distant cousins. My mother was the granddaughter of one of the Queen's older sisters. It's very complicated."

"I think I'm already confused."

"Don't worry, I'll explain it all in detail when there's time. I grew up with the twins and my other cousins at the court of Kellendra for a long while." She hesitated.

"But you do need to know that there was a time when Prince Valandin and I were...betrothed from birth...to be married."

David tried not to let his mouth fall open.

"You're engaged to the crown prince of...wherever. Does he know?"

Jerriel shook her head again and chuckled. "Of course he knows. I mean, he knew full well. He released me from that silly obligation years ago, but he still teases me about it unmercifully. Although he has had several lovers since we were together. Last I heard, he was engaged to a quite stunning princess from Darshia."

David choked. "When you were together? You dated this guy? Were you two...?"

Jerriel smiled sadly. "Daeved, you must understand that Valandin and I were young, foolish, and quite fond of each other. It was the first time for both of us. Very sweet and awkward. It only lasted for a few weeks.

"I had to travel with my parents and my family for a time. We tried to write to each other. I busied myself with my magic studies. He met other pretty girls. I was sad for a time, but we let each other go and decided to remain friends."

She waved her hand at the prince. "See, it all turned out for the best. Now they have traveled here to become our allies."

The princes were almost up to them. Jerriel waved. David still hesitated. Although he rationalized that any feelings of jealousy on his part were completely idiotic and ridiculous.

He still felt them.

Between them, the two princes spoke closely with one of the linguists, Theo Miller, who rode up and met them on a farm horse. Compared to the grand war horses, it looked like a pony.

The princes finally spotted Jerriel, lifted their visors, and called out to her. Both of them were very happy to see her. But they had to keep going, obviously on their way to meet the town council.

Identical twin princes. Great. Both of them just happened to be incredibly tall, gray-eyed, and amazingly handsome. It figured.

Did he seriously expect them to be short, fat, and ugly?

No, Jerriel would never have a lover that was unworthy of her.

As they went past, the linguist motioned urgently to David and Jerriel to come along.

As if they were going to stay behind.

"What about the younger twin?" David asked.

"Alendel? Oh, he's the quiet one, usually. Valandin usually does most of the talking. Alendel is always there to defend and protect his brother. Even I had trouble telling them apart sometimes. They can mimic each other at will. Valandin says it's useful and sometimes they do it just for fun."

The knights had all gone past by then. More ranks of infantry and archers, and the supply train and rear guard for their force came up behind them.

"What good is an identical twin if you can't mess with people?" David finally said.

"Exactly. Come, Daeved. We'll be able to speak with them at the council."

"Right. And don't forget, we have ThulKazar with us too."

"Oh, don't worry. No one's going to forget about him. I'm sure he'll make his presence known." In fact, as they walked, the Thul champion looked in good humor. He broke out into a deep-throated song.

Everyone winced and covered their ears. In the distance, all of the dogs began to howl.

Under lantern light, the town council held a packed evening session for the newcomers at the Morris Theater. Militia units had to hold the public back, interest was so high. A full report was promised in the paper the next day. Only so many people could fit inside.

David and his friends tagged along with Jerriel and ThulKazar, weaving their way through the chaos. Tori was feeling better rested and joined them in the midst of all the excitement. She grabbed David by the arm.

"Dave, I wrote a letter to Mace and sent it to him. You should write something to him, when you get a chance."

He smiled. "I will, Tori. So much has happened today. I'm glad you're feeling better. You're staying with us from now on, under our protection. Stay together; we have to go in or we'll lose our spot."

Jerriel turned to Tori as they continued to shuffle along. "I've heard so much about Daeved's amazing friend Mason. The tales from the other side about him and his weapons are astounding. But what is Mason like as a person?"

Tori's face lit up from within whenever she talked about Mason. David grinned, happy for his good friend.

"He's wonderful," Tori said. "Sweet and romantic. We were so happy together. I really miss him. I can believe we're separated like this. But he is a bit of nut about all of the pistol shooting stuff. I practiced with him sometimes, and went with him to some of his competitions. We always had fun together."

"You know," Jerriel suddenly said. "There isn't time right now, but I should test you for a magical ability at some point."

Tori smirked and waved a hand. "Yeah, I don't think there's anything magical about me."

"You never know," Jerriel said.

Tori laughed. "I do. They say your hands glow at some point, if you're a mage of some kind. I've never had that happen to me. Not even a spark."

"It doesn't always work that way," Jerriel told her.

Jerriel and Tori lowered their voices and spoke quietly together. They even looked back at him once or twice. David kept them trundling along.

The town linguistics team was quickly being taxed to its limits with so many Tharanorians to speak with.

But at last the guests were ushered in and seated, those who wanted to speak crowded together on stage.

The council decided that ThulKazar should speak first. Then Prince Valandin. Both of them had urgent information to share with the council. They barely had time to meet and share words with one another.

Jerriel stood ready to translate, but just as ThulKazar was about to begin, the Marrandorian wizards called to her and produced a small chest of translation medallions. They gave one to her, another to ThulKazar, and the rest to the town council. It was an incredibly generous gift.

They functioned much like Jerriel's translation crystal, but were made slightly less for adornment and much more for durability. They consisted of a thick silver filet with a silver medallion hanging from it, covered on both sides with magical symbols in Marrandorian.

Jerriel held up several of the artifacts from the chest with many thanks. She pointed them out to the assembly, speaking into the megaphone. "These translation medallions will help our guests speak with us and greatly advance our language studies. When properly trained and attuned, people with these artifacts can also send messages to one another over great distances—up to hundreds of miles. The princes of Marrandor have brought many of these enchanted artifacts with them, and offer them freely to the town council as their gift."

That brought on a healthy round of standing applause.

The princes and their wizards already wore such medallion. Jerriel held one up to put it on ThulKazar. He almost had to bend in half for her to reach his head.

ThulKazar looked a bit apprehensive as Jerriel arranged it, setting the medallion barely around his thick neck.

The big Thul turned to address the assembly through the megaphone as he saw Jerriel do.

"Does this sorcery work? Do you hear my words?"

"Yes," the crowd responded

"Then hail and well met, friends of Michiana. Greetings from the Thulls of Tornhold!" He saluted them with his mighty fists.

A great cheer went up from the council and the crowd.

ThulKazar looked very pleased, and shoved his thumbs into his broad iron-bound belt and squared his stance.

"Leaders of the Urthers, noble princes and wizards, brave warriors. The lords of battle from Tornhold on the Great Eastern Sea have sent out myself and other champions from our people as messengers and emissaries to offer treaties of alliance with any who will stand against our mutual enemies in these dark times."

He still spoke with the same thick accent as before, and gestured as broadly as he always did, but it sounded as if he spoke English.

"Our worlds have been broken and the pieces jumbled up. Hordes of evil creatures roam the wilds at will. Countless people have died. Many others have been enslaved. Who knows what the losses are, both on Urth and on Tharanor? Chaos and despair hold sway in many places. Our magicks have been disrupted.

"But if we stand together. If we fight side by side, we can meet these threats and crush them. Even now, your human comrades east of here in Elkhart are in great danger. They are about to be overwhelmed by foes from within and without. The Dragon Cult there must be crushed, as well as the bandits allied with the cultists. But even worse, many other formidable enemies from the Dark Khabal Wizards have joined the battle in earnest!

"I urge you to gather every able warrior you have and rush to Elkhart's aid! If that city falls, you will find yourselves hemmed in by foes from the east, to the west. And it will be difficult for any aid from Tornhold or Kellendra to reach you. Do not delay. I am willing to march with your troops this very night!"

The crowd went wild.

Crown Prince Valandin stood up and took his place at the megaphone.

"ThulKazar, mighty champion of a mighty people. Good gentles. I also bear tidings concerning these grave threats to us all. My great friend and ally, will you yield the floor to me so that I may speak?"

ThulKazar bowed. "By all means. I have said most of what I came to say. This is not a time for talk. We must act. We must march. And we must fight!"

Prince Valandin took the floor and the big Thul stepped back.

"Good people of Urth. I fear that ThulKazar speaks true. These threats are real, and they are urgent. The evils of the Dragon Cult has spread. Worse, they have allied themselves with shadow sorcerers and necromancers from the Dark Khabal. They raise armies of undead minions to fight for them. They open portals to the Void and the Abyss, gateways to the Nine Hells, and seek to bring dark allies through to join their ranks: goat-like grun, ghool lords, slurgs, shadowspawn—even demons and horrors we cannot even name.

"We fought these creatures on our way here, and suffered hundreds of losses reaching you. They did not want us to reach this council to bring you these dire warnings. Our father, the courageous King of Kellendra, fears that these forces are attempting to seize power in this entire region. Your fight is the struggle of all Urthers and Tharanorians—to remain free. I agree with the champion of the mighty Thulls. We must rush to the immediate aid of your brothers and sisters in the city you call Elkhart. I implore you to gather together as many forces as you can muster and march forth this very night!"

Dirk Blackwood rose up after a quick review from the council.

"The town council concurs. Unanimously. We must leave sufficient forces in place to maintain our security, but let the word go out for our troops to prepare for battle and march toward Elkhart. The muster goes out at this moment. Our war council will need as much information as you can give us concerning the threats we'll be facing."

Valandin bowed again. "We will do so. We are honored to fight beside you, and beside the Thulls. Let us prepare for battle!"

33

Mason and Rodell arrived at Blondie's compound and found many of the guards there already blasted to death, and sounds of fierce fighting emanating from within.

Several large explosions rocked the old warehouse, blowing out the sidewalls and windows. The entire south end buckled and partially collapsed, cutting off the entrances and the stairs on that end.

Mason clambered up the slope of wreckage and debris, while the magic battle continued up above them on the third floor.

Blondie's floor.

Ice blades sliced through the walls and windows, showering down more glass and wreckage.

A violet lightning blast took out part of the wall on the opposite side. More of the roof collapsed within.

Mason covered himself with his shield. He still nearly got crushed to the ground when a large chunk of debris bounced off of it. Rodell took cover briefly under a section of fallen wall panel.

They finally climbed and crawled their way into the building on the second floor, and raced toward a section that was still intact, and debris wasn't raining down.

Then they headed toward the back stairs.

But then the battle on the floor above them carried back that way as well. They were racing up the stairs when powerful magic and spells peppered the structure from up above. The corner of the building seemed to burst from within, and the stairs lurched, filling with wreckage and dust. It threatened to topple over and collapse.

Both of them made a leap for the railing of the third floor landing. Mason grabbed hold of it. Rodell scrambled to hang onto Mason's armor. They pulled themselves up and went through the door on their hands and knees.

Mason rolled to the side with his spear as something whizzed past his head. Rodell tried to duck, but there were dozens of wooden spheres smacking into everything. One clipped Rodell on the head, a glancing blow; but enough to drop him to the ground, moaning and dazed.

When Mason had a chance to glance up, he saw Blondie dueling both Ettal and Tharin, holding them off, but just barely. They were all shouting at each other, but with half of the building collapsing and crashing down, Mason couldn't hear what was being said.

The distance was too great for a spear cast, and Mason wanted to stay out of the range of their spells. But there was an entire shelf of rock and mineral samples that had toppled over onto the floor. Some of them were a good size to throw.

Mason put his spear and shield down for the moment, and began chucking rocks at Ettal and Tharin, hoping to at least distract or possibly injure them, in effort to help Blondie.

He missed, but succeeded in getting their attention, and they both fired spells at him, most likely thinking him in his uniform and helmet to merely be another guard.

Mason took cover behind some old archery mantlets, stacked up to one side. A wood splinter spell peppered the mantlets. An exploding needle spell blasted the first two to bits.

He peeked out, another rock ready to throw.

Blondie emerged from behind a heavy metal desk and nailed Tharin with some kind of force bolts that drove him off his feet and hurled him twenty-five feet away, out the gaping hole in the third floor wall.

Now that it was just the two of them, Blondie stood up to square off with Ettal in a final duel.

"Mace, stay back," Blondie said. "This one's mine. I've been waiting to deal with him."

Ettal fumed. "Bloody, stinking traitor. I'll be the one to send your black soul screaming into hell. How dare you turn on your own kind for these stinking, worthless Urthers? You're all dead. All of you!"

Blondie shimmered in a strange way, kind of like a mirror.

Ettal cast one of those black ray spells that always seemed to end in some kind of messy death.

Blondie deflected it to one side. Then a second Blondie appeared to the right, just as the other image vanished. He deflected and banked the spell right back at his opponent. Ettal was impaled upon his own reflected attack.

Only Blondie curled his lip and added to the spell's power several-fold.

Ettal arched up on his toes and wailed as every organ and muscle of his body ruptured and exploded from within. For an instant, before his brain and everything else burst, he looked like a bunch of expanding, blood-filled grapes and small balloons, swelling up out of his rending flesh and snapping sinew and bone.

Blondie quickly placed the shield of a water barrier around Ettal to cut down on the splattering mess just before the wizard popped. Then Blondie used the water as a wave, to sweep what was left of Ettal into the pile of ruin in the far corner.

Rodell recovered, rose to his feet, and joined them. Mason ran over to the open section of the wall and looked down, searching for Tharin's body. "I don't see Tharin. He might have survived the fall and gotten away."

"He's only one mage," Blondie said. "I'll secure my place here and go to Major Bill. I'll summon reinforcements to secure this area and hunt down Tharin. You two must go to our stricken mages and protect them at all costs. They're still vulnerable in their condition. Even someone like Tharin could kill many of them all at once time."

"I think we should stick with you and get to Major Bill," Mason said. "No one has seen Gellonar, either. He could be out there, too."

"I can handle myself, Mace. I'll be all right. Go make sure that our mages are well protected. That's a direct order. Please, you know I hate pulling rank on my friends. Just go make sure they remain safe. That's imperative right now."

Mason hesitated, but nodded. "Okay, Blondie. If that's the way you want it."

They climbed down the swath of wreckage on the south side and raced away from Blondie's magical compound. Ettal was dead, at least. Tharin and Gellonar were still at large somewhere in town. Perhaps they were now trying

211

to escape on their own. Maybe they were searching for the other five enemy mages, including the necromancer, Gultor.

And with the chaos of the monster attack that night and most likely into the morning, most of the militia units were on the line or near it, just in case this attack turned into a major enemy pushed.

They intercepted a runner from the unit, a message sent for Mason himself. From all of the signs, Major Bill told him that these attacks seemed to be nothing more than heavier probes and feints to detect weaknesses in the militia defenses. And also to see how many battle mages Michiana had now, and where the Pistolero and the Shooting Stars were.

Mason quickly sent the runner back with a quick verbal update on what was happening. They requested more troops.

First, according to what Blondie told them, Mason and Rodell had to check on the poisoned mages at the infirmary. In their helpless condition, the new mages would, in fact, be prime targets for any attempt to kill them all and wipe them out completely. In hindsight, perhaps it hadn't been wise to keep them all together in one place.

But when they arrived back on the scene, the unconscious mages had already being trucked out to other safe areas, in heavily-guarded wagons. Major Bill had been informed and wasn't taking any chances.

There really wasn't that much for them to do.

"Doesn't seem like we're needed here, at all," Mason said. "Blondie slipped up. Bill beat us all to the punch."

"This doesn't make any sense," Rodell noted. "Why would Blondie deliberately send us over here for no reason, especially if he already knew that the mages were going to be moved?"

Mason suddenly had an incredibly bad feeling in his gut. "Perhaps the word didn't reach him, what with the attack and all. But just maybe, to be sure, we should go back and ask him."

"But he was so insistent that we stay with the mages and protect them," Rodell said. "In a way, maybe he was still right. He even gave us direct orders to do so. And how did he already know that the poisoned mages weren't going to die, but remain helpless for a while?"

"Now I know something's wrong," Mason said. "Blondie never issued a direct order to anyone in his entire life, I'd bet. Why would he start now by giving one to us? This stinks. Something's up, and we need to find out what."

"Hey, look," Rodell said, "the guy on that stretcher over there. Doesn't that look like—"

"Gellonar...one of our missing enemy mages." They went over to the medics taking Gellonar away.

One other odd thing. For an escaped prisoner, Gellonar still had his magic suppression gauntlets on him.

"What happened to this one?" Mason asked the medics.

"Dunno, Sergeant. He was brought in half dead, found by the night watch somewhere nearby. Someone knocked him out and then stabbed him in the back. They left him to die, and he would have by morning, if he hadn't been found by night watch searchers. We patched him up, and since he was dressed like a mage, we put him here with the others."

"Keep a special watch on that one," Rodell told them. "His name is Gellonar. Make sure Major Avery is sent word about his condition and whereabouts."

"Will do."

"Rodell," Mason said. "I don't think Gellonar was a part of whatever's going on. He might have merely wanted to escape, or he might have been dragged along by Ettal, Resh, and Tharin–against his will."

"That would explain a great deal, and why Ettal and Resh didn't have their suppressor bands on, and Gellonar still does. Perhaps he tried to get away, gave them trouble, or wouldn't go along with their plans."

"With Ettal and Resh dead, maybe Tharin has gotten spooked, so he decided to ditch Gellonar, and make a run for it on his own."

"Or perhaps he's freeing all of the other enemy mages, even while we speak."

"That's also possible," Mason said. "But I think we still need to hurry back and see what our good friend Blondie is up to. Maybe he's just securing his workshop, like he told us, before going to Major Avery."

Rodell nodded. "Let's find out for sure. Hey, does Blondie know where all of the enemy mages are being held?"

"Yeah. He does."

They raced back to the magic compound, as quickly as they could.

They climbed up into the additional magical research building still under construction, adjacent to the main one, across the street. They had a good vantage point to spy across the way, and there were still lights on in Blondie's private third- floor lab.

Mason watched with binoculars. Rodell simply looked over.

Nothing much happened for a few minutes. Just as he said he would, Blondie rushed around, securing papers, notes, and books. He seemed to be gathering a backpack full of stuff to take with him when he left.

The question was, where was Blondie going?

"Uh, oh," Mason said. "Who the hell is that who just joined him?"

Rodell sucked in a breath. "That tears it. Look, that's Tharin and three of the other enemy mages who were locked up before. All four of them are free now, and none of them have their armbands on anymore."

"Tharin must have busted them out. But how did he know where to find them?"

Even as they watched, the four enemy mages obviously argued with Blondie back and forth, very intensely. Blondie produced a map and began pointing at it to the other four. They were clearly shouting at each other.

Rodell grabbed for Mason's binoculars. "Let me see those damn things. I can read lips and tell what they're debating."

Mason felt sick. Blondie was clearly working with the enemy to help them escape. There was no doubt about that now.

"They're arguing about the remaining mage and the necromancer. Shaeddor has shown the four where the other two mages are still being held, but he's trying to convince them that it is too far away, and that they need to escape and get away now. They're out of time. And they're still insisting that under the cover of the monster attacks, they can still spring the others. Three of them are now departing to go accomplish that goal, whether Blondie likes it or not. And they're also leaving Tharin behind to keep an eye on Shaeddor. They still don't trust him entirely, and they're worried that somehow he's going to leave them behind. Now Shaeddor is warning them all that he's the only one who knows how to get them out of the city and to safety. I don't know how he intends to do that."

From what Mason could see, the other three enemy mages had already left in a big hurry.

Five minutes after they were gone, Blondie must have said something wrong, because Tharin got upset and started pointing his finger and gesturing violently once more at Blondie.

"They've turned so that I can't read their lips," Rodell stated.

Blondie drilled Tharin into the corner with a lightning blast; more wreckage crashed down around Tharin. Then Blondie continued sorting through his papers and books and stuff in great haste.

Mason sighed. "I think we need to go have a talk with our friend and find out exactly what's happening," Mason said. None of it made sense. Blondie seemed to be playing everyone.

"Wait a minute," Rodell said.

To complicate stuff even further, Thulkara suddenly came up the partially ruined stairs from the opposite side, and started talking to Blondie in a hurry. She seemed oblivious to the fact that the enemy mages had just been there a few minutes before. But then, how would she know?

Blondie said a few things to her, and then Thulkara seemed to head toward another exit in a hurry, drawing a weapon in her hand.

"I think Blondie's sending her away," Mason said.

"Maybe on the same fake mission he tried to send us on," Rodell noted.

"Maybe. Let's try to catch Thulkara down below and let her know what's going on. She'd be a big help if Blondie turns on us. Let's go."

Mason still felt sick to his guts.

34

With militia units already stationed throughout Michiana, in a matter of hours, thirty thousand troops marched on Elkhart, rode on horses or bicycles, or pushed or pulled carts, wagons, and supplies.

Tori made friends with ThulKazar, Jason, Al, and the Blackhawks as they marched together. She had to put up with Alejandro's flirtations, but she seemed as if she could hold her own.

David and Jerriel still hadn't rested much since returning to town with their unit. Exhausted, they took some rest in one of the medical wagons for a few hours.

Dirk came by later and woke them up. "I know that you two have been running pretty hard, but there's still a lot of information we're trying to process. Something was very odd about that elderly woman you brought in."

"Did she have Alzheimer's or something?" David said. "She seemed so confused."

Dirk handed him a copy of the report, including a summary of her statements. "Actually, no. When she recovered sufficiently, she was quite calm and intelligent. She gave us her address. But it didn't show up on *our* maps of the city."

"How could that be?" Jerriel asked.

"Her house is located in a place where there isn't anything but Tharanorian forest now."

David and Jerriel gasped as it hit them.

"She's another crossover from the other side," Jerriel said.

"How did she get here?" David asked.

"That's where it continues to get interesting. She went out her back door to bring her dog inside. She stepped into a pool of some kind of glowing, blue-violet water in her backyard. Next thing she knew, in the blink of an eye, she found herself lost in the forest on the outskirts you found her in. She'd only been wandering around for less than an hour."

"What's happening on the other side?" David said. "The last we heard, our counterparts were expecting a major attack."

"We need to keep working with Bergman to develop those portal ideas of our own to get there and back," Jerriel said. "Our trooper and the lieutenant weren't vaporized when they stepped into that same kind of pool. Now we know for a fact that they were transported to the other side! Some of the magic pools have the power to transport people from one side to the next."

David thought about it. "It makes sense. But does each pool only function one way? Otherwise, they'd come right back through. If they could, or if they even thought about doing so."

Dirk sighed. "Our counterparts on the other side are facing the same threats we do. The hordes invaded there as well. They sacked much of the downtown and the city.

"But at last the enemy was driven out, surrounded, and wiped out. There are similar problems in Elkhart, but no Dragon Cult on their side—and no moon from what I hear. They have made contact with Tharanorians as well. Like us, their enclaves are isolated, worried, and under siege."

Jerriel studied the report Dirk handed them. "We'll need to rely on Rabbi Bergman. Daeved, did you read this? He's made amazing breakthroughs in transport magic while we were gone. He even studied the enemy cave in astral form and went back and forth through it. He has a basic understanding of its principles and thinks that, with time, he can work with me and the other enchanters to duplicate them in some fashion."

"Jerriel, that's exactly what we don't have right now. Time. We're already on our way to fight one war. I think it's a question of where the enemy pours in their reserves, and we can't match those numbers."

"Not to mention two adult dragons," Dirk added.

"Shavalkathar informed us on just how formidable they are," Jerriel added. "They nearly killed him. And they'll be protecting their first clutch of eggs in their nest. They will fight us with everything they have."

Dirk laid out the initial plan of attack. "They'll eventually figure out we're coming, so at some point, it won't be a surprise. We'll break our forces up into four battle groups, attack from three directions and try to roll them up, with one group held in reserve."

They poured over the maps, troop placements, and supply lines. The plans looked sound to David, but everything would change, once contact was made. He knew that much. They would need to adapt on their feet to the way the battle shifted both for and against them.

So much could go wrong, and there was still a lot about their enemies that they didn't know.

David looked Dirk in the eye. "What if they pour their superior numbers at us on this side?" he asked.

Dirk sighed. "Then we'll fight like hell, and probably still lose. I'm guessing the enemy will crush one side, and the pour back through and crush the other."

Their first contact with the city of Elkhart went friendly. Yet the half of Elkhart not controlled by the cults and the gangs reeled in full retreat from within. Waves of refugees—wounded and dying victims—blocked many of the already broken roads. Misery, chaos, and despair—the byproducts of any war—seemed to abound. All after a few days of heavy fighting and conquest on the part of Michiana's new foes.

Elkhart simply didn't have the people or the resources to stand alone against the forces already amassed against them. And many times that could be on the way.

The allies held a planning session with the Elkhart militia commanders in an abandoned convenience store. Quick introductions went back and forth.

They looked pretty demoralized in their military fatigues and makeshift armor. Despite their combined military and leadership experience, the two men and one woman were obviously traumatized and exhausted from their most recent ordeal. General Ben Macomber led the three. A retired Army brigadier general in his fifties, he had short black hair shot with steel gray, and light green eyes set deep in a lined face that made him look even more haggard. Yet his determination seemed indomitable. He struck the map table with one hard fist in frustration.

"Every place, every time we made a stand, they sent these crack squads of mercenaries, monsters, and wizards against us. They're incredibly tough!"

General June Dillon, a colonel in the Air Force, spoke next. She was in her early forties, blond and tall, with dark gray eyes. She looked very tough and spoke in an up-front, no-nonsense fashion. "They have dozens of wizards. We don't have any. At night, the enemy pulls back and sends their zombies and undead against us. Our people can't get any rest."

Their last general was Anton Kennison, a former Marine captain who had been home on leave. Thirtyish and in excellent shape, he had very short brown hair, and hard black eyes like marbles.

"And then there are the dragons," Kennison said. "They decimate everything they attack. Our strongest weapons can barely scratch them. They swoop in fast out of nowhere, flying low, or down out of the sun or darkness."

From there, the briefing turned pretty grim.

The Elkhart generals gave Dirk, David, and the other South Bend commanders an update on the enemy positions and strong points. They studied current estimates on the enemy numbers—which seemed to be on the rise—the last known sightings of the dragons, and the locations of their three known lairs.

After their victories, the enemy pulled back and returned to the primary dragon lair to worship their new gods and pay homage with the planned sacrifice of hundreds of new captives, all the next day and into the night.

"This is when we need to strike," Dirk said. "They think they've already won. Their enemies have been crushed. The rest of the city is theirs for the taking when they get around to it. They're throwing a big party. They fully believe that they have the momentum, and we can't stop them."

"They could be right," General Dillon noted.

"They're vastly overconfident. We can use that against them. Many of them are going to get drunk. Let's hope that they do. Then they can't fight."

"Yeah, they're going to be busy celebrating," David said. "Definitely overconfident. Right now they think they're invulnerable."

"Pull back out of the city," Dirk said. "Let them think we're retreating. With all of these refugees streaming everywhere, we can't get in to do anything anyway. We got here too late to affect this current outcome, but we'll get our chance. For now, make it look like we're getting bogged down helping the fleeing and the injured."

"That won't be very hard to do," David said. "That's pretty much where we're at."

Jerriel pulled him aside. "I don't understand," she said. "We've come all this way and we're not going to fight them? I'm not a military tactician, but—"

"Great generals choose the place, and the time of their battles," David told her. "That's what Dirk is doing. Trust me, it's coming."

All that day, they allowed their supply people to help the refugees.

A huge sprawling camp sprang up for that purpose.

Meanwhile, sticking to the cover of the dense forests, Dirk and all of the South Bend fighters and their new allies from Kellendra made their way around Elkhart proper.

They covered a lot of ground fast, doing everything they could to stay out of sight and undetected.

Two hours before nightfall, they positioned themselves up one side of the wooded valley overlooking the primary lair of the dragons and the new temple set up just for them. The partially exposed site near a dense patch of forested hills and vales was little more than a mile away. If they moved up quietly or at night, they could be right on top of them, without the enemy even knowing they were there.

But David knew that their troops had to rest, weary and exhausted from the forced march throughout that night and next day. The Elkhart troops who could still fight went with them, given a place of honor at the front of the left wing on that main flank.

When the time to attack came, they would be among the first to go in. From their vantage point, using binoculars and telescopes, they could see the preparations for the big sacrificial ritual coming up that night.

David instructed the scouts to spread the word. "Be careful the setting sun doesn't reflect off any lenses or shiny equipment and give our positions away."

"You got it, Captain."

The enemy continued getting carried away with feasting and drinking, engrossed by tormenting their captives as the late afternoon advanced.

A lot of the enemy activity became very difficult to watch or report.

David gave the binoculars back to the scouts keeping an eye on the developing debauchery. He'd seen enough, and exclaimed to Jerriel in disbelief and disgust.

"How could human beings regress into this kind of depraved barbarism in just a matter of weeks?" he said aloud. "A few months ago, these were normal people, just like the rest of us. Now look at them. They have captives for the sacrifice penned up by the hundreds. Their own people. Their neighbors: men, women, and even kids. Old people. Those captives are terrified; you can see the terror on their faces from here. They know they're going to be killed in horrible ways…and fed alive…to actual dragons."

"The Dragon Cults give the followers a heady sense of power," Jerriel said. "With the dragons watching over them, the cultists delude themselves that nothing can harm them. They think they can do whatever they want, whenever they want, to whomever they want. What

219

they don't realize is that when such cults start to run out of victims—it usually turns upon itself."

"Sir, I can't look anymore," one of the scouts said. "They're beating, torturing, and raping some of the captives right out in the open. I don't want to watch that."

"They're coating some of them in sauce," another observer said. "They're basting and flavoring the meat in advance, for the dragons!"

"I understand," David said. "You guys don't have to keep looking constantly if you don't want to. But you still have to track any changes or new movement in enemy forces."

"Can't we go in yet, sir?"

"Yeah, when are we going to go in and attack these bastards?"

"I know it's hard to wait, but when the time comes, we'll hit them as hard as we can. Keep checking on them from time to time. The dragons have to show. We have to try to take them out first, or wound them at the very least."

The frenzy of the Dragon Cult celebration increased as darkness fell. They tied or chained several captives to stakes and poles at the huge stage-like area, near the front of the cave lair.

A mismatched jumble of stolen church pews were carted in and set up for the worshipers, with cultist priests leading the faithful in prayers and supplications to the great wyrms. This fervent idolatry stood in strange contrast to the drunken, gluttonous feast and orgy going on off to the sides.

Gang members and guards tormented and prepared other batches of captives nearby. These people were going to die anyway. What did it matter what anyone did to them?

Things quickly degenerated from bad to worse.

Some of the cultists even reverted to outright cannibalism. Scouts spotted the enemy openly feasting on cooked human body parts.

Even David had had enough. He never felt such revulsion for his own kind before. His rage was almost maddening. These were Urth people. How could they do such things after only a few months?

Drums pounded, horns blared. Weird music grew louder. The entire scene was like something out of a bizarre, horrific fantasy movie, but it actually unfolded right before their eyes.

The ground shook. Terrible roars erupted from the lair itself. Out of its dark maw came the two flaming dragon-gods.

35

Rodell suddenly looked at Mason with a worried expression. "I know Shaeddor is your friend, Mace. This is hard to take. But clearly he's the one behind all of this, and I think that he's obviously been planning everything all along. But it's out of his hands now; it's out of his control. These other foes simply don't want to trust him or let him run things. That seems to be the point where they all argue with him, from what I can tell."

Mason felt his own mood and his countenance darken. "I want to hear it from him, first. I want Blondie to admit to me how he has turn against us all and betrayed us."

"Are you kidding me?" Rodell said. "He's going to try to kill us the moment he see's us. He's clearly a member of the Dark Khabal. He's been waiting to do all of this; he's not going to stop now just because you think he's still your friend. And he's certainly not going to wait to have a little brotherly chat with you. This is what the Khabal does, Mace. They get us to trust them and then they betray and kill us. This is how they destroy people from within."

"He'll talk to me. He owes me that much."

"Let me slip in first, Mace. Don't take any chances. Maybe I can zap him, or capture him. Then you two can have your little talk."

Mason didn't say anything. They spent a little time outside and on the first floor, but they didn't spot Thulkara anywhere. If Blondie had sent her off in a hurry, with her speed and strength, she could have leaped down and already be a mile away.

They had no other choice but to go forward on their own, just the two of them.

As they made their way further up into the damaged building, all of the entrances and stairs from the second floor up seemed to be blocked or choked with collapsed debris now, cutting the building off from the outside.

The various observation booths were also blasted, crumpled, or otherwise ruined.

No other guards had arrived, either. If Blondie had sent for some from any of the nearby garrisons, why weren't they here yet?

The answer was pretty obvious.

Blondie never sent for anymore guards.

What was it that Blondie was planning? Just an escape with the other enemy mages, or something even worse?

Regardless, Blondie would be waiting for them on the third floor, if he had not already fled.

As they picked their way in, something else crash up above them, and a billowing storm of dust blinded them and nearly swept them back downstairs.

"Move forward into the dust cloud," Rodell said. "Use the cloud to cover us and our approach. Keep your eyes shut and feel your way along. Use your other senses. Feel ahead of yourself and don't fall!"

Mason tried to do so, but it was difficult. The damaged old warehouse building shook and shuddered violently, threatening to collapse even further.

He lost track of Rodell. Rodell was most likely ahead of him.

It sounded stupid, but Mason still didn't want Rodell to kill Blondie on sight. If they could capture him, there was still a lot that Blondie could tell them.

But at that moment, Mason felt so betrayed that a big part of him wanted to gut Blondie on his own spear. And the rest of him was just sick to his core about the whole situation.

A fireball suddenly erupted on the third floor ahead of him.

"No, Rodell. Don't!" Too late.

Yet some other power absorbed the fireball's power, sucking it up and keeping it from setting fire to everything up there.

Mason heard Blondie's voice. It was still almost impossible to see with all of the swirling clouds of dust within. And sounds were warped somehow, making it difficult to determine what direction they came from.

"Come out, Darshian. I knew all along, somehow, that you were not what you claimed to be. Your advanced powers and knowledge exposed you. You're certainly not an Urthun. Step forward, and let us duel properly."

Rodell called back, "I answer only to my masters, and the royal house of Darshia, Prince Shaeddor. We serve the Circles of Light, and those who are of the Dark Khabal are our eternal foes."

"You are indeed a fine actor, and a competent mage, Rodell of Darshia. But you mistake me; I am not of the Khabal, however things may appear."

"Yet you work for them and do their will. How is this not so? Khabalists such as yourself are always deceivers and liars. They have to be, in order to lie to and murder their own friends and families."

Mason called out, slipping in and taking cover behind an iron support pillar he found with his hands. "Blondie. It's Mace. I need to know what's going on, and why you've done all of this. Tell me the truth, in your own words. Are you betraying us? Are we all enemies now?"

Mason clutched his spear and shield, drawing closer.

"I know how your mind, works, Mace. You would never understand. Yes, I am betraying you, for now. I have no choice but to betray you. To make my plan work, I must return to the enemy and rejoin their top ranks. But not for the reasons that you might think.

"There isn't time for me to explain it all, or to convince you that I'm not lying this time, Mace. I accept the fact that you may never listen to my words, or trust me ever again. But that does not change what I must do, and how I must achieve it. That's just it. You can't do what I must do, and you would never do what I am going to do, or what I am willing to do. I am the only one who can."

"Blondie. It all still sounds like more of your preening bullshit to me."

"I know it does, my brother. Perhaps one day, when all is said and done, you will then see that there was no other way. I must do this."

A thermal implosion detonated, sucking up all of the available air in one space near where Blondie's voice was coming from.

"Got you!" Rodell shouted.

Thulkara appeared from behind an unattached door, almost directly behind a startled Rodell. She picked up the door, swung it around over her head, and flattened Rodell to the ground before he could say or do anything more.

"Got you, traitor!" Thulkara shouted. Rodell was unconscious, sprawled out beneath the door. Mason rushed forward and checked for a pulse.

Thulkara proudly dusted her hands off. "Take it easy, Mace. Blondie told me not to trust this guy, even if you did. You don't know it, but Rodell was a spy, sent here by the Dark Khabal to deceive and destroy you. He got you to trust him. That's how they do it!"

Mason yelled up at her. "You big goof! I did trust him. Rodell didn't betray us. And he's not from the Khabal. Blondie's the one behind this all!"

Thulkara looked more stricken that Mason was in that instant. She turned to Blondie. "My battle brother. You lied to us? Tell us this isn't true."

Blondie sighed. "I want both of you to take good care of Jen for me. Look after her, tell her to forget about me, and make sure she finds a nice guy. I won't be back for her."

Blondie nailed them both with red-violet lightning.

Thulkara shrieked and fell to her knees.

Mason had his shield blasted away to the other side.

He flung his spear at Blondie. With the flick of one hand, Blondie deflected it.

Then he nailed them again with bolts from both hands, gritting his teeth. "You will fall!"

Mason thought his bones were glowing for a second. He fell back against the wall and could no longer move his body. He couldn't even blink, just stare straight ahead of himself.

He watched at Blondie had to zap Thulkara a third and forth time to finally stun her.

Why didn't he just kill them? Why was he keeping them alive, and helpless?

Mason watched as Blondie carefully fixed the scene to make it appear that a tremendous battle had been fought there.

He brought out jars of blood and spilled them over and splattered them around the three of them. For all intents and purposes, they looked horribly dead.

Then Blondie filtered debris and wreckage over them to make it look as if they had all been crushed, blasted, and killed.

Who was he putting on a show for? Even Blondie's betrayal didn't make any sense. Why didn't he just leave? Who was he waiting for?

36

The cloudy sky went completely cold and dark. Torches and bonfires lit the Dragon Cult temple and the lair. Heavy smoke and fumes poured out.

The dragons came forth into the night. An enormous crimson male dragon nearly the size of Shavalkathar, and a sleek, azure-blue female, only a bit smaller. She had to be younger still, because Shavalkathar said that adult females were usually larger than the males of the species.

They flexed their muscles and spread their vast wings, roaring up into the sky.

The entire area shook and shuddered at their might and power. It was truly an awesome display. Looking upon them, suddenly David could partially understand why some weak-minded people might fear or even come to worship such powerful beings—in a time of uncertainty and collapse.

But that still didn't make what the cultists were doing right. Even more so, they had to be stopped. Such dangerous idolatry could not be allowed to spread. It needed to be put down with all the force that could be mustered against such wanton depravity.

David and the militia had committed themselves to that exact task.

New guests appeared, arriving late to the festivities. Several dark mages of the Khabal, no doubt, dressed in black robes. Some wore ornate, pointed hoods of red, gold, or purple or fierce-looking, demon-like iron and gilded masks.

"Those are the dark mages who've allied themselves with the Dragon Cult and the street gangs," Jerriel said. "They have mercenary guards with them."

David took up someone's binoculars again that were handy. He spotted heavily armed Tharanorian mercenaries, from Khairun, most likely. Even grun. And other creatures that he'd never seen before. Lizard humanoids, snake humanoids, dog-like humanoids.

"They have monsters fighting for them as well?" he asked.

Jerriel studied them through a borrowed spotting scope. "Those creatures are most likely the guardians and champions of the necromancers and Shadow Mages. They bond many beings to their service. I see mor-kahls and gozogs. Some have grun. The warrior with the serpent head is a shagga, from another plane. The lizard-like humanoids are slurgs from the Loshang homeworld on the fringes of the Abyss. The dog-headed humanoid is from the bughon people. The bull-man is a murtal. They are fighters and killers from several Shadow Worlds and dimensions where the Dark Khabal has traveled, recruiting them all to fight their vile wars. How they came here along with their masters, I know not."

"I know about the grun, Jerriel. How tough are these other beings?" David asked.

"Very tough," she said. "Do not underestimate any of these creatures. These are champions of their races. They may very well outmatch all but our best fighters. And the Shadow Mages employ some of the most destructive magicks known to exist, much of that magic forbidden and accursed."

The new guests still sat in honor with the high priests and priestesses of the Dragon Cult off to the side. Even the dragons paid some deference to the new visitors, and spoke with them briefly.

David tried to get his head around all that. Dragons, posing as gods. Showing deference.

Shavalkathar would be appalled.

As darkness fell and twilight faded, everything looked about ready for the main festivities to begin.

A messenger crept up to David and Jerriel.

"Sir, General Blackwood's given the word. Move forward quietly. Advance as close as possible. The attack's going to begin, on signal."

Good. The waiting frustrated him and a lot of pissed-off troops.

David looked around at his friends: Jerriel, Jason, Alejandro, ThulKazar, even Tori Nelson. He saw the set faces of the Blackhawks. Princes Valandin and Alendel and their knights and warriors held their positions with weapons poised. The threescore Marrandorian mages, led by their three leaders: Pharrio, Maelen, and Urnessan.

David spotted his friends Kevin Policinski, Pete Steiner, Robert Billings, and Brent Wolfe, among the cream of the South Bend fighters. Fred Hayward and his son Steven, led flights of archers, along with Graham Ivers, national archery champion. Even Pastor Bryan Doran was there, leading a unit of volunteer fighters. Everyone who knew how to battle had volunteered to help their beleaguered Elkhart friends.

Within forty yards, the scouts and archers took out the drunken sentries.

At thirty yards, the mobile ballistae they pulled along close to the ground on well-oiled wheels were set up and loaded. Four dozen of them took direct aim at the dragons.

Jerriel and their other wizards readied their spells, aiming both for the dragons and the dark mages.

All of their friends and allies poised to charge into battle.

The first assault wave crept forward slowly on their bellies. They would charge in after the initial volley. The Dragon Cult ritual grew louder and louder.

Cultists and mercenaries finally spotted some of the attackers and attempted to raise the alarm before getting cut down.

But the noise of the ritual remained too loud for their pleas to be heard. The dragons tore into their first victims as everyone watched. The throng of worshipers roared their approval.

Dirk rose up and swung down his sword. "Fire! Unleash death upon them all. Attack!"

The giant crossbows thrummed, unleashing a volley at the dragons.

Destructive magic erupted and detonated all across the entire temple.

Clouds of arrows rained down out of the darkness onto the dragon worshippers and their guests, sparing the captives wherever possible.

Torrents of magical fire, exploding magical ice, lightning, and blasting rings of weird energy struck havoc among the dragons and the shadow mages.

The Elkhart troops swept in and showed no mercy to their foes. They ripped into surprised cultists and put them to the spear, sword, and ax, until that area ran red with their blood.

Several large, metal-tipped bolts–larger than pikes–stuck out of the dragons in numerous places.

At a glance, the blue female dragon in front took the worst of the barrage, all along her right flank. She dragged herself back into the lair, snapping the hafts of the bolts off as she did.

The red male spouted fire in pain and rage, most of it to the sky. Some of it fell back, ruinous on the worshippers and the other waiting victims. Many of them burned to death where they stood.

Then the male fled, launching himself into the sky and out of further harm's way. The dragon had little choice; it was flee, or perish.

So much for their new "gods" protecting them. Under the pressure of a real threat, they very clearly only sought to save themselves.

Hundreds of newly minted cultists noted this fact, and cried and wept for their "gods" to return and deliver them.

Morons.

Others, less stupid turned, took up weapons and fought.

More cultist troops and allies regrouped. The street gangs were the quickest to react. They tried to outflank the attackers.

Dirk ordered a wing to curl around and roll them up, too.

The fighting quickly grew dense and heavy about the lair. Packed units went at each other up close, in grim hand-to-hand fighting.

But by far, the attackers were better organized and disciplined, and still held the advantage.

David and Jerriel led their troops toward the stage, trying to cut off the fleeing Shadow Mages and their allies. Half of their number were left behind, either dead or dying.

The entire area seemed as if it had been blasted, scorched, and feathered with arrows. Troops moving in actually began to recover many of the shafts for future use.

Yet the enemy mercenaries reacted quickly, skillfully shielding themselves with magic, using their battlemages to strike back with magic of their own to stem the tide. Some of them looked wounded, but not enough to withdraw from the fight.

The enemy mercs fought a well-organized retreat, disengaging to regroup somewhere else. They wounded and slew many of the Elkhart troops in front of them, enough to slow the advance down and blunt the thrust of such an initial, heavy attack.

"Get down!" Jerriel shouted. They instinctively clustered around her.

She cast a shield spell over them just as a tremendous blast of dark magic erupted overhead. The other wizards raised similar protections.

But the intense blast charred several troops and cultists fighting nearby, reducing them to blackened skeletons and ash.

David and the Blackhawks rushed onto the stage as the smoke cleared.

The enemy made good their retreat.

"Free the captives," David said. "Put down the remaining foes here and pursue the rest of the enemy as far as we can tonight."

The battle continued to rage as more and more of the enemy regrouped.

David and the others prepared to enter the lair and take out the wounded, female blue dragon. The mages would help shield them.

Fresh, glowing, reddish-blue dragon blood smeared and streaked everything nearby. They made their way into the manufactured cavern, mined and dug out by thousands of slaves in a matter of days.

The primary lair was set into the southern side of a steep, rocky, wooded hill.

The other wizards went in front to shield them all from the dragon's flame.

The blue dragon was badly injured, but Shavalkathar warned them about how much damage dragons could take and still remain dangerous. They could even recover and heal quickly, given time. They could be extremely difficult to kill and were only partially vulnerable to magic.

David and Jerriel led the strike force, walking deliberately into a wounded dragon's lair while she protected her clutch of eggs.

This was not exactly a very wise idea.

Yet such was their mission.

These dragons had to be destroyed, and the major threat of their dangerous cult eliminated. Such cults could not be allowed to spread.

"She can smell us coming, I'm certain of it," Jerriel said.

"Shield! Shield!" Pharrio cried.

The cavern grew intensely hot. A bright blue glow, like a gigantic gaslight, expanded at the end of the tunnel.

"Get down or flatten yourselves to the sides!" Maelen yelled.

37

Mason listened to what was being said, but he couldn't move, couldn't speak.

Why, Blondie? Why? Were you always on their side, the whole time? Thulkara and I…you were a brother to us.

Blondie laughed, checking Ettal's remains to make sure he was good and dead.

Mason heard Blondie's voice in his skull. *Think about it. I'm a telepath, Mace. None of you ever guessed that I could also read all of your minds—as well as those of the enemy?*

I guess not, you traitorous bastard.

Easy, Mace. They'll be back soon. Get a brain. I've got important stuff to tell you, and not much time. For once, just shut up and listen.

Why should I listen to a pathological liar like you, Blondie? You've betrayed us all, and now you're going to go back to working for the enemy, and leave us here to die.

Think hard, Mace. I could have killed all of you…easily. I could still kill you now, instead of talking to you so listen. I only stunned Rodell and Thulkara, all of the guards I could. I made sure I paralyzed you so that you could hear what was going on.

It was you who poisoned all of the new mages, wasn't it? They're all dying, if not already dead.

You'll see, Mace. It was just a drug that will put them in a deathlike coma for a while. They'll come out of it in less than a day.

What, you want me to think that you're going to go back to your friends in the Dark Khabal to destroy them and ruin their plans?

Exactly, Mace. I'm the only one who can. Remember, the enemy thinks you are dead. Keep it that way until we leave. I can't help you after this. I'd have to let them kill you, or blow my cover. There's going to be a massive attack within an hour or two after I depart. You'll snap out of it by then, but you and the militia will still have to find a way to survive that attack on your own.

Bullshit, Blondie. Why do you have to keep up this charade? In case we capture you again at some point, and you can pretend to be on our side, and convince us that you're just a double or triple agent? So that we let you go, again? Or trust you?

Mace, you were going to find out anyway, later. But I might as well do it now. I've got something to give to you that will prove what I'm telling you is true, and that you can still trust me—somewhat. Just don't get in my way.

Hah, there isn't anything in this world that could—

Blondie tucked a folded-up envelope down into Mason's shirt.

Mace. That's a letter from Tori. She's still alive and waiting for you, on the other side.

Blondie. I am going to kill you!

Listen, dammit! She wasn't killed. That body they found wasn't her. She's alive; I swear it. The Traveler from the other side was here a short while ago. He dropped off a bunch of stuff, but he was in a hurry and couldn't stay. They're under attack on the other side, as well. They're in just as much trouble as we are, if not more so. I went through the stuff and found this letter to you—from Tori—and I knew how much it would mean to you. It's dated a day ago and it's in her handwriting, I'm guessing. When you snap out of it, you can read it for yourself.

Blondie, if you were ever my brother in any way, you had better not be lying about this. I will hunt you down.

You know I wouldn't lie about that kind of thing, Mace. Now act dead. We're out of time. Here they come.

The necromancer Gultor came back in with a sack of stuff. He put it down to one side by his feet. The other four escaped mages lined up on Gultor's far left.

"Good. You did manage to spring them all," Blondie said. "I was worried you wouldn't make it. That's the only reason I was worried."

They couldn't help noticing the bloody bodies.

231

"I've finished taking my vengeance here. I'll open the portal outside of the city, and we can all rejoin our forces in time for the attack. I have everything I need. Let's be on our way."

The other four enemy mages raised eyebrows, studying all of the carnage around them. They all waited to see what the necromancer would do.

"Impressive," the necromancer said. "I had always heard what a powerful sorcerer you were, Black Prince. Yes, very impressive."

Blondie opened the transport portal for them to escape from the city. The four enemy mages promptly ran through it.

Blondie gathered his gear and waited to follow the necromancer through the portal.

Suddenly Gultor blasted Blondie across the room.

"I didn't tell the others, but I decided not to bring you back with us after all, Shaeddor. Even if you did finally recall your old memories and proper allegiances to your master and the Khabal, I don't really much care about any of that. I simply despise you and all of your family. I always have. It's going to be a pleasure killing you, and your little sister. Later on, once we catch her."

"My sister?" Blondie said in a daze, struggling to stand up against the wall. "What does she have to do with any of this?"

"Why, didn't you know? She's on the other side, giving us all sorts of trouble. And she never even lost her memories."

"You're making a big mistake, Gultor. My master, Gorrial, will never forgive you for murdering one of his apprentices."

"I'll tell him that the enemy slew you for your treachery. What's one more corpse left behind up here? Boo hoo, how I tried to save you, but it was too late, and I barely escaped with my life. But don't worry. You can join your parents in the Nine Hells, and soon your little sister will be there, and you can all burn and twist and writhe together. I hope they give her to me. I think I'll slice off her legs at the hips and rape her while she stares in to my eyes and bleeds to death."

Blondie dove to one side and showered Gultor with a crushing wave of jagged debris.

Gultor motioned with his hands, and several energized tables and doors rose up into the air, deflecting the attack.

When Blondie rose up to strike, Gultor cast dozens of black snakes at him, hissing and speeding through the air.

They speared Blondie and pinned him to the wall, transforming into the same number of iron spikes, impaling him.

Gultor came over to him to gloat in triumph, dragging the sack with him, and the weight of it bumped across the floor. The necromancer grinned wide and reached into the sack. "And don't think I've forgotten that other filthy Urth whore of yours."

The necromancer yanked Jen's bloody, severed head out of the sack and held it up by its long hair. Gultor grinned and pressed her open, frozen mouth to Blondie's lips.

The necromancer chortled with mad glee, "Give your Urth slut a kiss goodbye, Shaeddor–on your way to the Nine Hells!"

Then Blondie smiled and turned into sand. He drained away from around the iron spikes.

"Simulacrum!" Gultor shrieked. He tried to spin around and strike, but Blondie stood right behind him, and rammed two long short swords up through the necromancer's belly and chest, out his back–effectively nailing him to the wall instead.

"I see you like grim jests. See now. Indeed, they do not call me the Black Prince for naught–necromancer. For I, too, am well known for having a dark sense of humor."

Blondie stared him in the eyes without blinking, and heated the blades red hot until they sizzled and steamed. Gultor's eyes popped and he gasped, steam wafting up out of his mouth and nose as he twitched upon hot, sharp steel.

Blondie shook his head slowly, never removing his gaze. "It was a very grave miscalculation on your part, Gultor. A very grave mistake indeed, to threaten, or lay hands upon, or take the life of any whom I love–and allow yourself to fall under my power."

The necromancer began to shudder and moan, "Mercy...great prince."

Shaeddor laughed so close that he sprayed spit into the wretch's face.

"Mercy!" he screamed. "Mercy? You dare to ask mercy of me, now? Look, and ye shall not find it in my vocabulary."

Blondie pointed down at Jen's severed head. "You...did that, to my beloved? No. The torments of the Nine Hells will seem *sweet*...after what I do to you. I have yet a little time. First, I shall melt the flesh off your arms up to the shoulders, and then consume your bones to ash."

Gultor's arms caught fire and were consumed even while he jerked, and shrieked, and screamed.

"Next, I'll sever your right leg halfway up from the knee." It flopped down to the ground. "My, look how your black blood flows so fast, vile one. In rivers. In jets, from your black heart. We can't have that, now, can we? Let's seal it off...with fire!"

Scarlet flames flared. Gultor screamed like a demon being torn apart.

"There. The stump is all blackened and sealed off. Now, let's do the same exact thing...to your other leg.

Gultor continued to wail.

"I see into your sick, twisted, disease that you call your mind, necromancer. Isn't this exactly how you like to torment your victims? Your favorite way to violate others? I can see full well that it is. What is it now—thirty-seven…or is it thirty-eight people you've done all of this to? Why, you've lost track of the actual number, haven't you? And for shame, over half of those victims were children, even a babe of seven months. All while their parents looked on, offering to pay any price—commit any evil for you—and begging you to stop."

Blondie stepped back. "Gultor, you are indeed a perfect example of the Dark Khabal. This is what you all are. This is what you do, for you know nothing but senseless slaughter and destruction. You can only destroy. And that is exactly why you must all die—the same exact way that I'm going to slaughter you. I will start a bonefire up through your groin, and your leg bones, and it will burn, and consume, and explode your bones from within, incinerate your flesh and innards to charcoal, and reduce you slowly to ash while you still live, and feel…all of it.

"Gultor, I'm going to stand here and watch you slowly perish, until the bonefire dissolves your skull, boils your eyes, and reduces your screaming mouth and tongue to hot dust. I'm going to make sure that your infested, infected brain stays alive for as long as possible…to experience every, single, delicious moment."

"P-p-please…Shaeddor…"

"Buck up, wretch. Why, by your own Dark Ghods, you're a necromancer, for pity's sake. But you bastards murdered my parents, and you—my vile friend—will never lay hands upon my little sister, in this life or any other. I will make doubly sure of that." Blondie commenced the bonefire, and it slowly ate away at the necromancer's body and turned it to ash.

"All that you twisted necromancers know and understand is death. Where others do not even consider or think of killing, you kill the way that others draw breath. The way others take sips of water. How stupid and boring. A sick, monotonous, droning chant. Just another reason why you and your so-called Dark Ghods need to be eradicated from every universe, and exposed to all as the lies, and jokes, and nothings you truly are."

"And you—my vile friend—shall rue this day, for all eternity, for laying your filthy, stinking hands upon my precious Jen—you festering pile of burning shit!"

Blondie watched the bonefire as it slowly incinerated the necromancer and melted his eyes inside his skull. Gultor kept screaming, even louder and greater than he had before.

"I wish that you could tell the Khabal that I am coming for them, but then that would ruin the surprise. Wouldn't it? A traitor, am I? I will teach them new definitions of that word. Hear my vow. I will return, and plant myself into their deepest councils and plots. I will make myself indispensable to them and all of their designs. And when the time is right, I will bring all of their schemes to ruin, crashing down upon their accursed heads, no matter what the cost is to me."

Blondie crossed his arms while the necromancer continued to melt and be consumed as he shrieked. From down below in the complex, sounds came of militia workers and troops, trying to work their way up through the debris and destruction.

Blondie turned to Mason before ducking through the open portal.

"My Jen is no more, Mace. They have taken her life and she is forever gone to me. I know full well that you understand what that is like. I go now to seek out my vengeance—however long it takes or wherever it leads me. I no longer care if you believe me or not. Farewell, my brother. I make no plans to return."

With that, Shaeddor, Black Prince of the Royal House of Holleth, stepped through the dark portal yawning before him, and vanished into the shadows along with it.

38

The protective screens just barely went up around David and Jerriel and all of their companions. Blue fires engulfed the passageway.

They had to wait even longer, until more air sucked back into the tunnel, and the earth and stone cooled off.

The entire area smoked and steamed, some places still glowing hot.

"Advance quickly," Urnessan said. "She won't be able to breathe fire again for several minutes."

David put his shield up, readied his pike, and rushed forward. "Then let's get in there!"

ThulKazar and the princes raced right behind him. Then the others. They even pushed past their wizards.

As they poured into the lair, the wounded female let out a deafening roar and attacked. She whipped her massive tail set with huge spikes, at them.

David and Alendel dove under it. Valandin and ThulKazar sprang over it.

The tail crashed into the entryway and nearly demolished the stone arch. The entire cavern shuddered.

More troops poured in, including Jerriel and the other wizards.

They pelted the dragon with several spells, driving it back, distracting it, allowing more attackers to rush in.

David and Alendel set their pikes and charged at the dragon's exposed midsection.

It ripped at them with an enormous claw.

At the last instant, David shoved Alendel out of the way, spun, and sidestepped. His glaive pierced deep into the dragon's left arm, but the sheer power of the creature flung him aside like a rag doll.

He smacked into the wall thirty feet up. Pain exploded in his body. He scrabbled, dazed and breathless, to keep from falling backwards onto his head, down into the chaos of the battle.

From his vantage point, he looked down as he recovered.

ThulKazar roared his battle cry and leaped upon the beast, laying open a deep gash in the dragon's left flank with his battleax. He stabbed his broadsword deep into its belly.

The blue dragon turned and snapped at him viciously with its huge maw, teeth like swords.

ThulKazar laughed and faced down the dragon. He hacked and cut at its armored face and horns with his flashing weapons. Bashing, flinging, and snapping it back.

This allowed Prince Valandin to ram his spetum deep into the dragon's neck.

The long neck undulated powerfully, lifting Valandin off the ground until the weapon pulled free of his hands. He dropped back to the ground. Valandin jumped up and drew his bright swords.

Jerriel and the wizards shot lightning down the dragon's mouth when it tried to breathe fire again. The blasts knocked the huge head side to side. One great eye burst and went dark.

The dragon twisted and thrashed, rolling over some of the attackers, flinging many aside, crushing others. Its ferocity was incredible.

Alejandro thrust his sword deep into the remaining good eye, blinding the monster before it knocked him away.

Jason and Pastor Bryan led troops on the right side, cutting up the rear leg and crippling it with deft strokes of their swords. The dragon snarled and crushed them and twenty others against the wall for an instant. Only their armor saved them.

Two Marrandorian knights charged forward and tried to spear the beast in the throat. It snapped their spears in half and then clamped its jaws on them with the next lunging bite, flinging the severed bodies and their gore across the chamber.

ThulKazar climbed onto its back, hacking and cutting at its spines, trying to reach the backbone and sever the spinal cord.

The dragon reeled, gushing blood from multiple wounds.

Jerriel and the wizards advanced, hammering the monster with spell after spell. They forced it back toward the nest, where the eggs lay hidden under hot gravel and large flat, protective stones.

It reared up and engulfed the wizards with a torrent of flame, cut short when princes Valandin and Alendel rushed in and buried their weapons into its chest.

The dragon stumbled and fell forward, pinning the princes beneath part of its bulk for an instant, roaring in agony.

It bowled the wizards over and scattered them with a head thrust, crashing through their protective spells. Jerriel lay to one side, stunned and helpless.

The dragon's jaw opened and descended toward her.

David let go of the ledge where he clung, and plummeted down through the air, his long sword and katana drawn.

He dropped down heavily onto the dragon's head, knocking it to one side briefly, burying both blades deep into the monster's skull where it joined the neck.

"Zaka!" he shouted, activating the lightning runes on both swords.

Twin thunderbolts ripped through the dragon. It jerked violently and reared up, stricken by the electric blasts ripping into its skull.

One of the razor-sharp neck spines sliced into David's right leg, straight through his armor. His own warm blood flowed freely with that of the dragon.

Other attackers thrust their weapons into the monster's belly, chest, and throat.

With a final roar, the great beast collapsed. David rolled free, clutching his leg wound and trying to reach Jerriel where she struggled to rise.

ThulKazar already climbed the nest mound to get at the eggs.

"Stop him!" Jerriel cried. "Don't let him harm those eggs. The mages will deal with them!"

"Bah. Kill them all!" the Thul roared. "Let none of the accursed beasts live to trouble the world."

"No!" Pharrio said. "She's right. Let us deal with the eggs. They have great value."

ThulKazar spat on the ground. "A pox upon dragons and mages both. If these monsters become a curse, let it be on your heads, then. Not mine. Death to all dragons, young, old, or unborn. My people have suffered too much death and destruction from them."

He stalked off, enraged. No one hindered the big Thul.

The blue dragon lay dead at last. The other wizards organized troops to skin and collect all of the useful pieces of the creature, much of it brimming with potent magic, they explained.

David helped Jerriel up.

They saw to getting his wound stitched up and bandaged as best they could. Then Stacy Keller came along and gave them both a little magical healing to help the process along.

The princes had brought magical healers with them as well, and Stacy and other Urthers were already paired up and training with them. They did their best to learn what they could, as quickly as possible.

"What shall we do with the eggs?" David asked.

"Keep them here until they hatch," Jerriel said. "That is the best way. They must be kept hot. Then the hatchlings can be moved. Otherwise they might not make it."

"Can dragons be raised safely?"

"It depends. Sometimes, yes. Sometimes, no. It depends on many things, including the hatchlings themselves and the persons raising them. All dragons are naturally incredibly independent, and will eventually go off on then own. But if they are treated well, and fed well, it is possible that they may maintain a positive relationship and even a friendship with those who once kept them safe."

Jerriel smiled. "Did I mention that they make terrible pets and must be fed constantly?"

"And you must have one, right?"

"Yes. I've always wanted a hatchling. Ever since I was a little girl. I'll have my egg picked out before we leave."

David sighed. "I couldn't let it eat you, Jerriel, but now that we've killed it, I still feel sad. I wish that it weren't so. They're so amazing and beautiful."

"And among the most dangerous of enemies. This dragon made itself our enemy: it was either it, or us, Daeved. I choose us."

"I agree."

Jerriel with a baby dragon.

This was definitely going to be a new twist.

Alejandro chimed in. "Do you think the baby dragons will mind that you killed their mother and plan to kill the daddy as well?"

"We'll leave out that part," Pharrio explained. "You can only raise a dragon from an egg. You cannot adopt and raise a wild dragon once it has been hatched. They are willful and independent enough as it is."

David shook his head. "How wonderful. Jerriel; you're adopting a fire-breathing eating machine that could decide to kill us or our neighbors in our sleep. I'm fine with that. But right now we have a war to win. This isn't over yet. There's still another dragon to deal with out there, and lots of enemies. And the next time we won't have the jump on them."

Messengers reached them shortly thereafter.

"Sir, the enemy's regrouping. Several of our units have met heavy resistance while pressing the pursuit. One was nearly wiped out, barely able to retreat. The enemy wizards concentrated intense spells on our forward line."

"Sir," another said. "We're getting many reports of undead activity throughout the city. Their numbers are rapidly increasing."

"Order our people to pull back and secure our defensive lines. Use the undead fighting protocols. Cut them up and they are not a threat any longer. Don't worry about being bitten or scratched, except for disease and infection. Holy water works as good as burning them."

The enemy counterattack hit them with the hour.

On all fronts, hundreds of fast, vicious, weapon-wielding undead battered their lines. The Urth humans and their allies barely held them off, with only holy water sprayers, pickets, and the old reliable: muscle and steel.

These hyper-undead were definitely something new.

All night long, hit-and-run attacks continued, trying to keep them off balance, bleed them, keep them guessing.

Then the male red dragon struck out their lines from out of the darkness in several places, lighting the city on fire.

But reports said the red dragon was badly hurt, having trouble flying. Many onlookers said that it literally limped through the skies on damaged wings.

Yet parts of Elkhart burned all the same. Even injured, the dragon remained a tremendous threat—an enormous wild card. And David recalled how quickly such creatures healed. Who knew if the dragon's allies could heal or patch it up even faster?

Outside of Elkhart, among the low wooded hills, the enemy mustered their armies, and challenged the invaders to meet them on the field of battle. On the ground, the enemy chose positions they had fortified, hardened, and prepared.

And where they held the high ground.

Even Dirk agreed with the other commanders when they studied the maps.

"Their military people are superb strategists. We couldn't have chosen a better battlefield if we were them. They want to bleed us, and bleed us bad. I'm sure that they and those wizards and that dragon have some very nasty surprises in store for us. They know what they've heard of us. We're aggressive, up-front fighters who don't hesitate to charge in head-on."

"That's exactly what they're expecting us to do," Prince Valandin said.

ThulKazar shook the table with a blow of his massive fist. "Yes. Then let us go forward and ram steel down their throats and have done with them!"

"No." Dirk said.

David raised an eyebrow. "No?"

"No?" ThulKazar protested.

"Right. We're not going to do what's expected of us. We're going to cut them off, surround them, and bottle them up."

"A siege instead of a battle?" Pastor Bryan said. "They'll just dig in even more."

"Let them. Let them burn in the hot sun and rot for a while in their own juices. They won't be able to resupply very well if we cut them off completely from the city. If we rush in, we'll have the same problem with supplies, aa well as the wounded and refugees once they rout us. They'd chase our sorry asses all the way back to South Bend and kick our butts good. That's their plan. I'm sure of it."

Jason Inada nodded. "Clever. So, instead we contain them. Let them sweat it out and use up their limited supplies. Let the elements work on them."

"And what about the dragon?" Jerriel said. "Each day it will heal more; each night it will attack. Each day it will grow stronger and more angry."

Dirk frowned. "The dragon is a wild card—a thorn in our ass no matter what we do. You wizards need to put your heads together and figure out something. Track that red bastard and we'll send an army after it once we know where it's hiding. Then we take it out. In the meantime, we try to get lucky."

"The dragon will not stay trapped with its allies," the wizard Maelen said. "It will fly away to avoid death. But it will stay in contact with the enemy, and help them in any way possible. It will seek vengeance against us for the death of its mate and eggs. We must bring it down, somehow, and destroy it."

Dirk stood up, and the other commanders stood with him. "From this moment on, the enemy stays where they are, under our hammer. We keep building our power around them. If they move or try to break out, we bleed and crush them the same way they planned to bleed and crush us."

"Let's do it, then," David said. "Except for the dragon, time is on our side."

"I still say we should go in there and just kill them all," ThulKazar said. He sounded so disappointed.

David laughed and clapped him on the back. "If we had an army of Thulls, we could probably do just that," he said. "But we're just mere mortals. Dirk's right again. We get them almost for free in the end, and we lose fewer good people whom we can't afford to lose by rushing in."

"One other plus," Pastor Bryan said.

"What's that?" Alejandro asked.

"The City of Elkhart gets a breather, and can also try to recover a bit, without a civil war ripping it apart any further."

"Get the people on line and working in the fields," Dirk said. "Unless they want themselves and their children to starve this winter, they must be made to understand that food production is everything right now. And they must protect their crops, if they want to live. Has there been any sign of large enemy troop reinforcements appearing out of nowhere? Numbers that have not been spotted before?"

"I have not heard of any as yet," David said. Most of the others agreed.

Dirk shook his head. "I don't know if that is good or bad. If the enemy isn't piling on us here, it must mean they are about to do so on the other side. And we do not as yet have any way to help them over there."

Jerriel looked to the wizards. "Then, for now, we must deal with the remaining dragon, the Dark Khabal, and the Dragon Cult. All three must be completely wiped out."

"They will be," David said.

But that was easier said than done.

Hours dragged on into days. The early summer days were still mostly cool during the day and cold at night. The enemy held their high ground positions and simmered in their own juices. They sent out scouts and skirmishers at first, and stopped once they did not return. The dragon harassed the Urthers and their allies at will, mostly at night, keeping parts of the city burning.

Jerriel and the wizards struggled to try to track the beast, thus far without much luck.

Rabbi Yosef Bergman came to Elkhart and spoke before them all.

His news was very interesting.

Bergman looked to be in good health. His wizard staff held pieces of precious stone set in it in several unusual patterns. They flickered, winked, and glowed at odd intervals.

"Did you know," he announced, "that the two sides are not in complete sync with each other? I didn't bother to notice it at first. They are some hours off with each other. While here on our side, it is daylight. There it might be several hours later, in the evening or even at night. But within a twenty-four hour period I believe. I wonder what causes the time disparity?"

"Who knows?" Jerriel noted. "Both mixed up worlds now exist in separate dimensions. There's no reason to think that both would be on the same exact time."

"Still, it is curious," Bergman insisted.

"Never mind that for now. How's the transport magic development proceeding?" Jerriel asked.

Bergman suddenly looked very worried.

"I have been to the other side and back, more than a few times, now," he said. "I know the way. And that's not all. I can go back and forth on my own. But the big news is that the enemy has three such portable portals, and are already deploying them against us."

39

Mason realized that Blondie was gone, now–no matter what. Perhaps forever. If anything his friend said was true, the city would soon suffer a major attack. The paralysis magic was only starting to wear off. Mason could not merely wait for rescue.

His unconscious friends would recover on their own and be retrieved, cleaned up, and seen to.

When he could move more, he dragged himself to the nearest window. When his fingers began to work, Mason pulled out the letter Blondie said was from Tori–alive and waiting for him on the other side.

He opened the battered envelope and briefly read. He had enough energy to do that much.

Later, he would read it many times over.

All he needed now was to know that it was in fact, true.

It was her handwriting.

It was. And the date. It was her.

She told him that she was alive, in her own hand and in her own words. She said how she loved him.

How she could not wait to see him again.

Mason closed his eyes, bowed his head, and shook, nearly out of control.

That was all he needed to read. There was more, much more, and he would savor every word later, when there was time.

Mason let his tears flow as he folded her letter and carefully returned it to its envelope, and tucked the precious paper away safely in a closed pocket.

He shot to his feet, shook his fists at the sky, and roared, "Yes!"

Suddenly the enemy wizard Tharin sprang upon him, covered with dust and blood from the debris pile he must have woken up in. He was not dead, as they had all assumed.

He wrestled with Mason, trying to stab him with his long dagger.

But Mason was still weak, and had not regained his full strength. Tharin's dagger slowly descended.

Tharin laughed. "My reward shall indeed be great indeed, for slaying the Pistolero!"

Mason laughed right back at him with a sudden realization. "That's right, you sonovabitch. I *am* the Pistolero."

Mason drew his derringer without hesitation and blasted Tharin's head clean off his shoulders as it it were a blood-filled melon.

He flung the wizard's body aside and screamed at it, "And I want to live!"

He found rope and secured it, dropping it down to the ground. He cut another piece of rope and tied a quick harness seat for himself, just the way he'd learned back in ROTC rappelling. Even without a D-ring, he knew how to make a harness seat like this work.

He called to the troops below to secure his lines and belay him.

In a matter of a few seconds, he was out the three-story window, bobbing off the building, and then his boots touched the ground.

He gave orders and sent runners, even as he ran back to his old quarters.

Once there he quickly prepared for war. Armor, his old duster, and his armored outlaw hat.

Let the Pistolero ride again—into hell itself, if he needed to.

Tori was alive and waiting for him on the other side. Somehow, he would find a way to reach her, no matter what it took.

But with a major battle already on the way on their side, he needed all of his guns and his teams, and he knew where they were.

He raced up into the unfinished tower of the new primary fortress, heading for Major Bill's private armory in the keep.

A message reached Mason. Bill said that he would gather the old reloading teams as much as he was able at short notice, and send them to the tower.

At least Mason had his derringer and his Spillers from his quarters, but he needed all of his guns and his heavy weapons. All of the loaded guns, the shotguns, and his St. Louis rifle–all loaded up with the high-yield, uranium-laced annihilator rounds.

They had no time. Very shortly, the enemy armies would pour over and around the unfinished defensive walls.

From the sounds in the distance, it was already starting.

He found the heavy door to the armory vault. Shit! It was locked solid.

Mason backed off and shot the lock to glowing pieces and kicked his way in. He knew from before that there was only one unfurnished floor above this one, and then the exposed top, some sixty feet in the air.

That would give him some room to shoot, if he could drag enough of his gear up there.

The few tower guards in place took bows up to the top so that archers could shoot down at the foe.

Mason grabbed two black powder shotguns and his St. Louis rifle, and slung them over his shoulders. Next he grabbed a box of loaded pistols.

That was all that he could carry.

When he reached the top of the tower, about eleven guards were firing their bows as fast as they could. Things already looked pretty dire.

The advance wave of hundreds of slurgs leapt and swept over most obstacles with ease, like shock troops. Behind them came units of grun with scaling ladders, and behind them, mercenary infantry.

"I'm the Pistolero," Mason shouted. "I need four of you to break off your attacks and go down to the armory. Fetch every gun down there and haul them all up here. I don't care what it is. Do it. Now!"

Mason took up one of the shotguns, the 10-gauge, and took aim out at the enemy's massed ranks.

"Eat this…fuckers!" His first shot lobbed high out into distance like a bright flare.

He quickly aimed over to the left and fired off the other barrel. By then the shotgun was red-hot; he set it aside.

He took up the other shotgun and fired off a shot on the right.

The first round came down and detonated in the air above the enemy ranks.

They vanished in blinding white craters of fire, a hundred and thirty yards in diameter. The blast wave and its thermal effects flattened everything in the vicinity and set it on fire if it could burn.

Then the rounds on the flanks ignited, with similar lethality that barely overlapped.

For a moment, there was stunned silence on both sides.

The better part of the enemy attack–troops, mages, siege engines, reinforcements–were annihilated and removed from the field in those three concentrated blasts alone.

The defenders could not have done better if they had planned it all that exact way.

A great cheer went up from the militia, and they rallied, now that they were no longer hopelessly outnumbered. But there were still many foes, mostly slurgs, who had penetrated deep into the South Bend defenses.

Once the enemy recovered from the sudden sweep of devastation, they turned back and went on the attack once more.

"Pistolero!" one of the archers cried in fear. Mason came over and looked down.

Scores of slurgs were climbing quickly up the side of the tower to get at them. There weren't any more large groups of enemies within range to attack, so Mason turned to defending the tower with pistols.

Guns blazing, he went around the tower's perimeter, pouring direct fire from his pistols down at the attackers, mowing them down in fiery sweeps. But he had to be careful not to damage the tower itself.

It wouldn't do to topple the structure over or blow it up with all of them still in it. That would be bad.

He quickly depleted most of the pistols from the box.

"More guns!" he shouted. "I need more guns. And where are my reloaders?"

For this to work in any sustained way, he needed his teams.

Two of the archers put down their bows and rushed over to the empty guns, examining them. "Tell us what to do," the sergeant shouted.

Mason kept firing and moving. "I can't, there isn't time. I have to keep shooting. That's why we need the reloaders!"

Things were going to get grim and tight very quickly if he could only rely on his lesser, dry firing.

Several people boiled up from below, dragging tubs and tools and folding tables with them. Mason recognized his old friends from Reloading Teams 3 and 4.

"We're here, Mace!" Corporal Schnieder shouted.

"About damn, time! What kept you?"

"Just keep shooting. We'll have these pistols loaded directly."

"Use high-heat and flame-blast rounds like the iron oxide, aluminum oxide, and the magnesium," Mason yelled.

"Right," Schnieder said. "That way we won't blow up the tower."

Mason grinned like a devil.

Now he could really go to work.

First he had to sweep the tower clean before they were overwhelmed.

He raced around the tower, guns blazing down its length, spitting fire, cutting down the fast-approaching slurgs.

247

Some he shot right into their maws and faces as they were reaching out with their claws to try to rake at him.

He couldn't be everywhere at once. Slurgs tried to boil over the lip of the top. Militia troops drove them back with spears, swords, and point-blank archery fire. Mason rushed across to several points, trying to hold off the attacking waves and sweep them from the length of the tower.

The slurgs all seemed to sweep his way, trying to overwhelm that unfinished tower and destroy the Pistolero on top of it at all costs. All of the enemy had clearly seen what a threat he could be.

Down below, the militia hemmed in and reduced the slurgs still on the ground and among the walls, using disciplined shield walls and a range of spears and pikes. Once the attackers were encircled and trapped, the spears closed in.

Meanwhile, from up above, militia archers rained death upon the packed, exposed slurg ranks. Slurgs were shock troops and often fought with a weapon in each hand as true berserkers, but without shields, they were incredibly vulnerable to concentrated archery fire when they were trapped.

With minutes, the tower was secure, and the militia forces mopped up after the attack. Like the other monsters, slurgs were vicious brutes and had no value as prisoners. They were routinely put down. After that, the wounded humans could be looked after.

Mason and his reloaders geared up. Once they were ready, they made they way down and out into the city, past heaps and waves of dead slurgs piled up at the tower's base.

Thulkara raced up on Goliath with a hundred of her best Shield Maidens with her. She had Winger already saddled up and ready for battle. An empty wagon had been brought along for the reloaders.

"Mace, Bill is getting the rest of the reloading teams and wagons and their carriers rounded up and ready. He has ordered us and several companies of horse and infantry to go up the line and attack any massed units of enemy troops in the field with those annihilator rounds of yours. We must do as much damage to the foe as we can before they change tactics on us. They're already beginning to shift their forces and spread them out."

"Then let's ride. Send word out ahead of us to have the spotters and officers call down to us and let us know where it is best to stop and make an attack. Inform them that we can engage targets within about two hundred to three hundred yards, max. Make sure they understand."

Thulkara turned to a few of her fastest riders. "You got that?"

They nodded, and thumped their gauntleted fists over their hearts and their breastplates in a martial salute to their mighty leader.

"We obey," they said.

"Stay out in front of us," Mason told them, "and spread the word. Make sure they know what to do to direct our fire. We don't want to waste a single shot."

The two messengers charged off into the distance.

But the enemy was already adjusting to the return of the Pistolero–if, in fact, at least to their mind, he had ever really left.

Mason manage to get off two more uranium rounds, but by then the foe had completely pulled back from the front lines and was regrouping , well outside of the Pistolero's maximum range.

Once Mason had a chance to relax, he took a break in a small room by himself. The first thing he did was reread the letter from Tori that he had only scanned before.

Alone by himself, he broke down and wept at every word in her messy hand. Most likely, they had told her to hurry to write it.

Thulkara pounded on the door to let him know that Major Bill, Rodell, and Koden were all ready to speak with him and make plans in the nearest conference room that was set up.

Mason kissed his letter from Tori, brimming with emotion. He flung the door open and hugged Thulkara as hard as he could.

"She's alive," Mason shouted. "My Tori's alive, and she waiting for me on the other side! We just have to find a way for us to cross over." If Thulkara had been shorter, he would have kissed on the face, but he wasn't about to climb up her to do that.

Thulkara roared with laugher and clapped him on the back, nearly knocking him to the ground. "That's the best news we've had since…since…"

Even Thulkara couldn't say it.

They'd better get to that meeting and help figure out what they were going to about Blondie's betrayal.

Tori was back, but Mason had lost a brother. And now his brother had gone back to the enemy, and would most likely become their enemy. When they met next, he would have to try to kill Blondie, and Blondie would most likely try to kill them.

That was very harsh medicine to swallow.

40

They sat down in David's old green command tent, gathering around the map table. One entire side of the tent opened to let in the light.

"You've been to the other side repeatedly now? That's amazing," Jerriel said. "What more have you learned?"

"Where shall I begin?" Bergman said. He looked very concerned. "But here is the main thing we need to worry about. On the other side, the enemy nearly has the upper hand, and soon they may dominate this side, as well."

"But how?" David said. "How is that possible?"

"What about the enemy's portable transport portals you warned us about?" Maelen the mage asked.

"They came close to capturing me once while I spied on them in astral form. But I got close enough to see that they now possess three such magic gateways that they have been able to tune to open on both sides of the Merge. They can cross over back and forth at will now, use them as shortcuts, and transport supplies and even large units of troops through them."

"That is terrible news," Prince Valandin said.

"We'd better inform Dirk and the town council," David added.

Bergman rolled his eyes. "Already done. He sent me to tell you folks. And that's not all," he said. "As we know from our encounter with the demon in South Bend, the enemy also possesses magical enchanted mirrors. With these, they can communicate with their agents, and even pass materials and even people through them if the mirrors are large enough. And what's more important, it's clear that they were developing all of these abilities and artifacts well before the Merge."

Jerriel gasped. "More proof that they knew the Merge was going to happen and were planning to exploit the aftermath."

"Of course they helped plan it," Urnessan said.

"Bergman, you can confirm all of this? How do you know?" David asked.

"From spying on some of them and entering their dreams," Bergman said, "They caused it, with the help of the Dark Ghods. They've had to adjust their schemes and plots after the merge. But yes, it's obvious that they prepared for months and years before the Merge to put people and supplies in place—on both sides, mind you—to make a power play to capitalize on the cataclysm."

"That means they knew about the existence of Urth and its dimensional connections to Tharanor as an alternate sister world," Pharrio said.

"The theories are there, for all who know them," Maelen added. "A sister world would have to exist somewhere. The High Mages would need to anchor to it in order to save both worlds from the coming cataclysm."

"Perhaps the demon was their advance spy in South Bend," Jerriel said. "He worked with them for a long while."

"I'm afraid the implications are even more sinister than that," Urnessan said. "They somehow had knowledge of Urth and its natural laws. I don't think Urth's technology was crippled so completely by accident. I think that was a deliberate part of their plan somehow."

"That would mean..." Pharrio said.

"Yes," Jerriel added. "That one or more of the High Mages was not only involved in causing the Merge, but also specifically took actions to damage Urth and its natural laws during the efforts to control the cataclysm. Gorrial Lankorro might not be the only traitor among the Six."

"They clearly did so in order to make both worlds easier conquests," Maelen said. "It makes perfect sense from the standpoint of the aggressor."

Jerriel turned to Rabbi Bergman. "Maelen is the only other mage I know besides you who can travel in astral and ethereal form. Right now we need to find the red dragon. Do you think the two of you can track it to where it's hiding?"

"We might be able to."

Maelen shook his head. "It is possible, but dragons–being highly magical in their very nature–can sense astral and ethereal entities. They can even enter those planes, if need be, to pursue or attack an enemy."

"Yes," Pharrio said, "but doing both takes great concentration even for a dragon, and in any case, he is not likely to leave his body behind where it is vulnerable to attack while he travels into another plane during an ongoing war."

"Captain Pritchard!" a messenger called out as he approached. "Commander Blackwood requests that you and your forces meet him at the front. The enemy has unleashed an all out assault in an attempt to break out."

"Very well. Tell him we'll be there ASAP."

"Good, we've worn them down," Pastor Bryan said. "They're trying to escape before we weaken them further."

"We have them now," Alejandro added.

David thought about that for a moment, picturing the units on the field of battle in his mind. He knew what they could and could not do. "I'm not so sure. Think about it: up until now they've been clever. The enemy has reacted quickly and intelligently to everything we've thrown at them. Why would they stop doing that all of the sudden and play right into our hands? For once they're doing exactly what we hope they might do for our advantage."

"You're right, Captain," Prince Valandin said. "They've never been this foolish before."

"My guess is they have something planned for us. Something they think will shift the battle in their favor."

"A surprise?" ThulKazar said. "The dragon, perhaps? Under the right conditions, if they draw us out into the open, the dragon could inflict heavy damage on any of our exposed armies."

"Just be happy it isn't two dragons," Valandin said.

"Perhaps they are trying to break out," David noted. "But it just doesn't feel right. They're taking a serious risk of being wiped out. Think about it. If we were them–if we were trapped in their position–why would we take such a chance? What would lead us to think that we could act so rashly and win the day?"

David saw the realization awaken on several faces an instant after it occurred to him.

Jason Inada, was the first one to voice it. "They have help coming. Reinforcements that we cannot predict, flooding through the portable transport gateways."

Alejandro nodded. "Yes, right when we think we have them. They think that with more numbers, plus the dragon, that they'll surprise us and take us all down."

"Okay," David said, "so the next question is: where is their help coming at us from? Where are they setting up these gateways? They would have to be close. No scouts have yet to report any large bodies of enemies massing or flooding out anywhere near Elkhart."

"They will use the transport gates very soon, I would think," Rabbi Bergman said. "That's how they'll try to overwhelm us."

David nodded. "Yes, I think you're right. It's going to be something just like that. Their reinforcements will flood in on us out of nowhere to sweep over us."

"Where will they set up these gateways?" Jerriel asked.

"I'm guessing…the ends will open up on both sides," David said. "Perhaps they will be concealed in the wilds where we can't readily spot them. We'll need to locate them by following back from the troops pouring out of them. Come on. We must meet with Dirk and warn him about this. Rabbi Bergman, instead of finding the dragon–who I think is going to show up any way, do you think that you and Maelen can infiltrate the enemy camp and find out where their portable transport gates are? And figure out how we might be able to attack them?"

"We can try," Bergman said.

"Wait," Jerriel said. "We still have to get word to the other side. They must attack the other ends of the gates there, just like us, and try to capture and hold them. Then we can use them to help whichever side is being swarmed on."

Maelen nodded. "We will try to send warning. But first we must find the gateways. We will put ourselves in the astral traveling trance and depart our bodies with our minds. You must take us with you, and keep our bodies nearby and safe."

David nodded. "We will, I assure you. Return to us safely as soon as you can. I hope…with the vital information that we need."

They traveled with the two wizards unconscious in the back of a heavily guarded wagon.

It took several precious minutes to convince Dirk and the other commanders that the enemy played into their hands too easily.

Even as they reached the front, by all of the signs, the battle went their way.

The enemy struggled to cover open ground and break out, getting mauled by clouds of arrows.

"Within and hour or two, we should be able to outflank and crush them," Dirk said. "But if what you have warned us about is true? We can't commit all of our forces just yet. That would leave us trapped and surrounded by the new forces the enemy gates in."

He turned to his messengers.

"Send word. Press the attack, but half of our forces will remain out of sight and guard our flanks and rear. Contact the city. Have them rush up as many troops and reinforcements as quickly as they can. We might have need of them."

David and his friends watched the battle beside Dirk from the observation hill overlooking the vale and the plain it opened up into.

"They're circling to the north to try to get out of the range of the bulk of our archers," Dirk said. "That's where they'll try to break out. That's where we need to hold them."

"That's also a perfect spot for their new allies to come pouring in at us," David guessed.

"That would also make sense," Dirk noted. He gave orders for those positions to be watched and reinforced.

"We'll know within an hour or less if that's their plan. And thanks to you and your people, Dave. We'll still be able to react to it."

"Dragon! Dragon!" spotters cried.

The red dragon swept in low at incredible speed, scorching a wide swath of ground on the left flank. Archers and other troops scattered in disarray and panic.

Dragonfire engulfed, killed, and injured dozens.

Troops shot Ballistae bolts at him, but wasted their fire. The red dragon was just too fast for them to track it.

Jerriel and the wizards with David were too far away to attack the creature. And just as quickly, it was gone again.

They waited with their friends around the wagon where the bodies of the two wizards lay within, guarded and immobile.

Another quarter hour.

The enemy continued to circle, and fought to break out. The lines held, bloodying the foe even more.

The dragon swooped in low again. This time it blasted the right flank where some of the light cavalry waited.

Mounted archers did manage to wound him slightly with a flight of arrows and crossbow bolts, but it did not slow him down.

"Come on," David said under his breath, as the battle continued to unfold. "If something is going to happen, it's going to happen now or very soon."

A moment later, one of the wizards groaned.

Both men stirred, but as they did, burns, blisters, cuts, bruises, and claw marks appeared as if by magic on their faces, hands, and arms.

They came to their feet. Rabbi Bergman clutched his side around his ribs.

The wizard Maelen limped and staggered, leaning against the wagon. Blood streamed down his left leg.

"Medics. Healers! See to their wounds," David commanded.

"Listen to us." Bergman insisted through his pain. "You must listen!"

"Both of you are hurt," Jerriel said. "Let us help you first."

Maelen pushed the medic's hands away for a moment. "No, we're battered, but nothing serious. The enemy does indeed have all three gateways set up. Troops pour through them, even as we speak!"

"A map. A map of the area!" Bergman shouted. "Show us a map. Even now, their forces keep charging through!"

Troops brought a map up. Bergman and Maelen studied it briefly, still wincing and groaning from their injuries.

"There is a magic mirror gate erected in these heavy woods here, to the east," Bergman said. "Get over there in force and capture it if you can. Destroy it if nothing else."

"To the west," Maelen said, marking the spot with a bloody fingerprint, "they have a magic oval gateway in a shallow cave in this steep rocky area. The gateway is fashioned out of some kind of metal or polished wood. You'll see a glow, perhaps, or the other wizards can sense its power when they get close enough. Bottle them up there. Same thing. Capture or destroy the gate. Go!"

"There's a third gate here, to the northwest," Bergman shouted, pointing at the map. "Between two tall copper pillars, the largest of the three gates, set into a hillside."

David called to his runners. "Tell Dirk the breakout to the north is a feint. Reinforce the left and right flanks and guard the rear. We're closest to the gate to the west. Come on, people, that's where we're heading. Have Dirk send other strike forces against the other gates in the forest and out of this hillside, in the tall grass."

"Let's take them down!" Jerriel shouted.

41

Mason spent the time just after sunrise reading and rereading Tori's letter.

At the moment, there wasn't much else to do, and he really liked that letter. The current battle was over, and he was exhausted. For some strange reason, the enemy had pulled way back. Not only out of range, but several miles out of sight. Apparently they had no intention of renewing their attacks at any point very soon.

Then, another shocker. That afternoon, the mercenaries approached under a flag of truce for a parlay.

They actually wanted to negotiate a peace treaty, and begin formal talks within the week.

Nobody knew what to think about that.

Then Rabbi Bergman appeared again in the magic compound on the third floor while it was still being clean up, repaired, and put back into shape. Mason and his troops assisted.

Bergman looked around while Rodell, Mason, and several guards surrounded him.

They didn't know, at first, who was popping in on them. Not after everything that had happened.

They did relax a little bit and lowered their weapons when they saw who it was. Bergman was an amazing person, and a Traveler, but he wasn't exceptionally frightening or imposing as an individual.

"Where's Shaeddor and Koden?" he asked. He carried another backpack full of communications and data. "My apologies, I was slightly wounded myself during the battles on our side, recently. But now I have fully been healed. We knew you were also under a pending attack, and we feared the worst.

"Were you able to make any headway with the magic data we sent over? Did the new transport spell work? Have you been able to study the design for the transport gateway prototype? We've already begun construction on our side, but it most likely will not affect the outcome of our present situation."

Mason and the rest continued to stare at him.

Bergman went on. "The principles of the applications were designed to duplicate the effects of the enemy transport cave in a device, activating two ends of a portal, and allowing transport between them."

"How much time do you have?" Mason asked Bergman.

"An hour or two, this time. I can go back and forth on my own now…once or twice each day…before needing to rest for a time. But I'm still having trouble transporting others. That is extremely difficult and exhausting."

"A lot has happened," Mace said. "Let's go have a quick chat with Major Bill Avery."

"Good idea. I have vital military information to pass on as well. Much has transpired on our side as well. I have military dispatches for your commanders on the grave situation unfolding in Elkhart on our side."

It took some time to explain all that had so recently occurred. When that was done, they skimmed over the packet of new information that Bergman had brought with him.

Bill gave him the latest prepared responses from their side, and the exchange continued.

They determined that Blondie had withheld Tori's letter to Mason, the information on the basic transport spell, and the prototype plans for the two ends of the first, functional transport gateway. The latter two things were still missing. More vital time would be lost, while copies were sent back over to replace them. Apparently, Blondie had hung onto them for his own personal use.

Intel advised, thereafter, that each packet include a list of contents as a security measure, and that both sides confirm the contents upon receipt, and send copies of the confirmed checklists back and forth. Such a basic safeguard would ensure that the right items were reaching their proper destinations, that nothing was forgotten by accident or stolen, and that deliveries of vital information could be confirmed and double-checked by more than one person handling them. And the proper records could be kept and maintained.

The worst notices were the military updates.

Major Bill announced that the enemy numbers on the other side continue to grow and expand at an alarming rate on an almost hourly basis. If this continued, eventually the other side would be overwhelmed.

So why was the enemy parlaying for peace on their side?

"I think I have the answer to this mystery," Mason offered. "Blondie and I spoke of this once in the past. He said that this was a standard military ruse that we were not to fall for. Say an invader had two large cities surrounded, but they did not have enough forces to take them both at the same time.

First, they would make a show of force at one city or even stage a preliminary attack, and then withdraw and pretend to sue for peace and negotiate terms. While they did that, they left a skeleton force behind, and raced all of of their troops over to the other city to lay siege to it, and take it by storm. Once that goal was accomplished, they would then regroup, return to the first city, break off the delaying tactics of the negotiations, and overwhelm that city next."

"Economy of force ratio," Major Bill noted. "It makes sense, and it costs little to delay an opponent who isn't going anywhere. As the invader, you are free to hit the defenders whenever you are ready."

Rodell nodded and agreed. "Historically, this is the way that mercenaries and even some Tharanorian militaries campaign, fought, and took territory. Yet it would also mean that the enemy already possesses the portable means of funneling troops back and forth between the two dimensions. That would be key to their strategy."

"We're already well aware of their transport cave in the mountains," Bill said.

"No, Rodell is right," Mason noted. "That wouldn't be enough. This strategy would require something different. These new portals or devices that Bergman has warned us about would be portable, and could be set up in different places. Even now, they might already have two or three of them in use. The enemy has been steps ahead of us all along the way. We should assume that they still are. They're containing us here, and sending all of their forces over to defeat the other side. When they're finished over there, they will flood in back here to wipe us out."

Major Avery stood up. "So, then, how do we defeat such a strategy?"

Rodell shook his head. "We don't have time enough to develop such devices of our own, even if we were certain that the prototype device would work. There's really only one option."

Bill and Mason and some of the others lifted their heads at the same time.

"We do what they least expect," Rodell said. "We commit an all-out attack against the enemy forces here, and seize control of the enemy devices on this side that are already set up and working. Or at the very least, if we cannot capture and make use of them for our purposes, we disable them so that the enemy cannot keep using them."

Bill jumped in. "We cut off the flow of reinforcements to the other side, eliminating their force multipliers."

"Not only that," Mason said. "Once we seize at least one of those devices on both sides of the Merge, we turn the tables and multiply our forces by sending our armies flooding over to the other side to help our allies defeat the enemy wherever they are needed."

Major Bill grinned like the Cheshire Cat. "Then we reverse the process, bring enough forces to this side, and crush the enemy here. Let's start planning our attack immediately."

"But wait," Mason said. "How do we locate the enemy's devices in order to attack them? We have no idea where in the hell they are."

The Traveler stepped forward. "Allow me to be of service, there; I have done the same thing on my side. Provide me with a quiet place under guard, where I can place myself in a astral trance, I can go out and review the enemy lines in my astral form. I will be like a ghost among them—most of them won't be able to see me. But it should be easy to spot the transport devices, and the huge number of troops and supplies being rushed through them. Allow me to study some of your maps for a bit to orient myself. Once I learn the locations of the three devices on this side, you can make plans to take them by force."

"Please, get going as quickly as you can," Major Bill said. "Every moment we delay means more troops bloating the enemy's lines on the other side. There are a number of rooms nearby. Just pick one, and we will guard you with our very lives."

Bergman nodded his thanks. "I must take certain precautions. I have learned that certain mages and persons—even children and some animals—can see astral forms. But do not fear. I have become an adept astral spy. In less than an hour, I should have your answers, and you can finish planning your attacks."

It only took Bergman a few minutes to settle in and go into his trance.

The waiting was the problem after that. The seconds and minutes ticked by with maddening slowness.

Mason left Rodell and the guards, and went to help Major Bill with the planning, sending letters and runners to all the leaders of Michiana on that side. This would require everyone's cooperation and timing. As certain units surged forward and went here and there, other forces would need to rush in and hold vital parts of the area behind them. The enemy could prove tricky as well.

Then word returned with Bergman, less than half an hour later.

The enemy was indeed utilizing the same three such transport devices on this side. All of them were spread out along the western flank, six miles back in the open wilds, and they were each heavily protected. Yet not so well-protected that they would be impossible to assail.

The only thing Bergman did not know was how long it took the enemy to set each of the different devices up, get them attuned to the other end, and have them open and functioning. These three devices were already set up and working, and long lines of troops were strung out in the distance behind each one, waiting for their turn to pass through.

Even worse, what if the devices could be shut down, dismantled quickly, and carried away in their waiting wagons? If they could be shuffled around rapidly, that might defeat any attempt to capture them.

Major Avery heard back from the militia leadership. They had to risk it. Making such an attack to capture one or more of the devices was their only hope of victory for both sides.

"Did you know," he suddenly blurted out, "that the two sides, our two dimensions are out of sync with each other by several hours? A curious thing, that. Anyone who crosses over back and forth will eventually notice it."

Avery waved a hand. "I can't change time, but we do need to know what each of those portal gatweays looks like."

Bergman was given some paper and started to make basic sketches of what he had seen, while he described the three devices and their locations.

One portal took the form of a wide oval of gold, which could be set in the ground, and had a short, portable ramp of wood and iron leading up to it. Wagons, horses, or infantry six abreast could march through it, and then appear shortly on the other side.

The second device was a mirror, set in a bright red metal frame. This device wasn't as wide. Two or three troops could squeeze through, but it was kept to two in order to speed things up. A horse and rider could pass through carefully, or a narrow, specially constructed wagon. The enemy had produced such wagons in abundant numbers and used them, pulled by a single draft animal or even by troops in a line using ropes.

The surface of the mirror looked like rippling quicksilver as troops, wagons, and supplies passed through it.

The final device was nothing more than two tall, copper posts set at a certain distance apart on heavy pedestals of iron and copper to support their weight and keep them erect and properly aligned. Each post looked to be about a foot and a half around, which would make them very heavy. They were engraved with strange, magical runes and symbols that glowed and flickered now and then. They were placed about twenty feet apart, and when activated, what looked like a lightning field or energy screen of some intense form, ten feet wide, filled the area between them.

Anything passing through that glowing field came through on the other side.

Militia artists quickly made many copies of those sketches to pass among the field commanders.

In proximity to their forces at hand, the golden oval was the nearest portal to attack. The mirror portal was the next closest, but it was also deemed to be the smallest and the most fragile. If it could not be seized and held or retrieved, as a last resort, it would be destroyed. If that was possible.

Rodell reminded them that they could not just think in Urth terms any longer. Magical devices that one might assume to be fragile could be enchanted with enough powers and protections to make them nearly indestructible.

The portal with the two copper posts was the furthest away from them. They would make an attempt to coordinate their attacks enough to assail and capture all three positions at once. But something could always go wrong. At best, they hoped to at least capture two of the three, and drive the enemy off long enough to send help to the other side.

Bill glanced over at Mason. "The Pistolero is going to be integral to these attacks, backed up by the Shooting Stars and all of our new mages. Everyone is going to have a hand in this one. Mace, your job is to get up as close as you can and first use annihilator rounds to reduce the enemy ranks of troops waiting to pour through the portals. That will confuse and dismay them."

"I get it," Mason said. "A little old-fashioned shock and awe."

Bill nodded. "Affirmative. Then we hit all three locations simultaneously and mow them down with all of the firepower we can muster. Our forces surge past them to set up pickets and portable defenses and mantlets to hold back the inevitable counterattacks. Our forces selected to go through and help out on the other side start to pour in. Once they aren't needed, they return, and bring friends back with them if we need help here.

"The development people have some new tricks up their sleeves that we want to try out—devices such as net shields and screens to repel and entangle the high-leaping slurgs and grun. Some of these obstacles will even be coated with pitch and tar, and can be set on fire, if we get enough foes trapped in them."

"You must excuse me. I have done all that I can, for now," Bergman told them.

Bill shook his hand with both of his. "Many thanks, Traveler. You've been a huge help. We literally could not do any of this without you. Watch yourself. You're simply too valuable to lose."

"Don't worry about me. I'm the careful sort. But I must return, let them know what you are attempting, and help out on my side. Thank you all." He picked up his pack to take back with him. "I will return as soon as possible, to check on your progress and bring you further information. Luck to us all!"

They waved to their brave friend and watched him vanish as he left them.

Mason finished checking his guns, and spun them into his holsters.

He had to stay alive long enough to reach his beloved Tori again. And one of those enemy portals could make that possible.

Damn anyone who got in his way.

"Time to get this done," he shouted. "Let's ride!"

42

David and Jerriel and their friends rode with Prince Valandin, Prince Alendel, and their knights. They were all given mounts, including a big draft horse to carry ThulKazar. It still looked like a pony underneath him.

Dirk sent a cavalry regiment with them to guide them among the hills. Jerriel, the two wizards, and their other friends rode with them as they raced to disrupt the enemy's plans.

They charged into that rocky target area and immediately came under enemy attack.

Torgs, ka-torgs, mor-kahls, and gozogs rose up out of the rocky landscape and pelted them with arrows, javelins, and missiles.

"Keep charging!" David shouted, lifting his shield.

A large rock blasted his shield. It nearly knocked him off his horse. An arrow glanced off, deflected by his leg armor.

"We have to reach that cave." Prince Valandin said. "The troops behind us will fill in and deal with these other foes!"

"Which cave is it?" Pharrio shouted. "I don't see a glow of any kind."

"There," Jerriel said, pointing with her staff at a distant spot. "Powerful magic. I sense it there, and it's growing!"

They sped in that direction.

The heavily armored Marrandorian knights and their armored horses, impervious to most of the attacks, spearheaded the way like thundering tanks.

As they neared their objective, hundreds of grun rose up out of the rocks and roared down the hillside to attack and cut them off.

"Lances at the ready!" Valandin commanded. "Tear through them and break left and right. Trample and destroy at will!"

He turned and smiled at David. "Captain Pritchard, your people and our wizards must take that cave and hold it. We will clear the way as much as we can!"

"Get us up there!" ThulKazar roared.

The charging knights ripped into the grun, tearing through and crushing them as the enemy tried to block the way.

In moments, they had almost reached the cave.

The knights and the cavalry lancers behind them wheeled to the right and left, dividing the enemy defenders, splitting them off. Only a few grun remained in the center.

Suddenly, the ground exploded right before them.

Rock and earth burst in every direction, scattering friend and foe, and horse and rider alike.

David rolled off his horse as an enemy spell flung it back screaming. He came to a crouch near Jerriel and the wizards where they sprawled, tangled up with some of the others.

As the dust cleared, Jerriel sprang to her feet, clutching her staff and stood beside them.

Both of them looked up.

The ground had not exploded from an earthquake.

The male red dragon had plummeted straight down at them from above and landed heavily on its feet and tail. Right in front of them, ready to defend the cave mouth.

It reared back and lifted its head, looming over them like a great shadow.

Jerriel and their wizards struggled to react defensively.

Intense dragonfire engulfed the entire area. People, and horses, and grun screamed and perished under that withering hurricane of heat and flame.

Even the hasty magic shields the wizards put up were barely enough to keep them alive for the moment, and collapsed even as the waves of dragonfire abated.

The dragon spun around and lashed at them with its massive tail.

Almost two dozen troops and horses, including Jason and Pastor Bryan, were swatted aside by the attack—some more than a hundred feet out of view.

David and Jerriel flattened themselves to the ground. The enormous tail passed over them.

They rose to attack and cast magic, but the dragon reared up again and beat its mighty wings, blasting them back yet again with fierce, gale-force winds.

The wind swept them off their feet and flung them back. ThulKazar caught them.

"You vermin helped kill my mate!" the red male hissed in rage. "Prepare to die!"

His eyes glowed again. He made ready to breathe fire.

Jerriel struggled to cast a protection spell. David knew about how long it took to cast such a spell.

This time, she wasn't going to make it.

The sky darkened. The ground exploded again, even more forceful than before.

The shock wave flung them all back forty feet or more.

The red dragon cried out in the erupting dust cloud.

Shavalkathar rose up on top of the other dragon, roaring in the ferocity of battle and ripping and tearing at the red male with his tremendous teeth and claws. He wounded the red dragon several times on the neck, throat, forearms, and wings.

"So, pretender," Shavalkathar raged. "The wyrm has indeed turned, now that you face me one on one. Your mate is dead and cannot help you overwhelm me this time. Soon, you shall join her!"

The red dragon roared and managed to pull free by sheer force, but it had taken serious damage. It backed off for more room to fight, not caring what or who it trampled.

But more importantly, its right wing looked severely damaged.

It couldn't fly away.

At a glance, the red male was longer than Shavalkathar, but not as heavily muscled.

It laughed, and croaked, "Come then, forest dragon. I've beaten you once and you are still weak. I will best you again and feast upon your carcass while you still live!"

"Unlikely," Shavalkathar said, and took to the air to crash down upon his foe once more.

They tumbled together, fighting, clawing, biting, and burning each other as they fought their way down the rocky vale, laying waste to much about them. The entire area shook and shuddered at the shocks of their deadly combat.

David noticed that Shavalkathar made every attempt to carry the battle away from them and their objective.

The way to the cave was nearly clear.

Yet nearby on the battlefield, friend and foe alike on the fringe of the area ran for cover, faced with two enormous dragons squaring off and fighting to the death.

But once their fierce battle carried the two dragons away, heads popped up again.

"Follow me." David shouted, drawing his swords. "Take that cave!"

Three large, hairy grun jumped down out of the rocks and blocked the cave mouth once more.

More charged in from either side.

ThulKazar roared his battle cry and rushed the three foremost grun.

The two to either side actually cried out in fear at the sight of the big Thul charging them. They dropped their weapons and ran.

ThulKazar ripped into the leader with his broadsword and battle-ax and tore him apart, flinging the severed head one way, and cutting the body in two and knocking the pieces aside, as he rushed into the dark cave.

David led the others behind the mighty Thul.

Within the cave David blocked a grun swordstroke even as he passed from sunlight into darkness. He impaled the goatman straight through the heart and kicked the body free. He dodged a spear thrust from the side.

Alejandro had his back, and slashed open the spear-wielder's throat, nearly beheading that grun.

A hooded wizard in dark robes stood next to a glowing, golden oval frame at the back of the cave. More grun tried to push their way out of the transport portal every moment.

The dark mage pointed a jet black rod at ThulKazar and spoke a strange word of command that split the very air.

Jerriel shielded the big Thul just as two grun sprang at him.

The black ray from the rod caused the two grun to implode, tearing them apart from within.

The next instant, Pharrio paralyzed the dark mage in a coating of magic ice.

Urnessan pulsed out orbs of grayish magic from his palms, that raced forward, struck the gleaming doorway of the golden oval, and drained it of energy for a few moments, deactivating it.

The shining metal ceased glowing and went dark, and looked tarnished almost instantly.

Several emerging grun imploded, sucked back through the portal in pieces.

"MOZHURRA!" Jerriel commanded. She closed her eyes and lifted her hands powerfully.

The remaining grun sank into the ground as if it turned liquid, struggling and shrieking as the stone of the cave floor closed over their heads.

Jerriel gasped and sank to her knees.

"Are you hurt?" David asked, covering her with his blades.

"I'll be all right. That was a powerful spell; very costly. Secure the transport gate."

Pharrio and Urnessan busied themselves trussing up the enemy wizard in some kind of magic bonds so that he couldn't escape.

Outside the battles still flamed, sweeping in several directions.

"Protect the cave opening." he shouted. "Don't let any of the enemy in!"

He examine the door frame of the transport gate.

Some kind of bonding material or weird mortar fastened it to the ground.

He jabbed at it with his sword. It broke apart and fragmented like brittle, unfired clay.

The other two wizards joined him, along with ThulKazar.

"That's just a bonding spell to hold it in place," Pharrio said.

"My negation blasts rendered the gate inert for a short while," Urnessan told them. "Right now, there's no danger in touching or moving it. We need to break it free and get it out of here so we that we can set it up again and reactivate it for our use."

David pried at the base with his longsword, busting up the bonding material even further.

ThulKazar dropped his weapons and grasped both sides of the large oval.

With a mighty heave, he yanked it free all by himself, and handed it toward the amazed team of wizards.

They almost toppled backwards into the wall. David and many others rushed forward to help steady the thing. The big Thul snatched up his weapons and strode outside into the sunlight to let forth his war cries and rejoin the battle.

Troops wrapped the oval in tarps and rope, securing it to drag it out. Then attached the lines to horses and pulled it out, placing their new prize on a prepared sled of logs with roller wheels. They carted it off under heavy guard to its new location behind their lines, to set it back up. Maelen and many of the wizards went with it.

Urnessan also went along briefly to help protect it.

Jerriel recovered, feeling better by then.

The reports from the continuing battle still came in mixed.

267

The fighting slowly bogged down. Thankfully, the two dragons carried their titanic battle into the adjacent wilderness.

"Captain Pritchard!" a runner called out. "The other strike force didn't reach the other gateway in time. It's still open, and hundreds of enemy reinforcements are continuing to pour out."

They checked out that area of the battle on the maps, and then with binoculars.

"Mercenaries, from Khairun," Jerriel confirmed.

The fresh enemy forces put up a stiff resistance and swept out onto the plain. They were expert fighters. Not only did they hold their own, but bolstered by their battlemages, they started to dominate portions of the field.

"We have to get over there and close that other gate." Jerriel said. "Who knows how many troops they plan to send through? Or what else?"

Dirk brought up reinforcements that helped push back the grun.

They explained the situation quickly, and gathered the Blackhawks and other units for a new assault.

Into the teeth of the most hotly contested part of the battle.

43

Mason helped lead the attacks on the enemy transport portals. That night, the sky was cloudy, with the rumbling threat of thunderstorms sweeping in from the southwest, on the horizon. Not only was the night dark, but in the lowlands and the shallow vales and forest hills and sloughs, a heavy fog was out.

Mages increased its reach and density to help mask the militia's movements.

Back in South Bend, the people there held a fake celebration over the peace talks, being as loud and as boisterous as they could to give them cover over any noise.

The advance troops of the first assault wave went in light. In fact, for the last half mile, they practically crawled in on their bellies, signaling each other by touch when they could advance more and when they had to freeze.

The enemy seemed secure in their power, from what could be seen. They had guards out, but no more than usual. Most of their troops did what most troops did—sat around fires, and gambled or talked in their camps.

Mason took up a vantage point in a high tree platform that the scouts and spotters used. It was more or a less an expanded deer stand, set higher up, but it gave him a wide view and perspective of the three primary enemy encampments, established around the portals.

In the distance, Mason could see the lines of troops still filing into all three of the portals without fail.

He waited there while his long guns were pulled up to him on tethers. Then they could be lowered quickly for reloading. Mason was on a lifeline as well, to avoid accidental falls. When the signal came, he was to fire three annihilator rounds at the packed troops marching in.

Then he would zip back down on one of the scout tree lines and join the attack on the mirror portal.

The first wave was in position without detection so far. Thus, an attempt was being made to move up the rest of the attack waves. Having them in place closer would make the attacks go that much smoother and faster.

Yet something went wrong, as it often did. On Mason's far right, the enemy detected the Urther troop movements somehow and raised the alarm.

Ready or not, and like it or not, they had been found out, and the battle was now joined prematurely. Mason had already fired his first round at the left and was about to fire on the middle column when the signal for him to shoot and commence the all-out attack went up.

There was already no reason for him to delay his attacks.

He got off his third shot on the right, when the first round whumped in the air and detonated in a blinding half globe of destroying fire, taking down hundreds, if not thousands of enemy forces in one swoop. Then the second round erupted in the center.

He buzzed down the line with his gloves, and his feet hit the ground as the third round ignited. He ran to Winger and leaped into her saddle, and sent her into a run as the attacking waves swept forward.

It seemed weird not having Blondie and Thulkara on either side of him. His militia buddies protected him now. He had his friends from Team 3 all around him. Blondie was now branded as a traitor, or whatever he was becoming—betrayer, revenant—none could know that guy's mind. Mason had sent Thulkara off with Rodell on the right. Rodell was good, but he was going to need her to watch his back.

The mages of Michiana had divided up into three separate attack elements, and would come in quickly with the second wave. The Shooting Stars led the attack on the left.

What they soon learned was that the enemy had allowed a bulge of their forces to gather in the middle, for whatever reason. This meant that the middle assault group, the one Mason was in, faced the largest number of troops in one place, almost twice as many as the groups on the right and left flanks had to deal with.

The Pistolero reached the front where the main attack wave had been halted in a shield wall stalemate. Both sides clashed, pulled back, and then clashed again. Mason rode up with his guards and his reloading wagons and teams behind him.

He started using his guns and devastator rounds to punch holes in the enemy defenses. Then several enemy mages charged up, peppering the attacking militia lines with destructive spells.

Mason switched tactics, and started targeting all of the enemy mages that he could spot within his range.

The second militia attack wave came up. They could not do much for the moment, but at least they brought the new mages with them. Spells ripped into the length of the enemy lines and began punching and driving them back by sheer force. They also engaged the enemy mages and took them on, at least keeping them busy.

The militia commanders cycled the line, sending in the second wave of fresh fighters, and drawing out the first attack wave to give them a break and form them back up behind the second.

The third and fourth waves behind them were heavier forces, meant to expand beyond the portals and set up defenses for the next lines to join. They would do this even while the portals were still surrounded and being hotly contested. Their mission was to prepare for the eventual enemy counterassault and hold them off, at least until the portals could be secured.

Even more armies would march up then to support the others, and to march through the portals and go forth to aid the Michiana forces on the other side.

That was the initial plan, but things continued to keep working out differently.

Unfortunately, it was taking much longer to seize the portals than anyone had predicted.

By now, they had thought that they would have seized at least one of the objectives, but the enemy stood fast and fought with discipline and ferocity.

The enemy sacrificed good troops trying to hold out. Mason blasted through their mantlets and shield walls methodically, dueling with enemy mages and ducking arrow waves, just like the old days.

But every time the Pistolero cleared a path, the enemy would surge ahead to try to fill the breach, and they advanced slowly, at half measures. And in the press, it was difficult to direct his fire so as not to blast any of his own people.

Clearly the enemy thought that if they could hold the defensive perimeter around the portals, that they could endure out long enough for their fresh forces to drive the Urth attackers away and back toward the city.

Then word from Major Avery up ahead of them told Mace that the enemy was close to accomplishing that very feat.

The third and fourth militia waves had been hampered by more attackers and resistance than had been expected. They had only advanced about half as far as they had originally intended to, and barely enveloped the backside of the enemy defensive perimeter around the portals.

This left the portals dangerously exposed and open to the enemy retaking them, if they counterattacked hard enough.

Bill wanted Mason to take up another vantage point and fire off three more annihilator blasts to degrade and delay the enemy's massed forces once again.

Mason obeyed his orders, and saw no rational alternative himself, yet it still delayed them reaching the middle portal again, and left the forces there locked in a deadly stalemate.

As he fired off the rounds from another spotter position, Mason noted that the attack on the left seemed to be doing about the best, almost as they had originally intended. Rodell and Thulkara's position on the right was even more behind than the middle by their positioning. But they had been hampered by an additional attack of monsters that had come out of the dark, and threatened their exposed right flank. Their third and fourth attack waves were busy holding off the sudden rush of monster hordes that had swept in. More militia forces swung even wider, to the left and the right, trying to encircle the mercenaries and the monsters.

He was ready to fire the third round on the right when a massive fireball shot their way, hurtling directly at the spotting tree they were in.

"Incoming!" one of the spotters shouted. A handful of people tried to zip down on lines and get away.

"We're dead. Get out of here!" The scout behind Mason said, and shoved him off the platform and out of the tree with both hands. He dropped the shotgun and it got tangled up in its own line as it fell. Mason plummeted after it, crashing through lesser branches.

His lifeline jerked him in half and almost winded him, as the fireball struck the upper part of the tree dead center and exploded.

Mason jerked back up as the blast wave of magical fire and exploding heat expanded. His lifeline either snapped or was melted.

As he fell to the ground backwards, he drew his pistols and tried to negate some of the magic blast with two of his own.

He gutted the fireball from below, and took out about half of it, saving himself and several others. But anyone who had been up in that tree, including the scout who had save him by throwing him down, were already dead. The magic fire reduced them to nothing but charred skeletons.

Mason hit the ground hard right after he fired, and was completely winded.

Hands of the people he had saved grabbed him and dragged him back, pulling him away while more enemy spells peppered his former position.

"Those annihilator rounds sure piss them off," one of his reloading runners said.

"Can you blame them?" Mason said. "Hey, when the smoke clears, see if you can send some people in to retrieve the shotgun I dropped. It still has two annihilator rounds in it. We can't lose that gun, and they still need a round or two fired on the right."

"Will do, Mace. Bring up the other shotgun and try firing from just behind that hilltop! Get the reloading wagons over there to protect them."

He didn't know where his horse was in the confusion, so he started running up the slope of that hill. At some point, a runner shoved one of the other shotguns into his hands.

By the time he crested the hill and looked out on the right, things looked pretty bad. He sent off both rounds, one to reduce the troops pouring in on the right from the enemy's rear, and another to take out some of the dark sea of monsters.

They all ran down the back of the hill as soon as he fired. As they expected, several devastating enemy spells peppered the front side of the hill and the hilltop where they had just left.

The enemy was constantly adjusting, also. Yet how had they increased the range of their magic so dramatically, by nearly twice or even three times as much as they had been before?

Mason had done what he could to help all three attack units once more.

Other riders raced in and returned Winger to him. More word reached him. They had to rush him up to their forward line, in back of the portal area. The third and fourth lines were barely holding out against a determined enemy assault up the middle. The Urthers there could not last much longer without additional support.

The Pistolero was the backbreaker they needed to charge in, blast the enemy to perdition, and break the spine of their massive counterattack.

He still missed having his brother Blondie, backing him up.

Once more, Mason obeyed his orders, and charged forward to help avoid disaster, but the Urthers still seemed no closer to seizing the middle portal or either of the other two. And that was not good.

44

Within minutes, David's strike force disengaged and led their troops in an outward spiral, through the forest and out of view from the clashing, main battle lines.

They stumbled into skirmishers, scouts, support units, and even enemy troops spreading out from or fleeing the battle in panic and chaos.

They blasted through those obstacles and kept going, follow-up forces racing up behind them.

Their objective: reach that mirror gate, and capture or shut it down.

Rabbi Bergman joined them at the last minute, directing them with his attuned senses to almost exactly where the gate lay concealed.

On a high ledge, up a steep, forested hillside, mercenary troops continued to march down the hill trails, feeding into the battle proper. Estimates were that a thousand or more had already done so, with more on the way.

"How large are these mercenary bands?" David asked.

"Some are entire armies or navies in the tens of thousands," Pharrio said. "Some fight with order and discipline, others as rampaging, looting hordes. Remember, Khairun is a nation of sellswords and mercenary clans and bands."

Enemy troops spotted them. Heavy missile fire slowed their approach up the hillside. The mercenaries had a very effective defensive position established.

"You have to admire their tactics," Pastor Bryan said. "They'll be able to hold this position for hours, against superior numbers, and bleed anyone sent against them."

"I see that," David said, and ducked behind some big trees to study a map while the arrows whizzed around them, and their troops fired back.

He rolled the map back up and tucked it away in his belt.

He peered out from behind the tree and pointed up at the higher ridge line. "We need to get a small group up there above that gate, preferably myself and some picked fighters, Jerriel, and some of the other wizards. And we need to move fast."

"Get us closer," Rabbi Bergman said. "If we can get within line of sight, I can spot-blink several of you about a hundred yards up, before I pass out."

"That's a new technique," Jerriel said.

"And its very exhausting," Bergman said.

They struggled to work their way up the back side of the hill and up onto the ridge line, while the strike force kept the mercenaries distracted.

"They know we're trying to outflank them," David said. "Because that's what they would do in our position."

Breathing heavily, they reached a high saddle across the way. No enemy troops there. But they did spot some skirmishers moving up from below to cover even that position.

The mercenaries could also read maps and terrain.

"We've only got the jump on them for a few, crucial minutes right there. Rabbi, whatever you're going to do, do it soon. Me, Jerriel, the other two wizards, ThulKazar, Jason, Al, maybe Pastor Bryan if you can."

"Half a moment; I need water and a quick breather."

David turned to Tori and the others. "Tori, please stay here with the rest of our troops and follow on in, once we crack the way open."

"Got it, Mace. Will do," she said with a sigh. "Too bad we don't have Mason and his guns with us here on this side."

David smiled along with her. "Maybe someday, if we capture these gates."

"You know, Mace taught me how to shoot at his events, and some of his practice sessions. I'm a good shot, Dave. I just wish I could do some of things that we hear he does."

"Maybe once we get him over here, Tori, he can teach you how."

"That would be something," Tori added.

Bergman guzzled some more water from a canteen, already red-faced from their uphill trek. He was an older man, after all, but he had done very well keeping up with them thus far.

"Half a moment. I just need to catch my breath," he said.

"Whenever you're ready, Rabbi."

Bergman had them face the position they wanted to reach and focus on it. He stood behind them with his hands on their shoulders, focusing ahead until his eyes began to glow.

He gave David a light push.

David zoomed through the air, covering the space within a split instant as the land raced past him.

The rush was very unnerving. It took his breath away.

He tumbled to the ground and rolled into a brake filled with leaves and pine needles. Several seconds later, Jerriel appeared nearby, tossed in next to him.

Across such an uneven distance, Rabbi Bergman could not guarantee a soft landing or putting them on their feet.

"It's still an experimental technique," Jerriel said, wincing.

Pharrio and Urnessan came in next, and tumbled together just above them.

ThulKazar smacked into a tree, grunted with a low laugh, and got back up.

The tree took the worst of it.

Jason Inada flashed in next. Then Al. They tried to hit the ground running, but only pitched face down into the leaves and dirt.

Finally Pastor Bryan tumbled in. ThulKazar stopped and steadied his tumbling bulk. Otherwise his momentum might have even carried him down the hillside.

"I think I'm the last," Pastor Bryan said. "The rabbi was pretty exhausted and ready to pass out."

"Everybody up and okay?" David asked.

"Now I know how a rag doll feels when a child tosses it across the room," Alejandro said.

"Let's move out," David told them.

Jerriel looked back. "I hope Rabbi Bergman is all right."

"He did his part," Jason said. "He can rest in the back of a wagon somewhere, while we still have to risk our butts getting to that fricking mirror gate."

"Then let's get to it," David said. "Take point, Al."

"Me? Why me?"

David placed his hand on Al's shoulder. "Because, my friend...you are the Eagle!"

Al shook his head and raised his chin high. "Yes. I am indeed. I am he who soars!"

They picked their way down the hillside, keeping to cover whenever possible. The enemy mercenaries continued to move up from below.

They tried not to watch how the rest of the battle went, but the mercs were tough disciplined fighters, and maneuvered with speed and precision.

No one spotted them from below, as yet.

Then a few stray arrows whizzed down at them from higher up.

Other enemy troops had made a similar climb after them, spotted them, and commenced an attack. They also gave away the strike team's position to the troops further down the hill.

"Great, just great!" David said. "We still have to reach that mirror!"

"We're almost there." Al shouted. "No need for silence anymore. "I can see where the enemy's rushing out. Less than sixty yards down and to our left. That must be it."

"Jerriel," David said. "You and the wizards blast that area with all the magic you can. Break the mirror if you have to."

"We'll never capture it against such numbers," Jason observed.

"Wait," Jerriel said. "We have to be sure. Just because the troops are coming out at that point, that doesn't mean that is where the gate is. If I was as good at strategy as you say these mercenaries are, I wouldn't leave my weak point exposed like that at all."

"She's right," Pastor Bryan said. "Look, further down on the right. There are almost as many troops streaming out at that point as well."

"Spread out then and we'll charge down the mountain side," David said. "We'll be harder to hit and cut off. Whoever spots the mirror, give a shout to rally everyone else over to that point. Go. They're already closing in on us from above and below!"

They moved out from their position. An air blast leveled a handful of the big trees like a cyclone and scattered them even farther apart, right where they had been standing moments before. They dodged debris, but the resulting cloud of dust and smoke actually helped conceal their descent.

They tried not to cough at the dust and dirt whirling around them.

"They have at least one battlemage with them," Pharrio noted.

"Right," Urnessan added. "That was a pretty good jolt of magic."

Forming a broad skirmish line, still in sight and earshot of each other for the most part, they raced down the mountain side with the dust cloud before and around them.

They had to reach the mirror gate ahead of the enemy reinforcements.

Then David realized that he didn't have any plan for what to do after that.

Even if they captured or destroyed the mirror…

They would still be surrounded and outnumbered.

First things first.

And there would be many troops guarding the mirror gate. Not to mention those still rushing out of the gate itself.

Running down the steep mountainside gave them speed.

Pharrio tripped and rolled forward, finally coming to a stop against another tree.

They couldn't slow down to help him where he caught his breath.

Hopefully, he wasn't badly injured.

The dust from the explosion swept over the area where the mirror should be. The enemy mage was apparently smart enough not to unleash any more wild magic that might give the strikers further cover.

David heard more shouts of dismay and cursing among the enemy in one place twenty yards to his right and straight down—much more so than in any other pocket nearby.

That had to be the location.

He leaped forward, cracked his head somewhat on a low tree branch. Protected by his helmet, he skidded forward in the leaves and pine needles.

Suddenly he tumbled down through the open air. But not far.

He fell directly onto a flamboyantly dressed soldier holding a map in one hand and a telescope to his eye, trying to look down at the unfolding conflict. He had a small pocket of horsebow archers clustered around him, either scouts or runners.

David heard Jerriel unleash an area of affect spell thirty feet to his left, just as he flattened the mercenary leader who broke his fall. The enemy troops cried out in dismay.

More spells went off to his right as he lay on top of the struggling leader. David rose to his feet and used his pommel to further clobber the leader clutching the map and telescope. He spun and lashed out wildly, knocking the others aside, scattering them more than wounding them.

Finally he spotted the mirror gate, tall and rectangular, and set in a strange, glowing frame of some kind of red metal, secured between two huge pine trees, almost out of sight in a deep copse of the forest.

"To me, Blackhawks. To me. I see the gate. It's over here!" David cried. "I've found the gate!"

Mercenaries also drew their weapons and rushed at him from all sides.

More enemy archers emerged from the gate.

And another enemy battlemage.

David spoke the command words rapidly activating all of the energy runes in his longsword, and charged the enemy.

Spells flared from his swords, blasting and scorching his foes in all directions as his blades wheeled, cut, and smote.

45

Mason shouted to his mantlet troops, "Get ready!"

He aimed his St. Louis rifle and fired for maximum distance. He handed the rifle off and quickly took up his 10-gauge. He fired a shot off to the far middle, and then adjusted and let one arc in dangerously close, approximately ninety to one hundred yards away.

The three annihilator rounds pounded the enemy forces straight ahead like a trio of blows from a massive, fiery hammer, blasting the earth as the explosions walked in.

Whumpf! Whumpf! Whumpf!

"Get down!" Mason screamed.

They were going to get flattened anyway. The foremost militia lines fell back beneath their protective mantlets, shields, and any cover they could find like rows of collapsing tiles. They held on to the ground itself for what was coming.

Less than a second later, three consecutive blast and thermal waves roared over them, even sweeping some of the exposed enemy troops bumping along over them and scorching everything that could burn within two or three miles. Trees, grass, buildings, troops, and wagons—the core of the battlefield was set ablaze, and the resulting grass and forest fires became an inferno. Smoke obscured the entire region, whirled around by the threatening winds.

As the fighting continued, lightning flickered and continued to flash in the distance as the wind increased, fanning the flames. Mason didn't like laying waste to the countryside that much, but with the enemy mixed in with it all, there was no avoiding such collateral damage. Their foes had to be reduced, at all costs. And besides, big parts of those new patches of the dark forests were going to be scheduled to be cleared out that way.

The pressure dropped and ozone mixed with the smell of smoke, blood, and monsters.

A great cheer went up from the left, and the mages there sent up red signals of victory. The Shooting Stars and their forces had finally taken the Golden Oval Portal intact. Mason craned his neck and saw ranks of militia troops lining up and waiting to pass through to aid their allies on the other side. The side Tori was on.

The enemy left broke, and now the middle was wiped out, so the massed militia forces raced at top speed to flow out from the left and the middle, to surge forward and seize the field in those directions.

The enemy right lines still held, and tried to spread out to delay and engage the surge, but the militia troops refused to halt or be held back, and spread out over three miles, with more reinforcements pouring in behind them. Finally they came about to the right, anchored their new left flank, and engaged the enemy's thin right line with showers of arrows to break them further.

It was only a matter of time now, but the enemy still held out stubbornly.

To make matters worse, Mason's people informed him that mercenary troops were starting to reverse, and pour back out of the mirror gate.

They couldn't let that happen. If enough troops came back out of the two remaining gates, they could turn the tide on this side and ruin everything.

They were close to mirror gate, even though no one had seen it yet or gotten within fifty yards of where the troops were pouring out. The mercenaries had constructed two thick stone walls on either side of a narrow roadway that hairpinned and dead-ended into the raised, forest hillside up a seventy-foot leeward slope. Using the trees as part of their defensive position, they also had pits, trenches, barricades of wood and stone, and fighting positions heavily entrenched all about that position.

It made a tough knot of enemy defenders to dig out, with more troops were still joining the mercs to defend it.

"I'm ordering an all-out assault on that position from every possible side and angle," Mason said. "We can't let them gut us up the middle and keep pouring out reinforcements. One way or another, we need to shut down that gate. Send in everyone and keep sending them in until we overrun that position!"

Word reached them. With the left side secured, Major Avery was bringing the Shooting Stars and the other mages with him to help out. Their center had to hold.

Mason would destroy the mirror if he could see it, but the enemy was too clever to leave it out in the open for that. Any attackers would have to fight their way in close through a hornet's nest just to try to get to it–while fresh troops continued to flood out.

"Bring me pistols with incendiary rounds again," Mason told his runners.

They moved up and around in a winding arc. They'd fight their way above that position and then loop back down around the other side.

Weapons, blasts, arrows, and magic went off, sweeping and tearing back and forth. Troops withered and fell on both sides. The mantlets and shields held for a time, were torn aside, and new ones came up to replace them. The scorched hill quickly ran red with blood.

The Pistolero kept up his advance, and blasted the hill with fire and flame. Troops leaped into pits and trenches, and locked with the enemy in deadly, hand-to-hand combat. By the time Mason came down the hill on the far side, everything seemed to have been set ablaze, and they fought within a nightmare that seem like something from hell itself.

He raked the mercenary troops rushing out with blasts of devastator fire, smearing them to either side in burning, red waves. It was slaughter, pure and simple.

He and his vanguard leaped down right among the shocked and stunned enemy survivors, and went toward where the mirror gate had to be.

Troops screamed and rushed at Mason with weapons set to charge. That close, Mason's rapid firing pistols shredded them into strings of burning meat.

Finally he spotted the mirror up ahead, still glowing and drenched with gore from the last score of mercs who had just vanished in flame and death.

Such carnage could not continue, and there was no way that his forces could push through and fight their way through foes packed in this dense tunnel.

Mason made a tactical decision, and drew his Howdah Hunter shotgun pistol from the holster in his duster.

He leveled both barrels, even as several more troops rushed out of the mirror, slipping and sliding on the red human meat and mud.

The Pistolero fired both barrels, not at the hapless men, but high up at the mirror gate itself. The tungsten-and-titanium-laced rounds were penetrators. They could sheer through solid concrete and steel.

The twin blasts struck the mirror gate dead center, and blew it straight to hell and glittering pieces. The gateway portal flashed brightly once and collapsed. The middle gate was taken down and almost completely destroyed.

The enemy defenders lost heart after that and surrendered readily. Mason had to hand it to the mercs. They had put up a stiff fight, right up until the very end. Some of the angry militia troops began to knock the prisoners and the wounded around.

Mason shouted to the officers to put a stop to that in a hurry. These people were the enemy, but they weren't monsters. They were brave soldiers who knew their business and had held up their end of things. They didn't deserve to be abused or murdered.

A few of the captives had heard his orders and even thanked him, staring up at him in fear and awe as they were led away.

Mason suddenly realized that he was drenched all in red, from head to foot.

He asked a mage to wash him off a bit with a water spell.

He sat down after that and had a breather, taking some water. He gave his reloaders time to reload all of his weapons. He had new rigs on his thighs to go along with his Spillers, which allowed him to carry four more of his smaller frame revolvers, and they all worked as well as the larger ones, it seemed.

These new rigs were working out well.

He couldn't sit down very well in a chair, but on a horse he was just fine. Mason had discovered that during the course of most battles, he was mostly standing and running anyway. There wasn't a lot of chair sitting, and having four more guns kept him shooting longer. Perhaps he could work a few more holsters into the side of his duster. He just couldn't make himself too heavy.

Just as he expected, Major Bill arrived, flanked by the Shooting Stars. Gosh, those pretty young girls were a such fierce little pair. He could see the light of battle blazing in their glittering eyes. They were young, but they were fighters all right, and veterans by now. Both of them had made it plain that they were hoping to find survivors from both of their families on the other side, once all was done.

The two young women—still only nineteen, one with long blond hair, and one with long, curly brown hair—had fought like Valkyries. Their courage was beyond question, and the people adored and practically worshipped them wherever they went.

The troops were cheering them now.

"Hey girls!" Mason shouted. "Glad to see you, sweeties!"

Both Minnie and Hannah leaped off their horses and rushed up to hug the Pistolero. Hell, he was only a year or so older than them, and they were Tori's age. Why did he feel so old now?

Minnie Patterson stared up at him, an extremely sad look on her face. "Mace, we're still heartbroken about Blondie."

Hannah Masters jumped in with her. "We still don't believe it, even after they told us. Did he really betray us all?"

Mason shook his head. "Ladies, it kinda looks that way for now, but let me tell you the full story when we have time. I think there's still a bit of fighting to do. Hey, did you hear they found my sweet Tori alive on the other side? She sent me a letter that made me so happy, I cried."

Minnie touched his face. "Oh, Mace. That's wonderful. We know how much you love her."

"We wanna meet her!" Hannah said.

"I hope you girls find your families there, too."

"Aww...thanks, Mace," Minnie added.

Major Bill stood by as long as he could. "All right, you three. Back to business. Rodell and Thulkara are still having a helluva time capturing that last gateway. With the middle gate destroyed, we need that one intact, more than ever. The enemy has all of their remaining forces surrounding it, and they look like they intend to hold onto it, no matter what."

The shooting stars leaped up onto their horses and readied their bows; they slipped on their helmets and set their faces to return to war.

Thunder rumbled behind them still, and lightning flashed even closer.

The wind swept around them and through their hair, making them look like bright warrior goddesses in their shining armor.

"Let's get over there," Hannah said eagerly. "Between us, the Pistolero, and the rest of our mages, the enemy won't stand before us for long. Let's put them down!"

Mason jumped up on Winger. It was all he could do to ride hard and keep up with the two gleaming warriors racing ahead of him.

46

From above, with a by now customary earsplitting battle cry, ThulKazar careened down the hillside. Like an avalanche of armor and steel, he slammed into the enemy and flung mercenaries in every direction.

He literally grabbed the battlemage by the head and hair with one huge hand and tossed him down the mountainside. Just before the wizard could blast David.

The hapless mage bounced off a tree and lay groaning in the weeds.

David attacked the gate.

Magical blasts punched into his foes with every sweep of his longsword. He had nearly reached the mirror.

Then the emerging troops pulled a small wagon through.

Battering weapons aside and dodging arrows, David leaped forward.

"Shit!"

An expanding ring of spirit force pushed them all back.

He climbed and kicked his way over the surprised troops before they could react.

He topped the wagon.

With his left hand, he flung a tomahawk at the gating mirror.

Foes raised weapons and batted it down.

Jason, Al, and Pastor Bryan fought their way to his position, but the rolling wagon carried David further away from the mirror. More surprised troops clambered up the sides and filled in behind. As soon as they came through and spotted foes, the mercs attacked.

ThulKazar jumped onto the wagon with David, nearly shattering it as the wheels and axles cracked and buckled under his great mass.

Urnessan engulfed one entire flank of the emerging troops in a gray-green choking gas to help immobilize them. Then an arrow struck him in the shoulder, knocking him back.

David looked up at the big Thul without hesitation. "Toss me at the mirror!"

ThulKazar grinned, snatched him by the collar and belt, spun around once on the wagon, using David's armored body to knock foes aside and let fly, almost without effort.

David cartwheeled through the air, barely able to hold onto his weapons. He passed over the heads of the choking troops and crashed directly into the big rectangular mirror and the glowing, red metal frame. He attacked the gateway with his sword.

The top section of the frame and the mirror itself crunched and shattered, bursting into many pieces. The energy within it swelled back up and exploded just as another wagon started through.

Fragments of glass, splinters of woods, and bits of debris and supplies raced ahead of the blast wave. It took out the two big pine trees on either side, and flattened friend and foe in a fifty-foot swath down the mountainside.

Stunned, David gasped and choked, struggling to breathe and stand at the same time. His smoking limbs wouldn't respond.

Mercenaries closed in, clubbing and beating him into the mud before he could recover. Rough hands stripped his weapons away and painfully secured him, holding him fast.

They half-dragged, half-carried him back and then tossed him to one side.

Some of his friends already lay on the ground nearby, blasted and battered, but alive.

Jerriel struggled against her bonds until a spear point appeared at her throat. Someone told her to lay still in Tharanorian. Her face was scratched and covered with mud, her right eye bruised and swollen.

Jason, Al, Pastor Bryan, Pharrio, and Urnessan—all captured and tied up.

ThulKazar was the only one David didn't see anywhere nearby.

The first enemy soldier he had initially flattened, still clutching his shredded map and a now-bent brass telescope, pointed the damaged instrument at David's face.

"Do you speak my tongue?" he asked, in a completely new Tharanorian accent.

David struggled to remember. Jerriel said the mercenaries had their own lands. They were from…Khairun.

"Sah…" David said. "A little." Actually, wearing one of the translation medallions, David could understand the fellow almost perfectly.

"Good," the man said. He had a crooked, aquiline nose and a proud, haughty air. "I cannot speak much Urther, yet, but I am learning. Yehess, as yoo shay?"

David smiled and nodded.

The leader drew himself up. "I am Field General Hatto Varrakarsus of the Scarlet Vipers, the Crimson Swords of Morrad. I have come to this place within the last month to personally lead my forces. I congratulate you on your courage and determination. You have successfully taken out our mirror gate."

"That was our mission."

"I know. Such bravery shall not go unrewarded. I will give the order shortly for my men to cut all your throats and end your lives quickly. You will not suffer…much."

"Where is the Thul?" David asked.

Hatto paled. "Oof! I tell you I'm going to keel you all, and you have no thought for yourself, eh?"

David laughed out loud. "Hey, Al. Get this. He's going to 'keel' us!"

Al snorted. "At least we won't be creepled."

All of them laughed, even Jerriel.

General Hatto Varrakarsus stared at them all in wonder. "I am liking you already, my brave fellow. You inquired about that blasted, bloody Thul? Hah!" He spat on the ground at his feet.

"That gigantic, unstoppable fiend is bellowing somewhere down the mountainside, hacking and hewing his way to your approaching lines by now, I believe. He and some of your friends saw that you had been taken, and were out of their reach after the explosion. They tried to make it down the hillside and get away. That cursed Thul was the only one of you that we could not drag down." He paused, frowned, and then shrugged.

"You cannot stop Thulls like that, once they are in their battle fury. Better to just get out of their path and let them go. You lose fewer troops that way. And I, for one, will not be the one who has to feed that giant glutton tonight, or slake his bottomless thirst and get him drunk, or find him a woman crazy and willing enough to be flattened beneath his massive bulk."

He smiled and looked around at his grim men. They all shared a harsh laugh.

"At least let us die on our feet," David asked.

"No pleas for mercy, then?" Hatto asked.

David looked him straight in the eye. "None. We are warriors. We did our duty, what we came to do."

"Again, verry brave." He passed a scarred hand across Jerriel's smooth cheek and looked her up and down.

"I might have something to say," Alejandro began. The others shot him looks that told him to shut up.

Hatto clucked his teeth in displeasure. "What a waste to cut such a pretty throat. Sylurrian, by the looks, and that is a surprise. She fights for you, eh? Yes, most exquisite. Come, my pretty little mage. Say that you will warm my bed tonight, and I shall let your glory live on. Cast your spell of love on me and see another dawn."

Jerriel spat at him and tried to sink her white teeth into his hand. "Do your worst. The only way that I will warm your bed is with your blood!" She tried not to send David a fleeting look, but she apparently couldn't help it.

General Hatto could not have helped but notice that glance as he and his men laughed once more. "This is all too much. So, the fair wizardess is not only your companion, but your lover as well?" he said. Jibes and hoots from the other mercs. "Most interesting. Again, I commend you, my amazing friend. Not only for your skill on the field, but for your taste in young women. Salute. But please, before you die, I must at least know your names, my brave people."

David smirked. "Then I will not tell them to you, and all of us shall live."

"Tut, tut, tut." Hatto shook his head and chuckled, wagging a finger. "No, no, my friend; it doesn't work that way. Take your names to your graves, then, if you insist upon doing so. It was mere curiosity on my part. I still have a battle yet to win."

"This one day may yet be yours," Jerriel said. "But you have lost the battle already, from the moment we shattered the mirror gate. You know this to be true."

"Captain Areglio, put sharp steel to their throats. Upon my signal, slash them ear to ear."

Rough hands pulled their heads back. Keen blades scraped and nicked their flesh.

"Now," General Hatto said. "Tell me again why I shall not win the day, and the morrow, both? What doth thou knowest, that the mighty Hatto Varrakarsus does not?"

"Our dragon has defeated yours by now, and dines upon its molten heart," David said. "The Dragon Cult is crushed, and shall never rise again."

Hatto waved at some gnats in his face. "Piffle. We do not need such weak fools. Go on."

"By now, our first wave of reinforcements have you surrounded and hemmed in," Pastor Bryan said.

"Only the first wave? I have tested the mettle of your troops. No better than my own, except for some elite strikers such as yourselves. We can break out wherever and whenever we like, and go wherever we please."

"And go where?" Jason Inada asked. "I'm guessing you're days, maybe weeks or even months from any other allies you might have. Otherwise you would not have used the magic gates to bring your people in."

"And we know that you weren't able to bring through all of your forces and supplies," Alejandro added. "Not by far. We saw to that. Our troops will wear you down and crush you. Actually, I advise that you surrender quickly. To us. Right now."

The mercenary holding Al nicked him again.

"...or not," Al squeaked.

"I did not entirely follow what that one said," General Hatto noted. "But I did not like the way he said it."

"He merely stated the facts," Jerriel said. "Both of your remaining gates are down, and one is destroyed. We've captured one and will be able to start using both gates ourselves, very shortly. Then it will be our reinforcements pouring through to bolster us. We still have a dragon, and you don't. You're cut off from your supply lines and any further reinforcements."

General Hatto lifted his hand. "Then I suppose I should finish with all of you and get back to winning my battle."

David laughed. "It's not your battle any longer. It's ours. You've already lost. You just won't admit it. And killing us? Big mistake, all around."

The general paused. "How so? Who are you again? I have given you my name. Step forward and speak to me, as a man."

David drew himself up and clenched his fists. "I'm Captain David Pritchard, leader of the Blackhawks. You can kill us if you like, but I'm telling you right now that General Dirk Blackwood will show no mercy

289

on you if you murder us, and pursue you to the end. He'll have your heads on pikes, and your skins nailed to trees, drying in the wind."

"Hmm, very unpleasant. Sounds like a rare man whom I need to meet and share a drink with. Perhaps not under those exact conditions that you named…the flaying and skinning and all."

Jerriel spoke up. "I am a royal cousin of the House of Marrandor. Prince Valandin and Prince Alendel are my relations and our allies. You know their troops are on the field playing havoc with your lines. Our deaths will enrage them, and they too will pursue you and all of your men to the death. You don't have a chance."

General Hatto thought an instant. "Lower your blades," he told his men. "Do not harm them…yet. So, my brave new friends. What is it that you are telling me? That you will all make better hostages than casualties of war?"

"Si," Al said.

"Sah," David corrected him.

"General, no more of your command need die," Jerriel said. "They will continue to perish every moment that you hesitate. Call a truce and pull back. You know your blood contract with them is now voided; you've done all that you can. The agents of those who hired you are dead or captured."

"This battle is lost—it is only a matter of time," David added. "There is no way that our forces will let you win, or even survive. We can help you negotiate an honorable surrender. We aren't like those filthy necromancers who hired you. We understand the concept of honor."

General Hatto sighed heavily. "Let me assess the field…before I decide your fates."

"Every moment, you lose more of your troops," David said.

"Silence!" He pointed his sword at David and Jerriel.

"If either of these two say another word. Gag them."

"May I speak, then?" Al asked.

General Hatto rolled his eyes.

"Gag that one right now."

47

Mason rode in to find Thulkara and Rodell. Major Avery and the Shooting Stars raced around to take up positions and attack from the far side, catching the enemy between them.

For good measure, they sent the mages at the head of an entire army to finish cutting the enemy forces off to the west and north, and completely surround the final portal.

A three-pronged attack developed. Four, actually, counting Rodell and Thulkara, if they didn't team up with Mason and his troops. Then they could hit the enemy from all sides at once.

The foe, of course, was in another dandy defensive position, and not by accident. A rocky, forested hilltop dominated the lower vales and hills all around it. A natural fortress of thick trees and large rock outcroppings afforded great protection against both magic and arrows. The trees were even of the kind that were resistant to fire. Rodell's most powerful fire attacks had only singed them. Great.

The backside of that broad hilltop was too steep to attack. The front side was less steep, but still at a high incline, and already littered with hundreds of dead and wounded from several failed militia assaults.

There were two narrow saddle ridges running down the hill to either side of the crest that could be easily defended by archers and a few mages–just as they were doing.

But there was one flaw. The room up in that fortress was finite. Even if they wanted to, they couldn't keep pouring troops through the magic gateway, and defend the hilltop at the same time. Any troops who exposed themselves out in the open now, could be quickly set upon and destroyed. And if the hilltop became too crowded, there wouldn't be enough room for the defenders to maneuver and fight.

Thus, a three-sided attack was planned.

From Mason's vantage point, he would help lead the assault straight up the middle. His guns were the heaviest firepower anyone currently had, plus could negate magic. Rodell and Thulkara and their mages would back him up, with not one but two armies. Bill and the Shooting Stars would blast their way across the saddle ridge on the right. The Michiana mages would do the same from the left.

It would be brutal, but it could be done.

And so they began.

Mason and his forces advanced behind mantlets, working their way up the vale behind layers of mantlets, foot by foot.

Waves of arrows and spells crashed among them. On they came, slow but certain. Brave flights of exposed archers dueled with the enemy, accepting their own losses while inflicting casualties on their foes.

The mages attacked on the left, magic blazing. The Shooting Stars came in from the left and slightly above, raining magic arrows upon the crest. They focused on using freeze and stun-gas magic in an effort to put the foe down quickly and in large numbers.

The battle raged for half an hour.

Then, without warning, the enemy resistance not only withered, but seemed to almost completely break off.

The attackers rushed in.

At first Mason couldn't tell what was going on as they charged up the vale to the top.

The enemy wasn't simply retreating–they were fleeing through the portal itself. Once enough of them made it through, they could cut the portal off or even possibly destroy it, from one side or the other. Perhaps even both.

Mason converged on the scene with Major Bill and the Shooting Stars.

"We have to seize that portal!" Bill yelled.

"More than that," Mason said. "We have to chase them all the way through and seize the other gateway, on the other end as well."

"What if they shut it down or destroy it?" Rodell said. "Anyone trapped inside will be lost or killed!"

"Mace is right," Thulkara shouted. "We have to risk it."

The enemy made one last concerted stand while their mages and leaders poured through. Other battlemages stood nearby, their hands and arms glowing, ready to either deactivate or destroy the portal itself.

The Pistolero charged in and gunned them down, firing accurately and with deadly precision. He negated spells, he maimed, slew, and killed any foe near the portal.

More enemies rushed up to try and stop him. He negated four more spells fired directly at him, right before magic from the allied mages and arrows from the Shooting Stars cut those fresh foes down.

Then Mason hit the fizzing lightning field of the portal's screen running and passed directly through it. Thulkara charged in right behind him.

Something went wrong. Rodell did not join them. There was a bright flash from behind, and they were suddenly sucked forward while strange lights and bursts of energy erupted around them.

Within the matter of a few seconds, both of them were spat out alone onto a sandy hilltop and road leading down from another high hill and cliff.

They had made it through to the other side, but just as the portal had been deactivated somehow. The copper pillars did not glow or flicker any longer. The opposite lightning field shut down as soon as they passed through it.

Mason saw a spear come at him. He dodged drunkenly to one side. Other hands and weapons came toward him, but he was still too disoriented from being tossed through the portal. Foes remained clustered around both pillars.

Of course, the enemy mages who fled through to this side must have turned it off, once they made it through.

They weren't expecting a few enemies to squeeze in behind them. And especially not the Pistolero and a Thul.

There was still heavy fighting nearby, and all around them by the sounds of things and the dust being whipped up. A great battle for the control of that gateway still raged on this side. The enemy was just barely holding onto the portal and the position.

That was probably why they turned it off. Perhaps they would even try to move it, if they had time. Although at a glance, that seemed unlikely.

Thulkara chopped, cut, and held the enemy off, while Mason staggered back up to his feet and cleared his whirling vision.

More enemies spotted and turned on them.

Mason drew his pistols and did his best to gun them down. Every shot needed to count. He was cut off from his reloaders and other gear. He only had enough supplies tucked away on his person for one, maybe two sets of reloads. If he even would even find time for such.

Urth troops in Blackhawk uniforms swept in from all sides up that way.

Hell, Mason even caught sight of his old buddy Dave, fighting like a champion, wheeling and cutting down foes two and three at a time–trying to reach the portal as an objective.

Holy crapola! Was that another Thul down there among the trees? This one was a dude. And he was even bigger and flashier than Thulkara.

"My Prince!" Thulkara roared, saluting her countryman with her gory weapons. "Yo, ho!"

The male Thul finished cutting down two full circles of monsters all about him, and started–amazed to hear the cry of another Thul. He spotted Thulkara and grinned wide, saluting her in return. "Yes! Yo-ho!"

A new wave of enemies swept toward Mason and Thulkara, retreating back up the hill. Enemy mages started firing spells at the copper pillars on that side, trying to damage or destroy them.

Mason and Thulkara weren't about to let that happen.

They would hold this side of the portal, or go down fighting.

Then Mason spotted her, charging up with some of Dave's forces and right next to the stunning wizard girl.

He spotted Tori.

48

Without warning, a massive explosion tore up the landscape southwest of the fighting. A hurricane of what appeared to be swirling dark energy and magic formed a vortex over that entire area. A glowing crater seemed to have formed beneath that maelstrom, hundreds of yards in diameter.

Almost everyone was flattened to the ground, and struggled to rise back up to their feet.

If that wasn't chaotic enough, an all-new host of enemy reinforcements raced up from the south as the sun went down on the horizon and twilight coated the lands in shadow. Thunder and lightning erupted within the advancing thunderstorm across the sky, as the enemy hurled their final numbers into the fray.

David saw monsters, mercs, dark mages, grun, slurgs. They swept in on an attack arc to smash into the Urthers and their allies, and push the defenders of Michiana toward that vortex hovering over the strange crater.

He looked over at Jerriel, trying to spot her and his friends among the dazed mercenaries, still being held at General Hatto's mercy.

Some had broken free or cut themselves loose. They even retrieved their weapons at hand where they had been stripped away and piled up. Jerriel had her staff back. She came to him with his swords, and used one to cut him free. The next thing he knew, they raced away from their enemy captors toward the militia lines.

Tori and a large group of the Blackhawks, now led by the two princes, Valandin and Alendel, absorbed them and skirted the crater, fighting valiantly all along that edge.

David gathered what troops he could and they fought their way toward the main group to join up with them and make their stand amid the confusion.

Finally he reached Jerriel's side once more.

"Daeved!" she yelled, pulling herself to him briefly.

Together they assessed the newly evolving battlefield. They had no idea what had caused the big explosion, or what purpose it served. And they were now even more outnumbered than they had been before the blast. The enemy's fresh forces slowly forced back and down toward what looked to be a long rectangular pond of glowing water at the center of the crater.

Lightning from the oddly boiling sky continued to arc down, drawn into that water.

"Jerriel," David said. "Why are they driving us toward that pool? What's in it?"

"Wild Magic," she shouted of the din of battle. "I think they mean to either drive us into it, or use its powers against us, somehow. Perhaps our mages can use it as well. I can't tell what the enemy is planning!"

Screams and frightened shouting erupted on their right, and David looked up that way with the others.

An advancing wave of marching necromancers in their black robes and masks came over the rise, arranged in formations of wedges, concentrating all of their powers together. Six of the foremost funneled all of their concentrated dark powers into the six floating, burning skulls above and before them.

The floating, burning skulls were blazing red or black—three of each—emanating a combined barrier of destructive force, drawn from the Negative Energy planes and the Nine Hells themselves, with the necromancers as the channeling conduits.

"A Dark Force wall!" Jerriel shouted. "What a terrible thing this is. Don't let the force field touch you. It destroys everything it comes into contact with."

Friend and foe quickly learned that as the enemy mages came on, vaporizing anyone in their path.

Pharrio the wizard went down on one knee and gasped. "What an evil. Not since Age of Legends has such a force been unleashed upon the Prime

Material plane of any living world." He looked about them. "And, alas, we surviving mages are now too few to stand against such dark might."

Maelen and Urnessan helped their brother back up to his feet.

"Courage, man," Maelen said.

"Verily," Urnessan added. "Come, brothers, let us try to devise a way to use the Wild Magic against them, before they do so to us!"

The Dark Force wall cleared a path before the Shadow Mages, and behind them came their leader, floating within what looked to be a sphere of shadows and dark lightning. Both the wall and the sphere were impenetrable, and deflected, vaporized, or absorbed any kind of attack made against them.

Then bolts, and blasts, and rays of dark magic began shooting out of the eyes of the six burning skulls.

Anyone struck by them was not slain, but had nearly all of their energies sucked out of them, the power of their very lifeforce drained and added to the swelling power of the enemy.

Scores of troops and mages dropped. Jason Inada and Pastor Bryan were struck, and lay helpless and dazed, drained and weak.

Alendel step in front of his older brother, and took a darkbolt meant for the eldest prince. The younger prince dropped, convulsing in his brother's arms.

Jerriel led the remaining mages. Together they attempted to throw up their own magical shields and barriers, layering them before the small band of defenders, who drew back toward the rectangular pool, which absorbed lightning from the heavens each second.

David was struck by a darkbolt that blasted through a weak point. He went to his knees.

Yet for some strange reason, the blast had little effect upon him. Why was that? He felt weak and dizzy for a moment, but he was not drained.

"Daeved!" Jerriel shrieked, rushing to his side.

Then a blast of dark power from the leader's shadowstaff drilled into her from behind and stunned her, flinging her back into the dangerous pool of Wild Magic itself.

Even if the Wild Magic did not kill her, the water was deep enough that she would drown in her feeble condition.

"Jerriel! Grab her. Pull her out!" David shouted.

He and Tori and two other troopers sprang into the glowing water to rescue Jerriel without hesitation, even as her stunned form sank beneath the glittering surface.

The trooper on David's left gasped and turned to dust.

The trooper on the right's scream was cut off as she vanished.

More lightning struck the pool at that instant, and both David and Tori grunted and gnashed their teeth as an agonizing power surge tore through their bodies.

They had laid hands upon Jerriel, but were frozen in agony for a moment and could not draw her out.

Tori's arms and legs began to glow with swirls and whorls of strange energies within, even while she and David dragged Jerriel out.

"It's burning me!" she screamed. David only felt numb, after getting zapped.

At last they were all out of the Wild Magic.

They dragged themselves and Jerriel back to the right, as the defenders prepared to make their final stand. Tori thrashed on the ground in pain, but the glowing energies within her finally faded, doing her no further harm.

Transparent bands of energy ribboned and rippled out of the pond of Wild Magic, forming waves and lines of protective energy in front of them, like layers of multicolored glass.

Pharrio and the other wizards harnessed the Wild Magic itself to defend them all, at least for a time.

Then the shadow mages halted, and for a moment, they stopped trying to penetrate the defensive barrier.

Instead, the enemy mages and their leader focused all of their energies up into the stormy sky, even drawing upon the Wild Magic as well.

Stacy Keller and some of the healers rushed up and zapped Jerriel and those stricken with some healing energy, bringing them all out of their weakened states. The others also began to come around.

"I'm feeling better now," Jerriel said. "Help me to my feet, my friends. I can stand and fight once more."

David pointed up to the sky. "Jerriel, why did the enemy break off their attacks? They all but had us. What in the hell are they trying to do now?"

Jerriel looked up and gasped and seemed to comprehend. "It cannot be!"

"What is it?"

"What in Hell is right! The fools are attempting to tear open a rent in reality itself—a gateway to the Nine Hells. They could summon or bring anything through such a gate in order to destroy us all!"

49

An entire battlefield and a variety of fierce enemy forces separated Mason and Thulkara from Tori and their allies after the big explosion, but that mattered little.

Then even more enemy units swept in from the east and south, pushing David and the Blackhawks to the right by sheer force, finally driving them over the lip of the enormous, steaming crater and down into its depths.

Mason lost sight of them and Tori, but it was all that he and Thulkara could do the hold back the foes flooding in at them. For the moment, they faced mostly mercenaries with the addition of a few grun and slurgs.

Because of the narrow trail and the built up defensive screens of stone set around the portal, the two of them could just barely hold that opening. Enemy dead piled up before them in mounds and waves. Mason had to waste precious shots clearing them away so that they weren't heaved back in upon them, to bury them under piles of corpses.

Out of the corner of his eye, Mason saw Rabbi Bergman flash in and rush over to one of the copper pillars, and then the next. He fiddled and did something with each, trying desperately to reactivate them.

Mason hoped something was going to go their way for once. He was down to his last two pistols, and there sure wasn't going to be any damn time to reload.

Finally, both pillars flared and the lightning field fizzed, flashed, crackled, and then hummed as it came back up. Bergman was weak by then and stumbled through it.

The enemy forces nearby saw the field come back up and made a determined push to drag the two defenders down, no matter what. They came at Mason and Thulkara like a human wave of flesh and superior mass, trying to sweep over them and take them out.

Mason heard a voice shouting and what sounded like a stampede. "Get out of the way!"

Mason dove to one side, and Thulkara to the other.

A charge of heavy horse rumbled and tore through the portal with lances set. They pierced and crushed the dismayed foes, and trampled right over them in an onrushing, destroying wave.

After they passed on down into the vale of the raging battlefield, Rodell came through, leading more mages and infantry columns behind them.

"We're here to help," Rodell shouted. "Lets get with the helping!"

This meant that the militia now controlled two of the three transport portals on the other side, and soon the tables would turn once more.

Mason and Thulkara clapped arms with their friend. Then Mason was even more relieved to see one of his reloading teams push through along with the infantry. He called to the runners and met them halfway.

They already had reloaded pistols all set and ready for him. He quickly exchanged them for his empties, racing them back to the wagon.

"Hurry! Bring the two shotguns loaded with annihilator rounds. I'm pretty sure we're going to need them against these numbers we're facing. Thanks, guys. Perfect timing!"

"Will do. Go get 'em, Mace."

"We'll bring 'em right to you. Put it on 'em, man!"

Reinforcements were just starting to form up and make a difference, but the enemy still seemed bent upon driving the Blackhawks and their allies down into that crater for some reason. What kind of strategy was that?

What the hell was down there?

"Rodell," Mason said, "order our forces to line up on the enemy's exposed right. We have to get down into that crater and relieve our forces, who are still being pushed back. Then, as more of our people come on line, we can press hard into the enemy's flank."

"Sounds good. I'm on it."

"I want three companies with me as a strike force."

"You got it. Companies 29, 34, and 40—fight beside the Pistolero and protect him and his reloaders!"

A cheer went up from those three companies as they came about and pushed ahead, around, and behind Mason and Thulkara. He nodded at some of his buddies from Team 3.

Together, they all hit the lip of the steaming crater in less than a minute, charged over, and down into a massive battle unfolding near the bottom.

The ground they passed over was a mixture of sand, dirt, and blackened ash, packed down somewhat, hard and cracked and splintered as if the crust of the surface had been partially fused by intense heat and pressure.

Down in the center of the crater was what appeared to be a long, rectangular pool of glowing water. Wild Magic. Mason could sense it from where he was.

What's more, the thunderclouds swept in on this side as well, and as they passed over, their lightning seemed to be inexorably drawn to the surface of that weird glowing pond of unpredictable energy.

And the Wild Magic continued to grow in intensity.

David's Blackhawks and their allies had formed two defensive lines right and left, like a spearhead, their shield walls several hundred strong and set. They defended the closest end of the pool, staying well in front of it. They clearly did not want to be driven into that water, and yet they also seemed determined to keep the enemy from reaching it.

David, the wizard girl, Tori, and the rest of their elite fighters and mages seemed to be holding out at the very tip of their defensive spear.

But thousands of foes swept down toward them, filling up half of the crater and charging straight for the defenders. Even though many other friendly forces attacked the enemy's far left from the portal on that side, and now even more fresh troops from the other side were also helping to attack the entire right.

Leading the enemy forces was what looked to be a wedge of Shadow Mages from the Dark Khabal. And at the very head of that wedge was a powerful necromancer, obviously the leader. He floated and surged forward within a sphere of dark energy that crackled with black lightning and destructive power. Even other mages and troops who got to close to that field shrieked and vanished suddenly in flashes of dark vapor and exploding black lightning and flames.

Just a quick spurt, and they were slain and gone.

Out in front of the leader, six triangles of six necromancers each comprised the very front of the enemy's wedge. The necromancers all chanted in some foul tongue or speech that was all their own, of some dark or hellish origin. It was sickening and maddening even to hear it spoken.

Trails of dark vapor and negative energy roiled off each necromancer and each triangle and seemed to be sucked up by the glowing, flaming, red and black skulls floating before and slightly above each set.

Three of the floating skulls were wreathed in flames and crackling lightning, as red as an ocean of blood. The other three skulls were enveloped in dark fire and black lightning–unlight–deeper than the shadows of the Abyss itself.

And the enemy formation appeared to be projecting a protective barrier of some kind before them that was invulnerable to all attack.

Waves of arrows struck it and vanished into hissing ash and flame. Various spells–fire, ice, lighting, blasts of magic–all struck the barrier and were dispersed or even absorbed by its powers.

From the front, the defenders had no way of stopping it or breaking through. Bolts of energy began to shoot out from the skulls and take out the defenders.

"Come on!" Mason yelled. "We'll hit them from behind and within on their flank once we penetrate their ranks. We must break up those lead formations and cut down those necromancers!"

Mason led his friends in a determined charge to do just that. Tori was still down there. The fury of the storm unleashed itself all around them, falling upon friend and foe alike.

The final, key battle was joined at last.

50

Jerriel and the allied mages attempted to interrupt the enemy efforts to tear a hole in reality. All of their attacks had no effect.

"You cannot do this!" she screamed at the Shadow Mages. "You know that what you are doing is utterly wrong!"

The foremost enemy necromancers looked back down and locked eyes upon her.

"Traitorous whore. All who defy the Dark Ghods must die!"

"Prepare to die, you filthy, stinking witch!"

They started laughing at her and all of the defenders.

"Fools!" Pharrio shouted, attacking the Dark Wall barrier in vain. "You know not what you will unleash. You cannot open such a gateway. You will destroy us all!"

"Not us. Just you, wyrms," another necromancer chortled.

Another foe joined in with knowing laughter. "Once the Kolugtathuloth breaks free, it will feast upon you all, and your petty little towns shall be swept away by its vast and limitless hunger."

The allied mages gasped, hearing what was said.

"Jerriel, what are they talking about?" David asked.

"They mean to unleash a colossus from hell upon this entire region! It can only survive here for a few weeks, but in that time, it will lay waste to everything it touches."

"Sheesh, how big is such a thing?"

"Up to several miles."

"Several...miles?"

The enemy leader rose up high in his protective sphere of shadows and black lightning. "I am Gorrial Lankorro, High Necromancer Supreme, the Favored One of the Dark Ghods themselves. What power have you insects to stand before our naked might?"

All the while, the rent in the sky shrieked and groaned and tore open.

"Surrender, pitiful fools. Accept the yoke and chain of my fell masters, or be consumed by the terror that we have summoned!"

The defenders shouted back, as one.

"Never!" they roared.

Gorrial laughed, certain in his power. "So be it. Then be crushed by the might of darkness. Great Kolugtathuloth, Champion of the Dark Ghods. Come forth!"

51

Mason raced up toward the edge of the pond, just as the gargantuan, horrific nightmare the head necromancer had summoned began to lurch and thrust itself out of its hellish portal above and to one side of the pool, half a mile up into the tortured skies.

Just the first section of the thing alone was fifty feet or more in diameter, and seventy feet in length, ending in a vicious maw.

How huge was the entire abomination?

Lightning continued to lash down at it from the sky, and the pool of Wild Magic flashed and flickered next to the open, floating wound in reality itself from which the mighty beast emerged.

The leader of the necromancers cried out, "Great servant of the Dark Ones, of the Mighty Fallen and the Elder Ghods of Darkness and Destruction. Destroy these fools! Lay waste to this entire region in your vast wrath. Before your time on this plane ends, slaughter and devour everything you can find. Show them thy fell power!"

The colossus continued to emerge, threatening to destroy everyone.

"To me, my servants," the leader roared. "Let these mortal wretches perish together in their precious little towns. The beast shall claim them all, and leave them all stripped bare and waiting for our purposes, in the wake of its passing."

The ginormous beast put out tendrils and pseudopods, fastening and grasping onto great trees and the rocks of the hillsides themselves, to anchor and pull its humungous bulk in to the living world to consume everything it could touch.

From atop one of those mighty trees, nearly two hundred feet up where he had climbed, ThulKazar roared his war cry and dove down toward the lead necromancer with both of his flaming battle axes spinning. "Die, filthy necromancer!"

Gorrial Lankorro turned casually and nailed the Thul prince with a freeze spell with the wave of one hand, encasing ThulKazar in clear, magical gray ice.

And sent him hurtling into the gullet of the beast.

"No. My prince!" Thulkara wailed in horror. With a running start, she leaped off the edge of the high cliff nearby, and fell upon the chunk of ice, hacking at it furiously as both of them sailed into the wide open maw of the Kolugtathuloth.

It gulped them down whole, as if they were but flies.

Mason managed to get to his knees and draw his Spillers to fire. Tori reached him, helping him stand and steady his aim with her arms around him.

Another swipe of his hand, and the sneering enemy leader flung Mason and Tori into the Wild Magic, where both of them gasped and floundered. Illuminated from within.

The necromancer leader shook his head in utter disgust. "Thulls and Urthers…how tedious and unimaginative." The leader unleashed some kind of power at his will. Waves of shadow pulled him and the remainder of his followers out of that reality, transporting them to some other place.

Rodell and many of the mages were still stunned and drained, crawling and groaning in the mud, barely able to lift their heads. The healers rushed to them, trying to get them back up.

David and Jerriel also looked spent, but struggled to rise and possibly help the others regroup, form some kind of strategy, or flee if nothing else remained.

The last thing Mason saw as he sank down below the glowing water was the enormous beast, emerging even more and coming for them all. Even as he sank, Tori pulled at him, trying to drag him back toward the shallows, as the concentrated Wild Magic continued to rip and tear through them.

Were they…dying?

In desperation, before any end could claim them, Tori put her lips to his.

52

The mercenaries saw that they had been abandoned to die. Half of them fled in all directions, and the other half started to attack the beast up in the sky. By then a huge section of it had oozed out of the rent. Who knew how big the entire creature was, if this was, in fact, only part of it?

The colossus was like a gigantic, devouring worm, covered with enormous, ravenous maws rimmed with sharp, jagged teeth the size of trees, which could snap out from lipless black gums. It ripped at and bit off huge chunks of whatever it came into contact with and swallowed with vast, gluttonous hunger, gulping everything down its huge gullet.

David saw it swallow more than a hundred mercenaries in one gulping bite. It ate rock, trees—even the sandy dirt of the crater.

David turned and called out to General Hatto, "It seems that your employers have abandoned you here to share our fate."

The general shrugged. "At least that breaks our blood contract and we can keep all of the money," Hatto noted with a smile. "Whether or not we live to spend it. Attack, my warriors! Call up every siege engine we have. Use the fire and magic bombs!"

Everyone hurled and fired weapons at the beast. None of the attacks seemed to do much damage to the creature, even magic, and merely alerted it to the best directions to propel its gobbling maws.

"We must pull back!" Hatto cried. "We must retreat and regroup."

"We cannot," Jerriel said. "If the entire beast emerges, it will lay waste to several regions before it finally dissolves. That could take weeks. Everyone will die!"

"How big are these things, again?" David asked Jerriel.

"Legends say that they are up to several miles in size. They can only last on the Prime Material plane for a month at most before dissolving, but in that amount of time they can roll and flip around, crushing and devouring everything. The beast will leave behind a defiled wasteland!"

"The rent," Rodell muttered. "Seal off or destroy the rent to the Abyss. Then it cannot fully emerge!"

Pharrio shook his head. "I wish we could. We don't have enough mages, and most of us are too weak. And even if we could cut off this section, it would only continue to feed and grow once more to its full size!"

"Jerriel," David said. "We have to try. We cannot simply stand by and do nothing."

She nodded. "Very well. Gather all of our mages and those of our allies. Use fire arrows, siege engines. Hit it with everything we have. We shall try to channel Wild Magic out of the pond, even if it destroys us!"

With each second the beast continued to ooze forth. The defenders rallied and stood their ground on either side of the rectangular pool of Wild Magic. The beast came for them, roaring and shrieking with its great maws, teeth snapping and gnashing.

The primary, vast mouth at the end of the head descended toward them like a dark tunnel of destruction, ready to consume them all.

The mages fired their enhanced magic at the thing's web of hundreds of eyes above its main mouth. Jerriel and the lead mages tapped into the Wild Magic and sent a surge of blasting energy surging through them, and scorching and scoring the beast's exposed length.

That did damage, and got the beast's attention finally.

For an instant, the thing reeled back, screaming in pain so great that everyone dropped to the ground, clutching their bleeding ears.

Then it came at them once more, enraged, stretching the open rent in reality to another breaking point.

Two glowing figures stood up and strode out of the Wild Magic pool's pulsing waters. The Pistolero rose up and set his feet. He flung open his coat, and Tori stood next to him, and looked up, wearing his outlaw hat upon her head.

Both of them looked fierce, set, and defiant.

They lifted their glowing shotguns and fired both barrels down the beast's vast gullet, as it descended toward them all like a huge tunnel.

Four destabilized annihilator rounds arced into it like flares shot down a vast cavern.

Then they detonated, deep within, near the rent.

The enhanced blasts of Wild Magic tore the emerged part of the colossus into enormous fragments that crashed ruinous to the ground, but horrifically, even the pieces still continued to fight and kill.

"Concentrate all fire on the rent!" Jerriel yelled.

A storm of fire and exploding bombs shot up from the massed, mercenary siege engines.

Mason and Tori flung their white hot shotguns into the hissing water at the pool's edge, where they sent up geysers of steam. Mason unslung the St. Louis rifle off his shoulder.

Tori pulled out the Howdah Hunter shotgun pistol from Mace's flapping, fluttering duster.

They fired three more annihilator rounds at the rent, even as more of the beast tried to surge forward and through. Everyone concentrated their fire with them.

The rent in the sky exploded and consumed itself, finally collapsing and imploding, sealing off the gateway to the Abyss itself.

The Wild Magic pool faded, reverting back to mere water.

"Come on!" Jerriel told them all. "This fight is far from over! We must kill all of the big pieces before the thing reforms again. Each one could become another adult, given time!"

In an instant, Mason reholstered his Spillers, after he and Tori threw down their hot, empty weapons once more. Reloader runners came straight for them, carrying fresh weapons.

Mason took Tori in his arms and kissed her for a long, delicious moment, while the Wild Magic still glowed within and flowed through each of them.

"Sorry," he said, nearly breathless. "I just had to do that."

Tori grinned up at him, her brown eyes literally shining from within. "Let's do it some more…later." She drew two more pistols from his holsters and cocked the hammers back with each hand. "I'm so glad you taught me how to shoot, honey. Come on. Let's finish killing that goddam thing. If we survive, we can fool around!"

Mason drew and whipped out his Spillers, spinning and flashing them in his hands. "Wahoo!" he yelled. "I'm all for that!"

The two Pistoleros raced forward, blasting at the biggest pieces of the beast wherever they still flopped around and tried to eat everyone.

Even fighting the pieces took more than an hour.

The grim task at had was nearly finished, when two large, gore-covered blobs hacked their way out of one of the last quivering sections of the beast. Everyone pulled back, not knowing what to expect.

The blobs were so covered in black beast blood, jelly, and ooze that no one knew what the heck they were at first.

Everyone stood ready to fight them.

"Wait, wait," Mason and David both cried together. "Don't attack them!"

"My friends," Jerriel cried out amazement. "You're alive? We all thought you dead!"

The two goo-coated blobs blinked their eyes at the fading sunset and saluted their friends, singing out together, "Yo-ho!"

"Why of course we're alive," ThulKazar said.

Thulkara flung down her weapons and tried to shake off the glop the two were covered in. "This stuff…is so disgusting!" she cried.

"Ugh!" ThulKazar said, trying to strip the layers of it from him "I agree. What we really need is a fine bath!"

Thulkara paused and then looked at him pointedly. "An excellent suggestion, my prince. I could use a dip myself. Just to freshen up a bit, of course. I just happen to know a great spot at the river nearby."

"Lead on, my beauty!" ThulKazar roared. "Whilst our blood still boils from the fire of battle! Yo-ho!" And with that he began to sing.

"Yo-ho!" Thulkara shouted, and sang right along with him.

Both Thulls ran toward the river, chasing each other and singing at the top of their lusty voices.

People who listened and looked on covered their ears.

Oblivious to all else, the two Thulls stripped off and flung aside their weapons, armor, and sticky clothing, until they streaked through the twilight naked as deer. They laughed and sang to reach the river and dive into its cleansing waters.

No one in their right mind tried to stop them.

Truth be told, it had been a rough couple of months.

Even the next night after the battle, David and Jerriel were still so sore and exhausted that they could hardly move around. They celebrated returning back to their home, with no missions to pursue. No battles to fight, at least for now.

A simple, hot meal was a luxury.

"We need to know more about our enemies," David said. "Why and how they keep coming after us. Why do they want you dead? Where are they based? How many are there? Why do they want this area so badly?"

Jerriel pulled him close and kissed him soundly, driving all other thoughts and worries from his mind.

"Tomorrow, my love. Tomorrow. We can hardly stand up." She staggered into her room, and crashed onto her bed for the night.

David sat up thinking for a while.

The chaos around them made it very clear that life could end for either of them at any moment. Life was short, and David loved Jerriel, with all that he would ever be.

There would always be more work to do.

They rested and recovered that night, as best they could.

David spoke with Dirk the next day and took some leave time he had ignored. He tracked down a couple of specialty items—including a few things he'd been saving in cold storage in one of the ice houses.

Personal treasures—just for such an occasion.

Now that the proverbial cat was finally out of the frickin' bag between him and Jerriel romantically, for once they were going to take the time to have a nice, proper, romantic evening together. Their very first, that very night.

And David planned on doing everything right.

Both of them had more than earned it.

Barring any further monster or assassin attacks from the depths of the Nine Hells, of course.

But as a young guy, officially in love, David made some plans all his own.

Before they reached home that next evening, David asked the Blackhawks to do him and Jerriel a few kind favors to help set the mood and tone for that night.

Some of the troops filled the small Jacuzzi in the sunroom with clean water pumped from the garden well. They did so with a bucket brigade.

David thanked them, and then ordered the troops a little further off, closed the shutters, and lit some candles. He opened a bottle of wine to let it breathe, and got out two glasses.

Jerriel was already up and around, and quietly studied her father's magic journal and her mother's soulstone in the family room.

They both clearly smelled even worse today, not having had any time to clean up.

Little more than washing their hands and faces.

Without running water, and Jerriel still too tired and weak to do simple magicks, even cleaning them up was difficult. There was a lot of that going around.

But David fully intended to remedy that.

Stacy Keller and a team of healers dropped by and healed them both some more. Their wounds all but faded, and both David and Jerriel felt much better, and much of their normal energy returned.

All part of David's master plan.

Stacy smiled wickedly and winked at him when she and the healers said their goodbyes and left the two alone. David winked back.

While Jerriel studied and then napped a bit, David prepared his special dinner. A delicacy from the bottom of the ice house. Little did Jerriel know what he had squirreled away there.

Crab legs.

Alaskan king crab legs to be precise. About five or six pounds, all for the two of them, still pretty much frozen, even from their trip home in the summer.

Into the boiling pot they went, with a little salt and some bay leaves.

Mmm…

He opened a small bottle of lemon juice, and melted some of their small hoard of butter. He used those little metal stands with the white ceramic cups with tea candles burning underneath. These were the same kind that the restaurants couldn't use anymore because of stupid insurance reasons.

Yeah, right. Welcome to Urth as it was now, everyone.

As if there were any restaurants open anymore like that, after the Merge. But he could be wrong. There were still pubs and places and eateries that the town kept open for people to enjoy.

People could still barter and trade goods and services for a great meal. Even with the food rationing.

Out of his backpack, David took out his own personal crab shears with the red handles that he had once purchased. This was serious business, with crab legs being one of his most favorite, decadent delicacies.

And one he wasn't likely to enjoy again for a very long time.

That night, he would share all of that with Jerriel…and much more.

He set the plates. Napkins. And a "bone-bowl" for the empty crab shells.

All right. Now he just needed his lady.

He went into the family room.

Great timing. Jerriel was awake again, and had just finished reading. She came to him and put her arms around his neck. She snaked against him for a long, decadent kiss.

He finally had to pull away slightly just to breathe. "Hold on, honey," he said. "You keep kissing me like that, and I'll need to sit down. I swear. You make my knees weak."

Jerriel grinned at him very intently. "Then perhaps we should lie down," she suggested.

She suddenly wrinkled her nose as the scent of enchantment in the room was replaced with the wafting smell of boiling crab.

"What is that smell, Daeved?"

"I'm afraid part of that reek is us. We still need to clean up."

"I don't know if I can work my magic yet."

"Don't worry, my heart. I have it all taken care of." If David had his way, they were going to enjoy cleaning each other up, the old-fashioned way.

By hand.

David led her by her pretty hands. She laughed slyly. "Where are you taking me?"

"Come with me. Let's find out."

Cooking crab did kind of stink up the house also while it boiled, especially if you weren't used to the smell. The scented candles in the sun room helped mask some of that.

He led her into the sun room and showed her the tub full of water. "Jerriel, I'll go finish getting the food ready. In the meantime, do you think you can summon enough magic to heat this tub of water up for us?"

She nodded. "I'm starting to feel much better. I think I can manage that. I like the candles, David. Very much. They smell wonderful."

Jerriel waved her staff over the hot tub water and chanted. A bluish-green glow roiled the water's surface.

David went to the kitchen. With tongs, David scooped out the crab legs, drained them, and piled them all onto a glorious platter.

He brought their feast into the sunroom in triumph. A visual check made certain that the windows were all shuttered. The doors stood securely locked.

Jerriel sat in front of her plate. Her deep, violet eyes grew both wide and worried at sight of the platter. "Daeved? We're eating…bugs. Big spider legs, perhaps?"

David put the platter down and burst out laughing. They did kinda look like bug legs.

"It is all right, Daeved. I did not know your people…ate big spiders."

His face turned red. "Stop…stop…you're killing me!" She only made it worse. He couldn't stop laughing.

"Do your peeple raise these big spiders somewhere, or catch them in the wild? I have not seen any on your farms."

That she was totally serious made it all even funnier. Tears squirted out of David's eyes at that point. "Oh, God…honey, they're not spider legs."

She stared at them, looking worried again. "You don't eat demons or shadowspawn...do you?"

"Crab. Jerriel, they're crab legs," he told her.

"Kra-hab?" She gave him her confused look again.

David pulled the visual dictionary that the linguists had given them over from the coffee table. He flipped open to a picture of the entire animal and showed it to her.

Her eyes widened once again. "Shochi? You raise and eat Shochi?"

"Yes. Crab. These are crab legs."

She picked one up and nodded. "I see. These must be the babies? On Tharanor, Shochi are a great danger to all. About once every century, they march out of the sea in huge numbers. Shochi are enormous, bigger than houses. They eat everything and everyone in their path, laying waste to everything until they select a place to mate. They often choose a deep lake to spawn in, and then some return to the ocean to lay their eggs, while others do so in the lake, or even on land or an ocean shore."

David still chuckled. "These are Alaskan king crab legs. They're of a smaller, less calamitous variety. This is as big as they ever get."

"Oh, that is a good thing, then," Jerriel noted.

"Yes it is," David finally agreed.

He cut one leg open and drew out a thick tube of red and white succulent crab meat. He added lemon juice to the melted butter with a spoon and dipped the leg meat into the warm lemon butter mix with a tiny fork.

With that small, metal fork he offered the first tempting morsel up to Jerriel's luscious, pink lips, holding his other hand under it.

She still looked a little worried, even as she smiled and nibbled on the end. Jerriel made squeals and happy noises as she gobbled down the rest.

Seconds later, after a little more cracking, she moaned in ecstasy when he gave her her first taste of of lemon-butter crab-claw meat.

She quickly lost all apprehension after one taste. "That is so good, Daeved! " He showed her how to use the crab shears. She immediately yanked them out of his hands.

He laughed and took up the other pair.

In moments, they fell to feasting in earnest, gorging themselves on delicious crab. Lemon and warm butter and juice ran down from their hands to drip off their elbows, over their chins and down their necks. They were sticky with it.

They almost forgot about the wine until they grew thirsty.

Finally, the bone bowl was full of empty shells. And six pounds of Alaskan king crab legs were history.

David almost shed a tear, wondering when he would ever have them again. Unless the Shochi marched across the New World someday soon, and they managed to drag one of the big bastards into a boiling pit of water. And they could find a lot more butter and lemon.

David poured wine for them again. "Enjoying the wine?"

She took a sip. Then shrugged. "S'okay."

She nestled in with him in the candle light on the love seat after their decadent meal. "I liked the crab better."

"Me, too." He looked over at the hot tub where the water still steamed. "That water isn't boiling, is it?"

"No-no," she said. "It will be very nice." She set her wine glass down and started to pull off her boots.

David put down his glass and protested. "Oh, no. I've been waiting for this moment. That's my job. Let me assist you, my lady."

She smiled wickedly and held one boot out, biting her lower lip, her white, oval face shining with joy and happiness.

David slowly tugged her boot off and briefly rubbed her shapely legs, then her white feet and her pretty toes.

He found everything about Jerriel extremely beautiful.

She pulled her foot back and giggled. "That feels nice."

A shiver went through him. Now the other boot.

Jerriel turned around and pulled her long dark hair up, revealing her luxuriant neck and shoulders.

David unlaced her leather bodice from the back. His hands shook slightly. He drew in his breath with delicious anticipation.

The bodice fell away.

He started on the line of dozens of buttons on the back of her robes. He kissed her neck and her ears, smelled her hair.

All the while his fingers worked down through those many buttons.

His hands slipped over her strong, white shoulders. Her gown whispered to her slender waist in a gathering of linen. Her ornate undergarments, or smallclothes, consisted of a black lace under-bodice, the Tharanorian version of a bra.

All of that spectacular enough.

But elaborate, almost lifelike tattoos of fierce, mythical creatures covered her back, in deep shades of black and gray. They were so three-dimensional that they almost moved.

David remembered the shadows that sprang from Jerriel to defend them against the mob of traitors.

"Tell me about these tattoos and markings of yours," David asked. He touched each of them gently. They actually seemed to move.

"I have had them since I was very young," Jerriel said. "They are my protectors, my guardians. If I summon them, or I fall unconscious or am injured, or face some threat, they will come forth to defend or carry me to safety."

"That's pretty amazing. Like pets who can defend and protect you."

"They are more like friends than pets. They are a part of me. The winged mouse is Mubo, the serpent is Shazar, the black wolf is Nakal. The shadow owl is Osna. Jurn, the ironhulk, Thorok the winged Khimaera, and the mightiest of the seven: Zerezhal, the three-headed behemoth."

"Impressive," David said, placing soft kisses on her ivory shoulders, drinking in the fragrance of her dark hair.

Jerriel rose, turned around to face him, and stepped out of her robes completely, letting them fall to her feet.

"What of this?" she asked, lifting her fair face proudly. Her perfect form was draped only in a sheer black shift and shorts as thin as a veil of sighs and whispers.

David sucked in a breath and could not expel it. His eyes nearly sprang from his sockets.

No mythical creatures were on the front of her, obviously. And none were needed, for Jerriel was the fiercest and most exotic of them all.

By heaven, she was stunning. High, peaked breasts, pink-tipped, straining against the sheerest black lace. Not too small, not too big, and perfectly shaped, as if by a master sculptor's loving hands. Black lace short-shorts clung to her hips. She still wore her long black leggings that looked as if they had been painted on her shapely legs, half-way up her thighs.

Just the sight of her in that instant made David stare, stammer, and ripple with passion and desire from head to toe. He had never felt this way with any woman he had ever been with.

His veins felt like red-hot lightning bolts, forking through him.

"What now?" she asked. Her grin wicked in a flash.

David matched that smile with one of his own, and leaned back with his hands clasped behind his head.

"Now...you undress me. Then I wash you. You wash me. And then...we see what happens next."

Jerriel smiled, trembling slightly. "I love you, Daeved. A lot."

"I hope so, honey. I know I love you. And I'm going to love you a lot, too."

She reached for one of his boots as he offered it to her.

It was not long before all of their clothing came off, scattered somewhere around the room out of the way.

A little kissing and touching. Actually, there was quite a bit of both of those.

He finally scooped her up into his arms, walked over, and got into the tub of warm water with her.

Damn.

Jerriel. So beautiful. In his arms.

The fact that he loved her so much made her even more beautiful in his eyes. Even if that were in any logical sense possible. He wanted her so much that even their passion could wait.

Neither of them were in any hurry.

He had some natural sponges, body wash, shampoo, moisturizing soap, wash cloths, towels—everything handy for two stinky lovers who wanted to clean up, and have lot of fun doing so.

He started with the sponge first.

His hands shook just touching her.

Oh, man…how long could he hold out?

Wow. How did her skin glisten like that in the candle light? Water ran off of her as if down alabaster. Ivory was gray and dull compared to Jerriel's radiant skin.

Magic.

The Tharanorian word for magic was Zahi.

That dragon had been wrong after all. Dragons weren't magic.

Jerriel was magic.

The mythical creatures fused to her shapely back liked the warm water, too. He swore that they…they danced as he bathed her.

Jerriel cooed, enjoying her sponge bath and David's strong, loving, gentle hands caressing her. Very much so. She stretched and leaned this way and that as needed, dripping with water. Just watching her move in the slightest ways gave David intense pleasures he could never have imagined.

He lingered here, lingered there, softly, firmly, carefully attending to every lovely inch of her. Both of them relished every rapturous second.

Up and down each arm, over the hands, the slender fingers. Up and down each long, shapely leg. He got in between her pretty toes.

Jerriel laughed. He tickled her again.

Why was her laughter like the finest music ever made?

He put the sponge down and slipped in behind her. She arched her head back for another long, luxurious kiss.

Then he had the fragrant shampoo in her long black hair, slick and wet. He massaged her scalp with his fingertips while she murmured a song in Tharanorian.

Lather. Rinse. Repeat.

It all took a lot longer than magical cleaning, but it was a hell of a lot more fun.

Efficiency wasn't always everything.

He pushed her shoulders down again. She dipped her head under the warm water and he rinsed her hair off. Waves of soap and lather rippled out from her as she stayed under for a moment and let bubbles rise.

She turned around and rose up out of the water slowly in the candle light. Jerriel parted her long, wet black hair to either side of her radiant face with her slender hands like long, dark veils of the night itself.

And revealed her radiant body.

Only a goddess could move and look the way she did.

She smiled and tilted her head. "Your turn, Daeved. Now I get to wash you."

David laughed. Then sighed. "I am a dead man."

She grimaced in confusion. "What? Yoo are not."

"Yes. I am. But no man will go happier into this good night."

She giggled and started with the sponge. "You're funny, Daeved. So very strange as you say."

Now he laughed out of pure pleasure and joy as the beautiful young woman he loved more than his own life, slowly, gently bathed him and gracefully stroked him into shivering madness. He tilted his head back, closed and opened his eyes, and continued to gasp and sigh as the fire of her touch passed over him.

"I'm living with the prettiest wizard girl in the universe. She casts lightning blasts. Her tattoos come to life and rip our enemies apart. Yeah. I'm the strange one, here."

She giggled. "You are. But I still love yoo, my heart. Verry much."

He never thought he could enjoy having his hair washed so much. Her hands, her fingertips massaged his scalp. All of it was incredibly pleasurable. The fact that Jerriel was firm, wet, and gloriously nude, pressed right up behind him, only made it all the better. He asked her to lather and rinse three times, just as he had done to her.

He could wait no longer.

David pulled her around in front of him. Face to face. Their eyes locked and melted into each other.

In the flickering candlelight, in the warm, scented water and air, Jerriel straddled him and entwined her lithe legs over his narrow hips. Her slender arms wrapped around his broad shoulders to caress his head, face, and neck with her warm, inviting hands.

He drew her close to him. To his waiting arms, his lips, his entire body.

They became one, and both of them began to gasp. Through the skylight overhead, the stars slowly smiled and wheeled in their eternal dance.

And the hours of the night turned magic.

Zahi…

53

Hours after the final battle, Mason and Tori both collapsed and started going into convulsions—a violent reaction, Rodell and Jerriel said, from being exposed to so much concentrated Wild Magic.

They passed a bad day of chills and fevers, but they refused to be parted from each other. Each one constantly reached out for the hand of the other for comfort, even when things were at their worst.

Then their fevers broke and the convulsions left them. It appeared that they were going to survive after all.

Once it was certain that they were out of danger, Mason gave orders that they didn't want to talk with anyone else for a while.

He and Tori simply wanted some time alone to recover and get reacquainted after all that they had been through.

Major Bill and the others respected their wishes. Their friends found them a nice little quiet home to use and make their own, if they chose to do so.

From what they heard, Thulkara and ThulKazar had more or less taken over a section of the river and refused to leave it—threatening to fight off anyone who even suggested that they move away from that place.

They pretty much lived there, naked and singing to each other and together. Major Bill sent wagonloads of food and drink there, direct from Ravenwood. The militia guards and the Shield Maidens watching over that area gave that place a wide berth.

Shortly after six that first night, after they had recovered, Mason and Tori went back to their rooms to clean up, get dressed, and celebrate.

After eating a late lunch, they had planned a late dinner at eight p.m., and soon it was already seven. Both of them had waited for a quiet moment together like this for a very long time.

Both of them deserved their happiness, and their time alone together. Both of the desperately needed it.

Mason finished shaving, and was about to get dressed in one of his better suits of clothing.

His good boots were polished, and he was leaving his armor and most of his weaponry behind. He would only take his Spillers and his pocket derringer with him.

He was still running around looking for clean socks when someone knocked on the door.

Who the heck could that be? Both he and Major Avery had left explicit instructions for them not be disturbed in any way, unless something dire had happened.

Mason felt a little frustrated and angry.

He snarled as he went to the door and grabbed the doorknob. "Whoever you are, this better be good!"

Tori stood in the doorway, in a bright orange, short dress and matching shoes that showed off her awesome legs, her great curves—everything.

She also wore her own holstered pistols, her own brown duster, and her new Pistolero hat. All gifts from Major Avery and the reloading teams. They had had the outfit made just for her.

Mason stood there with his mouth hanging open, completely stupefied and stunned.

Tori grinned at him. "Good enough, pardner?" she asked.

Mason had to catch himself from drooling. He wiped his wet mouth with the back of one hand.

She laughed slightly. "I'll take that as a yes." She removed the hat and duster, and tossed them aside onto a chair.

He glanced at her eyes, her lips, neck. He felt dizzy.

He wanted to kiss her.

He was going to kiss her, and touch her, and everything else that was naturally going to follow. Even just anticipating it all was the greatest kind of torture in the world. And the sweetest.

For that matter, the rest of both worlds and all the males therein could have whoever they desired, but the only woman Mason wanted to make time with was this ravishing young vixen standing before him. End of story. Period.

At that moment, nothing else and no one else mattered but the two of them. She unbuckled her gunbelt and slipped off her iron. They joined the hat and the duster.

"Sorry, Mace. I couldn't wait. You know how impatient I am. I had to see you. You gonna ask me in, or do you want me to just dance around a while for you out here so that you can watch?"

Damn. He'd enjoy that, too. Decisions, decisions.

Nope. "Sure, honey. Come on in. You surprised me. I was just getting dressed. I'm still in my T-shirt and shorts."

Tori's eyes twinkled and she had a sly grin on her face as she kept her huge eyes on him the entire time.

She slipped the door closed behind her and locked it.

"Good," she finally said. "That will save me the trouble of undressing you."

Mason walked back in from the doorway, smiling himself. "But I like that part–almost as much as I enjoy undressing you."

Tori smiled and walked past him. She sat down on his bed and crossed her shapely legs. "Then I hope you won't be too disappointed. All I'm wearing now is this dress...and these shoes. Nothing else. Oops!"

Mason looked at her. "What about dinner?"

"What about it?" She kicked her shoes off. "Guess it's just the dress, now."

And there wasn't much of that bright orange dress, either.

It might as well have been made out of flames, from the heat Mason felt.

Before he could take a step, she stood and came to him once more.

She reached for the bottom of his gray T-shirt and pulled it up over his head.

Then Tori was in his arms, right up against him. His strong arms were around her, and hers around him. They just couldn't wait anymore, and there was no reason to.

She rubbed her cheek against his broad chest and listened to the hammering thunder of his heart. She kissed his breast and sighed, melting into him.

He could smell her—her hair, her perfume, the taste of her lightly freckled white skin.

Mason had waited to be with his beloved for so long. At that moment, he wanted to kiss her, and lick her, and devour every inch of her right then and there like the finest meal. And savor every bite.

At that moment, he never wanted to let her go, never wanted to stop touching her—ever again.

Mason unzipped her dress.

She helped him lift it off her and toss it aside.

He smiled so hard he thought his face was going to pop.

No.

There was no need to hurry.

He tugged off his shorts and kicked them away, both of them gloriously naked. Both of them on fire for each other.

He wondered that they both weren't glowing, that all of the combustibles in the room did not instantly burst into flame.

They stretched out on the bed together, side by side, smiling and sighing.

Tori giggled.

He loved to hear her laugh.

They kissed slowly at first—deep, long, gasping, hot, and wet.

Then Mason kissed every inch of her lovely face; he lingered on her ears, her neck, while he caressed her with his hands and pulled her close.

The lovers took their sweet, sweet time.

They took the rest of that day, the night, and all of the next morning into the next day making love as they wished.

Mason and Tori went without sleep, they went without food or drink, far into the next night, neither wanting nor needing naught but each other.

And still, it would never be enough.

THE END

Please Post A Book Review Right Now

Please post a review of this book if you enjoyed it. Twenty little words are all that is required. Twenty words that say what you liked about this book while it is still fresh in your heart, mind, and soul. Please do so now before something else makes you forget.

Here is the link for *Mergeworld, Book Two* if you purchased it on Amazon:

http://amzn.to/1neuq0x

Please click on the link and post your review now.
Done? The authors would personally like to thank you very much.

In this busy world, everyone is pressed for time. Our time is so important, no doubt. It has reached the point now where authors of nearly every stripe compete not only for sales, but to garner reviews from their readers. Some authors even stoop to "purchasing" reviews in social media that some services now offer in bulk.

In the publish or perish work of competitive fiction, book reviews from readers are golden, they have now become a commodity even.

Many in the business even consider book reviews as important, or even more important than book sales in some ways. As crazy as that sounds.

So therefore, trust us in this. If you have authors whom you adore, and you want to read more of their books in the future, please post as many reviews for them as you can in all of the forms of social media that you use.

Doing so will help your favorite authors in numerous ways that you cannot even possibly imagine. Never forget that fact. Book reviews matter a great deal.

And if by chance, if you find that there is something about this book that you don't like, and you really do want to help authors, before you slam them with bad reviews, try briefly contacting them instead with your concerns through their contact info that is always readily provided, or through their publisher. Most authors, especially new ones, are usually happy to get constructive criticism that will make their books better. Only hating, online trolls slam authors with bad reviews without giving them a chance. Real pros and fen contact authors directly with any valid concerns. That is the current, accepted etiquette. Please don't be a troll.

Amazon Kindle Review Link for *Mergeworld, Book Two*:
http://amzn.to/1neuq0x

Barnes & Noble Review Link

http://bit.ly/1qCuR0H

Smashwords Review Link

http://bit.ly/1xDboBc

Other Review Sites

Good Reads

Google

Pinterest

Reddit

Delicious

Stumble Upon It!

Please post one or more reviews for Mason & Garan and each of their books, everywhere that you can.

Thank you once again.

Cheers and many thanks,

Mason Elliott & Garan R. R. Faraday

Please enjoy this teaser for *Mergeworld*, Book Three:

Mergeworld

Book Three

by Mason Elliott and Garan R. R Faraday

David and Jerriel's friends charged down into the valley toward them in the fierce battle's lull. Jerriel rose up out of the ground pocket where she had been healed and kept safe by the Urth entity. The wizard appeared fully recovered and ready to fight, but she also looked extremely confused.

The Spectral Urth spirit Khia seemed to be waiting eagerly for the wizard's return as well.

David smiled at Jerriel, his eyes still glowing intensely green. He showed her the equally glowing gauntlets that he wore. "These gloves are magical, but I cannot use them properly in conjunction with her. There's something wrong with me. This Spectral entity made these artifacts to fuze her powers together with a willing human host—a partner. Her name, is Khia."

"Keys," Jerriel said in wonder. "I understand now. They are indeed Spectral keys; I can sense the raw power from here. Entity Khia, I am a wizard," Jerriel said, turning to the energy spirit. "I offer my services to you, Khia. Not as your master, but as a partner, friend...and ally."

"A partnership?"

"Yes," Jerriel said. "Fuze yourself with me and our joined powers shall increase tenfold. I know that you need to link best with a willing mage against these dire threats that we both face. Let us face them together!"

Khia's voice and her essence forced its way out of David's mouth. "There is wisdom in what you say, mage Jerriel. And I truly sense that a union with an actual wizard such as yourself would be far more powerful than with this null human."

David shuddered, feeling the entity withdrawing from him.

"No," he insisted, part of him not wanting Jerriel put in further danger, another part not wishing to separate from Khia. "I can still help you with my abilities!"

"Not as well as she," Khia said. "Your null energy field is incredibly strong, David. But it is still not the same as fuzing with an powerful wizard. Yet, I do thank you for helping protect us all, for a time."

"My what field?" he asked.

"You possess a powerful null energy field inside and all around you, David," Jerriel tried to explain. "Most likely, it has awakened and grown stronger each time that you stepped into pool of Wild Magic and absorbed more of its properties. Now that anti-magic field is part of you."

"I have come in contact with a number of such pools," David said.

"Your null field should reduce or negate all but the most powerful magickal energies," Khia said. "Command your forces on your own, mortal. That is your gift. You will be more help to us in that capacity by yourself."

David fell to his hands and knees, and watched helpless and weak, as Khia withdrew her spirit essence from him, and fuzed fully with Jerriel.

Jerriel's eyes glowed bright green. So did her staff.

She held her hands out, reaching and yearning for the gauntlets. "The keys, David. Give them to me. Hurry. Khia and I will be able to make use of those much better than the two of you," she said.

He tugged them off and handed them over.

Jerriel slipped them on. Both gloves instantly formed to her hands and arms, and blazed with increased emerald might.

Jerriel gasped and turned to the northwest as the verdant aura spread over her entire body.

"THEY ATTACK US ONCE AGAIN, AND THIS TIME—A GREAT POWER COMES WITH THEM," Khia and Jerriel spoke in unison.

Jerriel plunged both gauntlets into the ground and drew power directly from the ley line sources. "WE MUST LINK WITH THE NEXUS NEARBY IF WE ARE TO HAVE ANY HOPE TO SURVIVE THEIR GREAT ONSLAUGHT." They looked at him directly.

"DAVID. ASSEMBLE A SMALL GROUP OF YOUR FINEST WARRIORS TO TRAVEL WITH US, TRANSPORTING DIRECTLY TO THE NEXUS. THE REST WILL NEED TO FOLLOW ON AS BEST THEY CAN. THIS BATTLE WILL BE DECIDED AT THE NEXUS ITSELF!"

David turned to their friends. "Prince Valandin, we are going ahead. Lead the rest of the vanguard in after us; I'm guessing a few miles. Strike down any foes who get in your way. Send word to the army concerning our situation."

"Captain," Prince Valandin said, "we are too few for a major battle The bulk of our forces are still a day away or more."

"I know. That cannot be helped. This conflict is going to occur now. But we must keep our side informed, even if we fall or fail here in this place. They must know what has happened."

"This battle will be long over and already decided by then," Prince Alendel said. "In hours, if not minutes!"

"My good and valiant lords, we have no choice but to fight on and do our duty in this place at this hour. I am following Jerriel and the Entity Khia to the nexus. They cannot flee, nor can they take all of us with them to the nexus. Follow on as best as possible and provide what aid and support you can. Good luck to us all!"

David turned to his troops. "Blackhawk Strike Team One, assemble for battle and follow me. The rest of you, follow your unit leaders and the princes into combat. Fight hard and do your best to win the day!"

Fifty spears, swords, and archers stood with him in the strike force. All of his friends and best fighters, and with them–ThulKazar.

"GATHER CLOSELY TOGETHER AROUND US," Khia-Jerriel said.

Green energy from her staff enveloped them all, lifting them off the ground a few feet. They slipped over the land, picking up speed. Terrain rushed past them.

A dark mass of gathering shadows appeared behind them, swelling and sweeping over the land, blotting out the broken clouds and the few stars that could be seen in the sky. The moon was already down.

"What is that growing menace gaining upon us?" David shouted.

Khia-Jerriel did not look back. "WE FEAR THAT ANOTHER POWER SUCH AS OURSELVES HAS COME TO CONTEST WITH US FOR THE MASTERY OF THIS NEXUS," they said. "WHATEVER THIS FORCE IS, A MIGHTY SHADOW MAGE CONTROLS IT."

"Another Spectral Entity?" David said. "Another mage who has fuzed with one of the Spectral Keys?"

"UNCERTAIN, BUT THAT IS MOST LIKELY. IT IS EXTREMELY FORMIDABLE. PREPARE YOURSELVES. THEY'RE TRYING TO INTERCEPT US!"

They lifted up over the trees and sprang through the air, clearing almost an entire mile in one leap. David and his troops tumbled through the air and crashed into each other.

The next thing they knew, they were on the ground, trying to get back on their feet.

Khia-Jerriel stood directly over the glowing nexus point. It was like a beacon, and they drew upon its power, completely encased in green flame.

But their eyes burned white-hot.

"PROTECT US ON EITHER SIDE AND FROM BEHIND." Khia-Jerriel shouted. "GIVE US A CLEAR FIELD OF FIRE TO THE FRONT!"

David and his strike team peeled around them, taking defensive positions, readying their weapons.

A sudden gale like that of a hurricane swept in as the shadows descended upon them.

For an instant, David thought he saw the vast darkness take on the form of a gargantuan bat, with eyes black and deep as the Abyss itself.

The shadow crashed to the ground, and the blast wave and following storm of blinding dust and debris flattened them again, even as the ground shattered and broke up under their feet.

Khia-Jerriel steadied themselves, anchored to the nexus itself.

"SHALLI-HAKKAL!" they cried.

A massive storm of emerald lightning ripped through the shadow, disrupted it and flung it back. Many dark shapes were revealed within for the barest instant.

Then the darkness concealed them once more.

"They'll attack out of the shadows," David warned. "Set all weapons against a charge!"

He and his troops raised their shields and weapons and braced themselves.

Out of the darkness of horde of enemies appeared close by out of the darkness and at full run. They crashed into and deflected off David and his defensive lines on both flanks. But the defenders held firm and dealt damage.

David deflected a Grun spear and split open the goat face with his long sword.

ThulKazar laughed aloud, slaying and flinging foes to either side of him, his battleax spinning like a huge black saw.

Khia-Jerriel nailed the enemies in front of them with blasts, tendrils, and ribbons of slicing, green Urth energy.

But a phalanx of Shadow Mages marched up directly behind the enemy shock troops, all bearing glowing skull staffs.

And behind them an even darker power walked, veiled in shadows, but like a black hole in reality itself, its true form and nature still masked.

Khia-Jerriel valiantly stood their ground, backed by the nexus, swatting the lesser enemies away, scattering the necromancers like bowling pins.

Khia-Jerriel unleashed a storm of magic upon the Dark Mages, pressing their attack, crushing the enemy's defenses and killing some of them outright.

The hidden shadow shot up into the air, spread its vast wings, and opened its enormous maw as if meant to swallow the world itself.

A wide beam of black energy shot down and rammed into Khia-Jerriel, driving them back several feet and ramming them into the ground. The earth cracked and cratered around them.

Friend and foe alike scattered in all directions from the sheer force of such an assault.

David clawed back up to his hands and knees, still clutching his weapons.

"Jerriel!" He shouted.

Could anything survive a stroke like that?

Khia-Jerriel shot up out of the crater. Rapid fire pulses of force punched into the shadow, blasting holes through it and flinging it back to plummet and tumble back out of the sky from where it had blotted out the stars.

The Shadow Mages regrouped by then and charged Khia-Jerriel once more.

Waves of glowing dark vines whipped and whirled up out of the blackened ground, churning and lashing at the foes of the Dark Mages. Those who did not flee were ripped off their feet and slammed against the ground and held fast.

"Face us, Dark Terror. Come on!" Jerriel challenged. "I do not fear you! I wield the might of the Urth and the power of the nexus. I was trained by the greatest mages of Tharanor!"

A tall shadow strode out of the darkness, and it took the form of a man with long golden hair and spoke at her. "As was I...*sister*."

Scores of tentacles of burning shadow rippled out from the darkness, and battered and slapped Khia-Jerriel off the ground, breaking their connection with the nexus and transfixing her high up in the air where they encircled her like snakes.

Jerriel's eyes bulged in terror, rage, and shock, as she glared at the blond young man and spat her words at him in her own voice. "Shaeddor...my dark brother!"

He curled his lip at her in abject hate. "Indeed. I am the Dark Prince. The merry chase is at last over, little one. I hereby claim you, this nexus, and another Spectral Key for my dread lords of the Khabal—and the Dark Ghods themselves—soon to be Masters...of *both* worlds!"

MERGEWORLD, Book Three: TBA

SF Author Mason Elliott's Contact Information

<u>Please Join Mason Elliott's New Releases Email List</u>

Use either of these:

Mailchimp email listserve sign up Bitly link:
http://bit.ly/1L2QpUL

Direct Mailchimp link to listserve sign-up:
http://eepurl.com/FgQzv

Be among the first to learn about my writing projects and new releases. I promise that I will not share your info or spam you. I will use the list only to inform you about matters directly connected to my writing projects.

<u>About the Author</u>

Mason Elliott grew up loving Science Fiction and Fantasy in all of their myriad forms. That love has transferred into his dedicated writing. Like most writers, he lives a spartan lifestyle and yearns to devote his life even more to his writing, and someday retire on the Pacific Coast. So be a fan, buy his stuff, and enjoy!

Like, friend, and follow Mason on Facebook, where he does most of his blogging at
https://www.facebook.com/masonelliott731

or use the shorter link:

http://on.fb.me/1mQkv0B

Mason's full link for friending him on FB:

https://www.facebook.com/?ref=tn_tnmn#!/mason.e.elliott.9

Mason's shorter link for friending him on FB:

http://on.fb.me/1E466TV

And on Twitter at
http://bit.ly/1nsqOSs

Visit Mason Elliott's website at
www.masonelliott.authorcontacts.com

And for even more information on Mason Elliott and his works,
visit High Mark Publishing online at

www.HighMarkPublishing.com

Fantasy Author Garan R. R. Faraday's Contact Information

<u>Please Join Garan's Publishing Update e-List</u>

Garan's Publishing Update e-List sign-up form link:

http://eepurl.com/YHOS5

I promise you that I will only send you emails connected to my writing projects and new releases. I do not spam.

<u>About the Author</u>

Garan Reginald Remington Faraday was fortunate to be the child of loving parents who adored all things Fantasy, and passed that love onto their son. It has been said by some that with such a name, he was born to become a Fantasy writer. Garan, or "Reg" to his closest friends, has written Fantasy stories since the Seventh grade, and completed his first Fantasy novel at the age of sixteen. If you enjoy anything Fantasy, you most likely have something in common with Garan. His lifelong dream has always been to publish as many Fantasy novels and stories as he possibly can.

Garan's Facebook fan page link:

https://www.facebook.com/pages/Fantasy-Author-Garan-R-R-Faraday

Garan's FB friends page link:

https://www.facebook.com/GaranRRFaraday

Garan's Twitter link:

https://twitter.com/GaranRRFaraday

Garan's website and blog link:

http://garanfaraday.authorcontacts.com/

And for even more information on Garan R. R. Faraday and his works, visit High Mark Publishing online at

www.HighMarkPublishing.com

Mason's Acknowledgements

My head is still in a whirl. This collaboration to craft this book and this series has been a joy and a delight. I must forever be grateful to the staff at High Mark Publishing Fantasy.

I have to cheer my companion author and my writing group buddy, Reg. Together we have shared so many laughs and had so much fun. Cheers! And here to many more!

And finally, let me thank all of our cameo friends, and my beta readers, and the rest of our amazing writer's group, as always.

Garan's Acknowledgements

High Mark Publishing Fantasy is great. None of this magic could happen without your adept guidance and advice.

Once more, I would also like to praise my superb writer's group and all who assist me and comprise my readers. I cannot love you all enough.

And always, I cannot praise my dear friend M enough. It is not possible. We are brothers until the very end.

Cheers forever, mate! To the both of us, and every continued happiness and good fortune!

Please enjoy the following teaser from the first Spacer Clans Adventure, Book 1:

NAERO'S
RUN

NAERO'S
RUN

Amazon Link to Naero's Run: *http://amzn.to/1eRKCOb*

by Mason Elliott

"We've got more than enough to consider here," Aunt Sleak said. "We'll post our final decisions on the Spacer ClanNet. All crew, take a breather. We're out of jump in less that two standard hours. Everyone on duty needs to be at their ready stations. Dismissed."

Naero went back to her quarters to do some laundry and a little more reading before they emerged. With regular effort, her quarters were less of a disaster than usual. She'd kept her bunk and her floor more or less cleared off, and slept in her bunk regularly now, instead of on the floor or in zero-G or a float bag.

And definitely not in her flex chair, as she had for years because she either couldn't get her bunk panel out or it was too piled up with crap.

Being small had its advantages. She could curl up like a cat and get comfortable almost anywhere for a snooze.

But keeping her quarters in better shape was a promise she made and kept–to herself–and her parents.

They emerged from jump with the customary shuddering of the ship. The fleet spread out into is standard formation, emerging back into real Space-Time.

Naero punched up their positions on one of her screens, even though she didn't have bridge duty for several hours.

The Shinai flanked *The Dromon* on the port side, with *The Slipper* posted starboard. Their two smaller ships, *The Nevada* and *The Ardala*, brought up the rear this time.

A red hot scarlet particle beam, 60mm in diameter, lanced through Naero's walls like they were paper, disrupting her wallscreens.

A direct hit from a big gun.

At the very least, from a heavy destroyer.

Warning lights flashed immediately.

The rupture in the hull led to an immediate explosive decompression.

Naero held on tight to her bunk and went flat on the floor as the hull sealed itself.

All ships were vulnerable coming out of jump. They couldn't activate their shields until right after they emerged.

Someone had been waiting for them.

The Dromon continued getting rocked by multiple hits from what felt like several spinal guns and secondary batteries.

But the big planetoid could take it and give back plenty, her quad main guns humming and whining to life, coming online.

Naero hit her wristcom. All her screens down.

"Bridge. Status?"

"We stepped into it. They were waiting for us. We're under heavy fire. Multiple bogeys."

The general alert sounded.

"Battle Stations. Battle Stations."

Aunt Sleak cut over the com. "All hands. All hands, to your stations. Prepare for battle. All ships, all batteries, return fire. Launch all fighters."

Naero suited up and raced to the drop bay of her fighter. She met Jan along the way.

More intense fire. *Dromon* reeled and fired back.

She and Jan almost got rocked off their feet again.

A security team intercepted them at the launching bays.

Their fighters had already dropped with their backup pilots.

"The fleet captain wants you two at your secondary defense stations, not out in the mix."

Jan started to protest.

"Orders are orders. Get to your stations."

They ran to their remote gunnery stations, small secured cubicles with a chair and a console, operating triple pulse turrets on the hardpoints above them.

Naero brought up her autotargeting displays, weapons already powered up and humming.

The secondary battery gunnery stations operated independently and were well-protected. They were also fully automated, but they still functioned more effectively with a human interface.

Coordinated targeting profiles came online as she watched.

Jan operated a torp turret nearby.

Directly ahead of the fleet. Twelve elite Matayan destroyers, each with a dozen escort fighters.

Half of their number pursued and attacked a convoy of two dozen independent mining freighters.

Aunt Sleak's fleet scrambled, launched, and deployed a total of threescore fighters in a standard Alpha-Charlie-1 defensive screen.

They were outnumbered two to one.

"All batteries make ready. Incoming torps," the bridge com sounded.

Countermeasures took out half of the blips heading their way.

Spacer fighters and the forward defensive batteries blasted the rest.

"That attack's a diversion," Naero muttered.

Shinai's fire control and com computers fixed on and monitored all channels–including those between the hapless freighters and the corsairs.

"Mayday, mayday, we are under intense corsair attack. All ships. Assistance, assistance. Heavy damage and casualties."

"What do you want?" another panic-stricken voice cried out. "We'll surrender. You can board us. We have no goods and few supplies. Please, stop firing. Our ships are full of workers–full of people. You're killing civilians. We're on fire!"

Scanners displayed an awful, one-sided battle among the transports.

Most of the old bulk freighters didn't even have weapons.

Each of the heavily armed Matayan destroyers was more than a match for them or most of the ships in Aunt Sleak's fleet.

Except for the 6m quad spinal guns of *The Dromon*.

One crippled freighter broke apart and exploded under concentrated fire from three destroyers. It didn't have any shields, and only minimal armor. Its two turrets either didn't work or had been taken out already.

Static and Matayan battle language rang out in triumph.

Dromon's four primary guns cut loose, lighting up the entire sector. Its blue-white blasts ripped into the lead corsair flagship and its wingships, disrupting their shields.

The starboard wingship took two hits and listed to one side. Its aft section exploded.

"This is Captain Sleak Maeris of Clan Maeris. Enemy vessels, be advised: Cease hostilities and vacate this system or be destroyed."

Matayan curses and laughter her only reply.

"Clan Maeris," one of the freighter captains cut in. "This is Captain Philsen of *The Botaru*. Help us! Our situation is desperate. The corsairs are trying to destroy us. We don't know why."

"Acknowledged. We're coming in. Disperse if you can. You're still too bunched up. Scatter and concentrate on defensive actions. Jump if you're able. We'll try to draw them off. We're boosting your distress call."

Three more corsairs turned on the fleet, with all twelve dozen fighters full front on intercept.

The other trio of Matayan attackers kept after the freighters.

Naero heard the pleading and the screams on the open channel, just before another freighter got blasted to oblivion.

Naero realized she had tears on her face.

Was that how her parents went? Blasted to death by Matayan guns?

The rage she felt nearly overwhelmed her reason.

She checked her systems, gripped the controls of her gunnery station, and forced her emotions to go cold.

Against superior numbers, Naero and her Clan Fleet closed for battle.

Amazon Link to Naero's Run: *http://amzn.to/1eRKCOb*

Please enjoy the following teaser from The Citation Series, Book One, *Naero's War:*
The Annexation War

NAERO'S WAR:
THE ANNEXATION WAR

Annexation War Amazon Link: *http://amzn.to/1gmxGQk*

by Mason Elliott

Naero's flagship, *The Hippolyta,* was one of the latest, Dromon Class dreadnaughts. These warships were fashioned out of dense, iron-nickel planetoids, not less than half a kilometer in diameter. Incredibly tough and rugged on their own.

It took the most powerful mining plasma-borers–working in precise conjunction with construction fixers and an army of teks–months to hollow out armored crew quarters, lift and transport tubes, launching and loading bays. Next came space for power cores, sublight engines, jump drives, backups, gravitics, life support, sensor arrays, communications, navigation, weapons, main bridge and backup bridge.

Set in the exact heart of *The Hippolyta* were its signature big guns. A quad of the largest production guns ever constructed on any ship of war: Four, *16 meter*, rapid-fire, particle beam cannons.

Cannons any larger than that exploded, melted, or otherwise were not feasible within the limits of current tek and materials. Thirty-six secondary batteries, assorted specialized weapons and gun emplacements, and forty-five advanced fighters.

Seven hundred and forty able crew, including a full Rifle Company of two hundred and forty Spacer Marines, and all of their equipment, vehicles, and gear for ship's security and rapid response deployment. Strike Fleet Six's Marines came from the 3rd Spacer Marine Division–known as *The Death Eyes*–because of their superb snipers and their overall, excellent marksmanship ratings. Marines made up a third of the warship's complement.

Their motto: *If We Can See It...We Can Kill It!*

The main bridge was a massive armored dome constructed on top of the dreadnaught's big metal, rough-hewn orb, protected by heavy blast doors, and the latest, most advanced shielding in the fleet. Within, the circular bridge was laid out in four levels under the huge dome, a dome sixty meters high.

Each bridge tier was separated by the height of a few steps from one to the next. The inner three levels could rotate in any direction, independent of the others.

The fleet captain's command nanochair and station occupied the highest tier. Each bridge station had its own secondary shielding, in case enemy fire penetrated the shields, the blast screens, and the hull.

In combat, bridges were routinely targeted, for obvious reasons.

From that primary vantage point, the strike fleet captain could direct battles in three hundred and sixty degrees, through an advanced, battleholo display surrounding her, full zoom data-feeds, constantly updated by battle AIs. Naero could manipulate the displays by nanosensors programmed into the fingertips of her nanosuit gloves.

The battle display system also recognized her voice pattern, and would respond to voice commands, or commands punched in manually through pads on her command chair, or via other backups.

The next bridge level down from hers held the secondary bridge stations: Helm, Weapons, Communications, Navigation, and Scanning, spaced out equally along their ring.

The third ring held all of the twelve tertiary bridge stations, that monitored, controlled, and coordinated all of the ship's other important functions:

Engineering
Gravitics
Life Support
Power Supply
Security
Shields
Medical
Jump and Sub-light Drives
Damage Control
Alliance Fleet and Intel Communications
Main Computer
Launching Bays

The fourth ring went to the two powerlifts, leading from the bridge to the other movers, decks, and levels of the ship. All lift and access points throughout the ship were constantly guarded by two battle-ready Marines, stationed on either side.

If a warship was boarded by enemy assault craft during a battle, invaders could be cut off and eliminated between decks, before they could reach a vital area.

Today, Strike Fleet Six had a mission–a simple one.

Captain Naero Maeris and her fifty warships proceeded to probe the next system on the outer, port arcwall of the Alliance advance at Beleron-4.

A routine run. Current intel assured them to expect little or no Triaxian presence or resistance.

By any stretch of the imagination, Beleron-4 was a nothing world, in the middle of nowhere, with zero, nacha–absolutely no strategic or tactical value whatsoever.

Checking it off the list on the pacified worlds of the Alliance system-hopping schedule was more-or-less just a formality.

But it still had to be done. And Naero and her lot drew the duty at random.

So why did Naero's sense of warning go bonkers?

After they jumped in, simple three-stack, Delta-India-3 formation, the reasons for alarm grew perfectly clear.

They came in right on top of twenty Triaxian fleets of the enemy's latest warships.

And a gigantic new flagship–as huge as *The Hippolyta*–the advanced design of which did not even register as existing.

It had never been seen before.

Naero shot to her feet, kicked her command nanochair back out the way and sent it down into the nanofloor of her top-tier bridge control station.

She instantly called her battle display holos up in spinning, horizontal glowing ribbons and rings all around her.

Data relays went wild. Her fingers flashed among the highlighted screen arcs, taking control of them and their parameters.

Multiple warnings sounded, and with excellent reason.

Nothing about this was good in any way.

Haisha! Twenty enemy fleets could chop them into confetti–well before any other Alliance forces could even jump in to help.

No strategy, no formation could possibly save them against superior numbers such as these.

"All ships, full withdraw. Emergency retreat on this vector, in Charlie-Romeo-7, cone-ring formation. Shields and all weapons full front and hot. Maximize all targeting profiles on the lead attacking enemy elements–they'll be on us in seconds. Whatever happens–we fight until our carriers and some of our ships can break free and jump out behind us. Get the carriers out first!"

For a split second, everyone braced for the sheets of flame that would quickly overtake and overwhelm them.

Annexation War Amazon Link: *http://amzn.to/1gmxGQk*

Please enjoy the following teaser…an excerpt, from the next Spacer Clans Adventure, Book 2:

NAERO'S
GAMBIT

A SPACER CLANS ADVENTURE

NAERO'S
GAMBIT

MASON ELLIOTT

NAERO'S GAMBIT

by Mason Elliott

Klyne set the huge Mystic testing room on board *The Kathmandu* to muted gray. Smartwalls, floor, and ceiling, Naero saw no equipment, no padding.

The lights were set low.

From experience, Naero knew that in a training room, just about anything could pop up out of anywhere.

She wore nothing but her black Nytex flight togs.

To her surprise, Klyne and his two adepts wore dark gray Nytex togs also, but with hoods and masks pulled up over their heads. Only their keen eyes showed.

All three of the Mystics appeared to be in top physical condition, including Klyne.

One of the adepts was female, with huge green eyes and light freckles across her nose. The other was male, with the black slanted eyes of the Lii-Kim Clans.

If black was the color of Spacers, the Mystics traditionally wore gray.

They all sat with their legs crossed in lotus fashion, focusing their abilities through meditation, and mental discipline. They formed a triangle, each side about three meters apart, with them at the points.

"Follow our instructions," Klyne said. "Take your place among us. Sit in the center; sit as we do. Face the instructor."

A circle of white light appeared at the center of the triangle. Naero walked over and sat down in it, facing Klyne. Her skin barely began to tingle.

A wider ring of similar light appeared, including the instructor and his two adepts.

Every hair on Naero's body went stiff with electric force.

"You have chosen to come before the circle of Spacer Mystics to be tested for Mystic training. Speak your name."

"Naero Amashin Maeris."

"You agree to be tested?"

"I do."

"I am Klyne, the instructor. My assistants are Adept Iselle, and Adept Makita. We shall refer to you as Adept Candidate Naero. Follow our instructions. Respond only if asked to respond. If you require any medical attention, it will be administered at the end of the testing. Until then, you are expected to endure and continue to do your best. If you understand, say yes."

"Yes."

"The training will begin. Defend yourself."

Without warning, Makita's attack smashed into her.

She blocked one or two out every four or five blows.

A snapwheel kick sent her flying twenty meters, nearly winding her.

The only things that saved her at all, once again, were the experience and knowledge she gained from her training sessions with Baeven.

Makita proved stronger and faster than her, but he still paled in comparison to the outcast's terrifying prowess.

Makita charged her.

Naero met him part way.

She took several punishing strikes, but flipped him hard to the ground.

He swept her legs.

They tangled on the ground, wrestling, slipping out of holds, twisting like snakes. They pummeled each other all the while.

They broke, crouched low, and launched themselves at each other again, like Telurian fighting blue cranes.

Naero landed a whipkick on the side of Makita's head.

He clipped her under the chin, grabbed her leg and ankle and swung her hard into the floor, stunning her.

She struggled to get up.

For a few dizzy moments, she couldn't.

She rose up and staggered back into her fighting stance.

She half-smiled.

"Come on."

Makita bowed his head, just slightly, and drew back.

"Defend yourself, "Klyne said again.

Naero whirled to face Iselle.

Too late.

An invisible force slammed into her arms and torso, flinging her back.

She rolled with the strike and came back up into her stance.

Iselle fought her from a distance, punching and striking with her hands in rapid combinations.

Naero struggled to advance, to close the distance between them, while heavy, unseen blows rained down on her from every direction, knocking her one way, and then the other.

"Telekinetic combat," Klyne called out. "Try to sense and block the blows. You cannot see them. Reach out with your battle senses, with your mind. Feel them coming. Counter and deflect them. True masters can fight thus, without even moving, simply by concentrating."

At least Iselle still had to physically move in order to project her attacks. That was some help.

Closer. Get closer.

Iselle thrust both hands forward violently.

A wall of force drove Naero slowly back. She pushed against it, slowing it even more.

"Resist. Focus on the energy before you," Klyne told her, "before it smashes you into the far wall. Fight back. Defeat it."

She rolled to one side and then the other. The barrier felt solid.

Naero leaped up four meters, felt the top, and flipped herself over it.

Iselle withdrew a step, cupping both hands loosely on the sides of her face.

Spinning orbs of pure telekinetic force shot out, rapid-fire.

Naero barely perceived them where they warped through the air; they made explosive popping sounds.

She tried to dodge them. One whirred past her head like an invisible ball at high speed.

The next clipped her left shoulder, spinning her aside.

Another knocked one leg out from under her.

She kept her feet and ducked, weaving to either side in turns.

Iselle directed her attack at Naero's feet.

Naero lost her footing, slipping and sliding on what felt like a bunch of invisible ball bearings cast beneath her.

She tried to roll back to her feet, but panes of force battered her from all sides, keeping her off balance.

It felt like being a rubber ball, bouncing around in a box that someone shook.

The sides of the box rapidly closed in.

They tightened all around her, threatening to crush her.

She couldn't breathe.

Iselle released her without warning.

Naero sprawled, gasping, face down on the floor.

"I'm somewhat surprised," Klyne noted. "Preliminary tests demonstrate no psyonic aptitude or innate talent to my trained senses whatsoever. That in itself is very rare. After your battle with the former Danner entity, we simply assumed that you would exhibit some kind of psyonic ability."

"I burned myself out dealing with the entity. I burned both of us out. I'm a nud once more." She admitted it openly. "None of my former abilities have returned."

So she wasn't psyonic anymore. Not even a teknomancer. Disappointing, but not the end of the universe.

"Yet I sense something incredibly strange within you," Klyne said. "What could it be?"

Was it Om? He was still inside her somewhere. He had not emerged again either.

"Take your place at the center of us once more. Face me again."

Naero did so, resisting an urge to massage several bruises.

Klyne positioned himself directly in front of her, sitting lotus fashion just like her and the others.

"I'm going to attempt to merge directly with your mind telepathically, one of my gifts. I'm also an Auralcognitor. Once I link with your mind, I can sense any type of psyonic energy field you might have, active, passive, or latent. I might even be able to trigger or bring them out to the surface. There might be some discomfort. Shall we proceed?"

"Sure."

"Do as I do. I will show you how to place your hands to effect the mind merge."

Klyne cupped his left hand firmly behind the base of her skull.

Naero followed his lead.

He placed the fingers of his right hand on precise spots on her face.

Thumb on her forehead, directly between her eyes.

Index finger on her left temple.

The next two fingers curled slightly in front of her left ear. His smallest finger hooked at the point of her ear and jaw.

As soon as Naero placed her right hand the same way, she gasped slightly.

Thin hairs of what felt like burning hot energy threaded their way slowly through the layers of her awareness.

She could feel Klyne connecting with her thoughts, joining their two minds.

The dull ache continued to grow.

"You should be feeling the initial discomfort. Hold still. Keep focusing. Almost there. Almost..."

A spike of pure agony exploded within her skull.

Naero screamed, transfixed as if by lightning.

Through the torment, a voice awoke in her mind full-force.

Protocols unlocked and engaged. We...are.

Interface...partial.

Om awoke, reacting instinctively with fear and vast power.

Threat detected...Protect all access.

Neural net...INTRUSION. UNWARRANTED.

LEVEL 1.359 DEFENSIVE RESPONSE.

An intense blast wave of white-hot psyonic energy fanned out rapidly from the epicenter of her immolated mind.

Naero continued to scream.

As if far away in the distance, Klyne and his two adepts also shrieked.

*

Naero blinked, her eyes and mouth frozen open.

She lay with her head to one side, in a puddle of her own mixed blood and spittle.

More pain struck her when she attempted to move.

Blood continued to stream from her eyes, ears, nose, and mouth– a bloody mess.

It felt as if a fusion grenade had blown her head open.

She reached up with her hands, to make sure her skull was still intact.

Some kind of noise.

Warning alarms sounded.

A ship. Yes, they were on a ship. The Spacer Intel Ship *The Kathmandu*. She was...being tested, for the Mystics.

Something had gone terribly wrong.

Naero focused, getting to her hands and knees.

She heard other voices, groaning and whimpering.

Makita lay sprawled in a broken tangle, blasted across the room. His gray clothing had been shredded and scorched into tatters. He choked and coughed.

To the other side, Iselle fared little better. She lay convulsing, blasted, scorched, a yellow-white bone of her forearm sticking out of her wrenched flesh. One side of her face was blistered, her red hair burned, some of it still smoking. She trembled and shuddered in pain and terror.

Naero looked around for Klyne, and found the instructor in a burned, bloody heap, lying beneath a dark red smear on the far wall. His hands were charred black, and he was missing fingers.

Naero could not walk. She couldn't even stand. She crawled to Klyne as quickly as she could.

He still lived, just barely.

Then she noticed the intense effects of the blast, all around the room, less than a meter up.

A massive expanding ring of Cosmic force had sliced into the duranadium hull of the smartwalls, punching a deep crease right through them where they buckled, all along its full diameter.

The force of the strike disrupted all systems. The entire training room was compacted, crushed, and heavily damaged.

Rescuers struggled to force their way through the various ruined doors and access panels.

Naero's Gambit Amazon Link: *http://amzn.to/1lx5Tyy*

Please enjoy the following teaser from the next book in The Citation Series, Book Two:
The High Crusade

NAERO'S WAR:

THE HIGH CRUSADE

by Mason Elliott

General Walker's Marines from Bravo Command maneuvered into position under the cover of darkness using their stealth gear.

Naero agreed to slip in ahead and bait the trap, in her battlefield role as Shettana–*The Dark Angel of Death.*

Get ready, Om. The show's about to start.

I will need some time to prepare, concentrate, and focus enough of our energies in reserve, before you deplete them all.

Just get ready and keep us ready. I'm going to set our game plan in motion.

I will do all that I can to assist. Call upon me when you require me. Good hunting, Naero.

Thanks, Om.

The invaders would do anything to have a chance to destroy or capture her.

She was–in fact–the actual, literal bait, and the trap was being set for an entire invasion force of Ejjai elite, ravaging the Corps border world of Tholos-4.

No local planetary army, military, or militia had been able to stand before the horrific onslaught of the alien invaders.

The Ejjai hammered the local landers into submission with advanced artillery, orbital bombardment from Ejjai fleets, and close assault gunships and gravtanks.

Then the terrifying collection process began, and all the living, wounded, and dead were hurled into the shrieking, whining processing blades of the robotic meatships.

The horrible sounds of the meatships warred with the screams of their countless victims.

Given time, Ejjai mass cloning factories and robotic ship and weapon-building factories would also be established onworld.

The murdering bastards had already wiped three major cities and their mixed populations off the surface of the hapless planet, before Naero and the Marines could even deploy on world.

The enemy left those lost cities little more than red, blackened, burning scars and stains that could be viewed from orbit.

Nothing left alive.

Ejjai hyaenanoids loved carrion.

Every man, woman, and child of any kind, species, or age that the enemy captured was routinely tortured, killed, and processed into rotting ration blocks in the horrific, robotic meatships of the invading aliens. That included any sentients, pets, livestock—anything and everything that was meat.

The meatblock rations were only frozen to keep them from breaking down, and decaying completely.

Hatred was too gentle a word for what most humans felt for the Ejjai invaders and their extreme methods. Spacers, landers, and each of the other known races that encountered the Ejjai quickly learned to feel the same way.

This vile, uplifted, intrusive and opportunistic species needed to be completely exterminated, wherever it was encountered.

The invaders proved that they were incapable of co-existing with any other living things.

The Ejjai could only dominate, torture, and destroy all life that they encountered, anything they could sink their teeth and claws into. Uplifting them, and giving them advanced weapons and starships had only turned them into a galactic abomination, an interstellar menace, a virulent plague.

An utter nightmare.

One that needed to end for the poor people of Tholos-4.

Naero and her Marine allies were here to see to that.

It was amusing that the Ejjai always saw themselves as invincible, the supreme warriors.

Shettana and Bravo Command quickly intended to disavow the foe of such jaded notions, time and time again.

The Marines of Bravo Commander were the textbook picture of professional warriors. A legend among all the known systems.

Naero loved serving with the elite of the elite. Together they made a fantastic team.

Even the Ejjai had learned grudgingly to fear them from their initial engagements, and the proof was there.

Every invader force that came up against Bravo Command had been completely wiped out–in record time. And then Bravo quietly packed up and headed on to the next world, ready to do it all over again.

The enemy struggled to halt the Spacer advance and throw it back.

They tried everything they could think of.

Increased enemy numbers.

Different tactics.

New weapons–traps and tricks of many different kinds.

The Ejjai generals turned themselves inside out trying to find a solution–way to achieve victory against the Spacer advance.

Bravo Command slipped in and ruined the invaders' sick, twisted party, every single time.

And Shettana, The Dark Angel of Death, used all of her amazing, Mystic powers and abilities to help the Marines keep up the pressure, and drive the enemy to terror, madness, and distraction.

General Walker worked closely with Spacer Intel, always making sure his leathernecks had the latest high-tek toys, weapons, and armor that came online.

As a result, they landed an entire Marine Division on Tholos-4 and slipped into position, without the enemy even knowing they were there yet.

By the time the Spacer Fleets swept in to destroy the enemy naval forces–Bravo Command would already be implementing their plan to put the foe down hard and fast on the ground.

Three Marine infantry regiments, one artillery regiment, plus specialized units of meks, armor, and air-to-ground support.

The ghosts of Bravo Command spread the impending Shadow of Vengeance and Death over their foes like an unseen net, without any knowledge or awareness among the invaders themselves.

Bravo and Shettana prepared for another stunning series of lightning attacks.

All became poised and ready, while the heedless enemy celebrated their vile victories and atrocities.

Naero struggled to remain silent as she slipped in among the foe. Death and damnation to any invader who thought they could invade the human sectors with impunity, death, and Cosmicide.

On every world, the invader needed to be taught that bloody lesson.

Naero strode right into the belly of the beast.

Alone.

Defiant.

Confident in her skills and abilities and all of her comrades depending on her and backing her up.

Her cloaked combat armor made her virtually invisible. The Ejjai could not even smell her.

She used her gravwing to slip into the most heavily guarded command and control bunker the enemy possessed. With her skill and her tek, she could crawl upside down on the ceilings like an unseen insect.

Her miniature vidcams and audio collectors fed data to Intel in real time, covering everything she saw.

Naero's small contingent of cloaked Intel fixers and microdrones stayed close, ready to disrupt key enemy systems and communications when ready, planting microbombs and detonation devices as they went.

The Invader High Command celebrated their latest triumph with what one might expect from them–a huge, decadent, disgusting feast–held within a shielded bunker.

They set up their victory celebration within a huge underground arena, probably used by the Tholosians for some kind of urban or regional sporting event.

Ejjai got drunk on stinking, fermented grog made from human blood. They shipped it in from the meatships by the tankerful.

Under the bright lights of the hi-tek arena, tens of thousands of Ejjai feasted and celebrated their latest victories. The enemy generals praised their troops and used the huge arena vidscreens to plot out their next attacks on the three nearest Tolosian cities.

On the center of the playing field, Ejjai transports and appropriated trucks had also hauled in and dumped huge piles of human corpses from the local population for their undefeated troops to feed on.

Piles of fresh and not so fresh meat, diverted from the enemy meatships to help sate the troops in large numbers.

One of the piles was all dead children and infants.

Even worse, to Naero's horror, some of the bodies in the various meat piles were somehow still alive. They twitched or cried out in pain and terror. Some weakly attempted to crawl away, despite broken or missing limbs.

The Ejjai quickly seized them and began tormenting them even further, laughing hysterically at the sport. They stabbed, cut, and skinned them alive—or otherwise got creative.

As Ejjai were wont to do.

Ejjai were among the vilest, most disgusting creatures Naero had even encountered.

She resisted the very strong impulse to cut loose on them right then and there.

But she couldn't–not yet.

These monsters needed to die. Every single one of them.

And very soon, she would have a direct hand in launching the attack that would accomplish just that.

The timing had to be just right, so she steeled herself.

The generals. Reach the generals and stay ready.

Six Ejjai generals held court like warlords at huge tables overflowing with comconsoles, sensor stations, map screens, and piles of loot. And the bloody remains of horrific, eviscerated meals.

All Ejjai clone troops were female. Smaller male Ejjai concubines were kept around on leashes for fun, for the leaders. They even dressed them in human clothing and poorly fitting human lingerie.

As an oddity, one of the generals even had a human male dressed up as a concubine. But the poor guy apparently had to be kept in a heavily guarded pen off to one side–to keep all of the other Ejjai from devouring and murdering him, most likely in that order.

Naero circled around the generals and studied the arena, trying to devise the best way to take them all down.

She listened intently to the plans the enemy generals were making, feeding it all to Intel.

"So, are all of the atomics and genocide devices in place yet?"

Another general pulled up a mapscreen displaying all of their installation of such devices planet wide.

Naero instantly transmitted all of that data directly to Spacer Intel as well–priority alert.

Intel and Bravo Command were most likely already neutralizing the most vital elements of the enemy plot. These genocide devices could be scanned and located from orbit. But it was always good to be sure, and to know their exact locations.

The Ejjai generals scoffed. "We will be ready for anything the enemy can throw at us in less than a day," one of the other Ejjai generals boasted.

"They won't know what's going to hit them until it's too late."

"Good, very good. Speed things up if you can. Get it all up and ready."

"Don't worry, sir. We will be more than ready to deal with their so-called Bravo Command—and their spack witch."

All of the Ejjai generals had a good laugh and congratulated each other.

The lead general stepped up to a waiting podium and addressed the crowd.

"Great news, sisters! We have it on good authority that the spacks are sending their precious Bravo Command and their spack witch Shettana against us."

Lots of cursing and booing about that roared up.

Their lead general continued. "This time, we are more than ready for them!"

Huge rounds of applause to that.

"Let me just say that we have some heavy duty surprises of our own ready and waiting and in store for our enemies. We can't wait for them to get here—and have them all for dinner!"

That brought an even bigger round of cheering, cursing, and applause.

"We will engage the spacks in a matter of days, and with our increased numbers and new weapons—I say we're going to kick their asses and stomp them bloody. We will gut them! I want all my girls out there to feast on spack Marine flesh until you puke!"

Further rounds of cheering and vile responses.

"We will ferment their blood in our huge vats and get drunk on it!"

More horrendous rounds of cheering and applause.

"And once we have captured their filthy spack witch, all of you will watch as I personally cut her up and rape her with red-hot knives, and torture her to death over the course of an entire week. She'll sing to all of us with her screams. Then I myself will feast upon her guts, and eat her heart while the light in her eyes fades. I'll crack her skull open and eat her brains!"

The Ejjai went crazy.

"Wait until we post *that* on the webnets for the spacks and the skinners to watch! I promise you victory. We cannot be defeated. And we will sweep the human skinners and all the other inferior races into our meatships and out of all existence. They are our prey! Yet another galaxy that shall fall to us and our mighty masters!"

More about their mysterious masters. Interesting.

Furious cheering continued in waves.

"So my warriors. Feast on meat until you vomit, and then feast some more. Then prepare for battle as we crush our foes and ravage the rest of this world. We shall drown it all in blood and swim in it! Prepare for our ultimate victory! Our time has come. None can stand against us!"

They erupted in an orgy of celebration and vile gluttony.

Fights broke out among the meat piles, and the Ejjai fought with and murdered each other in their frenzy.

The lead general returned to the others, rubbing her claws together eagerly in the midst of the chaos.

"My sisters, I have a special treat that I've saved just for us, at this exact moment. Please, enjoy my precious gifts to you all." She motioned to a large knot of troops off to one side among some gravtanks.

A full squad of Ejjai in heavy battle armor led out six terrified human women, all of them naked, and extremely pregnant.

None of them had a mark on them. Yet.

But from the looks on their pale faces, they all knew very well what the enemy generals intended to do with them. Each of them was heavy with child in the later stages of pregnancy.

That they had remained unspoiled and unharmed up until now would quickly change for the worse–the worst fate imaginable.

Although they were unbound, there was no chance for any of these captives to break free or escape on their own against so many foes.

The generals each glared at them and gloated. The Ejjai generals slavered and drooled, snapping jaws and smacking lips.

Each general had a set of rusty, bloodstained butchering tools that they began to place out in front of them in heady, eager anticipation of their coming feast.

Then the squad of Ejjai troops guarding the six women suddenly staggered a few feet away as if drunk.

Some melted into slag where they stood.

Other Ejjai troops exploded.

The six human captives looked around in confusion.

The next instant, they all vanished.

The six Ejjai generals shot to their feet in stunned surprise.

They couldn't even speak, but a few flung cleavers and knives at the spot where the captives had stood.

Their weapons fell harmlessly to the ground.

All of this was captured and displayed on the big arena screens, and slowly attracted the attention of the astonished crowds.

Then Shettana appeared as if by magic, right before the lead Ejjai general, resplendent in her full Angel of Death mode. She was all dressed in black, shining black hair flowing in the wind, violet eyes burning above her mask.

Twin blood-red katanas crackled and hissed in the damp air, at the ready in either hand.

Every eye fixed on her—while the mini-gravpods from her fixers whisked the six cloaked, female captives away to safety.

Naero only had to buy few more seconds for them to make it out. Fierce Marines waited nearby to take charge of them and keep them safe.

With the six captives out of the way, at last Shettana could go to work.

"I have come for you, filthy Ejjai cowards. I am Shettana!" she cried.

She rammed both of her swords through the lead general's eyes and out the back of the Ejjai's scorched skull.

Two of the generals tried to run.

The other three tried to attack her.

It did not matter.

Bolts of scarlet lighting tore forth from both her blades, ripping and blasting the other five into charred pieces of meat and bone.

Naero cloaked and shot away, as the area around the tables was engulfed in torrents of enemy weapon fire the very next instant.

Then the gravtanks, gunships, transports and other vehicles lined up nearby began to explode.

Naero projected multiple holos of herself all over the arena and in the in the air, drawing fire in all directions.

She used *the voice*, her words booming and echoing from several directions.

"EJJAI FILTH. PREPARE TO MEET DEATH. FOR SHETTANA IS THE DARK ANGEL OF DEATH, AND HAS NO FEAR OF MURDERING COWARDS."

The Ejjai fired in panic from so many angles that they cut down each other by the hundreds—just as Naero planned.

Fear began to infect them.

Gouts of red lightning lashed into the arena stands from several directions like gigantic whips of destruction. The devastation flung dead and dying Ejjai everywhere in a cyclone of slaughter, adding to the total chaos and confusion.

"NO MERCY, EJJAI SCUM. NO ESCAPE. FEAR IS MY MOTHER, DEATH MY SIRE, AND I THEIR DAUGHTER! YOU CANNOT HARM ME. THERE IS NO ESCAPE FOR YOU!"

Just as the enemy started to figure out they were shooting at holos and murdering each other wholesale, Naero merged with one in her mirror images in the midst of hundreds of Ejjai in the arena stands.

Multiple thin rods of red Chaos energy shot out from her, fanning in a diameter of thirty meters.

First she impaled hundreds of the shocked invaders.

When she spun, the red blades chopped them all into smaller gory chunks and pieces.

Torrents of unleashed Ejjai blood suddenly gathered and swept down the arena, carrying others away in a sudden red rushing tide of gore.

Naero cloaked and flashed away again.

More enemy fire stormed and tore at her former position.

She took the place of another holo, and sent forth a sweeping hurricane of of Chaos bubbles and orbs of every shape and size into another section of the stands.

The explosions collapsed that entire section. Wreckage toppled inward.

Next she appeared on the field before the horrendous meat piles, in the midst of hundreds of more frantic enemies.

Half of them flung their weapons away and ran in terror before her as she raced toward them. So much for the valiant Ejjai.

"STAND AND FIGHT, SCUM!"

Naero surged and fought with the mob of foes, sweeping one way and then the other, cutting them down by dozens, by scores.

She moved among them so fast they could not focus their attacks.

Then she would abruptly change direction and sweep another way before they could hem her in.

She unleashed more scarlet lightening strikes.

She sent random Chaos blasts into packed pockets of foes.

At times she just whirled and passed through them with her swords fully extended, mowing them down in lines and bunches.

Once she had shattered them completely, she merely turned her back on them and began walking away quickly and with determination, toward the nearest exit.

Naero set her shield pod full on.

Three enemy tanks roared at her, cannons blazing.

Naero dodged and deflected their blasts into the stands.

Two gravtanks she exploded with Chaos bombs.

The last she sliced the last in half with her swords and kept walking calmly, straight through the burning wreckage as the gravtank exploded directly behind her to either side.

She ignored all enemy fire directed at her, kept walking, and cut down anything stupid enough to attempt to stand before her.

She crackled with destroying red lightning as she passed into one of the exit tunnels, laying waste to anything before her.

The enemy regrouped and poured into the tunnel in hot pursuit.

Just as Naero hoped they would.

Another kill zone. How convenient of them to all bunch up for her.

She turned at bay, just before exiting, and focused all of her energies in an intense Chaos blast cone.

The massive detonation tore the tunnel apart and blasted shredded pieces of the packed invaders out the other end, right before a massive fireball that followed hard thereafter.

Naero cloaked, and called out over her secure link.

"You guys ready? I've got them primed, but I'm also almost out of juice."

"We're in place and ready to join the show, Shettana. You okay? Do you need us to extract you?"

"Negative. I can finish my part. It just takes a lot of energy to sustain attacks at this level. You guys know that. Did Intel take care of those genocide devices?"

"Almost all accounted for."

"All right, I'm setting up for my final show. They'll take the bait, all right. You guys hit them hard when they do."

"Hard as we can, Shettana. You know us."

"I sure do, and I can't wait to watch it all go down–right from the front row. Copy that. Make the legends proud, Bravo."

She took up her position in the center of the fallen city nearby, just outside of the shattered arena.

She formed a Chaos construct around her that duplicated her and her every move.

Her construct became a scarlet, giant version of herself, semi-transparent and fifteen meters tall, red and glowing with huge blazing swords.

She stomped on a meat ship and slashed at it until it exploded.

Then she attacked the clone ship factory next to it.

"FACE ME, COWARDS. SHETTANA SHOWS YOU HER MIGHT. SHOW ME YOURS. FACE ME AND PERISH!"

Yet in actuality, her energies waned with each passing second.

It wasn't like being back on Janosha where there was limitless Cosmic energy to tap into. Away from the Mystic Homeworlds, Naero's energy levels and her abilities were not infinite or limitless. She made a good show of it, but even she could not sustain these levels of attacks for very long.

The entire enemy invasion roared to life , and locked on, bunching and sweeping her way, to engage her from all directions.

The Ejjai went insane with fury.

Up in the skies above and beyond Tholos-4, the Spacer navy sent the invader fleets spinning down in flames.

Thousands of Spacer Marines suddenly materialized out of the black at key points and positions.

Phantoms who owned the night.

The black was their domain, their element, and they surrendered it to no one.

Bravo Command unleashed a torrent of concentrated, interlocking fire against the bunched up invaders. Veils of destroying fire, artillery, and ordnance–a deluge of precisely timed destruction that no living thing could possibly survive.

Within a matter of minutes, a quarter of a million Ejjai invaders flashed and flared into a sweeping typhoon of white-hot death that overtook them.

Naero had done her job.

Completely drained of all her mystic energies for the moment, she could barely stand.

Even as she staggered away, a full platoon of gigantic Sterodans in phaze armor appeared all around her.

They piled on and overwhelmed her with their greater mass, and several shock charges that hit and rippled through both them and her. The shock charges rattled Naero's teeth in her skull.

The Ejjai and their mysterious masters still wanted her and the KDM alive and intact, apparently.

Naero grinned.

Yet another trap, and she had stumbled right into it.

This time, the enemy thought they had her at last.

Yet Naero knew something they did not, and called out into her own mind.

Om–you're up. They've got me.

Take these bastards down hard and fast!

Amazon Link for The High Crusade: http://amzn.to/1DbFD5F

Please enjoy the following teaser ... and excerpt, from the next Spacer Clans Adventure, Book 3:

NAERO'S FURY

NAERO'S FURY

Amazon Link to Naero's Fury: http://amzn.to/1hLrPpO

by Mason Elliott

Naero still hadn't done it much, but going into a direct trance to enter the Astral Plane shouldn't be all that difficult. Master Vane had shown her how once. And she had gone there lots of times in her sleep, in her mind, to speak with Khai, using their astral crystals.

Before her friend Khai had vanished without a trace.

Yet she had never been completely trained in astral travel, and didn't know that much about exploring or moving around. Master Vane had taken her there once, just to teach her the basics and give her his marker. Many other times later to spar with her.

If nothing else, she could probably focus on his marker and locate him.

Zhen had roused Naero and reminded her it was time. And that she and Shalaen would monitor her while she was in the astral trance.

Naero focused her mind and abilities, controlling her breathing. Remembering the little she had recently learned.

Within several minutes of focused meditation, she open her eyes and found herself floating in the Astral Miasma, the nebulae of energy. She hugged her knees to her chest in her astral form.

Om spoke to her, even more easily here than in her own mind before.

I have accessed some of the Kexxian Matrix's data files on The Astral Plane. Like everything else, they explored it quite extensively.

Om, I'm naked here. I'm not complaining–but just tell me–how do I put astral clothing on again?

You control everything here by imagination, and force of will. Concentrate on your favorite clothing and they'll appear.

That's easy.

She looked down and saw her favorite Nytex flight togs, programmed just the way she liked them.

Naero blinked, spinning and twirling in one spot, turning upside down.

Why can't I move more than a meter at a time in front of us?

You're not used to this reality. So it's not clear to you.

The air around her looked opaque. Not mist. Not smoke or vapor. And it glowed slightly with its own bluish-gray light.

In the twilight she glowed softly blue-white with her own light. From within.

"I once heard rumors that the Mystics could travel and send messages this way, but I thought it was all just a myth."

Since the other planes are entire universes within themselves, it is said, they are all nearly infinite. Thus, it is difficult to pin point any kind of location or person unless you already know them.

Naero instinctively tried to stand up, but there was nothing to stand on.

Then she recalled Master Vane's Marker, and it appeared right before her. Where she found him, she would find the other High Masters.

At least she deserved a chance to be heard by them all. To try to explain herself and her actions. What happened with the obelisk was clearly not her fault.

But they would still blame her for it–especially Mater Vane, who seemed to blame her for everything since Hashiko's death.

Naero could not simply stand by and let the High Masters decide her fate without herself being present at her trial, in some way at least.

She focused on the crimson and black star more and swept forward, seemingly at great speed.

She came to an abrupt halt, like a starship coming out of jump at its destination.

The opacity around her partially melted away. She proceeded forward, opening her visual field far wider. She made out the area around her as the miasma peeled back.

Slightly below her, she saw spheres within glowing spheres, all spinning within greater spheres.

Her own sphere, glowing white-blue, suddenly surrounded her like a glittering soap bubble.

Yet it did not pop when she poked at it.

One sphere in particular, the largest, glowed and pulsed blood red, containing a withered old man with a long beard, pacing impatiently.

Burning eyes vanished and re-appeared at random all over his bald head. The red sphere absorbed Master Vane's marker.

Was this his true form? What he really looked like?

His scarlet sphere was also flanked by two smaller spheres with figures inside them.

Om made a calculated guess.

His current guardian adepts, no doubt. The ones you rescued from the enemy Darkforce generators on Janosha.

I think so, Om.

At most times, every High Master had at least two champion adepts protecting him or her, each of them very close to mastery themselves. Just as Hashiko had been.

Naero studied Vane's new guardians for the very first time, and tried to see into their spheres.

Something about each of them did seem strangely familiar.

One of Vane's adepts, the male, appeared to be so deep dark black, he could be a singularity. This adept's sphere was flat black on the surface and barely transparent.

If Naero had been able to breathe, she would have gasped.

Instead she simply raised her hand to her mouth.

She recalled that she had seen many of these adepts long before.

In her dreams, nightmares, and crazed visions. Perhaps even on the Astral Plane somehow.

Vane's other adept was the white female, the exact opposite of the other. So brilliant and blindingly radiant, she could be a pulsar. Her orb was like a high intensity bulb, blinding and almost completely crystal clear.

It occurred to Naero that during her initial testing, Klyne had male and female assistants as well.

She couldn't guess what the significance of that pattern was all about. Perhaps just some weird Mystic, egalitarian tradition.

Then why weren't any of the High Masters female?

Everyone seemed to ignore her where she floated.

The next larger sphere, farther away, glowed silver-blue.

If she focused intently on it, she discovered she could zoom in with her third eye–her mind's eye.

Within that silver-blue sphere, a silver man sat serenely, neither young nor old. Master Tree, in his purest form of order.

Two smaller guardian spheres flanked him.

Master Tree's female adept glowed with intense blue energy in a deep blue sphere.

The male likewise glowed with vibrant green force within a green sphere, a shining sword sheathed down his broad, athletic back. He seemed very familiar somehow.

Naero did a double-take. Long blond hair. Green skin. Big glowing sword.

Yep. In the flesh–or–astral form at least.

It was Khai! She was sure of it. He was alive.

Had he actually succeeded in his great task of forging his mystic sword in the heart of a gigantic pulsar? Was that it on his back?

Naero gasped again. Now that she knew what he looked like, Khai was also the dreamy green hunk from many past, pent up nightmares. The one who kept sticking his astral sword through her head.

What did it all mean? She wasn't nuts enough yet?

Now she knew for certain she needed serious help.

And to do some serious dating at some point, once-and-for-all.

If the Mystics continued to let her live.

Khai must have sensed her inner turmoil, or thoughts, or maybe just her concentration on him.

Mr. Green-god even glanced her way for a second, looking just as confused and puzzled by her sudden appearance.

Neither of them had ever met the other in person.

Naero covered her face with one hand and looked aside, withdrawing her sphere suddenly further away.

How fricking embarrassing.

She crept forward again. Slowly.

The third and final sphere glowed golden, and contained an equally golden child within, energetic and bristling with lightning. He bounced back and forth inside like a gigantic electron.

Master Jo of course.

Two flanking spheres.

One of his adepts had no clear form, eyes gleaming within a shifting, flickering miasma like the Astral Plane itself. His female counterpart shifted shape from one fantastic creature to another.

When she suddenly made out their voices, she could sense that an intense debate had been doing on. One that still continued.

"We cannot be certain in this matter," the golden child insisted. "We do not dare act in any rash way."

"Agreed, High Master Jo," the serene silver man added. "She might yet be another Trickster from what I can tell."

"Yes. Quite possible, High Master Tree."

The old man in the blood red sphere blustered impatiently. "Fools! Always conspiring against me. Taking positions opposite of mine for no reason but to anger me. I've been telling you all along, this child is clearly the Great Destroyer–long foretold. Our duty is clear. She is a threat to all existence. To multiple dimensions. She must be eliminated, at once, before she can grow even more powerful."

"High Master Vane," Tree said. "None of us can be sure of that fact. Including you."

"I am."

"You are always certain when it comes to destroying someone," Jo added. "Your pure Chaos answer to everything. Destruction or Creation."

"It works."

"No. It doesn't. It only delays and worsens the inevitable," Tree said. "The Universe shall have its way. We all know this. You were mistaken with the last savant when he appeared, and now he remains at large–a renegade beyond even our control."

Baeven? We're they referring to her uncle?

Vane rolled his eyes. "Idiots! The Renegade is the Trickster, I say. This child must in fact be the Great Destroyer. Just look at the powers roiling within her. They will surely corrupt and overwhelm her entirely and drive her mad in the end. She will go berserk on a scale that makes her recent outbursts feeble and puny by comparison. She must perish now, while we have a chance to put an end to her. While the only crimes she has committed include destroying an entire planet, and another of the vital obelisks!"

"We still don't understand the purpose of the ancient obelisks. And we've studied the mysterious disappearance of Janosha, and we still cannot be certain in any conclusive way, that she had anything to do with it."

"Really? Who else could it be then? Planets like Janosha aren't in the habit of just obliterating themselves suddenly for no reason at all. Everywhere she goes, destruction follows!"

I cannot allow this.

Quiet, Om. Don't do anything. I'm trying to listen.

Naero...they're discussing our destruction. The Chaos Master means to destroy us.

Master Jo continued to protest. "You can't just kill off every entity that manifests Cosmic Abilities such as these. Our universe is peppered with them. We must continue to locate and guide them–not find excuses to execute them. Like the Others have told us, Tricksters often appear to oppose Great Destroyers. Without the former, final victory is never possible. "

"High Masters," Tree said. "This young woman also possesses the Kexxian Data Matrix. We cannot destroy her without destroying it. Intel and The Spacer Council of Elders value our wisdom, but even they would not agree to such action."

"Regrettable," Vane said. "Yet I cannot take the risk. I have decided this matter on my own."

"You have no such authority on your own," Tree insisted.

"Idiots! I cannot stand by and allow our galaxy–perhaps our entire universe to be destroyed–just to satisfy your foolish, philosophical, and theoretical whims."

Master Vane turned to his adepts. "My finest students, obey me. Delay these fools. Keep them occupied whilst I act for the good of all existence."

More rapid than thought, the male dark ensnared the blue sphere and its satellites in coils and tendrils of darkness. While the bright female enveloped the golden sphere and its companions in waves of of pure light.

Naero tried to pull away, but in her panic she did not know where to go.

High Master Vane sped straight at her with impossible speed.

I must act, Naero.

No, Om. Please, this is already bad enough. Don't do anything.

I cannot comply. I must defend us!

Naero went down on her hands and knees before Master Vane. She called out, using *the voice* to project her words.

"Please, Master Vane. Do not attack me. I only wish to be trained to control my abilities. I have struggled hard to do so. I still don't understand what happened with the obelisk."

Vane bore down on her, arcs of pure scarlet energy bristling around him.

"Far too late for that, monster. Nothing is ever your fault, is it? Now, you must perish for the good of all. I told you this hour would come."

Instinctively, Naero drew back again, trying to evade his attack. She rose within her receding sphere.

Vane closed in once more, gathering his powers.

"Don't do this," Naero begged. "Please. Help me. I know I can't fully control all of my abilities yet. I'm trying as hard as I can. I can't be responsible for what will happen if you attack me. I can't control myself."

"Yes, and look at the results? Countless lives crushed and eradicated. Janosha vaporized–an entire planet. You must never be allowed to reach your full potential. Now–monster–hold still and embrace your fate."

Naero put her hands out before her, holding her palms out defensively. Pleading.

"No. Don't. I can't–"

"I know, Maeris. You can't help yourself. That is why you are *an abomination*!"

Vane smashed into her, piercing all of her defenses as if they were shattering glass.

In the distance, she sensed that Master Jo and Master Tree finally broke free.

Too late.

Master Vane attacked, trying to overwhelm her with raw power.

He pummeled her with impossible blows.

In the end, he beat her up badly, but only succeeded in knocking her around once more.

Om roared in their mind.

Kexxian defense protocols unlocked and on line.

An energized, glowing armor of some advanced origin formed around Naero like a hi-tek battle suit.

Naero saw out of her third eye as it awoke and burst into radiance like a blue-white star.

Master Vane came at her once more, all of his powers focused through his primary scarlet, burning eye, centered in his forehead.

All of his other flaming eyes closed as he concentrated, his skull wreathed in weird cosmic flames like a mane of cosmic fire.

"See how powerful you have already become? No adept could have withstood those lethal attacks. We must finish this now, before the others can interfere."

"Please, Master Vane. Please–I'm begging you–please, don't do this."

"Maeris, just as I foretold–you shall fall before the greatest of all Cosmic attack techniques. And I am one of the few who have ever learned to master it: The Eye of Annihilation!"

The same Chaos technique that had destroyed Hashiko–even she couldn't control it properly.

A massive blood red beam of destroying Cosmic force shot straight at her.

It all happened so fast. Naero heard Om screaming.

Reflection defense. Analyze incoming cosmic assault. Duplicate and reflect attack tenfold!

Just before the incoming blast vaporized her, a blue-white beam shot out of her own third eye to war against Master Vane's powers.

The Cosmic flows flared intensely.

Naero screamed as if her body and soul were being sucked through the eye of a black hole's needle.

The wide blue beam quickly drove the red beam back to its source.

At the last instant, High Master Vane cried out in terror.

"Impossible! There can be no such–"

The destroying energy ignited on contact.

A massive detonation on the Astral Plane blinded the area within a few light years.

High Masters Jo and Tree barely managed to withdraw and shield the others. All of their spheres shattered.

Pure cosmic energy punched into High Master Vane right before Naero's eyes.

It drove him back like a white-hot comet.

He struggled against it with all his might.

To no avail.

The reflected attack obliterated High Master Vane to glowing ash and dust, screaming in the wake of his own annihilation.

Vane's dying force of will echoed off into the universe.

Naero would have caught her breath if she had any.

The outcome left her completely stunned for a shuddering instant.

Om…what did we just do?

We had no choice, Naero. My sole purpose is to defend our current form.

Naero stared down at her hands in terror. Tendrils of Cosmic energy rippled and still curled off of her body and her sphere like smoke.

Om…*Haisha!* We just killed a High Master of the Spacer Mystics!

Amazon Link to Naero's Fury: http://amzn.to/1hLrPpO

Please enjoy this teaser for The Citation Series, Book 3:

Naero's Trial Amazon Link : http://amzn.to/1oaMNE3

NAERO'S
WAR:

NAERO'S
TRIAL

Naero's Trial Amazon Link: http://amzn.to/1oaMNE3

by Mason Elliott

On the third day of Naero's trial, the Prosecution and the Defense made their final, closing statements.

Master Jo spoke first, for the Defense.

"In the final analysis, I would both conclude and insist that Naero Amashin Maeris has proven herself time and time again to be an honorable Spacer, and that her word is without question. She is also vital to the survival of her people in many important ways. Naero Amashin Maeris is a noble, invaluable warrior and a proven leader who has served the Clans and the Alliance well, in both peacetime and war. A Mystic Champion who is now part of the great and mysterious Cosmic Prophecy, long foretold. There is still so little that we do not know about those prophecies; who can say what her role will be in the end?"

Master Jo paced a bit. "And on a very basic level, she is a Spacer. As such, she has the right of all Spacers and all sentients to defend herself, to the death, against anyone who attempts to kill her. Reluctantly, she only resorted to lethal force when High Master Vane attacked her with the intent to destroy her, and take her life. Even after she had tried to get away from him, and begged him repeatedly not to attack her.

"She cannot not be convicted of murder for defending her own life against someone trying to kill her. Those are all many good reasons why you must see fit to exonerate her of these erroneous charges. We cannot take the life of this hero."

The Defense finally rested.

Master Tree was given the final word in the trial for the prosecution.

"Hero? First, let me also revisit the reckless side of this renegade, outlaw Spacer, who fled from justice and had to be brought back by force to face her crimes in shackles, in order to keep her from getting away once again. On several occasions, Naero Amashin Maeris has proven herself to be dangerous, unpredictable, and out of control. By her own words, she has more than once declared that if she ever lost control and became a threat to any of her people, that she herself agreed that she should be put down–and destroyed.

"The cold blooded murder of a High Mystic Master has not demonstrated this fact readily enough? Beyond all doubt? If she can slay a High Master of the Mystics so easily, how much more is she a danger to all? And she even admits that she cannot control her abilities. Her very existence has become such a clear and present threat that it cannot be ignored and must be dealt with. I repeat, she has admitted on several occasions that her powers can go out of control and be very dangerous.

"Next, she also clearly admits that she killed Master Vane. Now, of her own accord, she claims that she killed him in self defense. But she has thus far presented no single shred of proof of that. She claims that Master Vane attacked her, attempted to kill her, and that she killed him, as she now conveniently claims–in so-called self defense. And I remind everyone in this court, once again. It does not matter who she is, what she is, or whatever else she has done. No one is above Spacer Law.

"Not even the infamous, Naero Amashin Maeris."

Tree took in a breath and clasped his hands behind his back. "What are the facts, therefore? A High Mystic Master lies dead, murdered by his own student, who openly stated that she could not stand him. Who openly admitted that she killed him. Nothing else can be proven, beyond those facts. Nothing else exists as fact. And this case must only be decided, based solely upon the facts. Nothing else.

"A Spacer on trial for her life could readily claim and say anything. Merely stating something does not make it true. That does not prove it to be fact. According to the facts of what is known, Naero Amashin Maeris is clearly guilty of murder, and will undoubtedly say and do anything possible in order to get away with her crime. As anyone logically would, in order to escape punishment, justice, and execution."

Naero fumed. Haisha! What the hell did they expect her to say? Yes, I offed the asshole, I loved it, and I'm a fricking monster. Go ahead and kill me?

I wish that weren't so painfully funny, Naero.

Me too, Om.

Master Tree went on to demand that the jury uphold one of the key tenets of Spacer Law and Spacer society:

"Spacers do not murder other Spacers and take their lives! Naero Amashin Maeris is not above that law. Naero Amashin Maeris broke that solemn law. And like it or not, the law demands justice. There is no way around that law and no way to escape it. That law demands that she face the ultimate punishment for her being guilty of committing the ultimate crime!"

Tree emphasized his final point with a single, upraised index finger. "That punishment is immediate Death, by execution. To be carried out by beheading, at the hands and the blade of the Mystic Enforcer!"

The Prosecution rested its case.

Admiral Klyne looked slightly pale as he instructed the jury of Mystic Elders to decide the case and announce their decision after their period of deliberation.

Naero went back to her cell in silence feeling sick, unable to meet Khai's utterly heartbroken glance. She felt stunned and numb. She didn't know what to think. All that she could do was await the jury's decision, along with everyone else.

Yet it was her fate alone that was being decided.

But when she thought about it further it wasn't just her fate.

Everyone waited for eight long hours.

Naero could neither rest nor sleep.

Then everyone was summoned back to the court room.

A decision had been made. The jury had arrived at a verdict in her case.

Admiral Klyne announced, "All rise for the verdict to be read."

They did so.

The jury leader stood up and read their decision.

"According to Spacer Law, and based upon all of the facts and evidence presented, we the jury find the defendant, Naero Amashin Maeris, of Clan Maeris…guilty of murder in the death of another Spacer."

Naero gasped, nailed to the bedrock of the planet itself in almost complete shock.

Guilty meant…

Master Tree rose up. "This Mystic trial has ended; it is over. A verdict has been reached. Without question, this grim crime is punishable among our people by death. Under the circumstances, the sentence is to be carried out immediately and without delay."

Naero, I can–

Shut up, Om.

Naero gasped and covered her mouth with both hands as she sobbed and went down on one knee.

Then she dropped her hands to her abdomen and her eyes met Khai's in explosive waves of desperate horror and regret.

Their child from their love within that distant star barely grew within her. Now, no time remained to tell Khai all that she needed to before he performed his duty as the Mystic Enforcer.

Before he took her head…ended her life, and the lives of his own family.

Naero Amashin Maeris clenched her fists, and rose up with her head held high to meet her fate with her eyes clear and wide open, if that was what must be.

Amazon Link for *Naero's Trial*: http://amzn.to/1oaMNE3

Enjoy this teaser to the Fantasy novel Mergeworld 1, by Mason Elliott and Garan R. R. Faraday.
Amazon Link:
http://amzn.to/1uboBDC

Mergeworld

Book One

Mergeworld 1 Amazon Link: http://amzn.to/1uboBDC

by Mason Elliott & Garan R. R. Faraday

David Pritchard woke up gasping from one nightmare and went straight into another. A terrible agony tore through him as if the universe twisted him inside out.

Then he snapped back again.

What in damnation had just happened? Something…was very wrong.

Startled, groggy, it only took an instant for his bleary mind to figure it out.

Flames engulfed the front of his college apartment building. The stench of smoke, and the sounds of screams and breaking glass outside, only confirmed it.

He felt dazed, and blinked his scratchy eyes. The first thing he instinctively reached out for was the framed picture of his dead parents.

That was the last picture he had of them, taken a few years back, right after he started college in South Bend.

They hugged and smiled at each other in medieval garb at the Bristol Renaissance Faire up in Wisconsin. The picture froze both of them happily in time, retired in their forties. Unlike many parents that age, they weren't divorced and they still loved one another. One of their Ren-Faire pals had taken that picture for them on their digital camera.

The same camera retrieved from the car accident on the Illinois highway on their way back home from Bristol. A tractor-trailer jackknifed in the heavy rain and took them away.

The same weekend David begged off going with them.

He had blown that picture up in Photoshop, printed out an 8 x 10, and bought a nice oak frame for it. He kept it with him wherever he went. He'd die before he'd part with it, fire or no.

All that history and pain flashed through David as he clutched their picture close to him in the dark. He didn't even have to see it, just cling to it in his hands. That picture always sat prominently behind his small alarm clock on his night stand with his smart phone and wallet while he slept. That was how he found it, even in the semi-dark. He also grabbed his phone and wallet.

His clock normally flashed bright green. Power outage, probably from the fire. And the backup battery must have gone dead. Light switches? Nothing, of course, due to the fire.

The growing reek of smoke triggered his desire for self-preservation. Once he got out, he could call his friend Mason Tyler, who lived in a duplex over on Allen Street. His buddy Mace would help him.

Somewhat more awake now, David struggled not to panic. He staggered out of his room like a robot. His lanky, five-eleven frame stumbled down the hall toward his front door. He stubbed his little toe hard in the darkness. A second later, he grunted and cursed the sudden blinding spread of pain, but kept moving.

Oh, hell. No way out the front.

Dangerous ribbons of smoke curled violently through the metal front door frame and snaked up across the ceiling like an upside-down waterfall. The paint of the metal fire door already bubbled and blistered. David choked and swallowed hard.

If that door had been wood, his entire apartment might have already been completely engulfed. He might not have even come to. He saw no sense in touching the steaming door knob.

The apartment building stairs acted like a natural chimney, funneling the fire and heat straight up.

A window—climb out a window. He was only on the second floor.

His three richer roomies were already off on spring break for the next week, to the Bahamas or some such. Their parents could afford such junkets. David could not.

He suddenly realized two very important things. First, the fire hadn't spread to the back part of the apartment building yet.

Next, he was only wearing navy boxers and a gray T-shirt over his shaking frame.

Early April in South Bend, Indiana, could be any weather from sun and sixties to a flippin' blizzard.

Clothes. Only seconds to throw some on. Even in the dim, flickering orange light spilling out of the thick curtains, he spotted his laundry basket on the couch.

The smoke in the living room grew thicker. He put his precious picture, smartphone, and wallet down for only a few moments.

Jeans. On. Socks. On. He snatched up his thick blue, gold, and green hoodie from the back of the old couch where he usually left it, and pulled into its soft, warm comfort. Stocking cap. Popped on his head. Wool scarf. Around the neck. He sat down and jammed on his old gray Nike running shoes, feeling a pair of thin gloves and keys in his hoodie pockets still when he bent over.

Ready to ride, or, at least, climb out the back window to escape burning to death.

He stuffed his folks' picture, wallet, and smartphone into his dark green Jansport backpack with his pad, gel pens, and a few books. He zipped it all up.

To the back window. He pulled the curtains aside and yanked the big panel open.

He jumped slightly at the sight of some guy who had already climbed down the back of the building from the third floor. Their eyes locked, only a window screen between them in the dim, pre-dawn light and the cold morning air.

The guy looked utterly terrified.

"Watch out!" he warned, trying to keep his voice low. "Those things are killing people. They're everywhere!"

"What things?" What was this guy freaking out about?

The guy jolted, wide-eyed, and then choked.

A bloody iron arrowhead jutted out the front of his throat. In the time it took them both to blink, another arrow punched through the front of his chest, out of his T-shirt. The poor guy's mouth gaped and worked. Then his eyes rolled up white. He fell backwards, head down.

David grabbed for him but missed, his hands blocked by the barrier of the screen. He tore it away and stuck his head out the window.

He spotted strange movement down in the darkness.

Two dark, twisted, hunched-over figures loped in on bandy legs and clawed feet wrapped in fur and rags. They were smaller than humans, about four to five feet tall, and very skinny and wiry.

Whatever they were, they were definitely not human.

One of them slit the dead guy's throat from ear to ear with a long, wicked-looking rusty knife.

Blood spurted bright black in the night.

The other creature sniffed the air and snarled up at David with a greenish-black, twisted, inhuman face. Long pointed ears stuck out of holes in its ragged hood. It had a big warty nose, and gleaming green eyes. It gave full draw to the same kind of short, black bow of jagged horn that the other one carried.

The creature took dead aim at David.

And fired.

Mergeworld 1 Amazon Link: http://amzn.to/1uboBDC

Edition Notes

If you do not see this edition note here in this spot on the copyright page and on the very last page of your ebook or print version of this title, then you are not getting the final, polished version of this novel that the publisher, editors, and author intended for you to receive. Please contact either the publisher or the author via their emails or websites if you do not see the following update code:

High Mark Publishing Update Code K2428E